SHADOW
RANCH

— · —

CHILDREN OF THE LIGHT SERIES BOOK ONE

REBECCA CAREY LYLES

PERPEDIT ✓ PUBLISHING, INK

PERPEDIT PUBLISHING, INK

Perpedit Publishing, Ink
PO Box 190246
Boise, Idaho 83719
http://www.perpedit.com

First eBook Edition: 2022
ISBN: 978-1-7341439-6-6 (eBook)

First Paperback Edition: 2022
ISBN: 978-1-7341439-7-3 (print)

This is a work of fiction. Names, characters, places, organizations and events portrayed in this novel are either products of the author's imagination or are used fictitiously.

Cover design by 100 Covers: https://100covers.com

Published in the United States of America by Perpedit Publishing, Ink

Shadow Ranch is dedicated to my three favorite
Children of the Light—Maverick, Dakota and Grace.
May Jesus' light always shine bright in you!

You are all children of the light and children of the day.
We do not belong to the night or to the darkness.

1 THESSALONIANS 5:5

PROLOGUE

F OR AS LONG AS she could remember, Kasenia Clarke had harbored a love-hate relationship with Arizona weather. Tonight, she tilted toward love.

A spring breeze drifted over the hillside patio, teasing her hair and carrying a sweet citrus-blossom tang from a nearby orchard, a smell so delicious she could taste it. Below her, Mexican poppies blanketed the rocky slope, their golden petals luminous in the sunset's waning rays. Saguaro silhouettes, dozens of them, rose above the poppies and creosote bushes. Kasenia imagined the tall cacti with their barrel arms raised heavenward to be prickly desert warriors welcoming the night. Babushka Irina, her Russian grandmother, would say they were praising God.

"Kasenia...a penny for your thoughts."

She smiled and turned to her host.

Across the table from her, just beyond a candle flickering in a lantern, Brewster Wiley winked. "I'd swear you were a thousand miles away."

Tall and slender yet buff beneath his fitted suit jacket, the University of Arizona professor had a trendy blond haircut—short on the sides with a bit more on top, a reddish-blond five o'clock shadow, and a smile she couldn't resist. As always, the pocket handkerchief in his silver-gray Armani jacket matched his silk tie, this one a blue paisley print.

"Such a beautiful evening." Kasenia lifted her wine glass, twisting it to catch the candle's shimmer through the ginger ale. In Russia, she drank wine, but here she was too young. "I always enjoy sitting on your patio with you, Brewster. The view is amazing."

He raised his glass in response. "A view made even lovelier by your presence, my dear."

"You can barely see me." She laughed.

"Oh, but I remember..." His eyes glittered in the candlelight.

She didn't blush easily—in her industry, beauty was expected—but something about his tone triggered a flush of heat. She patted her cheeks. "You're embarrassing me."

"Good." He chuckled. "I'm that kinda guy." He drained the glass, set it on the table and stood. "I'll be right back." With his long-legged stride, he was across the patio and inside the condo in moments.

Smiling, Kasenia shrugged the light-weight beige shawl her babushka had crocheted for her off her shoulders and settled into her chair to savor the peaceful evening. But as often happened when she slowed long enough to relax, the dissonance that plagued her soul surfaced, a dissonance never more apparent than when she sat on this patio.

It wasn't Brewster's fault his concrete-and-steel condo was a far cry from Babushka Irina's cottage on the north bank of Russia's Usva River. Or that her little village by the same name was the only place Kasenia could picture when asked about a hometown. Tucson had become a somewhat permanent residence after she entered the University of Arizona. Yet, she had no special attachment to the city. To any city. Her entire life, she'd been caught between cultures.

From birth, she and her brother, Sergei, had been shuttled around the world until their photojournalist mother tired of homeschooling them. Her solution was to leave them with her parents in their isolated Ural Mountain community. But their American father, a mining engineer with clients on almost every continent, had objected. "Nadia, no...nyet."

Kasenia giggled. Her father, who knew a mere handful of Russian words, used *nyet* whenever possible.

"They can't learn anything useful in that two-horse hamlet," he'd insisted. "They need an American education to be somebody and get somewhere in this world."

Nadia had bristled at the insult, but he was adamant. Their compromise was for their children to live in Tucson with their paternal grandparents from January through June and in Usva with their maternal grandparents from July through December of each year.

Below the patio, Tucson's lights twinkled to life across the valley, one after another, like reborn fallen stars. Kasenia blew out a long breath and let her shoulders relax. She could watch this light show every night. It was a great way to unwind.

Now nineteen and a U of A senior, she only returned to Russia during school breaks. But fourteen-year-old Sergei continued to be shuttled back and forth every six months, an unfortunate arrangement that made them both sad. She was her brother's best friend as well as his stateside guardian. No one understood the impact of their rootless upbringing like they did.

Neither their parents nor their grandparents grasped how the two of them didn't feel at home anywhere. How from their early years, they hadn't fit into any particular culture. How they didn't have a sense of belonging in either Russia or America. They were outsiders on both sides of the ocean, no matter how hard they tried to adapt.

Kasenia's solution was to avoid close relationships. The better someone knew her, the more likely they were to realize she was *not in her own plate*, as they said in Russia regarding awkward situations. She put on a confident facade but had a feeling her confusion and discomfort were obvious.

"We're freaks," Sergei had complained. "Our accents give us away, even though we speak English better than we speak Russian, better than my American friends speak English."

"Remember," she said, "they haven't had the years of language-acquisition classes the Tucson school district required us to take."

"They can still tell we're different." Her brother tried harder than she did to assimilate. He'd even undergone accent-reduction therapy. But living in Russia half of every year reversed any progress he made.

She sighed and turned to the wavering candle flame. Too bad Sergei's accent was such an issue for him. He hadn't mentioned it lately, so maybe he was outgrowing his frustration.

The mild zephyr wind—one her babushka would call a *veterok*—caressed Kasenia's shoulders and danced the candle flame to the smooth jazz wafting from hidden speakers. She adjusted her sundress straps and flipped her hair behind her shoulders. The dress was Brewster's favorite, a long sea-green chiffon he said matched her eyes.

Brewster...

Her heart skipped a beat. The man was an enigma, which was what attracted her to him. That and the fact he was the best-looking professor on campus.

Kasenia hadn't been searching for romance. She'd fast-tracked her degree program, which meant she devoted endless time and energy to schoolwork. She also monitored her brother's schooling and drove him to his activities. In addition, the two of them freelanced as fashion models. She hardly had time for friends, much less romance.

Somehow, however, romance found her. Never in a million years would she have pictured herself perched on a professor's patio with a wine glass in her hand, basking in a beautiful evening. Yet, here she sat, just because he asked her to proofread a book he was writing. According to Brewster, her papers outshone those of his other students, thanks to her "impeccable English." The language-acquisition classes had paid off as well as proofreading for her mother who, though she was Russian, wrote mostly for English-language publications.

He'd been so kind to her and Sergei and their Tucson grandpa, Gordon Clarke. At least twice a week, the professor appeared on their doorstep with a takeout meal in one hand, flowers in the other, and a baseball glove under his arm. Sergei's eyes always brightened when he saw the glove.

"This is for you, Kasenia," Brewster would say. "So you can spend your evening studying, not cooking."

After they ate, he'd send her to her desk, and he and Sergei would play catch until dark. Kasenia loved watching them through the office window. She knew how much her brother missed their dad. Though Brewster didn't attempt to replace their father, he filled a hole in Sergei's life. Now that she thought about it, he filled a hole in her life too, one she didn't know she had.

Due to university rules, they'd kept their professor-student romance "under wraps," as Brewster suggested. She grinned. Having their own little secret, just the two of them—and her family, added an extra zing to their relationship.

But then her friend Diane spotted them at a restaurant. Later, she said, "Kasenia, just because your father is overseas doesn't mean you have to hit on a prof for daddy love. Professor Wiley may keep his beard short, but I see a hint of gray in it."

"That's not how it is," Kasenia had protested. "When I'm with him, I feel tethered, no longer like a balloon bouncing from place to place, searching for a place to land. Please don't tell anyone you saw us together."

Her explanation didn't convince Diane, but that was okay. Kasenia was used to being misunderstood. And she herself didn't understand how easily the settled sensation gave way to her ever-present ache for stability when he wasn't around. And sometimes even when he was around, like now.

Despite her fickle feelings, Brewster's maturity was a refreshing change from her ex-boyfriend, Thad, who lived and breathed sports—and reeked like a locker room more often than not. Shaking her head, she remembered the night he took her to a high school wrestling match. He'd heard wrestling was big in Russia. Seated on the hard bleachers surrounded by a noisy crowd, they'd split a candy bar and washed it down with a shared soft drink. That was months ago. She hadn't dated anyone more than twice since then—until now.

She took another sip of ginger ale and swiveled her chair in time to see the first star emerge above the mountains behind Tucson. Then another, and another. *Whatever did I see in Thad, other than his sky-blue eyes?* She pursed her lips. Strange, she couldn't remember.

Hearing the glass door slide open, she faced the table again.

Smiling his wide irresistible smile, Brewster stepped onto the patio.

Ah... Kasenia's heart flipflopped. *Apparently, I haven't forgotten what I see in this man.* She watched him walk around the patio table. *Nice looks, sharp dresser, good taste, great conversationalist, generous, conge nial...* Well, most of the time. He'd snapped at her a time or two, but he always apologized, with flowers. He attributed his mood swings to post traumatic stress disorder resulting from trauma he'd experienced in a special forces unit.

Brewster didn't sit at the table. Instead, he knelt before her chair, bringing with him a whiff of aftershave. He must have added a splash when he removed his jacket and tie—along with the holstered handgun he normally kept on his belt. His blue silk shirt, now open at the neck, exposed a short chain with his initials in the center—BAW.

Kasenia grinned. After a bit of wheedling, she'd learned his middle name.

He took her hands in his. "I have a question for you."

She tilted her head. "A question, for me?" He'd dropped hints of a long-term relationship, but Brewster Wiley was a busy professor with a demanding side business, something to do with sales. She hadn't dared to expect anything more from him than their current clandestine intimacy.

"How much do you like the view from up here?" he asked.

"Oh, I, uh..." This wasn't the question she'd expected. "I like it, a lot. You probably never tire of seeing sunrises and sunsets without buildings to obstruct your view."

"My view can be yours, along with all this." Brewster released her hands and indicated the three-story condominium rising behind them. Its tall windows reflected the last glimmer of sunset. "When..." He pulled a velvet case from his shirt pocket and opened it, angling it so the diamond inside captured the candle's glow and refracted a brilliant burst of golden light.

"When...you agree to marry me. Will you marry me, Kasenia?"

To her surprise, "yes" was not the first word to come to mind. Rather, it was "home." Marrying Brewster would establish a permanent home for both her and Sergei, who'd love to live in this fancy condo on the hill.

They could finally put down roots, be *tethered* to one spot on the earth. Sam, as Sergei liked to be called in Tucson, could enter high school assured he wouldn't be forced to leave his friends behind after the first semester. Wouldn't need to relearn pop culture each time he returned from a village that hadn't yet joined the twenty-first century.

He could embrace his world and be a normal American teen. Transitioning to a different culture every half year had been hard, especially when their Russian dedushka and their American grandmother both died while she and Sergei were in opposite countries. Surely, their parents would let Sergei live fulltime with her and Brewster.

Wait... Kasenia sucked in a breath. How could she even consider his proposal?

Diane was right. At forty-five, Brewster was almost as old as her father. Marrying him could spark generational clashes as well as cultural clashes. Even now, he sometimes acted like a bossy big brother, certain he knew how to do things better than she did. Russians would say he liked to set the weather. And then there was his PTSD, which would likely affect a marriage.

Brewster leaned closer, probing her soul with his beautiful gray eyes. "Kasenia, sweetheart, did you hear my question?"

"I'm sorry. You caught me off-guard." She paused. "I am honored you asked me to marry you, but..."

"But what?" He looked so concerned, she couldn't help but smooth the worry creases between his eyebrows with her thumbs.

"You're a professor, Brewster. I'm one of your students, a foreign student at that, and much younger than you."

"You're a gifted, mature student, Kasenia." He took her hands again. "A woman weeks away from receiving an undergrad degree two years ahead of your peers. I'm proud to say I helped you achieve that goal."

Lifting a lock of hair from her shoulder, he studied it in the candlelight. "I know I've told you before—I love this color. It's natural, right?"

She nodded.

"It's like..." He released the strand and ran his fingers down her arm, sending chills along her spine. "Like burnished copper. None of my other—" He stopped.

She lifted her chin. "Other?"

"I tend to date blondes and redheads." Brewster's boyish grin never failed to cause a hitch in her breath. "Must be something in my DNA." He chuckled. "None of them have had hair quite this color, natural or otherwise."

"I'm glad you like it." She smiled. "Americans say redheads have more fun, but I didn't have much fun until I met you."

"Actually, Americans say blondes have more fun, but I consider your words a compliment." He removed the ring from the case. "I plan to have a lifetime of memorable moments with you, Kasenia. All because God told me you're the one for me."

"Really?" Kasenia gasped. "God talked to you about me?" She clutched her chest. "When was that?"

"The first day you walked into my class with your beautiful hair catching the light from the windows, and your long legs... Well, let's just say I was more than ready to obey when he spoke."

"What did he say?"

Brewster frowned, as if annoyed she questioned him. "Not much, just, 'She's the one,' but that was enough for me." He grasped her left hand in his. "Remember, Kasenia, when you marry me, you'll no longer be a foreigner. You'll be Mrs. Brewster Wiley, and through me, you can become an American citizen."

She didn't want to ruin the moment by mentioning she and Sergei already had dual citizenship, thanks to their parents. Or that she hadn't actually accepted his proposal.

He slipped the ring onto her finger, lifted her to her feet, and for the first time, said, "I love you, Kasenia Anya Clarke."

She wrapped her arms around his neck, sensing the weight of the ring. Did diamonds always feel so heavy? "I... I love you, too, Brewster Anton Wiley."

"Just remember, Kasenia, sweetheart..." He nuzzled her neck. "Until you graduate and leave the university, no one can know you and I are engaged. If anyone asks, tell them this beautiful ring came from your Russian boyfriend. The two of you will be married there this summer."

1

— ◦ —

K ASENIA ANYA CLARKE HADN'T meant to fall for Brewster Anton
Wiley. But when she began proofreading his book for him, he'd
insisted on weekly dinner meetings to discuss her findings. And she'd
seen no reason to refuse a night out with a handsome man who treated
her like a princess.

Their first meeting, he took her to one of Tucson's nicest restaurants,
where he'd reserved a table for two in a secluded patio corner. Over lob-
ster and steak, he inquired about her past. "I enjoy your accent, Kasenia."
Melted butter on his fingers glistened in the candlelight. "So rich and
exotic, yet you appear very American. Must be a story behind that."

"I wouldn't call my heritage exotic, but I suppose you could say it's
unique." She cut into her steak, inhaling the satisfying aroma. "My
American father is a mining engineer whose job has him circling the
globe. That's how he met my Russian mother. She's a photojournalist.
Traveling with Dad provides opportunities for her to write travel articles
and take pictures for magazines and websites."

"Ah, so you're half Russian."

"Yes, and half mongrel, as my dad says." She laughed. "My grandfather
doesn't appreciate that word. He says the family comes from..." She
imitated his growly voice. "'Good northern-European stock,' whatever
that means."

Brewster chuckled and wiped his hands with the linen napkin. "Having a mother who's a journalist explains why you're such an excellent
writer—and proofreader."

"I've proofed many an English-language article for her. But I had to learn to speak the language because I heard mostly Russian as a child." Kasenia tapped her chin then pointed at his. "Some butter on your—"

"Thanks." He dabbed with the napkin. "Did you grow up in Tucson?"

"Yes and no. When Sergei and I were young, we traveled with our parents. After that, we lived with our grandparents, alternating countries. Six months here and six months in Usva, Russia, each year."

"I've been to Russia but never heard of Usva. Must be small."

"It's a tiny village in the Urals. My Dedushka Abram was the mayor for thirty-two years before he passed away."

"Which do you prefer, Tucson or Usva?"

"I'm not fond of the desert." Kasenia wrinkled her nose. "Though it's, of course, warmer than Usva. Those bushes..." She indicated the Mexican fan palms and bird of paradise bushes that bordered the patio, their red-orange blossoms muted beneath the string lighting. "Those bushes would never survive a winter there. Tucson is also more modern. My babushka has indoor plumbing and electricity but no Wi-Fi or car. She says she doesn't need a vehicle because she walks everywhere."

"Sounds primitive," Brewster shook his head. "Not my cup of tea. What do you do when you're there, other than shovel snow?"

"Sergei and I make simple repairs, tend the animals and garden, trim trees, help our Babushka Irina bake bread and put aside food for the winter, and whatever else she needs. But as much as we love it there, we miss big-city life." She grinned. "Compared to Usva, Tucson is truly a big city."

"So, basically, you've lived in two worlds your whole life."

Kasenia nodded.

"Interesting." He steepled his long, well-manicured fingers. "I've heard everybody knows everybody in small towns. You must have life-long friends in Usva."

"Yes, but not close friends. They're both fascinated and disgusted we live part-time in America. They hear the difference in our speech, see it in our clothing. Someone actually said we walk like Americans, not Russians. But I think our walk comes from being trained fashion models."

"Fashion models, huh?"

She nodded and cut another piece of steak. "My friends ask about American movies, fashions and music, but their parents don't like us to spend a lot of time together. They're afraid their children will want to immigrate—or stray from their Russian Orthodox religion."

"How about your parents..." Brewster picked up his wine glass. "Are they in Tucson with you?"

"I think they're in South Africa right now." Kasenia shrugged. "That was the last place they called from, anyway."

A strange light came into his gray eyes. "Ever travel with them?"

"Now and then, if it's somewhere Sergei and I haven't been before. Last summer, we spent three weeks in Thailand. I loved it there."

He sat back, glass in hand. "Beautiful country."

"You've been?"

"A couple times with a special ops team."

"What did you do in Thailand?"

"Can't say, but I'm trained in all manner of undercover warfare. Nothing gets past me." His eyes darkened. "*Nothing.*" He dropped his voice. "I can shoot out a coyote's eyeball at fifty yards."

"Eww." Kasenia shuddered.

Brewster chuckled. "I'm that kinda guy." He opened his jacket flap and pointed to the pistol on his belt. "I carry, and I don't hesitate to use it."

She shivered. She'd seen coyotes wandering around Tucson and an occasional javelina. *Surely, he wouldn't discharge his gun in town. Would he?*

"Now you know, Kasenia..." He touched her hand. "You're always safe with me."

Disturbed by the coyote story, she shook if off, attributing it to male bravado. "Did you go directly to college after you left the military?"

"In the midst of inserting American *influence* into hot spots around the world..." He winked. "I acquired what I call a bunk-light education.

Got my undergrad while in the military and then later, my master's degree and doctorate in the States."

Lifting his glass, he drained the last of the contents and set it down. "I had military benefits, but I needed extra income to wine and dine the ladies." He waggled his eyebrows. "Moonlighted as a firearms instructor and also as a tactical advisor for law enforcement."

Their twenty-something waiter approached the table, a wine bottle in one hand, ginger ale in the other—and a big smile for Kasenia. "May I top off your drinks?"

He directed his question to Kasenia, whose glass was a quarter full, but Brewster answered, "Please do." After the waiter left, Brewster said, "Change of topic," and looked her up and down. "A pretty girl like you must have several boyfriends. Am I right?"

Kasenia swallowed a smirk. The waiter's interest hadn't gone unnoticed. "I have guy friends, but I'm too busy with work and school and acting as a surrogate mom to be romantically involved with anyone." She didn't mention Thad. He was old news. "I don't want Sergei to flounder because our parents aren't around."

She'd never told anyone her determination not to fail her brother like her parents had failed her and Sergei. Her mom and dad seemed to think they were on an endless, childless, international honeymoon with no responsibilities except to pursue their careers. Sometimes when they asked her to check their bank account or pay their taxes, she felt like she was parenting them as well as Sergei.

Grandpa Gordon was equally immature. He rarely helped around the house or with Sergei. All he did was play, whether it was golfing with his buddies, hanging out at the shooting range, tinkering with his old car, or traveling to car shows. In his seventies, he had a white mustache and goatee and wore his long white hair in a braid that fell halfway down his back. His daily uniform never varied—black t-shirt under a leather vest plastered with vintage-style car patches, faded blue jeans topped by a tooled-leather belt that had a holstered gun hanging from it, and brown lace-up work boots.

"How about you?" She grinned. "A pretty boy like you must have several girlfriends. Am I right?" It was an audacious question to ask a professor, but she was curious, and repeating his words back to him gave it a humorous twist.

Brewster chuckled. "Touché." He ran his fingers through his short hair. "I've had some fairly serious relationships since my marriage to Lorraine several years ago." As if counting the women, he tapped his fingers one by one. "Wanda, Veronica, Rachel, Chloe, Alana, Margo, Brittany..." He shrugged. "At the moment, I'm footloose and fancy-free. And that's fine by me. I've got my university work and side business to concentrate on as well as writing books."

"You're a busy man." Kasenia forked Parmesan cheese from a small bowl onto her roasted vegetables. She hated to see marriages disintegrate, but he seemed to have moved on. Still, his former lovers' names had come to him rather fast. Was he one of those guys who kept a record of his conquests? "Do you have children?"

"A couple teenagers." He smiled. "Great kids. They live with Lorraine. I see them occasionally."

"That's good. You said *books*, plural. How many have you written in addition to the education manual?"

"I'm working on five total."

"So, tell me..." She cocked her chin.

He arched an eyebrow. "Yes?"

"You're a business administration professor, you've been in the military, you have special training. Why write about education when you could write about business or your world travels and undercover experiences?"

"You'll be pleased to know I'm writing on all those topics and more." Brewster's eyes brightened. "My favorites are my two novels, *Traitor* and *Terrorist*. Both feature military assassins."

Kasenia grimaced. Neither title suggested a book she'd want to read.

"*Traitor* is two-thirds complete, *Terrorist* is more than half done, and I'm turning my doctoral dissertation into a book. I also have a companion workbook in progress for the education manual."

"Let me guess. It's two-thirds finished, right?"

The scowl that flicked across his handsome features morphed into a sigh. "Ah, you caught me there." He folded his hands and offered her a little-boy smile. "That's why I need your help, Kasenia. I have total confidence you'll get me over the finish line again and again, one book at a time."

Oh, so the professor planned to keep her on the payroll. A steady gig would be nice. She could only hope his fiction was better than his tedious nonfiction. "You're juggling a lot of projects along with teaching."

"That's why I live by myself, though I sometimes get lonely. Roommates can be distracting."

No wonder he'd been through so many women. He was a charming dinner companion. But if he was always writing, he probably bored his "roommates," as he called them, into the arms of other men. "Have you had any books published?"

"Not yet. Just articles for academic journals." Brewster aimed his trigger finger at her. "But with your help, it'll happen sooner than later."

"Remember..." She smiled. "I have a thesis to write, as you well know. I'll try to put a little time into the proofread each day, but my progress will likely be slow."

Brewster winked. "Fine by me. No matter how long it takes, I look forward to treating you to dinner once a week to discuss your findings."

"That's very kind of you." Kasenia grinned, already anticipating the next dinner date with the handsome professor.

By the time Kasenia completed her proofread, Brewster had learned her dream to establish her own modeling agency plus set up an import business to distribute Usva goods in the U.S. The village women created exquisite felt dolls, egg art and lace, along with beautiful quilts and crocheted items like Babushka Irina made.

She and Brewster had grown comfortable together, and their dinners, to her surprise, had morphed from business to romantic. He hadn't kissed her or asked to take her to bed. In theory, they didn't violate the university's mandate, although he sometimes held her hand when they were alone.

One evening during a stroll around the botanical gardens, he gave her a heart-shaped gold pendant necklace with *B+K* in the center. She'd been moved to tears. "Oh, Brewster. You are so sweet."

"Turn around, and I'll clasp it for you."

"Thank you."

When he fastened the necklace, he murmured in her ear, "I'm glad you like the necklace. I had it custom-etched just for you. If anyone asks about it, tell them your Russian boyfriend sent it to you."

She rubbed the heart with her forefinger. "I love it."

"I like to think you'll never take this necklace off."

Was he hinting at forever? Was she ready for forever?

"Because..." he whispered, "we have something special, Kasenia. Something we *never* want to lose."

Kasenia graduated on a Friday afternoon in an outdoor ceremony held at Arizona Stadium. The next evening, she married Brewster in a noisy helicopter as it circled above Las Vegas. The city's bright lights added sparkle to the brief ceremony. The wedding company provided the chaplain, a small cake, two champagne glasses engraved with *Mr. & Mrs. Brewster Wiley*, a bottle of champagne, and a dozen peach-hued roses tied with a matching ribbon.

The flowers added a hint of color to the chopper's utilitarian cabin and complemented Kasenia's simple white gown. She inhaled their sweet perfume, grateful for the attempt to enliven the cabin's dull gray interior and mask the smell of aviation fuel.

Brewster, who wore a camouflage tuxedo, didn't seem to notice the ambience, or lack thereof. He practically bounced with excitement. "This reminds me of my jumps from military birds. Those were the best days of my life."

Saying their vows inside a loud vibrating machine was not Kasenia's dream wedding. She'd agreed because Brewster didn't want to wait and had promised her and her parents—and more importantly, Babushka

Irina—a Russian wedding. Part of the story she'd been telling her friends was true. She would be married in Russia, even if it wasn't to a Russian.

Her grandmother's Russian Orthodox priest would officiate. Sergei would be the ring bearer *if* Kasenia could talk him into it. So far, he was less than thrilled by the idea.

Brewster had convinced her parents they didn't need to travel to Tucson to attend the graduation or the wedding. "You can watch both events live online and see us up-close and personal."

Kasenia, who'd agreed with him, found she missed her mom and dad more than she expected, even as she threw them kisses via the internet. Along with her parents, she found consolation in knowing they'd see each other soon.

Their Vegas honeymoon was short, just five days, but they made the most of it. They swam in the pool, strolled past water-and-light displays, enjoyed concerts and magic shows. And registered for ballroom dance lessons. Brewster loved magic, and he loved to dance.

On the way from their hotel suite to the street-level dance hall, he indicated their endless reflections in the mirrored elevator walls. "Without a doubt, we'll be the best-looking couple on the dance floor." He straightened the black bowtie on the pale-green silk shirt he wore beneath a black tuxedo jacket.

Kasenia giggled, and the sequins on her floor-length forest-green gown shimmered. "We wouldn't want to be vain about it, of course."

"Why not? It's true."

The band was excellent and so were the teachers. For Kasenia, dancing with her handsome husband beneath shimmering chandeliers was like stepping into a Russian fairytale. She reveled in how tenderly he held her during the slow dances. And how one thing led to another, and they soon found themselves back at their suite, enjoying their new life as a married couple.

The last morning of their Vegas stay, the hotel treated them to espresso, chocolate muffins and tropical fruit cups on the suite's private terrace overlooking the Strip. "We'll have a longer honeymoon in Finland, maybe a month," Brewster said. "Finland isn't far from Russia, and I've always wanted to check out their famous saunas."

"Don't you remember we decided on Bora Bora, sweetheart?" Kasenia touched his hand. "It's more romantic and relaxing than Finland. I've been both places."

"I didn't ask your opinion." Brewster jumped to his feet, bumping the table and rattling the dishes. "Leave it to you to ruin a perfectly good morning." He stomped into the suite. "Time to pack."

Blinking back tears, Kasenia stared straight ahead. *What just happened?* He'd always valued her opinion, or so she thought. Her parents and grandparents never said things like that to each other. She tried to smother the dreadful notion, but it surfaced anyway. *Is this what our marriage will be like?*

Almost as soon as the question entered her head, Brewster was at her side. "Sweetheart..." He sat in front of her and took her hands. "Sorry I'm a bit grumpy this morning. Worn out from all our celebrating, I guess." He winked. "It was worth it." He squeezed her hands. "I forgot we talked about Bora Bora, but I know you'll love Finland."

The day they returned to Tucson, Brewster moved in with Kasenia and her brother and grandfather, and life went on almost as if nothing had changed. He traveled often for his side business, and the rest of the family continued their usual routines.

One hot summer afternoon, Kasenia picked up Sergei from his guitar lesson. Instead of going home, they headed for a guest ranch outside of Tucson to do a photoshoot. Now and then, the agency found modeling work they could do together. People seemed to like their tall slender limbs, green eyes, and ginger hair, as their agency described it.

Sergei had recently overtaken Kasenia in height and was now a half-inch taller, an "achievement" he mentioned daily. He'd filled out and could pass for an eighteen-year-old, but he was still a juvenile. She never allowed the agency to schedule her brother when she couldn't be present.

When the city was behind them and they were on the highway, Kasenia turned the radio down. "How was your lesson?"

"All right." He bit into the apple she'd brought him.

"You're extra quiet."

"Just tired, I guess."

"You were supposed to memorize a song for today, right?"

He shrugged. "Aced it."

"Of course. You have an amazing memory."

He looked out the window. "It's too hot for a photoshoot."

Kasenia checked the dashboard thermometer. One hundred five degrees. She couldn't remember ever doing an outdoor session on such a warm afternoon. "According to the agency, we'll mostly be in barns or stables, with fans, or inside the ranch headquarters. Maybe a couple shots in the corral, but I'm sure no one wants us to drip sweat."

The apple's sweet scent filled the car. Kasenia drank from her water bottle, wishing she'd brought a second apple for herself.

Sam slid his favorite guitar CD into the player. "I heard Brewster complaining about this job we're doing today, like he was mad we didn't ask his permission."

"I told him we committed to it months ago."

"But why would we ask his permission?"

"He wants to start our own modeling agency with the three of us doing the modeling. Later, we'll hire more people." She didn't answer the permission question because she didn't know the answer. Was this how marriage was supposed to be? Brewster wanted to know her comings and goings, every nickel she earned, every penny she spent, and everyone she talked with or texted.

Rather than explain her interactions, she'd stopped answering calls and responding to texts. As a result, her friends no longer attempted to communicate with her. And she'd noticed Sergei's friends weren't coming over as often.

Her brother snorted. "First, Brewster thinks he's a writer. Now, he thinks he's a model."

"Sergei..."

"Call me Sam. We're in the U.S., remember?"

"Okay, okay." She rolled her eyes. "Sam, that's not a nice way to talk about my husband, your brother-in-law."

"He's no brother to me. You'd think he was my dad, the way he orders me around."

"Well, he is old enough to be your father."

"And yours."

Kasenia sighed.

"Just because he's old doesn't mean he has a right to be so bossy." Sam scowled. "He blows a fuse every time I open the refrigerator door."

The first time Brewster groused at Sam for searching for a snack, she'd said, "You were once a growing teenage boy. You know Sam's hunger pangs are real."

"When I was his age, I was fending for myself," he'd retorted. "I got used to being hungry. So can he."

Brewster's grocery hang-up was getting to her too. He wanted her to cook gourmet meals complete with elaborate desserts and expensive wines yet said she spent too much on food, though she used her money not his. He'd asked the university to deposit his paycheck in her bank account, but that hadn't happened yet.

"When we get to town..." Kasenia glanced at Sam. "We'll stop at a grocery store to buy some energy bars you can keep in your bedroom."

"I'll have to think of a better hiding place."

"A better hiding place than what?"

"Than where I hid my coin collection. I put it under my mattress, but now it's gone. I should have put it in the safe deposit box." He rubbed his nose with his knuckle. "Then my favorite t-shirt disappeared and my Xbox—and the drone you gave me for Christmas. I couldn't have lost all those things. Brewster must have taken them."

"Brewster? Why do you...?" She couldn't finish the unthinkable notion.

"Either he took my stuff or Grandpa did, but my things never went missing before you married the dude."

She'd had some items disappear, too, like a favorite dress and a new watch, even frilly underwear, and had chalked it up to misplacing her things. But underwear went from the laundry basket to the washer and dryer and then to her dresser drawer. How could she misplace it?

On the other hand, she couldn't imagine Brewster was a kleptomaniac. Her husband was too together, too smart. Surely, they'd find the items or learn the reason they vanished.

If she had to, she'd talk to him about the problem, ask if he was missing anything. But she'd have to be careful not to accuse him of theft, or he might have one of his all-too-frequent temper tantrums.

"Someone must have broken into our house, Sam. If anything else disappears, tell me and I'll call the police." She smiled. "That work for you?"

"Go ahead and believe what you want. But remember, if it was a thief, they've broken in more than once."

Kasenia shivered. The idea of a stranger entering their home uninvited and rifling through their possessions made her feel defiled.

A mileage sign indicated the ranch turnoff was a quarter mile ahead. She slowed and punched Sam's shoulder. "Ready to put your cowboy on?"

He combed his fingers through his hair. "Gonna be scorching hot."

"You'll get to be around horses."

He brightened. "I like horses."

2

O N THE WAY HOME, Sam slept and Kasenia contemplated her two-and-a-half months of marriage. She wasn't sure what she'd expected, but so far, it wasn't like her parents' marriage. When her mom and dad disagreed, they worked out a compromise. When she and Brewster butted heads, he had the final word, every time, which was crazy. She'd always been able to hold her own in an argument.

But something about his stony glare brought his boast to mind—*I can shoot out a coyote's eyeball at fifty yards*—and kept her from pushing to have her say.

She stared at the flat dry desert beyond the car window. Each time she tried to set a Russian wedding date, Brewster pushed it to the next season. First, they'd planned an early summer ceremony, then a mid-summer celebration, and then a fall wedding. Her parents and her grandmother begged for a solid date, so they could arrange their schedules, send invitations and begin preparations, yet he wouldn't commit.

The last time she asked, he'd yelled, "Get off my back," and stomped from the kitchen into the garage, where he jumped in his Corvette, slammed the door and took off. She could hear the tires squeal down the driveway, onto the street and out of the neighborhood.

That, she had a feeling, was her clue to stop asking. However, her babushka and her parents hadn't stopped asking. They also asked why Sam wasn't spending the summer in Usva, like before.

"Brewster wants the three of us to travel together for the wedding," she'd told them.

"But Kasenia," her mother said, "he keeps delaying the wedding."

Her father added, "We're Sam's parents. We decide when and where he travels, not Brewster."

"I know," she'd responded. "We'll come soon."

Two weeks into their marriage, she and Brewster had been getting ready for bed when he said his wedding ring made his finger itch. He took it off and placed it on his dresser beside his handgun.

"We could ask a jeweler to coat it," Kasenia said, "or we could buy one that doesn't irritate your skin."

"I don't want a jeweler to mess with it, sweetheart. They might ruin it." He pulled her onto the bed. "This one is the original ring. It has your initials and our wedding date engraved on the inside. I can't bear to part with such an important symbol of our union. I'll keep it on my dresser, where I can see it every day." Slipping the covers over the two of them, he'd kissed her and then kissed her again.

End of discussion.

Much of the time, the ring sat alone on Brewster's dresser because he was gone so often during the summer. For Kasenia, it symbolized the loneliness and abandonment she felt, emotions similar to what she'd experienced with her parents' frequent absences. He rarely told her where he was going or when he would return, got angry when she asked, and almost never called her or answered her calls.

Brewster taught a summer class, she knew that much, and his toned physique told her he visited the gym regularly. Yet he refused to jog or work out with her. He had a side business that required lots of travel, he said, by car and by air. Supposedly, the university let him distance teach when necessary, and supposedly, he promoted products handcrafted by Arizona artisans. However, she hadn't seen any of the items, not even pictures.

When he was in town and available, he was careful to let her know exactly what she should fix for dinner and what time it should be ready. Takeout meals and lavish dinners at pricey restaurants had ceased the moment they returned to Tucson. Instead, she fixed the food and washed the dishes.

He'd taken her to lunch once, the day he suggested they establish a family modeling agency, a dream he'd stolen from her. Edgy and out of sorts, he refused to hold her hand while they walked to the restaurant and acted like he didn't want anyone to see them.

From a far corner of the shaded mister-cooled patio, he'd watched everyone's comings and goings and seemed particularly interested in the three giggling college girls at a nearby table. But that could have been her newlywed jealousy at work.

Brewster's temper flared over little things, like the soap that fell from the shower caddy onto the shower floor. "You should have retrieved the soap," he said, "before I slipped on it." Not that he was hurt.

Anything out of place angered him. Shoes left in the living room, shirts not properly spaced on the closet rod, spices out of order on the spice rack. The only thing he "cooked" was cinnamon toast, but if the cinnamon container wasn't in the same spot every time he opened the pantry door, the entire household heard about it.

Once or twice a week, he butted heads with her grandfather over tools scattered on the garage floor. The 1933 Ford Roadster her grandpa was restoring and the accompanying tools consumed half the double-car garage. The "lazy man's mess," as Brewster called it, irritated him to no end. But he wasn't above using the other half.

He insisted Kasenia and her grandfather leave their vehicles on the street so his silver Vette with its black top and red interior could be parked in the garage. She couldn't count how many times she'd heard, "The Arizona sun is *merciless* on ragtops and leather interiors."

Though Brewster was rarely home in the daytime, neither Kasenia nor her grandfather dared to drive their vehicles into the garage. "Gotta tell you, Senya Girl," Gordon insisted, "I'd do what I want in my own home, but I don't wanna hear him bellyache. Gets on my nerves."

A roadrunner darted across the highway, its dark crest high and long tail straight out behind. Kasenia giggled at the silly bird with its swift stiffed-legged stride.

But when her musings returned to Brewster, her laughter dissolved into a sigh. One night early in their marriage, as she was rubbing sweet almond oil on his back, something he loved for her to do, she offered to travel with him. "I'd like to go with you tomorrow, sweetheart, to keep you company and see what you do on your trips."

"Nah." He bent his elbow behind him to point to a spot she'd missed. "Arizona backroads are dusty and boring. You need to be here to keep an eye on your brother."

"Sam's a good boy. Besides, Grandpa will be with him."

"Gordon's always hanging with his cronies at the club. Sam is *your* responsibility. You need to make sure he stays out of trouble."

Since that evening, sweet almond oil's nutty fragrance, an aroma she'd once enjoyed, no longer smelled so sweet. But while Brewster was gone, she'd made a point to treat *her responsibility* to a day at the waterpark. And a night at the movies, complete with sugar-free soft drinks and butter-free popcorn, thanks to a generous tip from a modeling client.

They also ate pelmeni meat dumplings and tart borscht at their favorite European deli, savoring every bite. Borscht was a special treat because Brewster despised beets. They never had the soup at home.

That night, she parked in the garage.

Kasenia didn't mind cooking and cleaning, but she missed her previous busy life. She'd been accepted into a master's program at U of A and would have registered for one or two summer classes to get a head start. Brewster, however, insisted she take a year off from school. "Like people did in the Bible," he said. "In modern terms, we'd call it an extended honeymoon."

She wondered if his real reason was for her to have time to fix the gourmet meals he demanded. "The Bible talks about honeymoons?"

"You can read it for yourself in Deuteronomy." He lifted an eyebrow. "That's in the Old Testament. Look it up. Chapter twenty-four, verse five."

"You memorized chapter and verse?"

"I'm that kinda guy." He winked.

Her husband was an endless marvel to Kasenia. He knew everything about everything, whether it was history, astronomy, biology or business.

And now, the Bible. She'd never seen him with a Bible, yet he could tell her a chapter and verse for what she assumed was an obscure passage.

The next day, she bought herself an English Bible—she'd left the Russian Bible her Babushka Irina gave her in Usva—and found the Deuteronomy verse.

If a man has recently married, he must not be sent to war or have any other duty laid on him. For one year he is to be free to stay at home and bring happiness to the wife he has married.

"What?" She read the verse again. The stay-at-home rule was for men, not women. Brewster had switched the roles, implying she was supposed to stay home for *his* happiness, when he was supposed to stay home for hers, something he'd never done.

Kasenia rubbed her neck. It was too much. A recurring contemplation surfaced again. *Should I leave him?*

Once again she reminded herself that when she married Brewster, she'd vowed to love and cherish him "till death do us part." She shouldn't be thinking about leaving him. The ink was barely dry on their marriage license. Kasenia sighed. She needed to try harder to please her husband.

In an attempt to stave off discouragement, she'd begun reading the Bible she purchased. The store clerk had suggested she read from the psalms in the Old Testament and from the first four books in the New Testament called the gospels. He'd stuck an additional Bible in the bag, saying the deal of the day was a free travel-size Bible with every Bible purchase. Now she had two English Bibles. She'd offered the small one to Sam, but he wasn't interested.

Though she didn't understand why, reading a chapter or two every morning lifted her spirits and gave her hope for happier times.

As she'd promised Sam, they stopped for snacks on the way to the house. Knowing Brewster was planning to be home that evening, she purchased a rotisserie chicken to go with the salad she'd left in the fridge. It wasn't gourmet, but it was the best she could manage tonight. Before they left the parking lot, Kasenia texted her husband to tell him they were on their way. She didn't expect a response because he rarely acknowledged her texts.

This time, however, she received an immediate reply. *Can't wait. I have a surprise for you.*

What that could be, she had no idea, but at least he was in a good mood. She shook her head to release her dark thoughts. Tonight would be a happy night with the man she loved. She just needed to show him how much she loved him.

Pulling in front of the house, Kasenia spotted Brewster on the swing at the far end of the front porch. She smiled and waved and said to Sam, "Don't take your snacks into the house right now. You can get them later."

"Why?" He frowned. "I don't..."

She aimed her chin at the porch.

"Oh, I get it. The food Nazi." Shoving the grocery bag under his seat, he grumbled, "The chocolate'll melt."

"Which do you prefer? Melted chocolate or..." She didn't want to say it, but she had a feeling Brewster wasn't above taking her brother's snacks from him. "I'm sorry—"

"Forget it." He jumped out of the car and grabbed his guitar from the backseat, slamming both doors.

Brewster met her at the porch steps. Dressed in a lavender shirt, navy silk tie and gray dress slacks, he had a Diet Dr. Pepper in his hand and a big grin on his handsome face. "I've got an amazing surprise for you two. Quick, pack your bags. We're leaving for a long weekend at my country place."

"Country place?" Kasenia squeaked. "You have a country place?" She narrowed her eyes. The week after they returned from Vegas, he'd had his name added to her bank and credit card accounts, her car title and her safe deposit box. It was where she kept paperwork related to Sam's guardianship, their grandparents' and parents' wills, and other important documents, plus the fifty gold coins her Russian grandfather left her.

Brewster's eyes had bulged at the sight of the coins. "You have gold? Real Russian gold?"

She didn't tell him about Sam's safe deposit box with his fifty gold coins or his savings account where she and her parents deposited money for his future education. And where she deposited his modeling checks. That was Sam's money, not hers or Brewster's.

As far as she knew, Brewster hadn't added her name to his bank account or to his condo title. Kasenia clenched her fists. *The condo.* His opulent hillside home had become a point of conflict the day they returned from their honeymoon. Rather than move her and Sergei there, he claimed it was his private writing getaway and insisted he never said they'd live there. He hadn't even invited her to visit.

And now, a country place he hadn't mentioned? What else did he own? What else was he keeping from her?

Starting up the steps, she was about to brush past him when he took a swig of soda, licked his lips and kissed her.

Kasenia pulled away. She hated slurpy kisses.

"It's a special secret," he said, "one I've been saving to share with you. I'm super pumped for you to spend some time there." He swatted her backside. "Hurry, get your things together."

After a grueling photo session, all she wanted was to eat a salad and a couple bites of chicken and go to bed. Yet, she hadn't seen Brewster this excited since their helicopter wedding. And truth was, she'd been wishing for a change of pace.

Inside the house, Kasenia dropped her purse by the front door and took the stairs to their bedroom. *A country home.* The idea was growing on her. It would be nice to have a place to escape the heat.

But... She crumpled her eyebrows. This was Arizona, not the Ural Mountains. A country home here might be located in the middle of the Sonoran Desert with rattlesnakes for neighbors and saguaros for shade. Nothing could be worse.

Leaning over the railing, she called into the living room, "Brewster, is it in the mountains?"

"I named my place Shadow Ranch. A cliff to the west casts a shadow over the lodge when the sun is setting." He grunted. "That's the only clue I'm going to give you, Kasenia. Now, you two get packed, and let's hit the road."

While Brewster loaded luggage into the rear of her SUV, Kasenia moved her brother's snacks from beneath the front seat to the pocket on the back. Sam, who was climbing into the back, saw what she was doing and gave her a thumbs-up. Whether or not he'd have a chance to eat the goodies, she didn't know, but she had an idea that might work.

Brewster slammed the hatchback closed.

Kasenia jerked, startled by the jolt to her eardrums. Did he not realize she and Sam were inside the car?

He slid behind the wheel and put the key in the ignition. "Shadow Ranch, here we come." He grinned. "You two will love it there."

She stared at his hands, now clad in thin disposable gloves. "Why are you wearing those gloves?"

"Saw the dermatologist today." Brewster pulled the cuffs higher on his wrists. "She said this was the best thing for my rash."

"What rash?"

"It broke out while I was traveling. Don't know what caused it, except maybe motel soap, although I've never had trouble before."

"Those gloves have to be hot. They could make the rash worse."

Eyeing the rearview mirror, Brewster backed the car down the driveway. "Drop it, Kasenia. Doctor's orders are doctor's orders."

Once they'd left the city behind and were headed south, Kasenia said, "I picked up some energy bars today. Would you like one?" Without looking, she knew her brother was cringing. He didn't know her purpose was to allow him to eat without Brewster throwing a fit.

"Just what I need to go with my soda." Brewster lifted his Diet Dr. Pepper from the center console. "Open this for me."

He never offered her or Sam a soda. Maybe it was because their modeling agency discouraged soft drinks or because he wanted her to stay thin. But Sam, being a growing boy, didn't have to watch his diet as closely as she did. Most likely, Brewster was just being his usual selfish self.

She popped the top and gave him the can. "You're welcome."

Brewster ignored her and tipped the can to drink from it.

Kasenia stifled a sigh. His rude behavior soured the soda's sweet scent, cherry mixed with plum. That's how it smelled to her. Brewster said it tasted like caramel with a hint of vanilla. She turned to Sam who gave her a discreet thumbs-up before he handed her an energy bar. She peeled down the wrapper for her husband. "Speaking of Dr. Pepper..."

Brewster scowled. "What does that mean?"

"Lately, I've noticed a tremor in your hands—"

"That's ridiculous. I don't have a tremor." One gloved hand on the steering wheel, he held out the other. When it quivered, he quickly closed his fist. "I've got the jitters 'cause I'm excited for you to see Shadow Ranch. That's all." He shifted in his seat.

She handed him the energy bar. "I did some research." Determined to pursue the subject while he was in a halfway decent state of mind, Kasenia kept talking. "Some researchers believe aspartame, the sweetener in many diet drinks, can cause or exacerbate diseases like multiple sclerosis and Parkinson's, and others. Diet Dr. Pepper has a lot of aspartame in it. You drink it all day, every day, so I thought you might—"

"I do not drink it all day."

"You know what I mean. Maybe you should get tested to see—"

"I'm fine. Leave me alone." He bit into the energy bar then added a garbled, "My health is none of your business."

"But you're my—"

"Subject closed." He raised his palm. "You keep harping at me, you'll ruin our weekend." Giving her a weak smile, he patted her bare knee with his rubbery fingers. "I want this time together to be special."

Kasenia closed her eyes and leaned against the window. She'd said what she needed to say. He could do with it as he pleased. Too bad he brought her and Sam along. They would have had a fun weekend without him.

He turned up the radio volume, and no one spoke the rest of the lengthy drive.

3

At the sound of her name, Kasenia opened her eyes.

"We're almost there, sweetheart." Brewster squeezed her arm. "Five more miles."

The sun had fallen behind the mountains on the west, backlighting the rugged peaks and coloring the clouds in rich fruitlike colors. Lemon, orange and watermelon with a hint of grape. She loved sunsets and had to admit dusty Arizona skies offered fiery iridescent displays like nowhere else.

Yawning, she sat up. "How far are we from the Mexican border?"

Brewster chuckled. "Close enough."

The color was fading from the sky when he slowed the car to access a dirt road. Before them, maybe a quarter mile ahead, a simple log portal straddled the road. As they grew closer, a wooden sign hanging from the crossbeam and lit by floodlights became visible. Etched in dark letters, it proclaimed the property to be the "BW Shadow Ranch."

"Here we are." Brewster took Kasenia's hand in his gloved fingers.

She wrinkled her nose, trusting he couldn't see her in the dark. His grip was like holding hands with a plastic-wrapped porkchop.

"Time to meet my family." He squeezed her fingers. "I can't begin to tell you how thrilled I am to introduce you two."

"Family?" She gawked at him. "When I mentioned hosting a wedding reception for nearby family and friends, you said you didn't have close family."

"That's the best part of the surprise." He grinned. "The reception is here."

Kasenia pulled away. If she'd been informed, she'd have dressed for the occasion, not in a sloppy t-shirt and baggy shorts. She sighed, her vision of a quiet weekend with just the three of them vanishing like a desert mirage.

Bouncing over a metal cattle guard, they passed under the ranch sign. Moments later, the headlights were shining on a tall chain-link gate. A long narrow building sat to the side. Brewster stopped the car and tapped a code into a keypad attached to a short post.

"What's with the high fence?" Sam asked.

The gate clinked and began to slowly, noisily roll across the road.

Brewster cleared his throat. "Living this close to the border has its challenges."

A horse stepped into headlight range. Kasenia gasped, startled by the animal's sudden appearance. Then she saw the big man on the horse. Like an Old West gunslinger, he wore rattlesnake-skin boots and had a holstered pistol on his thigh. A rifle butt protruded from a scabbard on the saddle.

Brewster lowered his window. "Hola, Marlin."

Marlin saluted in response. "Hola, Boss." He had a deep gravelly voice. *Boss?*

The gate rattled to a stop, and Brewster inched the car forward. "Marlin is our head security guard. In addition to the usual Sonoran threats—wolves, coyotes, rattlesnakes, Gila monsters, javelinas, bobcats, cougars—we have illegals passing through all the time. They were robbing us blind before we installed the fence. Also, small children live on the property, and we raise livestock here. I felt this was the best protection."

"Huh." Sergei yawned. "Gila monsters and cougars."

Kasenia couldn't tell if it was doubt or surprise she heard in her brother's sleepy words. Like her, he must have slept most of the way. She should have stayed awake, so she'd know how to find the ranch when she needed a break from city life. On the trip home, she'd pay attention to landmarks and junctions.

She opened her window for a better look at their country home and got a whiff of dust. As she'd feared, it was in the desert. But the nearby mountains gave her some comfort. She could go for hikes or try her hand at drawing cactus flowers or mountains or maybe even birds.

"It's a dangerous place," Brewster said, "but it's the spirit's—God's—chosen place for us, and we make the best of it."

Kasenia rubbed her eyes. When he proposed, Brewster said God told him she was the one for him to marry. Now, he was saying the ranch was God's chosen place for his family. Apparently, religion played a bigger part in his life than she realized.

"The razor wire faces inward," Sam observed, "like prison wire to keep people in, not outward to keep illegals out."

Kasenia glanced over her shoulder at her brother. How did he know about prisons?

"Oh, that?" Brewster snorted. "Contractor mistake. I blew my stack when I saw it, but they said it was too difficult and dangerous to change and gave me a substantial discount." He snickered. "I'm known for swinging deals 'cause I'm that kinda guy."

Ahead of them, yard lights illuminated buildings of various sizes and shapes, including mobile homes placed side by side. The car tires crunched over gravel and rolled to a stop before a sprawling three-story log structure with big windows and a long veranda. Tall cottonwoods towered above the porch, branches spread wide. A short pole fence divided the yard from the parking lot.

She peered between the tree branches. Several teens who'd been clustered on the well-lit porch ran into the house. Kasenia smiled. "Sam, I see kids your age."

"Oh, yeah?"

Piano music drifted through the open screened windows. People milled about inside. Brewster not only had relatives in Arizona, his family was larger than she would have guessed. The lodge must be the ranch headquarters where they all lived.

Their hired hands probably lived in the trailer houses with their families. She didn't envy them. She'd heard desert trailers became unbearably hot in the summer.

Brewster switched off the engine and vaulted from the car. Peeling the gloves from his hands, he called to a woman standing in the doorway, "Rachel, tell everyone to gather. We'll be right in."

Kasenia cocked an eyebrow. *Rachel?* She'd heard him mention that name before. Was the woman a sister? A cousin? She got out and stretched. What a strange situation. But then, she'd married a strange man, and she loved him for it. He was atypical, neither a macho jock like Thad, nor dull and starchy like some professors. He was one of a kind.

Sam came around to her side of the car. Shoulder against hers, he whispered, "This is weird, meeting relatives we never heard of."

"Right..." Kasenia murmured. "And having a wedding reception I wasn't told about..." She bent down to get her purse from the front-seat floor.

Brewster leaned into the car. "You can leave your purse, Kasenia. It's safe out here on the ranch."

"My cell phone, my tablet, they're—"

"You won't need them. The ranch doesn't have cell reception or WIFI. We're lucky to have a landline."

He slammed the door and walked around to the tailgate. "Get your bags. The others are waiting."

Each toting their own luggage, the three of them walked a flagstone path between peppery-smelling cottonwoods and sweet-smelling flowering shrubs. Without slowing, they climbed the stairs and hurried across the veranda, wooden floorboards creaking beneath them.

They'd barely stepped through the open doorway into a large brightly lit room when applause erupted and cheers resounded. Beneath balloons and colorful crepe-paper streamers, people clapped and shouted, "Welcome, Mr. and Mrs. Wiley."

Someone yelled, "You too, Sam. Welcome."

Kasenia adjusted the wide strap on her shoulder and waved. The room smelled like Thanksgiving dinner.

Sam muttered, "That's a big family."

"Uh-huh." Forty people, she guessed, maybe fifty, counting toddlers and babies.

Brewster brandished an enthusiastic thumbs-up. "You remembered my favorite meal, turkey with all the trimmings. The heavenly aroma hit me the moment I reached the porch."

Kasenia plastered an appreciative grin on her face, grateful for her modeling experience. She could fake a smile with the best of them. In her way of thinking, hors d'oeuvres, salads and fruit were more appropriate for a summer reception than Thanksgiving dinner, especially in the desert.

But no one asked her, and this was her husband's family. They obviously wanted to make the celebration special for him.

Gesturing to the onlookers, he said, "Family, I'd like you to meet Sam Clarke and his sister, Kasenia, now known as Mrs. Brewster Wiley."

Again, applause and cries of "Congratulations" burst from the group.

Kasenia nodded, her smile fading. She'd never thought of herself as *Mrs. Brewster Wiley*. Since their wedding, she'd gone by Kasenia Clarke Wiley.

A teenage girl seated at an upright piano with a large television screen balanced on top played a few notes and Brewster's family began to sing. Kasenia didn't catch every word, but each time they repeated "welcome to our happy family," they held out their hands.

Like Brewster, they were fair-skinned, except for a group of Latino boys near Sam's age bunched in the corner. Everyone was nicely dressed except for her and Sam. Brewster, who was attired in his usual finery, hadn't bothered to suggest they dress for the occasion.

When the song ended, he thanked the singers and motioned for Kasenia and Sam to set their bags with his beside a couch. Then he guided them toward a table laden with food, most of which Kasenia didn't dare eat.

Ambrosia salad thick with marshmallows, yams with more marshmallows, cranberry sauce, green bean casserole, turkey, dressing, potatoes, gravy, butter, pumpkin pies and sheet cakes. But no wedding cake, not even the word "congratulations" on one of the cakes. This was like no American wedding reception she'd ever attended.

The pendant dangling from a nearby woman's neck caught the light. Heart-shaped, it was similar in design to the one Brewster gave her. She couldn't be sure, but she got the impression it had initials engraved on it.

She looked into the woman's blue-eyed gaze. Like others in the room, the frozen smile on her lips didn't reach her eyes.

Kasenia surveyed the crowd. A woman with a child in her arms, two clinging to her skirt, another woman, five children, a cluster of teens, two women with babies, some with middle-schoolers... She scanned the room again. Several women, even more children, but no men. How odd. Ranchers were known to work long hours, yet they were also known to be family men. Surely, they took breaks for family events.

Brewster grabbed Kasenia's hand and held it high. "This lovely lady," he exclaimed, "is wife number nine. Three more wives to go, and we'll be a complete family!"

Wife number nine? Kasenia yanked her arm down. "What are you talking about?"

"This is my wonderful family, Kasenia, my wives and my children. And now that you're married to me..." He wrapped an arm around Sam's shoulders. "You and Sam are now members of the Wiley clan."

"Huh-uh." Sam wriggled from his grasp.

Kasenia gaped at him. "These women are your *wives*?" Comprehension twisted her stomach. These weren't former girlfriends. They were current bed partners, like she was.

"Yes, and these are my children, every last one of them. Right, my little ones?"

In unison, from the toddlers to the teens, they droned, "Right, Papa."

"Papa?" Fists clenched, Kasenia glared at Brewster. "You told me you were footloose and fancy free, when you were far from it."

"Ha-ha," hooted a woman on the far side of the room. "He used that line on me, too."

Brewster whipped around. "Shut up."

Kasenia couldn't tell who'd spoken because the women all cringed and shifted their gazes. The children stared straight ahead, eyes wide and unfocused.

She poked Brewster's arm.

He turned to her, eyes flashing.

She didn't care. "Only one of your so-called marriages is legal. The rest are illicit, including mine. Give me my keys." She held out her hand. "Sam and I are going home."

"*This* is your home."

"No, it's not."

Eyelids narrowed over gray eyes now dark as iron, he spat his response one word at a time. "Oh–yes–it–is." His jaw twitched and his corded neck muscles bulged. He looked every bit the menacing commando he once was.

"Brewster, please." Kasenia peered into his eyes, searching for...she wasn't sure what. Compassion? Sanity? "This is crazy. Let's just, let's just go home to Tucson."

Beside her, Sam pleaded, "Please, Brewster—"

He gripped them by their shoulders, squeezing until Sam yelped and Kasenia cried, "Stop, you're hurting us."

"You two are ruining the party." A purple vein pulsed on Brewster's forehead. "Shut your mouths, or I'll shut 'em for you. Understand?"

Kasenia blinked. She'd seen him angry, but nothing like this. He'd never before hurt or threatened her.

Shaking them like they were misbehaving children, he shouted, "Do–you–understand?"

A quick glance at Sam, whose green eyes were glassy marbles in his white face, was all Kasenia needed. "We understand."

He shoved them away before opening his arms to encompass the frozen bystanders. "Time to eat, Family. Let's party." With rough nudges, he steered Kasenia and Sam to the other end of the table. "The newcomers are first in line, with me."

Pushing paper plates into their hands, he hissed, "Smile, or I'll pop you in the kisser. Get a move on. I'm hungry."

Kasenia stumbled alongside the table. How did she and Sam end up in a nightmare with Brewster as the monster?

"Sis..." Sam nudged her. "Put some food on your plate."

She didn't feel like eating, but she lurched ahead, scooping this and that onto her plate, not caring what it was. She wouldn't touch Brewster's *favorite* food. The dressing had an overwhelmingly strong odor.

She might be only half American, but she knew too much sage when she smelled it.

At a separate table, a tall woman wearing a red-and-black dress identical to one of Kasenia's designer outfits was waiting at a punch bowl. She looked Kasenia over, from her bare legs to her shorts and t-shirt, and with a smirk, asked, "Fruit punch or Diet Dr. Pepper?" Dozens of soda cans surrounded the big bowl, every one of them Brewster's drink of choice. But these were caffeine-free, unlike what he drank at home.

Teeth clenched, Kasenia promised herself she'd never drink another drop of Dr. Pepper, diet *or* regular. Forcing words from her mouth, she stuttered, "I, uh...punch, please."

The woman reached for a paper cup. As she did, the pendant hanging from a gold chain around her neck swung to the side. Kasenia sucked in a breath. Heart-shaped, it had initials she could clearly see. *B+V.*

Had Brewster given every mistress—for only one of them could be his wife—the same necklace? How dare he? She loved her necklace. But now, she'd rip it off first chance she got.

The server handed Kasenia her drink, a half-smile on her lips. Her stony eyes suggested she wasn't as thrilled as Brewster was to add another "wife" to their bizarre family.

Kasenia glanced at the woman's ring finger, sickened to see a wedding set identical to her own. These women were the Stepford wives her friends joked about. Even more deluded, in fact, because they shared the same husband.

Brewster led Kasenia and Sam into an adjoining room with big windows and long rectangular tables. Desert sunflowers displayed in quart-size canning jars served as centerpieces on white paper tablecloths. "We're at the head table," he said. "Kasenia, you'll sit beside me. Sam will sit next to you. Wait to eat until everyone is here."

Without responding, they pulled out chairs and sat. Kasenia stared at the sunflowers on their table, despising Brewster's presence, yet hoping her body would somehow shield her brother from the volatile charlatan. They were in a world she would never have imagined whether in Russia or America. Was it real, or was it a bad dream that refused to release her to the safety of sunrise?

An ant crawled from a sunflower, down the side of the jar and onto the table covering. She was about to flick it off when Brewster reached over and squashed it with his thumb. He gave it an extra twist, presumably to ensure its death, tearing a hole in the paper.

He sniffed, and though he'd told them to wait, started eating. Kasenia had no appetite for the rich food, could no longer smell it. Dropping her gaze to her plate, she pictured the lone wedding ring on Brewster's dresser. Where did he keep the other eight rings? Could he tell them apart?

She pressed her lips together. Of course, he could. When he'd had her initials and their marriage date engraved inside his wedding band, she'd been deeply touched. Now she realized he did it to discern which ring went with which woman. But what did it matter? He never wore any of the rings. Why do that when he was always on the prowl for another woman to drag into his harem?

The women and children settled at the tables, chatting and laughing as if they'd forgotten Brewster's outburst. Were his tantrums a common occurrence? She looked around the room. From what she could tell, children sat with their mothers, no matter their ages, except the Hispanic boys who sat with a stern-faced redheaded woman.

Kasenia counted eight women, every one of them beautiful and at least two pregnant, and forty or so kids of various ages, far more than the two he'd mentioned. Did Brewster really father them all? He considered himself hot stuff in bed, but... Really? And why had he insisted she use birth control? Was his plan to wait until he sequestered her on the ranch before he got her pregnant?

Whatever his plan, she'd *never* have his baby. She didn't want an illegitimate child with genes tainted by his craziness. And who knew what kind of sexually transmitted disease he might have already given her.

No wonder he balked at paying Grandpa Gordon rent and didn't help her buy groceries. He had all these mouths to feed. But how did he afford his fancy car and designer clothes? His U of A salary couldn't possibly cover these people's needs plus his indulgences.

And where did he find the women? How did he convince them to join his supposed family? Were they all duped, like she was? Or did they choose to join? Whatever the case, she should feel sorry for them and their pathetic lives.

Instead, she longed to drive out the gate and put the horrible night behind her.

Brewster stopped eating when, one after another, small giggling children came running to him. "Hi, Papa." "I missed you." "I love you, Papa." Their high melodic voices rang with joy, and they smelled like they'd been freshly bathed and shampooed. He greeted them each by name. After he hugged the little ones and kissed the tops of their heads, they ran to their mothers.

All Kasenia could do was gape at him. Who was this chameleon? One minute, he threatened and shook her and Sergei. The next, he was a doting father.

What a fool she'd been to not delve into his background. The one time she questioned him, he'd been curt. "I don't discuss my childhood." She should have considered his response a red flag, like when he called her by the wrong name, a mistake that happened more than once. He also didn't appreciate questions regarding his travels.

Brewster's "side business," apparently, was impregnating Shadow Ranch women.

4

—·—

E LBOWING SAM, KASENIA WHISPERED, "First chance, we walk away." Although he was as tall as she was, he looked small and afraid.

"Sis..." His lip trembled. "I watched that big gate close—"

Brewster jumped to his feet. "Time to teach the newcomers our meal prayer."

Adults and children alike noisily pushed their chairs away and stood, arms raised.

He motioned to Kasenia and Sam. "You, too."

They looked at each other then stood and lifted their hands.

"Spirit Father," Brewster intoned, his eyes focused on the ceiling.

"Spirit Father," the women and children repeated, heads back, hands high.

"We invoke your power to bless this sustenance."

"Bless this sustenance, bless this sustenance." 'S' sounds hissed from one corner of the room to the other.

"And make us strong warrior gods and goddesses."

"Strong, strong, strong..." Their shouts reverberated about the dining room.

"That we may reach our highest potential on this earthly sphere and rule the universe with you."

Rule the universe? He's loonier than I thought. Kasenia snuck a peek at her brother, whose wild-eyed gaze shifted from Brewster to the others and back. Leaning close, she whispered in his ear, "We're in this together, Sam. We'll find a way out."

Women and children cried, "Please, Spirit Father, please, Spirit Father." Some yelled, "Potential, potential, potential. Highest potential."

"So be it." Brewster declared and sat, accompanied by a "so be it" chorus circling the room.

Kasenia was certain she hadn't read anything about people becoming gods and goddesses or ruling the universe in her English Bible *or* her Russian Bible.

Chair legs rasped against the wooden floor, and everyone sat.

Staring straight ahead, Sam muttered, "Freaky..."

Kasenia nodded. These people were worse than weird. They were polygamists ruled by a madman. She had to get her brother out of here. Fast.

The group started eating, and conversations resumed.

Brewster put an arm around Kasenia, drawing her close. When she resisted, he pinched her shoulder. "Smile, my love." He kissed her cheek. "This is our wedding reception."

Hands clenched, she fought the urge to knock him off his chair and kick his nether region so hard he'd never sire another child. While he was down, she'd dig her car keys from his pants pocket and drive Sergei home to Tucson. Far, far away from this sick, sordid, polygamous love nest Brewster had created for himself.

"I said..." Brewster spoke through clamped teeth. "Smile."

Swallowing her rising dread, she turned to face him. "We have nothing to celebrate." Her voice low, she added, "Our marriage is an unlawful sham."

He lifted an eyebrow. "According to mankind's rules, possibly. However, our people live by a higher standard."

"Oh, really? What's that?" He'd always been cocky, but this was ridiculous.

"The Good Book." Lifting his Diet Dr. Pepper, he sipped from it then wiped his lips with the back of his hand.

"You mean the Bible?"

Across the room, silverware clinked, women and children chatted, a baby cried. She glanced around. No one seemed concerned about her conversation with Brewster.

"Specifically, the Old Testament," Brewster said, "where having plural wives was not only practiced but endorsed by Spirit Father. Solomon had the most wives of any man who's ever lived, and Spirit Father blessed him more than any man who's ever lived. The one restriction is that we don't marry sisters. Leviticus chapter eighteen, verse eighteen. I've been careful not to do that."

"Who is Spirit Father? Sounds Native American."

"It's our family's name for the divine being some call God. We like to use a more appropriate, more reverent name to address the universe's deity."

"So, you believe you can flout the law and do whatever you want in the name of some made-up religion?"

He took her hands and leaned close. How his eyes could be iron-hard yet his words gentle was beyond Kasenia.

"Sweetheart, I and my family, including you and Sam, must submit to the Spirit Father's will. To receive his blessing, we have no choice but to be the family he expects, even when it means defying mankind's decrees. And he *has* blessed us, immensely. You'll see for yourself when I show you our many-faceted enterprise. And, for your information, ours is not a contrived belief system. Family groups around the world worship the way we do."

"Do they have a name?"

"We call ourselves Spirit Children."

Searching her memory for similar organizations, she lowered her gaze. "I've been a few places and haven't heard of—" She stopped. "Your hands, they're perfectly fine. They don't have—"

He yanked his hands away and stood, shoving his chair back. Fingers in his mouth, he blew a piercing whistle that turned heads around the dining room. "Time for introductions and entertainment. Alana, what do my progeny have for us tonight?"

A twenty-something pregnant woman with strawberry-blond hair pushed to her feet. "Children, front and center." She wore a long flowered dress over her bulging midsection.

The younger kids left their mothers and formed two rows before the head table, shorter children in front. Alana maneuvered behind Kasenia and Brewster to direct from there, one hand on Brewster's shoulder. Her cloying floral perfume revived Kasenia's sense of smell and triggered a headache.

The children's rendition of "Old MacDonald Had a Farm," complete with animal sounds, was probably cute. But all Kasenia could think was, *I can't believe these are Brewster's children. From multiple women.* Including Alana, who belly bumped her enough times she wondered if the woman did it on purpose. Was she flaunting her pregnant condition or letting Kasenia know she was not welcome at Shadow Ranch?

Next, two middle schoolers dressed as a magician and his assistant performed simple magic tricks. Brewster laughed and clapped and said to Kasenia, "They know I love magic. In fact, some who've observed my mushrooming empire call me a magician." He snickered. "I'm the envy of my peers, 'cause I'm that kinda guy."

She stared at him. He was a crazy, cheating conman, traits she should have seen earlier. How could anyone envy someone so manipulative and dishonest?

The piano player joined the final act to accompany three teen instrumentalists—a guitarist, a fiddle player and a bass player. When they announced the title, Kasenia recognized it as one of the cowboy songs on the CD her grandpa listened to while he worked on his roadster. They were just children playing a fun song for their father, yet she hated how they sullied a good memory.

Kasenia mentally slapped herself. The kids were innocent victims. Brewster was the one who sullied lives.

The applause subsided, and the kids bowed. Carrying chairs and instruments, they returned to their seats. Alana edged from behind the head table, jostling Kasenia one more time, and Brewster rose to thank the performers, his words kind and gracious.

Kasenia eyed him, dumbfounded. Did he have a split personality or what? She'd never been so confused—or frightened. What had she gotten herself and Sergei into, and how could she get them out?

When Babushka Irina first learned about Brewster, she'd said in her Russian way, "Don't rush the horses, sweet girl. Still waters sometimes shroud deep crevasses." Kasenia bit her lip. She should have listened to her babushka. And to Grandpa Gordon, who'd said, "Senya Girl, I'll only say this once. Always take a good look at what you're about to eat. It's not so important to know what it is after it's fancied up, but it's critical to know what it was beforehand." She hadn't understood then, but his meaning was becoming clearer by the minute.

"Time for introductions," Brewster said. "I'll begin with wife number eight, the lovely Brittany Wiley." He extended his hand. "Please stand, Brittany."

Hand on the table for balance, a young pregnant blonde stood. Like the other women, she was pretty and wore just enough makeup to highlight her natural beauty. Her cute maternity top appeared homemade. Ignoring Kasenia, she offered Brewster a demure dimpled smile.

He responded with a slow wink.

Kasenia clenched her fists. The woman was flirting with her husband, and he was flirting back. Choking down her fury, she shook off the useless jealousy. Brewster wasn't *her* husband or Brittany's. One woman in the room was his real wife, probably the tired-looking older woman in the far corner surrounded by teenagers.

"Twenty-four-year-old Brittany is our resident beautician," Brewster said. "She enhances our community's appearance with her expertise. She's also quite a seamstress, always busy with her fellow stitchers, making items for our family enterprise. In addition, she does the family mending.

"Not one to hoard her creativity, she assembled a talented team and taught them how to make jewelry. Our turquoise-and-silver necklaces, bracelets and belts equal Navaho Nation quality and are quite popular with the tourists." He pointed at her belly. "As you can see, she's expecting our third child."

Brittany blushed and patted her stomach. Her watch, much like Kasenia's missing timepiece, flashed, reflecting the ceiling light.

"You may sit," Brewster said. "Careful you don't disturb our littlest Wiley."

The others tittered. Kasenia wanted to vomit. Very likely, she'd been sitting alone at her kitchen table in Tucson, planning a Vegas honeymoon, the night Brewster got Brittany pregnant.

"Next, we have my beautiful seventh wife. Please take a bow, Margo."

The unsmiling redhead seated with the Hispanic boys stood. Dressed in a white blouse and a denim skirt, she had a no-nonsense air about her. A slender woman whose build was more wiry than ballerina-like, she ignored Kasenia, yet made no attempt to flirt with Brewster.

"Margo is our forty-three-year-old horse manager in charge of equine care, training and sales. In addition, she's a honeybee expert." He nudged Kasenia's shoulder. "Amazing how she never gets stung."

Kasenia could picture Margo taking a firm grip on reins or ignoring a swarm of bees circling her head. A strong-willed intelligent woman like her hooking up with a shyster like Brewster made no sense.

"Along with the honey, bee pollen and royal jelly we get from the hives," Brewster said, "we've developed several honey-related products." He dipped his chin. "Thank you, Margo."

He hadn't mentioned children, leading Kasenia to assume that was the reason Margo sat with the Hispanic boys. Were they the children of ranch workers?

Next, he introduced wife number six, the very pregnant music director, Alana. "Not only does our sweet Alana, age twenty-seven, sing like a songbird, she can play and teach every musical instrument on this ranch. She's our head baker and a talented photographer who does the photography for our advertisements and website.

Website? He'd told her the ranch didn't have WIFI. She'd assumed that meant it didn't have internet. What a liar. And what a fool she'd been to believe anything he'd ever said to her.

As you can see," he added, "sweet Alana will soon gift the family with our fourth child together, or possibly fourth *and* fifth. Just look at the size of that woman."

Alana grinned and patted her bulging midsection. "He or she or they are very active tonight. They love music. Come feel them bounce, Brewster."

"Later."

Alana's lips puckered into a pout.

Kasenia eyed Alana. Had Brewster gotten the woman pregnant before or after his candlelight proposal on the condo patio? Bile crawled up her throat. His proposal, their wedding and honeymoon...so romantic, and so wrong.

Brewster continued his introductions. "My charming fifth wife, Chloe, holds a very special position in our family. At thirty-one, she's the mother of five children and our family's nurse midwife who tends wounds and illnesses and delivers our babies. Please stand and say hello, Chloe."

Alana sat and Chloe stood. Though not overly so, her physique was a bit fluffier than the others. Her sleeves were rolled above her elbows, and she wore a paint-splattered apron.

"In addition to her medical duties, Chloe oversees the cleaning and laundry schedules and paints exquisite desert sunsets." Brewster blew her a kiss. "We love her paintings as do our customers."

Customers? Kasenia pursed her lips. Maybe Brewster's travels did include sales. That's what the honey products, jewelry and marketing talk was about. If people came to the ranch to buy pastries and paintings, she and Sergei could sneak into someone's backseat—

"Please be seated, my love." Brewster's smile was gracious.

Choe responded with a grateful, almost pleading, smile and sat.

Kasenia looked from her to Brewster. Was Chloe desperate for his attention? Kasenia knew from experience that once he made a conquest and the honeymoon was over, his devotion diminished. Now, she knew why. He'd spread his so-called love nine ways, not counting his children's need for a father's devotion.

"And now for number four..." Brewster crooked a finger toward the next table. "Our beloved schoolmarm."

A petite woman whose auburn hair had blond highlights, grinned and rose, revealing dimples in both cheeks. She wore a light-blue blouse tucked into a black skirt.

"Rachel is thirty-two and mother to five children. She teaches *all* my children right here in the big house as well as the foster children." He indicated the Hispanic boys then turned to the others. "You love your teacher, don't you boys and girls?"

"Yes," they shouted.

Rachel smiled and dipped her head.

"Rachel instructs all levels of students and monitors the childcare schedule. She's also our head gardener, a very important position, as produce sales account for a substantial percentage of our family's income."

As she sat, the woman in the red-and-black dress and the *B+V* necklace rose. She had strawberry-blond hair and a wary expression on her face.

"This is Veronica," Brewster said, "my beautiful wife number three I stole right off the farm. Right, Ronni?"

Veronica sighed. "So to speak."

Undaunted by her lack of enthusiasm, Brewster continued. "Ronni is thirty-seven, mother to seven, and in charge of our dairy products. In addition, she oversees our canning operation. You'll soon learn she makes excellent spaghetti sauce. Our clients can't get enough of it."

Kasenia surveyed the women. Interesting how they each had special skills that benefited the family enterprise. Or more likely, Brewster's bank account. No wonder he drove a Corvette and wore Armani suits and Stefano Bemer shoes, not to mention the diamond-studded Rolex.

Veronica sat, and a woman with white-blond hair stood.

"Ah, dear, dear, Wanda, wife number two, forty-one years of age and mother to eight of my children."

Wanda managed a small smile.

"Around here, we call her our very own Dr. Dolittle. We love her and so do our animals, from our cattle and hogs to our goats and chickens. She tends their needs, including injuries and diseases. You'll soon learn..." He elbowed Kasenia. "Wanda makes a mean tomatillo salsa, a family favorite and one our customers love.

"Please be seated, *pretty woman*." Brewster chuckled at his private joke, and several women snickered.

Wanda narrowed her eyes, apparently not amused, and resumed her seat.

Without further comment, Brewster motioned to the weary woman with the teenagers, and wife number one got up. Kasenia had the impression she'd forgotten how to smile.

"Sweet, lovely Lorraine, age forty-four, is number one in marriage as well as in management skills."

Kasenia gripped her thighs. *She's number one because she's your REAL wife, your ONLY wife, you arrogant, promiscuous jerk.*

"Lorraine is an administrative, accounting and bookkeeping wizard who oversees the ranch operations in my absence," Brewster said. "We stay in constant daily contact."

Kasenia gave him a side glance. *That explains those texts you didn't want me to see and phone calls you didn't want me to hear.*

"Lorraine makes our best-selling product, prickly pear jelly, from a recipe she developed when we first moved out here. In time, she formulated recipes for our other jellies—jalapeno cactus, raspberry chipotle, and blueberry habanero."

He dipped his head. "Thank you, sweetheart."

Without responding, she smoothed her gray-streaked red hair over one shoulder and took her seat. That's when it hit Kasenia—like Brewster told her the night he proposed, his women were either blondes or redheads.

Someone called, "What can number nine do?"

Now I'm a number? Kasenia cringed. All eyes were on her. Most faces were blank, though several women looked like they'd rather throttle her than include her in their fraudulent family.

"Kasenia..." Brewster pulled her up. She stiffened, but he didn't seem to notice. "My dear newest wife is one of my students who recently received her BS in business administration—with my help, of course."

Kasenia tightened her clasped fingers. She didn't like him calling her *his* student and taking credit for her hard-earned degree any more than she liked him calling her *his* wife.

"Smart girl, she was my best student." He patted her back. "For the past several months, she's served as a proofreader for my books. In the future, she'll take the lead to promote and market them."

"I am *not* a marketer." Kasenia pulled away. "I won't—"

"Oh, yes, you will." Eyes like flint, he declared, "I'm not going to let your degree go to waste." Turning to the group, he said, "Kasenia is also an international fashion model."

"That's not true. I—"

"From Russia, with love…" He smirked. "As the Bond movie goes. Isn't her accent delightful? First, it was her long legs that got my attention, then it was her accent."

Kasenia closed her eyes. What would he brag about next? Their sex life?

"Together," he said, "we're launching the Wiley Modeling Agency."

"What?" She gawked at him.

"She and Sam, who's also a model, will train our modeling team and arrange photo sessions."

Sam grunted, but the women and teens perked to attention.

"No need to volunteer for the training," he said. "I've already decided who's going to be on the team."

Though no one voiced disappointment, shoulders drooped and bored expressions reappeared on faces that had momentarily come to life.

Kasenia folded her arms. "I am not launching an agency with you."

"Of course, you are." He glared at her. "You must do your part to contribute to the family income."

"This isn't my family."

He grabbed her arm, squeezing hard. "These are your sister wives, Kasenia, your stepsons and stepdaughters. Get it?"

She had opened her mouth to say, "No, I don't get it," when he jabbed a finger at Sam. "You're no longer a spoiled only child. Now you have brothers and sisters."

"No way. I already have a sister."

Leaning past Kasenia, Brewster shoved his fist in Sam's face. "That's the last time you backtalk me, boy."

"Stop it." Kasenia clutched his arm. "Leave him alone."

He shoved her into her chair. "I'll deal with you two later." Smoothing his hair, Brewster turned to the others and calmly said, "Family, I have good news, exciting news."

All around the room, eyes brightened, and individuals sat taller, including the younger children. A small child exclaimed, "What is it? Tell us, Papa."

He held up a hand and waited for everyone to settle before he continued. "As you know, Spirit Father commanded me to be like the Jews and marry a dozen wives to replicate the twelve tribes of Israel." He paused.

Someone whispered, "And...?"

"I believe I've met wife number ten."

Gasps and shouts of "What?" "Already?" echoed throughout the dining room.

5

——— • ———

K ASENIA FUMBLED FOR SAM'S hand. "Let's go." They rose and
started for the doorway.

"Marlin!" Brewster bellowed.

From the other room, the big man she'd seen on the horse stepped into
view, blocking the exit.

Her mouth went dry, and all sound ceased, as if they'd been sucked
into the eye of a storm.

"Kasenia..." Brewster's voice punctured the silent vacuum, low and
menacing. "Remember the coyote?"

She released Sam's hand and slowly rotated, fearing what she'd see.
And she was right. Every inch of Brewster's body radiated fury. She knew
the signs. Pitiless glare, flared nostrils and tight lips above a jutted chin,
thrust chest, wide elbows and planted legs.

He held a gun in his hand. But it wasn't aimed at her. It was pointed at
Sam's head. Any lingering love for her phony husband, now her captor,
was replaced by a gaping terror deep as an Arizona canyon. She swallowed
and took her brother's hand, which shook as much as hers did.

Brewster brandished the weapon. "Sit."

They returned to their seats, the scrape of chairs loud in the guarded
hush.

Eyes glinting, Brewster patted her shoulder. "Good girl."

Palms pressed against her legs to control the shaking, Kasenia turned
her head. She'd seen that glint when she let him win an argument. But
she wouldn't give him the pleasure of a grovel or a verbal acquiescence.
And she wouldn't allow him to see the rage seething inside.

Scanning the room, she caught the fear on the children's faces and what could be interpreted as hatred on more than one teen's countenance. None of the foster boys displayed any emotion. Had their previous lives been so traumatic that Brewster's behavior didn't faze them? The women were a mix—frightened, shuttered or...gloating.

"As I was saying..." Brewster, who'd remained standing, chuckled.

Kasenia squinted up at him. *He just threatened us with a gun, and now he's laughing?*

"Wife number ten is in my sights." He grinned. "She's a cute little blond with blue-and-red streaked hair. But Brittany can restore the original color—"

"You mean Denika?" Sam blurted. "Our neighbor?"

"Yes, a true beauty, through and through."

"But..." Kasenia gaped at Brewster. The dreamy look in his eyes matched the longing in his voice.

Sam said the words stuck in her throat. "She's fifteen."

"Age is of no consequence..." Brewster lifted his palms. "When it's Spirit Father's will." He clapped his hands. "Speaking of Spirit Father—time for you to return to your divinely appointed duties."

Leaving the others to clear the tables and wash the dishes, Brewster led Kasenia and Sam out of the house and onto the veranda, luggage in hand. "Time for the royal tour."

"Not tonight." Kasenia trotted down the steps. "I'm going home. Give me my keys, please."

Brewster whipped around, his face like granite in the white yard light. "*This* is your home now. Shadow Ranch is where you belong."

She whipped around. "I do *not* belong here. You can stay with your pretend wives, but I'm returning to Tucson."

He slapped her, knocking her to her hands and knees in the gravel. When she lifted her head, another set of feet had appeared—clad in rattlesnake-skin boots. Was the man Brewster's shadow or what?

Brewster grasped Sam's ear.

"Hey..." Sam clutched Brewster's arm. "Let go."

"Stop it." Kasenia jumped up, wiping her scraped palms on her shorts. "I'll do whatever you ask."

He sneered. "Get your bag." Pulling Sam by the ear, he started toward the mobile homes arranged along the tall chain-link fence. All down the row, narrow metal steps led to narrow trailer doors lit by dim porchlights.

She grabbed her bag and hurried after him, tripping through the gravel.

Brewster stopped at the first trailer, a faded older-model camper, and thrust Sam toward the stairs. "Open the door."

Sam climbed the three steps to the landing, opened the screen door, then the inner door and stepped aside. Brewster directed Kasenia into the dark interior and followed close behind, blocking the meager exterior light. "The newest wife gets the oldest quarters. That's how it works."

Before she had a chance to look around, he said, "Leave your bag," and turned to Sam. "You're in the boys' barracks."

Kasenia frowned. "Why can't he stay with me?"

"Because I said so."

"We don't like to be separated."

"That's why he's such a baby. Time to grow up, *baby boy*." He shoved Sam, knocking him down the stairs.

When Kasenia started after her brother, Brewster stopped her. "From now on, he answers to me."

"I'm his guardian, not you."

Brewster yelled for her to shut her mouth and for Sam to stand up like a man.

Sam stood and brushed gravel from his forearms.

Brewster yanked Kasenia down the steps, grasped Sam by the neck and marched the two of them back the direction they'd come. Sam limped but somehow managed to keep pace.

When they passed the car, Kasenia vowed to sneak into it first chance she had to retrieve her phone. Shadow Ranch, she was convinced, had cell service. Brewster wouldn't be without it. Probably had a tower on the property. She'd call 911 to beg for help *and* to report him and his harem.

They entered a one-story adobe building with "Niños de la Noche" painted below the porchlight. Kasenia knew enough Spanish to know it meant *Children of the Night* in English. Inside the dorm, Brewster flipped a switch, illuminating an unfurnished sand-colored foyer. He led them into a hallway with doors on each side and sconce lighting. A fresh-paint smell underscored the building's new-construction appearance.

"You're in the last room on the right," Brewster said, "the first person to sleep there. We recently remodeled a storeroom to create this barracks."

Kasenia rolled her eyes. Of course, Mr. Military would call the dormitory a barracks.

At the end of the hall, Brewster opened a door and switched on the light. The room was small, with a bed, a dresser and three hooks beside the door. A beige roller shade covered the window. "Leave your stuff here," he ordered, "and let's go."

Sam dropped his bag on the bed.

Kasenia didn't like the forced separation but seeing where Sergei would stay helped. *Temporarily*, she reminded herself. *He won't be here long.*

From the dormitory, Brewster directed them to a lighted path that ran alongside the lodge. They walked past a huge garden, greenhouse and beehives illuminated by yard lights. People were working inside the lighted greenhouse. Then they toured a series of buildings that housed everything from sewing machines and jewelry-making supplies to refrigerators stocked with dairy products. One building had sinks and stoves, canning equipment, and shelves lined with Mexican salsas, Italian sauces, canned vegetables, and fruit jams, jellies and syrups.

Everywhere they went, Brewster's tribe was hard at work, sewing, stirring, chopping, pouring, soldering, stringing beads, and much more. A numb feeling, like when she learned of her grandparents' deaths, overtook Kasenia's senses, dulling her anger and fear, clouding her comprehension.

Focused on their craft, the laborers rarely spoke. Kasenia was reminded of the Russian idiom her babushka liked to quote when she and Sam balked at cleaning the barn. *The peasant sweats, and the nobleman is always right.* "I am the nobleman," she'd declare with a wink. "You are the peasants. Go sweat." No one would argue who the nobleman was and who the peasants were at Shadow Ranch.

A sweet-smelling building with a honey extractor and floor-to-ceiling shelves of the golden nectar had several work areas. Margo, the unsmiling redhead in the denim skirt, was at a stove, stirring a creamy substance. "This will be all-natural hand cream," she told them. With a wave of her free hand, she indicated her helpers. "They're packaging other honey-based personal care items, like lip gloss and wound salve, along with udder balm—for milk cows, of course, although some people use it for chapped hands."

The bakery hut, as Brewster called it, had a fresh-baked bread aroma and boasted commercial ovens and wide butcherblock counters and islands. Women and children were kneading and rolling dough, filling pie shells, packaging pastries and stirring batter. Like the other buildings, it was spotless.

They passed animal pens, barns and corrals accompanied by a manure odor that changed from place to place but never improved. Their presence was acknowledged with shuffling and grunts, but in the semi-darkness, Kasenia didn't get a good look at the animals. Most seemed to be bedded down for the night.

"The poultry pens are covered with chicken wire to protect them from hawks and eagles," Brewster said. "Pigs and goats don't need the wire, except when they have young ones." Fiberglass sheets over half of each pen provided shelter from the sun. Misters cooled the animals on hot summer days.

Whenever possible, Kasenia touched her brother to remind him he wasn't alone. His pale face and vacant stare scared her. Maybe it was because the yard lights washed his skin a ghostly white, but his jerky movements and rapid blinking were unnatural. She had her own twitches and had to clench her fists to keep her hands from shaking. Still, no matter how scared they were, she and Sam couldn't give in to panic. They had to keep a cool head. If Grandpa Gordon were here, that's what he'd say.

"Beyond those trees..." Brewster pointed to the barely visible trees that lined the south side of the compound. "Everything is powered by ground-mounted solar panels and those two wind turbines up on the ridge." Starlight glinted off the slowly rotating white blades. A red light blinked on the cell tower between them.

"Thanks to my superb use of natural resources, the generator I installed as backup has never been used." He squinted. "It's hard to see, but the satellite dish at the side provides our internet service."

Peering at the cliff as if trying to see the satellite dish, Kasenia scowled. *Of course, you have internet service, you liar.* Yet, despite his duplicity, Brewster had just shown her what she needed to see. A cell tower. The moment she retrieved her phone, she'd call for help.

Not only was the nighttime tour surreal, the immensity of Brewster's family enterprise appalled her. The women and children were lining his pockets while receiving little in return, from what she'd observed. A night in bed with him for the women, a pat on the head for the children, verbal assurances of his love now and then.

They returned to the dormitory to drop off Sergei. Margo, who must have hurried over from the honey hut, met them in the foyer.

"Margo serves as a dorm mother for our foster boys," Brewster said. "She'll introduce Sam to them in the morning."

The horsewoman didn't bother to return Kasenia's nod.

"Do what she says." Brewster shoved Sam's shoulder. "She reports to me every day."

Kasenia bristled. "Don't—"

Grasping her arm, he spun her away from the dorm before she could say goodbye to her brother and dragged her to the travel trailer. He stopped at the steps. "I'm leaving for Tucson now to set things in motion for your disappearance."

"What?" She gaped at him. "What are you talking about?"

"When Gordon gets home from his golf trip, your car will be there, but you won't be." He sneered. "Later, I'll return from my travels and tell him I thought you flew to Russia to plan the wedding with your babushka. You'd mentioned it several times."

Kasenia pulled from his grip, trying to comprehend the lies he must have concocted long before they left Tucson.

"He'll eventually call the cops, they'll search his house and your car and come up emptyhanded. I'll tell them I can't stand to be in that house without you, but they can find me at the condo anytime they need to talk."

His eyebrows puckered and the corners of his mouth twisted downward. "I can play the part of a grieving spouse as easily as I can play that of a lonely professor."

You dirty rat. Kasenia stared into his shadowed eyes. "This is a game to you, isn't it? Pulling the wool over people's eyes, collecting women, tricking authorities—"

"Oh, baby, you don't know the half of it." His maniacal laugh, unlike anything she'd ever heard, ruptured the night and shot a chill down her spine. "I'm that kinda guy." He seized her shoulders and kissed her. Hard.

Her instinct was to pull away, but her Grandma Clara's words flashed through her mind. *Remember, Kasenia, you can catch flies better with honey than vinegar.* She wrapped her arms around his neck and molded her body to his, smelling his sweat-soured aftershave. "Let's go home, Brewster." She rested her forehead on his. "Let's go back to the way we were."

With a snort and a shove, he extricated himself from her hug. "You take me for an idiot?"

"Please," she begged, "don't leave me here."

"Kasenia, darling..." He tugged the disposable gloves from his pocket. "You're far more useful to me at Shadow Ranch than you'll ever be in town." Pivoting, he jogged toward her car without a farewell or a backward glance.

"Useful?" Kasenia whispered. "You only care that I'm *useful* to you?"

He trotted across the compound, his blond hair briefly brightened by a yard light, and climbed into her SUV. The engine roared to life, thunderous in the quiet night.

The lights flashed on. Kasenia blinked, stirred from her stunned stupor. Brewster wasn't joking. He was really leaving her and taking with him her ties to the outside world—her phone, her tablet, her credit cards.

Her car.

"Stop." She waved her arms. "Brewster, stop."

Running after the SUV, Kasenia followed taillights clouded by tire-churned desert dirt. The gate opened, and the car was through the opening before she could leap onto the bumper. For a brief moment, the headlights illuminated a horse's head and chest. Marlin must have opened the gate. Just as quickly, it rolled shut.

Overcome by dust, she slid to a halt, coughing and struggling for breath. What good jumping onto the car would have done, she didn't know. But at least she'd tried to do something. Didn't just stand there, watching him steal her car and everything in it.

She sucked in another dust-laden breath and sneezed. Swiping a knuckle beneath her nose, she tracked the SUV's progress over the flat terrain. At the highway, Brewster turned toward Tucson and picked up speed. Kasenia watched the taillights until they faded and her heartbeat slowed.

A moan escaped her lips. *Fingerprints. That's why he wore the gloves. So he wouldn't leave fingerprints in my car.* He'd planned their "disappearance" down to the most minute detail.

Head in her hands, she whispered, "I have to get us out of here."

"Give it up, lady."

Kasenia jolted upright.

Marlin.

She recognized his gravelly timbre. Yard light reflected off a horse's rump on the other side of the gate, but she couldn't see the man.

"End of the road for you, *Missus Wiley*." He snorted. "Face it."

Never. Kasenia stood stock-still. She was Kasenia Clarke—not Wiley—and she refused to believe this was the end of the road for her or Sam.

"Go on, get inside the camper," he ordered, his voice harsh. "You're out past curfew."

Curfew?

She walked toward the travel trailer. By the rustling sounds behind her, man and horse were moving on. How had she come to be locked inside a razor-topped fence patrolled by a nasty guard, one employed by her husband?

Kasenia stopped. Brewster was *not* her husband. He was an imposter who'd conned her from the day he called her into his office to ask her to proofread for him. His women might not mind his deceit, but she'd married for love and for life. She'd promised to love him and no one else, only to discover he didn't love *her*. And she wasn't really married.

Reaching behind her neck, she unclasped the heart necklace and dropped it into her palm. *B+K*. What a joke. Worthless symbols of a love that never was. She pulled off her wedding set and placed the rings with the necklace. Meaningless cookie-cutter trinkets no better than costume jewelry. That's all it was.

She twisted her hand, letting the gold and the diamonds catch the yard light. Then, raising her arm high, she flung the jewelry at the fence. The pieces clinked and disappeared, covered by darkness and dirt.

One of these days, she'd take time to process her humiliation, anger and loss. And whatever additional issues she'd have by the time this was over. Right now, she had to focus on her brother. Maybe she should knock on the dorm door to make sure Sam was okay. She wouldn't wake him, just check on him.

Kasenia started that direction then stopped. Margo didn't seem like someone who'd appreciate being awakened. She'd call Brewster and he'd come barreling back, eyes flashing, fists ready. She couldn't do that to her brother.

Besides, her knees had turned to jelly. The adrenaline must have worn off. She could hardly walk.

Swatting at gnats that came out of nowhere to circle her head, she slowly climbed the trailer's three metal stairs. Without a handrail for support, balance was difficult, but she made it to the landing. She had no desire to go inside, but where else could she avoid the gnats—and the ever-present Marlin?

6

— . —

O NE STEP INTO THE hot stuffy interior, and Kasenia knew
she wouldn't be able to sleep. Between the heat, the lock-
er-room smell and claustrophobia—the ceiling was mere inches from her
head—she'd be a wreck within minutes. The other mobile homes, she'd
noticed, were not only newer and larger than this one, they were cooled
by air conditioners or swamp coolers.

She flipped on the dim light. The camper had AC—with a thermostat
set to "off."

Brewster's women knew she was coming and where she would sleep,
yet they hadn't cooled her quarters for her. One more indication the
sister wives considered her an interloper. She opened the curtains and
the windows, surprised but grateful the primitive camper's windows had
screens to prevent the gnats and other bugs from crawling inside.

The women's rejection stung, she had to admit, but that was okay. She
wouldn't be around long enough for them to accept her into their sick
sisterhood. Having Sam nearby helped. Her brother's wellbeing was far
more important than trying to win over the Shadow Ranch harem.

She switched off the light and stepped outside, leaving the inside door
ajar but closing the screen door to block the gnats that now swarmed
the porchlight. One by one, she made her way down the steps and crept
to the rear of the camper. But when she turned the corner and her shin
connected with something solid, she stopped.

In the sliver of yard light that shone between trailers, she caught a glint
of metal. The trailer had a bumper, a place to rest her wobbly knees. She
sat, closed her eyes and leaned back. Tomorrow would be soon enough

to deal with the AC. It wouldn't do her any good now. After the last few dreadful hours, sleep would surely elude her.

Propped against the trailer's metal siding, which still held some of the day's warmth, Kasenia lifted her gaze and gasped. "Oh, wow..." She'd never seen so many stars, except on a rare clear night from her babushka's back porch. As much as she disliked the desert, this pristine view of the heavens was phenomenal. The Big and Little Dippers, the North Star and the Milky Way were plainly visible. But what were those cloudlike clusters?

A satellite moved slowly across the expanse, and a meteor shot past like a speedboat on a lake. The sky was surprisingly vibrant.

A cool breeze lifted her hair and stirred the creosote bushes on the far side of the fence, releasing their distinctive aroma with its hints of citrus, pine and rosemary. Their Tucson neighbors had planted a creosote hedge because they loved the fresh scent, which was especially strong after a rain.

She scanned the sparkling canopy. Where was God? The first words in her Bible said God created the heavens and the earth. Was he up there with the stars or beyond the stars? Or maybe he was in everything, or everything was God, like one of her Russian friends believed.

"Animals, birds, insects, trees and plants are all part of God," he'd told her. "So are rocks, wind, rain and fire. God populates inanimate things as well as animate. Some people refer to him as Supreme Being or Universe."

When she told Babushka Irina what he said, she'd scoffed. "Nyet, ne pravda. Not true. Such a stupid boy." Though her words, spoken in Russian, were strong, her tone was soft and melodic, as always. "God is far more than a supreme being or a universe. He's above all beings, a holy Creator *separate* from his creation. His creation is not him, yet his infinite power holds everything together. He's a Creator who loves his creation, especially those he created in his image, people like you and me."

"Just remember..." She'd smiled her sweet smile then and repeated her priest's favorite Russian proverb, one Kasenia was still trying to understand. "God is always where we don't look for him."

Supreme Being. Universe. Creator. Spirit Father...

A cricket chirped nearby. In the distance, a coyote howled, and another answered.

Kasenia shivered, remembering Brewster's not-so-veiled threat. Now, she understood what he meant when he said, *I can shoot out a coyote's eyeball at fifty yards.* He'd intended to instill fear early in their relationship. And it had worked. More than once his anger had alarmed her. But he'd never gotten physical.

Until tonight.

An owl hooted from somewhere faraway. She pictured the bird perched in a mesquite tree or atop a cactus. But maybe it was calling from a hole in the ground or the edge of a cliff. Why her mind was wandering around the desert, she didn't know. Maybe that's what the desert did to a person. She'd heard stories.

But she wasn't lost in the middle of a vast wilderness. She was *imprisoned* in the middle of a vast wilderness.

Hands on the bumper, she gazed into the starry night. "God," she whispered, "wherever and whoever you are, Sam and I need you. We're trapped, we—"

Hearing a muffled noise, she held her breath. The sound came again. Swishing, then thumps. Her heart drummed her ribs. Was it a coyote or a javelina? She hoped the creature was on the other side of the fence. Encounters with either animal could be nasty, from what she'd read.

The intruder snorted. Or was it a growl?

Kasenia gripped the bumper and planted her feet, ready to run.

A shaft of yard light between two mobile homes down the row briefly revealed a moving horse with the vague shape of a rider's leg. She pressed her shoulders to the trailer. As many photoshoots as she'd done on ranches, she should have recognized the snort and darted into the camper.

With any luck, Marlin wouldn't see her in the dark.

The horse stopped by the fence, both it and the rider silhouetted by starlight. She couldn't tell much except the man wore a cowboy hat. He didn't look as big as she remembered.

Her inhalations shallow, her heart pounding, Kasenia sat rigid and silent, breathing dust, smelling the horse's musky scent. Trying not to cough.

"Hola, Señora Wiley." The man's voice was soft and accented. "Buenas noches."

"What?" The cough escaped. "Who are you?" He didn't sound like Marlin.

"I…Tomás, Shadow Ranch security. Welcome."

"I am *not* a señora," she hissed, "and you're *not* a security person. You're a prison guard."

"Shh," he whispered. "Others hear."

"I don't care. Brewster tricked me. I'm not his wife, and this is not my home."

He dismounted and came to the fence.

Kasenia flattened against the camper.

"Señorita…" He spoke barely above a murmur. "I want help, but must be…uh, tranquilos. Sorry, Inglés no es bueno…not good."

"You want to help me?" Was he baiting her? If she could just see his face…

"Sí."

"Will you…?" She tiptoed to the fence. "Will you open the gate?"

"No can." His hat moved in emphasis. "They no tell code."

"Then how can—?"

"I watch, wait."

Hands on her waist, she leaned closer. "Why? You don't know me."

"Su hermano, brother," he whispered, "y son of sister, mi sobrino, en Niños de la Noche."

"The dormitory?"

"Sí."

She knew some Spanish, though not much. If only Sam were here. He'd taken a Spanish class last semester. "Are you saying your nephew is with my brother in the Children of the Night dorm?"

"Sí, señorita." His hat brim moved up and down. "No es good."

"Why do you say that?"

He lifted an arm, and a wristwatch face glowed green below the night sky. "Me tengo que ir. I go. We speak mañana."

Mañana, she knew. *Tomorrow.* "But..."

He tipped his hat and mounted the horse.

Kasenia watched the horse and rider weave in and out of the yard light until she could no longer see them. *If God is always where we don't look for him, is Tomás a messenger from heaven? An angel, maybe?* Whoever he was, he gave her hope. But what did he mean by "no es good"? Should she trust him?

I trusted Brewster. Look where that got me.

The first hint of sunrise was seeping over the mountains to the east and a creosote-scented breeze was wafting from the desert before she reentered the trailer. Unable to sleep, she'd either paced the fence behind the camper or sat on the bumper. The outside temperature dropped during the night and the wind picked up, yet she hadn't been cold, and her headache had finally faded. Despite faint crackling and scurrying noises, she hadn't spotted any desert wildlife, thank goodness.

Kasenia turned on the light. The camper had cooled considerably and smelled slightly better. It featured a bed at one end and a bench seat at the other end near the door, a kitchenette of sorts, a narrow closet, and an impossibly small bathroom. The interior was well-used but clean with sun-streaked brown curtains on the four windows and a worn cushion on the bench seat. Faded wallpaper peeled from the corners, and the thin paneling had separated in places.

So, this was where Brewster's latest acquisition spent weeks or months or years? Had the other women started here? Surely, they weren't happy in the cramped trailer or with his supposed family. But they must have acclimated.

Fear clutched her throat. She could never, *would never* accept Shadow Ranch as her and Sam's home. With effort, she swallowed and renewed her vow to do everything in her power to free the two of them.

The thermostat was mounted on the wall that separated the stove from the shower. She turned the dial and the AC rattled to life then settled into a noisy vibration. The entire trailer shook, but maybe the temperature would be more tolerable tonight, if they hadn't escaped before then. She hated to think they'd spend one more hour, let alone one more day in Brewster's warped world.

Again, she asked herself the question that had plagued her all night long. What did Tomás mean by, "No es good"? What could be worse than Brewster tricking them into joining his polygamous family?

Face lifted to the cosmos, she'd asked God the same question, more than once. He hadn't answered.

Rifling through her bag's meager contents, she extracted a fresh tank top and shorts then closed the windows and pulled the curtains over them. She had changed her clothes and was brushing her hair when someone knocked. Opening the door, she peered through the screen door into the early morning murkiness.

Margo stood at the base of the stairs, vaguely lit by the porchlight. Several boys, including Sam, waited behind her. Kasenia pushed the screen door wide and stepped onto the narrow platform. "Good morning."

"Did you take your pill?" Margo demanded.

Kasenia squinted at her. "What pill?"

"Your birth-control pill. Brewster wants you to stay on the pill."

What? Brewster had discussed their birth-control method with another woman? And that woman was discussing it in front of adolescent boys, including her brother?

Margo scowled. "Go take your pill and be sure to limit what you eat. He wants you to be a decent-looking model. Then open the curtains and come with us."

"I closed them for privacy while I changed my clothes. They also block the sun."

"We don't have secrets here. Open them."

Kasenia stepped into the camper and shoved the curtains aside. *No secrets* was right, not even something as intimate as birth control. What they didn't know was she no longer needed the pill, for she would *never* let Brewster touch her again. She slipped into her sandals, flipped off the light and exited the trailer. "I'd lock the door, but I wasn't given a key."

"Why would you need a key?" Margo huffed. "Our fence protects us from the world's evil."

"You've got to be kidding." Kasenia closed the door so hard the trailer shuddered on its axle. "This is a prison, not protection."

"Brewster will hear about your ingratitude." Margo grabbed a phone from her belt and stabbed at the keypad.

Kasenia choked down a fiery retort and let the screen door slam shut. From now on, she'd keep her thoughts to herself.

"Let's go." Margo marched toward the lodge, phone at her ear and the other boys trailing behind.

A rooster crowed from the back of the property.

Sam fell into step beside Kasenia, trudging over the gravel. "That was rough. You okay, Sis?"

"Didn't sleep a minute, but I'm fine." She didn't mention she felt a little shaky from lack of sleep, topped by the Margo encounter. But she'd pulled all-nighters in college. She could do it again. With the help of coffee. "Did you get some sleep?"

"Slept a little. But it was hard." He lowered his voice. "I heard someone crying, and then that Margo woman yelled at him to be quiet. I felt sorry for the kid."

"Did she yell at you?" Kasenia eyed Margo, pitying the horses she trained. Was every sister wife as insensitive and rude?

"Just this morning when she pounded on my door and told me I was allowed five minutes in the bathroom."

"Generous of her." Kasenia rolled her eyes. "Did she tell you what we're doing this morning?"

"Setting up for breakfast is all I heard." He aimed a thumb at the parking area in front of the lodge. "What happened to your car?"

"Brewster took it." The previous night's madness surged through her and she sucked in a shaky breath. "He's planning—"

"Sam, Kasenia, get over here." Perched on the lodge steps, Margo jammed her fists onto her waist. "You have work to do."

The other boys were already entering the lodge.

Sam groaned. "Sorry about your car. Now, we'll never get out of this place."

"Don't give up hope," she whispered. "We still have each other."

Along with the boys, Kasenia filled juice and water carafes, stacked paper plates, cups, napkins and silverware on the serving table and spread paper tablecloths over the long dining tables. Breakfast smells wafted around them, triggering rumbles from her stomach. She hadn't eaten last night, but maybe she should today, whether the food was something she normally ate or not. Whether Brewster approved or not. She'd need strength for whatever she faced today.

They worked without speaking, though sounds of meal preparation surrounded them. The women in the kitchen issued orders and banged pots and pans. Occasional childish chatter broke through their noise. Were the Shadow Ranch kids immune to their deprivation? She was sorry Sam was old enough to realize he'd been kidnapped and imprisoned. Yet, when it came time to escape, she wouldn't need to carry him. He'd be able to run on his own two feet. The simple realization calmed the panic ricocheting about her ribcage.

Other than Margo, no one spoke to Kasenia or the boys. They sat together to eat, with Margo at the head of the table. But they had to wait until wife number one, Lorraine, rang a bell by her plate and led them in the Spirit Father prayer. Kasenia stood and raised her hands but did not join the petition to the mystery deity, did not proclaim a desire to be a warrior goddess or reach her highest potential.

Instead, she prayed silently, hoping the God who made the stars could hear her inside the lodge and send help. He was the one her babushka worshiped, not Brewster's Spirit Father. He couldn't be the same.

The group's half-hearted blessing didn't hold the passion of the night before. Was it because everyone had recently awakened or because Brewster wasn't there? Did they act happy and enthusiastic last night just for him? Was it because they idolized him or because they feared him?

Before she lost her mind trying to understand the polygamists' mindset, Kasenia determined to get to know the young men at her table. They looked lost and lonely, separate from the Wiley offspring, and could possibly be the only allies she and Sam would have.

"So be it." Lorraine declared.

"So be it," the others mimicked and sat amidst mumbling and the sound of chair legs scraping the floor. Heads down, the boys at her table dug into the surprisingly substantial breakfast. Scrambled eggs, sausage, toast, oatmeal, orange slices and juice. The food even smelled good.

Kasenia leaned in to catch Margo's eye. "Excuse me, Margo." Conversations around them had grown loud enough she had to repeat her words to be heard. "Excuse me, Margo."

The redhead looked up, eyebrows scrunched.

"I didn't see the coffee. Is it in the kitchen?"

The horsewoman's green eyes widened. "Spirit Children do *not* drink coffee. It's an addictive substance."

Kasenia winced. How would she stay awake today? "Then I'll go make myself a cup of tea." She motioned to the others. "Anyone else like—"

"Kasenia Wiley..." Margo stabbed a finger at her. "We do not allow coffee *or tea*, also an addictive substance, to taint our bodies. Nor do we drink alcoholic beverages. We are gods and goddesses with holy, sacred bodies destined to rule the universe. Spirit Father forbids us to defile them with harmful substances."

"Really?" Kasenia looked at Sam. "We've seen Brewster drink coffee, tea *and* alcohol. He has a coffeemaker in his office at the university."

Sam nodded. "He has a beer every night he's home, sometimes two or three. And he drinks Dr. Pepper all day long. It has caffeine, just like coffee and tea."

Barely moving their heads, the other boys shifted their gazes between Margo, Kasenia and Sam.

Margo jutted her chin. "Our husband is our intermediary to the outside world who must sometimes sacrifice his health to do as the pagans do. Without his sales abilities, our hard work would be futile."

Our husband? Two words Kasenia never expected to hear together. Afraid the next words out of her own mouth would trigger another text to Brewster, she switched her focus to the boy across from her. He had a shy smile, crooked teeth and dimples and didn't appear to be very tall.

"You probably know by now my name is Kasenia." She smiled. "What's yours?"

Head down, the boy mumbled something she couldn't understand. "Please tell me again." She bent closer.

He glanced at her and then away. "Benicio."

"How old are you, Benicio?"

He tilted his head, and the boy beside him translated, "¿Cuantós años tienes?"

Benicio responded, "Doce años."

The second boy said, "Twelve years."

Benicio repeated, "Twelve years," and squared his shoulders, as if proud to speak English.

"Thank you, Benicio." Kasenia turned to the translator. "What's your name, and how old are you?"

"I am Cesar," the somber teen replied. "Fourteen years." His thick dark hair was combed to the side.

"Leave them alone," Margo ordered, "and let them eat. They have work to do in the dairy barn this morning."

The boys began to eat again.

Margo shook her fork at Kasenia. "You took too much food. I told you Brewster doesn't want you to overeat."

All the more reason to eat as much as I want.

Kasenia counted the boys. Eight, including Sam. She'd ask one more boy his name and learn the remaining four at lunch. She motioned to the boy seated beside Cesar. He had heavy eyebrows and short-cropped hair. "How about you? How old are you?"

"I, uh..." He hesitated. "Twelve años."

She nodded. "Your name?"

"Ismael, same en la Biblia."

"That's cool, Ismael. Biblia is the word for Bible in my first language...our first language." She nudged Sam.

"What is it, your country?" Cesar asked.

"Russia," Sam said. "We were born there."

"Now live here?"

Not wanting to claim Shadow Ranch as her home, Kasenia said, "We live in Tucson."

"Oh..."

Seeing the confusion in his eyes and sensing Margo's frown, she concluded their conversation. "Thank you, Ismael. I'll be sure to look for your name in my Bible, mi Biblia."

She'd finished her breakfast and was downing grape juice when Lorraine stood and rang the bell again. "Announcement time. Hands in your laps."

Kasenia set the paper cup on the table.

"Tomorrow is Saturday," Lorraine said. "The first day of our weekend market. We have much to do to prepare. Most of you know your work assignments for the morning. Those of you who don't, come speak with me as soon as the tables are cleared." She clapped her hands. "On with the morning."

Everyone pushed back their chairs, the legs loud against the wood floor. The flatware was dropped into a tub of soapy water, and the paper products, including the tablecloths, were stuffed into trash bins and wheeled outside to be burned.

Kasenia was surprised they didn't utilize fabric tablecloths that could be washed again and again. After all, they used metal flatware, not plastic. In Tucson, Brewster had insisted she cover the dining room table with a spotless linen tablecloth.

"Kasenia." Lorraine waved her into a corner with another of the sister wives. "You'll be assisting Veronica with yogurt packaging this morning. She'll take you to our dairy room."

Kasenia recognized the tall woman as the one who'd served the drinks at the reception. Like the other so-called wives, she was wearing her Brewster necklace. She looked at Kasenia like she was a bug she'd like to squash.

Ignoring Veronica, Kasenia watched Margo lead the boys, including Sam, out the door. "Where's Sam going?"

"Not your concern," Lorraine said.

"It is my concern." Kasenia lifted her chin. "I'm his guardian."

"Brewster and I are his guardians now."

"That's not true, not legal."

Lorraine sniffed. "You'll learn." She tapped Veronica's shoulder. "Off with you two. Make sure she washes to her elbows and wears a hairnet, gloves and mask."

Veronica hurried out of the room, but Kasenia didn't budge. Lorraine lifted a cell phone from her pocket and brandished it like a flag. "Do I need to call Brewster?"

7

— · —

"P LEASE DO." KASENIA FOLDED her arms. "I want to talk with him."

Lorraine reared back, apparently shocked her threat had no effect. "No one speaks with our husband by telephone except me, and upon occasion, Margo. Next time he comes, I'm sure he'll want to discuss your belligerence with you in person." She arched an eyebrow. "It won't be pretty."

With that, she shooed Kasenia away like she would an annoying fly. "Get to work—and drop that pretentious accent."

Kasenia stumbled out of the lodge and down the porch steps. The thought of Brewster assuming Sam's guardianship sickened her. He and Lorraine had no legal right to supervise her brother, yet she was powerless to stop them. She had to get him out of Shadow Ranch.

She looked around the compound. Other than the mobile homes, none of the buildings were familiar in daylight. Where was the dairy? Brewster's nighttime tour had left her confused and disoriented. Of course, that might have had something to do with her bewildered state of mind.

Two girls dressed in t-shirts and capris came up beside her. She recognized one as the piano player and the second as the magician's assistant. Like most of the girls, they had long blond hair.

"Are you lost?" the shorter one asked. "We can give you directions."

"I don't remember where the dairy room is."

"We'll take you." The taller girl smiled. "That's where we're working this morning."

They had a unique way of forming their words, as if they rounded them between their tongues and the roofs of their mouths.

Kasenia asked, "Are you two sisters?"

They snickered and the first girl said, "Everyone here is our brother or sister."

"Oh, right." How could she have forgotten?

"We're half-sisters." The girl appeared to be around Sam's age. "But we do everything together and spend the night at each other's trailers. My name is Corrine, but I forgot your name."

"I'm Kasenia and my brother is Sam." She turned to the other girl. "What's your name?"

"I'm Glenise."

"You both have beautiful names." Though they were an evil man's illegitimate children, they were lovely girls with lovely names.

They thanked her, and then Corrine said, "Today is yogurt day. But before we bottle the yogurt, we have to sterilize the jars and lids."

"Question for you," Kasenia said. "Why are paper tablecloths used at meals instead of fabric that can be washed? Seems the paper costs would add up and burning them would be an environmental issue."

"Our closest neighbors are miles away." Corrine laughed. "They're not bothered by a little smoke. The reason we use paper instead of tablecloths is because water is limited in the desert, and we need it for so many things, like the garden and the animals."

They walked together toward the dairy room. The morning was already warm. If the ranch was anything like Tucson, it'd soon be sweltering. Kasenia was glad she'd dressed in a tank top and shorts.

"Snake!" Corrine pointed a shaky finger at a fat rattler winding across the packed earth.

Kasenia gasped.

"If we don't bother it, it won't bother us." Glenise kept walking, seemingly unconcerned.

The words had barely left her mouth, when with a whir of wings, a huge hawk swooped out of the sky, grabbed the snake, and flew upward again. The writhing reptile dangled from its long talons like a worm on a hook. They watched until the hawk landed on the cliff behind the satellite dish.

"That was...wow." Kasenia blew out the breath she'd been holding. "I've never seen anything like it, except on the Nature Channel."

"I don't know what the Nature Channel is, but I know what that hawk is having for lunch." Corrine wrinkled her nose. "I've heard rattlesnake meat is good, but you won't catch me eating it."

"Not unless Daddy *makes* you eat it," Glenise corrected.

"Well, of course, but I hope not."

Kasenia, who was still reeling from the close encounter with a snake *and* a hawk, eyed the girls, who seemed to accept Brewster's domination without question.

The cold dairy had a bleach odor Kasenia hadn't noticed the previous evening. It overpowered the milk smell. Within moments, chill bumps sprouted on her bare arms and legs. She regretted not wearing the sweat jacket and jeans she'd packed.

The closest thing to a greeting from Veronica was a quick glance when they walked in. Without a word, she lifted a box of jars off a shelf and set it on a table, then another and another. "Open these and we'll get started."

Four hours later, Kasenia's core was warm from the work, but her extremities were still cold, and she was more than ready for lunch. They'd packed over a hundred pints of yogurt in four flavors—vanilla, strawberry, blueberry and plain. "Most of this," Corrine said, "if not all, will sell tomorrow at the market."

Walking with the girls to the lodge for lunch, Kasenia slowed, partly to soak in the noonday heat and partly to ask the question uppermost in her mind. "Tell me about the market." She rubbed her arms. "Is it a flea market, a regular store, a roadside stand...?"

"I guess you could call it a roadside stand. We sell lots of stuff and have customers all day Saturday *and* Sunday."

Kasenia raised her eyebrows, trying to look interested, but not too interested. "They open the gate and people come inside to shop?" Was this the opportunity she'd been hoping for?

"They'd never do that," Glenise was quick to say. "The security guys open the stand—that little white building out front, and we haul everything to it on carts."

Kasenia nodded, remembering the building beside the gate.

"Just those who have permission go outside the fence," Corrine added. "The moms run the booths and some of us older kids keep them stocked with product."

"I see." Kasenia stretched her sore back. She should have known escape wouldn't be easy. Yet, this was a viable opportunity. She'd alert Sam to the possibility of slipping out the front gate.

Under Margo's disapproving gaze, Kasenia proceeded to learn the names of the remaining boys over a lunch of ham sandwiches, apples and potato chips. Jorge was a stocky boy with curly hair and chubby cheeks, the kind her Russian grandpa used to love to pinch.

When asked his age, Jorge replied in accented English, "I thirteen años yesterday."

"Wonderful." Kasenia clapped. "Let's sing 'Happy Birthday' to Jorge." She hoped her "hor-hay" pronunciation was correct.

"Huh-uh." Cesar shook his head. "He mean birthday last week, not yesterday."

"We can still sing to him."

Margo pounded the table so hard her plasticware bounced. "You will do no such thing. The Wiley family honors and celebrates Spirit Father, not mankind."

Jorge's gaze fell and his shoulders drooped.

Kasenia bit into her ham sandwich, the first she'd eaten in years. If she and Sam didn't escape soon, she'd find a private way to celebrate Jorge's birthday. But, she promised herself, they *would* leave soon, and she'd tell the authorities about the polygamy and how the foster boys were treated.

The boy next to Sam was Ulises. He was fourteen like Cesar but spoke limited English. A handsome young man, he had acne on his cheeks and wavy hair with yellow-orange streaks, as if he'd added highlights with hydrogen peroxide.

Sam introduced himself, and then came Mateo, a shy, slender boy. Like Ismael and Benicio, he was twelve. Though his English was broken, he answered her questions with ease.

Kasenia picked up a potato chip, something else she hadn't eaten since she became a model. Her mouth watered at the thought of biting into the thin, crisp, salty slice. One way to sabotage Brewster's plan would be to get fat. But then... She sighed. She wouldn't have opportunities to get out of the compound for modeling jobs.

The last boy, a slender kid with a thin strip of mustache above his scraggly chin hairs, was seated on her other side. She motioned with the chip. "What's your name?"

"I Raúl. I fourteen."

"Very nice to meet you, Raúl."

Kasenia turned to Margo. "I'm amazed at how close in age these boys are. Does this group only accept adolescent boys as foster children?"

"None of your business." Margo's eyes flickered. "Put that potato chip down. You know you're not supposed to eat it."

Kasenia looked at her, looked at the chip, and bit into the crunchy saltiness. "Mmm." Then stuck the rest of it in her mouth.

Sam and the foster boys ogled her as if she'd lost her mind. But Margo already had her phone in hand. Mouth set in a grim line, she punched the keypad like she was smashing ants.

With a shrug and a wink for the boys' sake, Kasenia grabbed a second chip. Her rebellious act added another infraction for Brewster to rag about, but she had to show some backbone, for Sam's sake. And for the other boys. The tiny smiles tugging at the corners of their mouths warmed her heart.

Lorraine rang the bell and stood. When everyone's hands were in their laps, she rattled off names for the afternoon chores and then motioned to Margo. "Margo, have the boys clean the chicken coop and pen. Wanda will show you how she wants it done."

Sam groaned. "I'm already sore." They'd spent the morning shoveling manure in the corrals.

Kasenia whispered, "Did you pack your hat?" The tops of his ears were pink.

He nodded.

"Better grab it or you'll be hurting later."

"A reminder for those working outside," Lorraine continued. "Take two water bottles with you and wear sunglasses and hats with brims. Anyone who invites a sunburn or dehydration will hear about it from Brewster."

Kasenia arched an eyebrow. Was this how the Wiley family showed love and concern?

Assigned to work in the garden with Rachel, the schoolteacher, Kasenia thanked her lucky stars she'd tossed her floppy sunhat into her overnight bag—for romantic country strolls with her husband.

What a joke.

Throttling her anger before it erupted in a primal scream, she heard her dedushka's calm voice reassuring the villagers after a heavy snow crushed the town hall roof. "No misfortune comes without a blessing," he'd said. "We've been patching that leaky roof for years. Now we can replace it."

No misfortune comes without a blessing. The sunhat was a blessing she'd wear for protection from the sun, not to please Brewster.

Inside the camper, which was stifling hot, she flipped on the AC someone had turned off and dug her hat and sunglasses out of her overnight bag. When she exited the trailer, Rachel was waiting at the foot of the steps. A satchel of water bottles rested against her leg.

"It'll be hotter 'n' blazes this afternoon." She squirted sunscreen into her palm and handed the bottle to Kasenia. "High of a hundred and seven, I heard."

Rubbing the lotion onto her arms, Rachel added, "Use as much sunscreen as you need to cover your arms and legs. After this, you might want to wear long sleeves and long pants. Eventually, you'll always wear sleeves. Brewster prefers we keep our brands private, especially when outsiders are present."

"Thank you." Kasenia set her water bottles on a step and began applying the lotion. "I had no idea where we were going or what I was getting into when I packed to come here. But I do have a pair of Levi's with me." Wearing jeans in intense heat was not appealing, yet sunburned legs would not be fun, nor would a confrontation with Brewster over a sunburn that was none of his business.

She returned the lotion. "What were you saying about sleeves?"

"When you get your brand, you'll need to keep it covered."

"My brand?" Kasenia squinted at her.

Rachel tossed the sunscreen into the satchel and moved the bag into the meager shade beneath the camper. "Let's step in your trailer for a moment." Once they were inside, she closed the door. "Whew, it's hot in here. Your AC isn't doing a very good job."

Kasenia was about to tell her someone kept switching it off, when Rachel pivoted and then slid the neck of her t-shirt down, exposing her left shoulder blade. "See?"

"Uh, that's quite a tattoo." Kasenia winced. She'd never seen such an ugly tattoo. The black **BWSR** was an inch-and-a-half high and three inches wide.

"It matches the brand on our cattle. Shows who owns us."

"Owns you? You believe Brewster *owns* you?" Kasenia rubbed her temples. The sunscreen's powerful scent in the overheated confines was giving her a headache.

Rachel shrugged her shirt into place and turned to face her. "You know what the Bible says regarding marriage."

"No, I don't know."

"Men are masters over their wives."

"Where does it say that?"

"I'm not sure. Brewster could tell you."

Kasenia lifted an eyebrow. "With chapter and verse, no doubt."

Rachel opened the door. "We'd better get busy."

They left the trailer, grabbed the water bottles and started for the garden. "I brought plenty of water,' Rachel said. "Help yourself whenever you get thirsty."

"Thank you." Kasenia eyed Rachel through her sunglasses. "Who did it?"

"What?"

"The tattoo."

"Brewster. He has the equipment."

What kind of man brands women to show he owns them, though his own body is tattoo-free?

"Was it painful?"

"Oh, yes. But it made Brewster incredibly happy, which made me happy...when I quit crying."

Kasenia changed the subject. She didn't want to hear any more about Brewster's sick control. "Thank you for talking to me and answering my questions. The other women act like I have leprosy."

"I'm excited to have someone different to talk with," Rachel said. "Besides, you're my new sister, and I want to get to know you and find out how you and Brewster met."

Children pulling weeds at a nearby trailer waved and chorused, "Hi, Miss Rachel." The teen boy who appeared to be supervising them saluted.

"Hello, my sweeties," Rachel called. "You're doing a good job with those weeds. Be sure to drink plenty of water."

Turning to Kasenia, she whispered, "My tattoo was worth the pain 'cause Brewster loves it. He kisses it when we're alone and says it makes him love me more because it proves I'm his."

Kasenia scrunched her eyebrows. "He really says that?"

"Yes. I think it's sweet."

"Surely, you don't believe—"

"You'll come around." Rachel patted her arm. "Once you get used to life here. And you get your brand."

8

— · —

"I PREFER MY OLD life." Kasenia scowled. Brewster was a sick, evil man, but branding women like cattle was a new level of crazy. She would never let him brand her.

"Listen..." Rachel hurried her away from the children. "I'm s'posed to report you for talking like that, but I won't. Not this time. I was miserable until I accepted the fact there's no going back. I love the children Brewster gave me, and I've learned to love the desert, my students and gardening."

"Did Brewster trick you into coming here, like he tricked me?" Heat rose from the packed dirt and wrapped around Kasenia's legs.

"I knew he had other wives." Rachel dropped her voice, talking as they walked. "But I adored him, and his family sounded wonderful, so loving and happy. My parents bickered constantly before they divorced, and my aunts and uncles were on their second and third marriages. I wasn't close to any of them. I'd always dreamed of being part of a *real* family. In fact, I thought it was going to happen, but then my fiancé broke our engagement."

"Where did you meet Brewster?" Kasenia couldn't believe she was asking another woman how she met the man she thought was her husband and hers alone. Could life get any weirder?

"We met in a Phoenix bar. I'll never forget that wonderful day." Rachel grinned. "I was hunched in a booth, feeling sorry for myself and drinking too much, when he asked if he could join me. He was so handsome and nice that, of course, I said yes. And, well, you can guess the rest of the story."

"How did you learn about the other wives?"

"It sort of slipped out one day after I said I'd always wanted a big family. I think he'd been feeling me out on the subject. We watched a couple documentaries together that featured poly families—for the fun of it, he said. I was super curious as to how people relate in those kinds of marriages, and everyone seemed to get along great."

"He didn't show me any documentaries."

Rachel laughed. "Brewster is a student of human nature and loves the challenge of wooing each woman with a customized approach. He must have realized documentaries wouldn't work for you."

Student of human nature? More like master of manipulation. Anger sat like a lump at the base of Kasenia's throat. She swallowed hard. "So, you knowingly joined his harem."

"Don't call our family that." Rachel frowned. "Pagans have harems. We have a *family*. I chose to marry into the Wiley family because I love Brewster." She looked around the compound. "I didn't expect the ranch to be so, uh, confining, but he's the father of my five children and this is our earthly home."

Kasenia followed her into a tool shed, trying to digest everything Rachel had just told her. She seemed content, but deep down, was she happy? And what if her children wanted to leave? Would Brewster allow them the freedom to go? Probably not because they'd broadcast the appalling truth about Shadow Ranch.

The shed was warm and stuffy, yet it provided welcome relief from the sun's rays. "The other women?" Kasenia asked. "How did they get here?"

"Except for Lorraine and Margo," Rachel said, "they came from a large poly community across the border. Oh, and Veronica came from a farm."

"So, this lifestyle wasn't a huge surprise for the women from Mexico."

"Alana says she misses the ocean, which is near her former home—and all the activity. They have a lot more people than we do. But she's glad Brewster bought her. If he hadn't, a really old guy with lots of wives and children would have married her. She would have been expected to help them clean their homes and care for their children, including cooking for them and doing their laundry."

"Brewster *bought* Alana?"

"That's how they do it where she's from."

"Does everyone here get along?" Kasenia asked. "Seems like jealousy would be a big problem."

"Our husband and Spirit Father *hate* jealousy." Rachel's eyes flashed. "We're *very* careful to avoid that most evil of sins."

"Then they're like your sisters or best friends, right?"

"I, uh..." Rachel hesitated. "I love their children as much as I love my own. Making this a happy place for them is what matters to me." She lifted her hands. "They're my reason to live."

"What about the kids? Do they leave when they turn eighteen? They can't marry each other. That would be—"

"Shh." Rachel touched her finger to her lips. "No more questions. The walls are thin, and we need to get busy." She handed Kasenia a hoe. "You'll find gloves in that box over there. Watch out for Theodore."

"Who...where...? She glanced around the shed.

"Theodore the Tarantula."

"Tarantula?" Kasenia jumped back. "Where?"

"On the wall above the gloves."

Eyes wide, she stared at the huge furry creature with its striped legs.

"Don't worry." Rachel smirked. "He won't hurt you."

Kasenia grabbed the gloves and jerked away, relieved the big spider didn't jump on her arm. She stepped from the shed into a wall of heat, certain she'd have plenty to think about to take her mind off the tarantula while she hoed. Like, what kept the "sisters" in this desolate compound, other than the fence? Did they ever regret their decision to "marry" Brewster? And why didn't Lorraine leave the instant Brewster brought the second wife home?

Two boys and two girls, all preteens wearing sunglasses and wide-brimmed hats, approached the shed with big grins for Rachel. One of the boys said, "Hi, Teach."

"Ah, some of my favorite people." Rachel hugged each of them. "I miss you when school isn't in session."

"We miss you too," one of the girls said.

"Everyone, say 'hi' to Kasenia." Rachel motioned to her. "As you know, she's learning the ropes around here."

They nodded and smiled. "Hi, Kasenia."

One of the boys said, "Welcome to Shadow Ranch."

"Thank you." Kasenia wasn't happy to be a Shadow Ranch resident, but unlike their mothers, the kids were friendly.

Rachel told the newcomers to get hoes and gloves from the shed. "Close the door when you come out or some critter besides Theodore will think it's the perfect place to escape the sun."

They passed the greenhouse, where big cooling fans mounted in the end walls blew at full speed to keep the produce from succumbing to the desert heat. Kasenia heard voices coming from inside and smelled the fertile plant life. When they reached the gigantic garden, Rachel told the kids to hoe between the beans and onion rows and then had Kasenia accompany her to the opposite side.

Hoe in one hand and her satchel of water bottles in the other, Rachel surveyed several long rows of light-green cabbage heads. "Almost ready to pick." Rachel pointed to a row of less mature plants. "We stagger the planting, so the heads don't all come ripe at once."

"All this cabbage..." Kasenia laughed. "I feel like I'm in Russia again."

Behind sunglasses that had slipped down her sweaty nose, Rachel's hazel eyes sparked with interest. "I remember Brewster saying you're Russian, but even if he hadn't, your accent gives you away."

"You have a bit of an accent, yourself. Uralic, right?"

"Ah, you guessed it." Rachel pushed her sunglasses in place. "My grandparents on my mother's side were Hungarian."

"What do you do with the cabbage?"

"We'll turn most of this crop into sauerkraut and sell it at our market stand after it ages. We keep some for ourselves, of course, but there's only so much sauerkraut the family will tolerate." She laughed. "I personally love it with sausage. I also like to make cabbage rolls, using my great-grandmother's recipe."

"Ah, the memories." Kasenia grinned. "My babushka makes wonderful cabbage rolls—halupki, she calls them—and delicious cabbage pie."

"Yum. You're making me hungry for old-country food." Rachel walked to the other end of the first row and dropped her bag beside the fence that bordered the compound's southern edge. A long row of trees on the outside of the fence—palo verde, mesquite and iron-wood—shaded parts of the garden. On the desert floor beyond the trees stood the dozens of solar panels Brewster bragged about, each one angled southward.

Kasenia studied the trees. They were tall enough that some branches hung over the fence. If she could reach a branch, she could—

"Have you ever hoed a garden before?" Rachel asked.

"My Babushka Irina always has a big garden. Sam and I normally spend summers with her, but Brewster..." No sense going into how he'd stalled on a Russian wedding date. "I've hoed weeds, lots of them. Or as they call hoeing in Russia, motyzhit'."

"Motyzhit'," Rachel repeated. "I like it. Makes hoeing sound fun."

Kasenia marveled at the woman's chatty friendliness. Although the sun's rays threatened to overwhelm her, working in the garden with Rachel was much better than the cold workspace and frosty brushoff she'd experienced earlier.

Rachel started chopping weeds. Kasenia stepped into the next row and followed her lead. The smell of dirt and vegetation brought sweet babushka memories to mind. "Rachel, do you think my accent sounds fake, like I'm trying to be somebody I'm not?"

"No, but you never know who Brewster will pick up—" Rachel gulped. "It's just that he's not particular where he gets..." Her neck reddened, and it wasn't from sunburn. "I mean, look where he found me."

"I have a feeling," Kasenia said, "it takes a while for Brewster's latest acquisition to be accepted. What do I need to do? Go through an initiation? Or is that what the tattoo is all about?" She didn't plan to stay long enough to gain true sister status, but she was curious to know their process.

"Acquisition..." Rachel pointed the hoe handle at Kasenia. "Brewster doesn't *acquire* us, he *marries* us because he's a unique man with enough love for a dozen women—*and* our children."

"Rachel..." Kasenia eyed her over the top of her sunglasses. "Brewster Anton Wiley loves one person in this world, and that's Brewster Anton Wiley. Period."

"Don't say that. The children..." She jutted her chin toward the kids at the far end of the garden.

"They're busy chatting and chopping. They can't hear us."

"Still..." Rachel clutched her collarbone. "You shouldn't say such things. It's a rebellious lie. Spirit Father hates rebellion."

"It's the truth. Besides, polygamy is illegal."

"Brewster says we obey a higher law. Jesus had several wives. Brewster has to follow his example."

"I'm not a Bible expert, but I'm pretty sure Jesus never married."

"You know the Easter story, right?"

"Yes..."

"All those women who went to his tomb, those were his wives."

"The Bible doesn't say—"

"Brewster has it on good authority."

"Whose authority?"

"Spirit Father told him."

"Rather convenient, don't you think?"

Rachel gasped. "You shouldn't talk like that."

"It's a free world."

"No, it's not. I mean, it is, but... Please don't let anyone hear you say mean things about our beloved husband, the man who loved us so much he married us. They'll report you in a heartbeat...." Her words dwindled to a whisper. "Like Queenie there." She aimed an elbow at Veronica, who was striding across the compound.

"Quick." She slammed her hoe into a clump of weeds. "Get to work before she sees us talking."

Kasenia stabbed at the base of a tall weed. "Queenie?" She kept her voice low. "I thought her name was Veronica."

"Queen of snitch," Rachel murmured. "Never misses an opportunity."

Veronica entered the canning room, and Rachel turned to Kasenia. "I'm glad you joined us because she'll aim her venom at you for a while. I know it's selfish, but I need a break."

"Now we look the truth in the eyes."

"What does that mean?" Rachel frowned.

"It's a Russian saying, like when Americans say, 'Life isn't all sunshine and roses around here.'"

"Well, it is what it is." Rachel pushed a stray auburn curl behind her ear. "We have snakes and scorpions on both sides of the fence, if you get my drift."

Brewster is the nastiest snake of all. Kasenia whacked at the weeds, venting her frustration. "Doesn't seem very sisterly." Sweat dripped into her eyes. She swiped it away. The heat was becoming more unbearable by the moment.

"Sisters fight." Rachel lifted her hat and wiped her brow with her sleeve. "It's normal to have disagreements. In fact, you and I will probably fight. I'm being nice right now because you're new."

Kasenia planted the hoe in the ground and straightened. "I'm used to being in an airconditioned classroom, not outside in the heat. Any chance we can take a break? I'm starting to feel lightheaded."

Rachel glanced at her watch. "It's early, but on an extra-hot day like this, we should hydrate often." She yelled across the rows, "Children..."

They lifted their heads.

"Hydration break."

They dropped the hoes and ran to the water bottles they'd left in the trees' spotty shade.

Walking with Rachel toward the fence, Kasenia couldn't help but wonder what preteens with no outside contact talked about. Brewster's latest lecture? Doubtful.

She eyed the beehives between them and the kids. "Is it safe to be near the bees?"

"As long as we don't bother them, they don't bother us."

"Good to know."

Seated with her back against the fence, Kasenia gulped half the water in her bottle before she stopped. The warm liquid didn't cool, yet it quenched her thirst. She leaned her head on the hard chain links and closed her eyes, smelling the earth, smelling her armpits. The heat made her sleepy, oh, so sleepy.

"I don't want to do it," Rachel said.

Kasenia opened one eye partway. "Don't want to do what?"

"If you disrespect our husband one more time, I'll have to report you for ingratitude."

There it was again, *our husband.* The ridiculous concept grated on Kasenia's psyche. "Ingratitude?"

"Ingratitude for everything he and Spirit Father do for us, for their provision and protection."

"Looks to me like you-all provide for Brewster." Though the lodge blocked their view of the front gate, she pointed that direction. "He's out in the real world, driving an expensive sports car, wearing Armani suits and..." The mental image choked her. "Wining and dining any woman who strikes his fancy. I hate to admit my shallowness, but that's how he snared me."

"You don't understand." Rachel shook her water bottle at Kasenia. "We have to build our family, whatever it takes. Three more wives, and we'll be complete."

"Who says?"

"Spirit Father."

"Where?"

"In the Bible. Sometimes Brewster reads to us from his Bible and other scriptures."

"Like the Quran?"

"That's a blasphemous book. Spirit Father gives our husband scriptures just for us."

Kasenia focused on the cloudless blue sky. "I've read some of the Bible, in Russian and in English. And I've never seen a command to have twelve wives, or any size of poly family, or to lock them inside a fenced compound."

"Be careful what you say, Kasenia. If certain people catch wind of your rebellion, you're in deep doo-doo."

"Meaning what?"

"They'll tell Brewster and... She paused. "He has a temper none of us dare cross. But..." She studied Kasenia for a moment. "If he wants you to do modeling, he'll probably go easy on your face."

"My face?" Kasenia touched her cheek. "He wouldn't."

"When he gets mad, he loses control. He can't help himself because he has post-traumatic stress disorder from his military experiences. But he doesn't like dentists, so he usually tries to go easy on our faces, as much as he can."

As much as he can? Kasenia had seen enough Brewster blowups to believe her. And she'd heard his PTSD line, yet she'd seen him rein in his temper. He had more control than Rachel knew. "Does he hurt the children?"

"Only the... I'm sorry." Rachel shook her head. "This is no way to welcome you to Shadow Ranch. I just wanted to warn you to be careful what you say. Tell your brother to watch his mouth, too."

"Thanks." Kasenia downed the rest of the water and opened another bottle, trying not to think about Brewster harming a child. "Who lives in the trailers, besides me?"

"All the lesser wives."

"*Lesser* wives?"

"Numbers one and two, Lorraine and Wanda, live in the big house. The rest of us live in the trailers. The one way we move up is if someone dies, which has happened twice. Or when we get a new cash cow like you."

Kasenia stared at her, mouth open. "Cash cow?"

"Oops, sorry, did it again." Rachel didn't appear the least bit sorry. "That's what Lorraine calls us. I didn't mean..."

"I get it." *And, apparently, so does Lorraine.* Did she and Brewster hatch the plural-wives plan for free labor? Seemed unlikely a woman would willingly share her husband, but greed made people do strange things. "Do you know how those women died?"

Rachel looked around then lowered her voice. "I wasn't here then, but I was told a woman named Beth and her two children disappeared without warning. Brewster searched for them out in the desert but finally gave up. He figured if dehydration and starvation didn't get them, wild animals did." She shivered. "I try not to think how terrifying it was for them."

"That's awful..." Kasenia groaned. "I can't imagine anything worse than watching your children die. Must have been horrible. Did the other woman die the same way?"

"Eva...well, hers is a different sad story. She was a nurse and she, uh, hanged herself."

"Hanged herself?" Kasenia gasped.

"I heard she was upset because Brewster asked her to treat someone outside our faith."

"And she killed herself over it?"

Rachel shrugged. "That's what I heard."

Kasenia shook her head. Is that what happened to women after they'd been trapped in the harem year after year? They took their chances in the desert or killed themselves outright? A passing breeze rattled the tree leaves and cooled her forehead.

"But there's good news." Rachel smiled. "Spirit Father allowed both women into heaven because they were married to a man who practices the plural principle."

"The plural principle? You really believe—?" Before the insanity of it all overwhelmed her, Kasenia lifted a long beige bean pod from the ground. "What's this? I like the purple streaks."

"It's a mesquite pod. We grind them and mix the flour into butter. Gives it a sweet nutty flavor and is quite popular with our customers."

A strange buzzing sound, louder than a bee, ended with a whine and then started again. Kasenia glanced around. The older kids still sat in the tree shade. The younger ones were huddled beneath a faded awning, sipping from water bottles. They weren't the source of the odd noise.

She pointed with the water bottle toward the north side of the compound. "Who lives in those big trailers outside the fence?" From her slightly elevated position, she could see three dumpy doublewides some distance beyond the singlewide trailers parked inside the fence. Dusty pickup trucks of various eras, makes and condition sat between the aging mobile homes.

"Those are where the guards and vaqueros live."

"Vaqueros?"

"Mexican cowboys. They do some maintenance, but mostly, they watch over the cattle and horses."

A crow cawed from the top of a tree. Amidst giggles, the teens imitated the loud bird.

"I hope their AC works better than mine." Kasenia took another drink. "Do the guards and vaqueros ever return to their real homes?"

"Most of the vaqueros are illegal immigrants. Brewster lets them stay here, so they don't get arrested and shipped to Mexico."

Was this more free labor, or did he pay them? Was the man she talked with last night an illegal vaquero? He'd said he was a security guard, not a cowboy. "What about Marlin?"

"Like the other guards, he's a creepy mercenary Brewster knew from his military days." Rachel made a face. "Stay away from him, from all the men, like the one over there."

Kasenia looked to where she was pointing and saw a dark-haired man trimming a palo verde tree with a chainsaw. His back was to them. "So that's what the buzzing sound is."

"Remember, you're Brewster's wife. You shouldn't speak with any of the men, even if they speak to you."

"I am not—"

"You are exactly what Brewster says you are, his ninth wife and a fashion model." Rachel's tone was stern, like a teacher at the end of her patience. "No more, no less." She finished her water and got to her feet. "I'm going to gather the empty bottles and get more water. You can start where you stopped. I won't be long."

9

— · —

F INISHED WITH THE ROW, Kasenia walked to the head of the next and jabbed the hoe into a thick clump.

"Psst."

She gasped and jumped backward. Had she disturbed a rattler? She backstepped again, wishing she'd worn her hiking boots. Her sandals were no protection from snakes.

"Psst." The sound came again.

Lifting her gaze, she saw a cowboy hat at the base of a tree on the other side of the fence and a booted leg where the bottom branch joined the trunk.

"No look, señorita. Es Tomás."

She lowered her head. "Hola, Tomás."

"We speak."

"Sí." Kasenia chopped at another weed. Slowly turning her head, she checked the kids to see if they noticed. They were farther away now, talking as they worked. No one else was around. However, Rachel could return at any moment.

She had a thousand questions for Tomás, yet she waited, unwilling to chance exposing her one possible ally by talking too much.

"Su hermano, your brother, he is...how you say...uh, trouble."

"What?" Kasenia peered into the branches.

"No look."

She hacked at the ground, heart pounding. "Did he do something wrong?"

"Los niños de la noche..." He paused.

"Children of the night."

"Sí. Un nombre...name, it is purpose."

"Purpose?"

"Por eso se llama así...why is called like this."

"Why the name is called like this... A reason for the name?"

"Sí."

Kasenia frowned. "I don't get it. Oh—" She gasped. "Are you saying—?"

"Silencio, por favor."

Clutching the tool handle, Kasenia fought for air, shaking her head. "No, it can't be."

"Es verdad. I don't like tell you...los hombres, they come una semana."

She didn't understand everything he said, but she knew hombres meant men, and they were coming. "Una semana—one what?"

"Uh...siete días."

"Seven days. One week?"

"Sí, they come one week. Por los chicos, the boys."

"Will they...?" Her heart stuttered. "Will they take the boys away?"

"Los hombres tienen mucho dinero, come aquí, here...Shadow Ranch por los chicos."

Mucho dinero, Kasenia remembered, was *much money.* The men would pay for the boys. She retched, losing her lunch on the dirt at her feet. Bent over, forehead on the hoe she gripped with both hands, she whispered, "That's horrible. I can't let Sam—"

"Lo siento mucho...I sorry."

She covered the vomit with soil and wiped her mouth with a cabbage leaf. "Tomás, it's unthinkable evil. But why boys, not girls?"

"Brewster, he say no quiere, no want chicas. Make bebés. Aborto big problema. Chicas hurt, no make dolares. Bad hombres también desean...also want los chicos."

Brewster didn't want girls because they made babies. Kasenia thought she caught the gist of Tomás's words. *Abortions were a problem. Brewster would lose dollars while the girls healed.* Groaning, she dropped the cabbage leaf. It was about the money. The man's capacity for greed and wickedness was bottomless.

Kasenia leaned on the hoe, weakened by the violent upchuck and by fear of what lay ahead for Sam. But then she straightened, infuriated Brewster planned to use her brother and the other boys in such a sordid, sick manner for his own gain.

"What can I do, Tomás? I have to do something."

"Con tu hermano y mi sobrino, nos vamos, we go...pronto."

"We can't take just those two boys. We must take *all* the boys with us."

"Sí. Llevar los chicos lejos...pronto."

Lifting her hat, she wiped the sweat from her forehead. *Niños* she knew and *pronto*, but... "Llevar and lejos, what do they mean?"

"We get boys...go...far."

"When?"

"No can say." He lowered his voice. "Señora Rachel, she come."

Following the dinner cleanup and final preparations for the Saturday market, Kasenia stumbled into the travel trailer after midnight. To her amazement, the AC rumbled, and the trailer was cool. The floor vibrated, but she didn't mind.

Still wearing her sweaty tank top and shorts, she closed the curtains and fell onto the bed. As hard as the mattress was, it felt heavenly. She wouldn't be able to sleep, but she could rest her eyes and brainstorm ways she and Tomás might thwart Brewster's evil plans.

She'd barely closed her eyes, it seemed, when a loud clatter jolted her upright. Kasenia stared at her surroundings until a strip of yard light between the dark curtains brought her to reality. The camper. Shadow Ranch. Sam and the boys...

What was that sound? Not the air-conditioner, which was momentarily silent. Or maybe it made a loud noise when it stopped.

The sound came again, like hail on the trailer. But it was brief, and rain wasn't pounding the roof. She crawled across the bed to the window, pinched a corner of the curtain aside and peeked out. The moonless night was dark, yet she made out what she thought was the outline of a horse.

Three steps, and she was at the door, slowly turning the handle. She opened it and then the screen door and checked both ways. Seeing no one, she tiptoed down the metal stairs to creep alongside the trailer. The porchlight cast her shadow ahead of her, something she regretted but couldn't change.

At the trailer's rear corner, she stopped. Hearing nothing, she whispered, "Hello... Anyone there?"

"Sí, es Tomás," came a soft reply. "Come, señorita, por favor."

Glancing behind her, she slid around the corner. When her eyes adjusted, she saw him at the fence.

"Sorry to wake, pero we hablar, speak."

She moved closer.

"You like caballos, uh, horses?" He patted the horse's neck.

"Yes, sí. I like horses."

"You ride los caballos?"

"Yes, I can ride." When she and Sam first started doing fashion shoots on ranches, they'd been skittish around horses, whether on or near the big creatures. One of the agency photographers had suggested they take riding lessons.

"They sense when you're nervous," he'd told them, "and get nervous, too, which can spell trouble."

After three months of twice-a-week lessons, both she and Sam were much more comfortable around horses.

"Su hermano?"

She nodded. "My brother knows how to ride."

"Bien." He mounted the horse.

Kasenia gripped the chain links. Was that all? He'd awakened her to ask if she could ride a horse?

"Wait, please." Her whispered plea was loud in the night, too loud.

His hat tilted downward.

"What can I do to—?"

"Shh, señorita. La paciencia es importante."

"Patience is important. That's all—?"

"También, rezar a Dios."

"*También* I know," she whispered. "It means *also,* but rezar a Dios...?"

A click of his tongue, and horse and man moved from the shadows into hazy light. Tomás twisted her direction, palms pressed beneath his chin.

Oh...pray to God.

From her perch on the camper's bumper, Kasenia watched the pair weave in and out of the light. Once again, she was wide awake, searching the stars for God. The unthinkable notion her brother could be horribly abused night after night by man after man tormented her heart and twisted her stomach. She couldn't let it happen, to Sam or the foster boys.

"God..." She scrutinized the heavens. "Wherever you are, please stop this horror before Brewster opens the gate to perverts. Show Tomás and me what to do."

She scuffed at the dirt with the toe of her sandal. Horses. Why did Tomás ask about horses? Was he planning for them to ride away? But where to? On what horses? Surely not Brewster's. He'd chase them down or have them arrested for theft. What if the other boys didn't know how to ride? How could that many people and horses not draw attention?

The only response was Tomás's final words ringing in her ears. "Rezar a Dios." She had prayed, like he said, but she needed to do more than talk to an invisible deity.

Pushing her sleep-tousled hair from her eyes, Kasenia remembered her dedushka's words. *The Christian faith is not complicated*, he'd said. *All people need to do is trust God's Son, Jesus, to save them from sin and walk with them through life's ups and downs.*

She huffed. Easy for him to say as mayor of a tiny sleepy village where nothing ever happened. Well, except for the raccoons that invaded the city center during the lean years. And the wolves that stalked the villagers' livestock. And frozen pipes every winter.

Yet, she had to admit, Jesus and God were all she had.

Kasenia returned to the trailer and, somehow, her fears faded into slumber.

⟨⟩ ⟨⟩

The morning came fast. Kasenia didn't feel the least bit rested. But she had hope, hope for los Niños de la Noche.

Her two minutes in the camper's cold shower thoroughly awakened her to her mission—deliver the boys to safety. Amazing how simple life had become. The boys' protection was what mattered now. She wished for freedom for each Shadow Ranch child, but Brewster's kids had mothers who were supposed to care for them.

Hearing voices, Kasenia peeked through the big window at the front of the trailer. The sun hadn't yet crested the mountains, yet people were wheeling carts to the open front gate and a well-lit building beyond it. Open gate? She hurriedly dressed, ran her fingers through her wet hair and exited the trailer. Two girls were passing the camper, one pulling and one pushing a load of what was probably produce.

Kasenia hurried to walk alongside them in the cool morning air. "What's happening?"

"Don't you know?" The girl pulling the wagon motioned ahead. "It's Saturday, market day."

"Oh, right. I forgot."

The other girl added, "It's where we sell our homespun products and homegrown produce."

Kasenia followed them to the gate, which was lit by a light at the top of the pole. A square-jawed man with a pistol on his hip raised his palm. "Present your badges." His harsh tone matched his stern features.

The girls showed him the badges pinned to their long cotton dresses, and he waved them through. But when Kasenia said, "I'm new here. I don't have a badge," he shook his head. "Only those with badges are permitted beyond the gate."

Kasenia returned to the camper to watch from inside. Maybe she'd learn something to help her and the boys escape or see someone drop a badge. Activity increased. Residents scurried back and forth, delivering cartloads of goods.

The day dawned with a cloudless shimmer. In the growing light, she saw Margo marching toward the camper. Before the austere woman could knock, Kasenia opened the door and stepped out. "Good morning."

"You're late." Margo put her hands on her waist. "You should be helping with breakfast preparations. Do you know what time it is?"

"I don't have a watch or a clock."

"No excuse. The sun is up. That's all you need to know."

Kasenia arrived at the lodge in time to help Sam spread paper tablecloths on the long tables. "Good to see you, brother. How was your night?" Bacon and pancake aromas filtered from the kitchen.

"Didn't sleep much, thinking about..."

Kasenia opened another tablecloth package. "Thinking about what?"

"Tell you..." He sent a furtive glance toward the doorway. "Tell you later."

Lorraine rushed them through a halfhearted breakfast prayer and then told them to eat fast, so they could support the market's frontline soldiers. Kasenia eyed the woman. *Soldiers?* As far as she knew, they were peddling potholders and potatoes, not defending the market against rowdy ranchers.

She took her seat beside Sam, annoyed they couldn't talk like normal people. Under Margo's watchful eye, she didn't dare ask about his night. The boys were quiet, focused on their food. Her attempts to draw them out fell as flat as the pancakes they ate.

Around them, people came and went, busy prepping for the roadside market. Lorraine's daily duty speech was short. Sam and company were tasked with cleaning more animal excrement, this time the duck yard. Kasenia's chore was to help Brittany load utility wagons with craft items, as needed, and deliver them to the roadside stand.

Surprised by an opportunity to get outside the gate, Kasenia whispered in Sam's ear, "Sorry you're stuck with duck doodoo, but I'll check out, you know..." She hoped he understood she'd look for an escape, and that she wouldn't leave without him.

Sam shrugged. "Poop is poop, just like at Babushka Irina's house."

Brittany was already in the craft room when Kasenia arrived. She gave Kasenia's t-shirt and shorts a onceover, checked her watch, and began opening cabinet doors. Her long maternity dress printed with tiny daisies reminded Kasenia of women's dresses in the old westerns her grandpa watched.

Her flashy timepiece, however, was a mismatch with the dress. Kasenia would have asked where she got it, but she had a feeling she knew the answer. Though it was once her favorite watch, knowing Brewster stole it to give to another woman ruined its allure.

Shelves in one craft cabinet were piled with brightly colored baby blankets, lap blankets, quilts, casserole cozies, potholders and aprons. Stained-glass pieces and framed paintings stood upright between cabinets. More cabinets held pottery, jewelry, Christmas tree ornaments, candleholders, leather purses, wallets and headbands.

"Does a craft exist that you don't do here?" Kasenia asked. The eclectic collection was a jumble of colors and aromas, the most obvious being leather mixed with paint, reminding her of her Grandpa Gordon and his roadster. Had he missed them yet? She missed him.

Brittany smiled. "Lorraine sometimes lets me search the internet. If I see something I think will bring in cash, and she and Brewster agree, she orders the supplies, and we learn how to do it."

Kasenia lifted an eyebrow. Evidently, the ranch had a computer. Had to be somewhere in the lodge, probably upstairs behind locked doors. "I'm impressed with your creativity, Brittany. You must enjoy your work."

"Enjoy it?" She shrugged. "Work is work. If it needs to be done, we do it."

"I assume Lorraine places your orders online. How does it get delivered way out here?"

"Like stuff is delivered anywhere, of course." Brittany's expression suggested she doubted Kasenia's intelligence. "UPS, Amazon, FedEx—they all come to the gate. Here, help me load the wagon. Blankets and quilts first trip, then we'll return for fragile stuff and use the smaller quilted items for padding."

Brittany took the handle to steer the piled-high cart toward the gate and the produce stand, and Kasenia pushed. Hearing music, she lifted her head. The stand's hinged panels were propped open, front and back, providing access as well as shade. Beyond the stand, teen musicians stood between picnic tables clustered under a large canvas canopy and bordered by a semi-circle of colorful awnings. They were playing the song they performed the night she and Sam arrived.

Kasenia sighed. Another Grandpa memory. Was he searching for them or believing Brewster's lies? Oh, to hear him call her Senya Girl again.

Cars were parked behind the awnings and other cars were driving the road to the ranch, stirring clouds of dust. What was wrong with people? Didn't they realize Shadow Ranch was a polygamist's lair, that its products were produced by slave labor?

Kasenia caught a whiff of sweet popcorn and spotted a teenage boy in knickers with a long wooden spoon. He plunged it into a big black cast-iron pot to stir what she assumed was kettle corn. A girl in a white blouse and long print skirt was bagging the popped corn. Next to them were two boys hovering over a big grill, metal spatulas in hand.

In a matter of minutes, Shadow Ranch had morphed from prison camp to county fair. But the guards hadn't gone away. Marlin and another man stood at each side of the gate. When they drew close, Marlin held up his palm. "You in the back, where's your badge."

"I don't have one."

"I need her to help me with the wagon," Brittany said. "She'll return as soon as we unload."

Kasenia straightened. "As you can see, she's pregnant. Can one of you help her?"

"Marlin," Lorraine called from the stand, "let them through. We need those items." She was wearing an ankle-length cotton dress with a wide white collar.

"She ain't got no badge."

"I'll give her a badge later."

"You're the boss." Marlin shrugged and motioned them through. To Kasenia, he said, "I'll be watchin' you, woman. Don't try any funny stuff."

She turned her head.

The other guard let out an appreciative whistle. "Who's the new broad?"

Marlin grunted. "Wiley's latest."

"Dang, he done good this time."

"Shut your trap, Smith. I told you to keep your hands and eyes off the boss's women."

"What's the harm in a little sightseeing?"

Kasenia stared straight ahead, feeling their focus on her backside and wishing she wasn't wearing shorts. The nerve of them to talk about her like she was a piece of meat. *But,* she reminded herself, *isn't that what Shadow Ranch is about? Dehumanizing women?*

Once she and Brittany were through the gate, Kasenia ignored the men and relished a tiny taste of freedom. For the first time in days—was it really less than two days?—she was outside Brewster's prison. So many cars, and more coming. With all those people milling around, Marlin wouldn't see her crawl into someone's backseat. She'd ride to freedom, call the authorities, and return by afternoon to rescue her brother. She hated to leave him behind, but this way she could report Brewster's atrocities and thwart his horrific plans.

They parked the wagon behind the quilt awning manned by Lorraine's daughter, Jacintha, who was in an animated discussion with a customer concerning a desert-themed quilt. Like Brittany, she wore an old-fashioned dress. Her blond hair was braided and wrapped around her head.

"First, we'll hang the quilts on the racks," Brittany said.

Kasenia didn't understand why pregnant Brittany was pulling a wagon and a teenager was waiting on customers, but that was a question for another time. "What are they selling in the other booths?"

"Baked goods, meat, dairy and produce are sold in the stand, where it's a bit cooler. Jewelry, pottery, paintings, stained glass, leather goods, metal art and Arizona t-shirts are under the awnings."

"Metal art and t-shirts? I didn't know you made those too."

"We don't. Brewster arranges the suppliers." Brittany twisted her blond hair into a bun at the nape of her neck and secured it with a hair tie. "But don't tell the customers. We advertise everything as being made by Shadow Ranch residents, which is mostly true."

Right... Kasenia could hear her Grandma Clara say, "A fib is a fib, no matter how big or small."

Leaning close, Brittany whispered in Kasenia's ear. "That guard Smith will pay for his comment, big time. Brewster will teach him a lesson he'll never forget, if he lives."

10

— · —

KASENIA BLINKED, EYES WIDE. "Are you serious?"

"Shh." Brittany grabbed a quilt and turned to hang it on a rack.

A moment later, Lorraine stepped inside the booth. "Kasenia, we need you over at the stand to fill the fridge. Every time we put out our half-price milk and eggs sign, customers buy dairy products faster than we can restock."

She turned to the two middle-school youth standing behind her with a wagon. "Leave the eggs and milk by the cooler, boys, then return for more. Put the milk in an ice chest and the boxed eggs in a flat on top. Be very, *very* careful with the eggs and glass bottles."

They nodded and headed for a glass-fronted refrigerator at the far end of the stand. Lorraine followed and then Kasenia. She assumed dairy products were positioned at the end so people would pass the other food items along the way.

After the boys unloaded the wagon and left, Lorraine said, "You'll arrange everything according to labels. "Cheese, butter—including mesquite butter—cream, yogurt, milk and eggs are displayed on the top shelves by product and flavor. The excess is kept on the bottom shelf. When someone buys a pint of yogurt, for example, one of us will take it from the fridge. Then you will replace it with another pint."

"Why don't I just hand the person the pint?"

Lorraine glared at Kasenia, her expression as horrified as if she'd suggested they bomb the ranch. "It's how we do it, Kasenia Wiley. Our methods are tried and true. This is your first time at the market, so keep your mouth shut and do as you're told."

Kasenia's mouth dropped open. She couldn't help it. No one had ever talked to her like that. Well, no one but Brewster.

"And stop seducing the men with that skimpy outfit. We wear prairie dresses on market days."

"I don't have one."

"Ask Brittany to get you one from the costume closet." With a parting scowl, Lorraine stomped away.

Kasenia watched her go. *Why would I want to be hot and sweaty and crabby like you? I may forget to mention the dress.*

Fists on her hips, she blew out a long breath, doing her best to dismiss the nasty encounter, and turned to the cooler. She surveyed the contents and then the cartons and bottles the boys had deposited nearby. Looked like an easy enough chore. She tackled the egg cartons first, carefully stacking the chicken and duck eggs separately.

The happy sounds around her—music, corn popping in the big kettle, meat sizzling on the grill, people chatting and laughing—all helped to calm her spirit. So did the realization Lorraine was an unhappy woman who took her anger out on others. *Lucky me, I just happened to be her latest victim.*

The kettle corn's sweet smell mingled with that of coffee, freshly baked pastries, and barbecued meat. Though the morning was warming, the temperature was tolerable, and stocking the cooler was the most pleasant Shadow Ranch work she'd done so far. Yet, she couldn't allow herself to get comfortable and miss an opportunity to escape.

She was placing two milk bottles on a shelf when she sensed someone watching her. Hands on the bottles, she turned her head, ready to give Smith a piece of her mind. But she didn't see him.

Sliding the door closed, she scanned the ever-moving crowd and made eye contact with a tall twenty-something man walking her direction. Turquoise-studded silver conchos ringed the hatband on his gray cowboy hat. She dipped her head but took a second glance in time to see him sit at a nearby picnic table. Coffee cup in one hand and a paper-wrapped pastry in the other, he grinned and lifted the cup.

Three people moved between them, blocking him from view.

Kasenia returned to her assignment. The yogurt jars appeared to have been hastily inserted into the fridge. She sorted them by flavor, all the while thinking of the cowboy. Who was he? And why had he focused on her? Couldn't he see her wedding rings? She held out her left hand. *Oh, right*. She'd thrown the rings in the dirt along with the necklace.

The next time she looked, the man was gone. Kasenia slumped with disappointment, which was silly because they hadn't even spoken. Stretching her arms, she surveyed the crowd and saw him talking with Marlin at the gate. They both seemed at ease, like longtime friends. In fact, she'd never seen Marlin so relaxed. They were too far away for her to hear what they were saying.

Was the guy a security guard? Was that why he was watching her? One thing she knew, any friend of Marlin's was no friend of hers.

Wanda walked past, cradling a chicken under her arm.

"Wanda..." Kasenia said, "can I ask you something?"

The woman sighed and turned. "What?"

Kasenia eyed her plain brown dress, already stained with sweat. "Why long dresses on such a hot day?"

"Isn't it obvious?"

"No."

"Come." Wanda led her between customers to stand beside an empty picnic table. "Read."

Propped on the stand's roof was a long white sign with green edging, a huge yellow chicken, and the words "Shadow Ranch Country Market" painted in tall red letters.

Kasenia gazed from the sign to Wanda.

"You still don't get it, do you?" The chicken clucked, and Wanda stroked its orange feathers. "Ranch. Country. Market." She lowered her voice. "Those words suggest old-fashioned, maybe Amish or Mennonite. We do our best to fit our customers' expectations. Why do you think we sell quilts? Why do you think I'm carrying a chicken around? It's about marketing. You, with your fancy business degree, should realize what's happening here."

Kasenia didn't respond. *It's about pulling the wool over people's eyes to blind them to Shadow Ranch's true nature. That's what it's about.*

Wanda looked her over. "You should be wearing a dress."

"I don't have one."

"Find one."

Kasenia had just unloaded a second cart of milk and eggs, when the boys brought produce to distribute. Peering over Rachel's lacy collar, she could see lettuce and cucumbers were low. "Excuse me."

Without comment, Rachel stepped aside, her bun-topped head held high.

Kasenia carefully arranged the produce on a tray. "How do you keep everything cool?"

"The trays are refrigerated, like those used for buffets, but we only run electricity on market days."

A woman with long frizzy gray hair and John Lennon sunglasses, wearing a rainbow-swirled floor-length caftan, hobbled toward them. "Girls..." She lifted a gnarled finger. "I'll take five pounds of tomatoes, three red onions and two basil bouquets. But let me sniff the basil before you package it. I love the sweet aroma."

"I can fill a bag for her, if you'd like," Kasenia said. *And carry it to her car.*

"That's my job, not yours." Rachel elbowed her aside. "Besides, you're not wearing disposable gloves—or a dress."

"Sorry. Just trying to be helpful."

"We stick to our assignments around here."

"Where can I find gloves?" Lorraine hadn't told her she needed them, but maybe that was because the dairy products were packaged.

"On the table back there." Rachel motioned with her chin.

Kasenia walked to the table and pulled gloves from a dispenser. The temperature would soon be in the triple digits. Despite the big fans spaced every few feet, the gloves could become uncomfortable. And a dress... she didn't even want to think about that. But maybe she'd get an opportunity to carry someone's purchases for them. She tugged on the gloves, all the while surveying the customers. The tomato lady was struggling to balance her purse and her bag of produce.

Kasenia hurried to offer her assistance and arrived at the counter in time to hear her say, "I'll put this in my trunk, so Bruno can't get into the tomatoes and make a mess."

"Who's Bruno?" Rachel asked.

"My German shepherd guard dog. He's my reincarnated husband who loves tomatoes, especially tomato-and-onion sandwiches with basil and mayonnaise. Bruno goes everywhere with me. One whiff of his breath—and maybe a growl or two—and people keep their distance. He wants to ensure no one gets their hands on our money."

Dipping her head, she glowered at them over her glasses. "The two of us worked hard to build our ranch."

"I'm sure you did." Rachel folded her arms.

Kasenia added two cabbage heads to the display, grateful she'd overheard their conversation. A confrontation with Bruno might not end well. But someone else would come along.

The woman set the sack on the counter and shifted her bohemian bag from one shoulder to the other. Appliqued with daisies and peace symbols, the fringed satchel was as colorful as her caftan. "I must hurry home to fix Bruno his sandwich. He hates it when I dawdle." She touched her finger to her nose then pointed upward. "Keep your eyes on the stars, girls. This *is* the Age of Aquarius, you know."

With those weighty words of advice, she hefted the produce and tottered off, the caftan's hem catching in the tops of her flower-patterned cowboy boots.

Rachel snickered. "Desert people sure have some strange beliefs."

"You can say that again." The words came out louder than Kasenia intended, and Rachel gave her an odd look before turning to a customer.

Her beliefs are weird, but yours aren't?

Kasenia replenished the carrots and beans, enjoying the produce's fresh aroma, and was reaching for snap peas when Rachel muttered, "Can't you see we need more tomatoes, now?"

"I'll go get some." Power games. Was that what the ranch culture was about? A bunch of women trying to one-up each other. Rachel was nice yesterday, but not so agreeable today.

Not your problem, Kasenia reminded herself. She was at the bottom of the pecking order, and that was okay. She had no desire to fit into their bizarre world.

With barely a moment for a drink or a bathroom stop, and no pause for lunch, Kasenia scurried from one end of the stall to the other, and from one awning to another. She restocked baby blankets and potholders, cucumbers and melons, keychains and Christmas ornaments. And kept the dairy products flowing until the milk, butter, eggs and yogurt were sold out, and most of the cheeses. All while wearing shorts and a tank top.

Just before sundown, the cliff's long shadow fell across the marketplace. Sale signs were removed from the highway and the booths emptied. Lorraine, guarded by Marlin, opened the cash register and placed the contents in a thick leather bag with **BWSR** tooled on the side. Limp leftover produce was delivered to the kitchen to be incorporated into omelets, stews or "Sunday night surprise." The remaining veggies were placed in cold storage to be offered for sale the next day.

Kasenia melted into her chair at dinner. The roast beef on her plate smelled good, but she wasn't sure she had the energy to chew it. Every muscle and joint ached. Her eyes and skin burned because she hadn't stopped long enough to get her hat and sunglasses or to apply sunscreen. For sure, she hadn't had time to don a dress.

The others had changed out of their old-fashioned outfits, so her casual attire wasn't a problem at dinner. But... Kasenia sighed. She hadn't snagged a ride away from Shadow Ranch, which meant she'd have to find a dress for tomorrow.

Sam looked as tired as she felt.

She nudged him. "I hope you get some sleep tonight. Last night, you—"

He kicked her ankle.

Kasenia switched topics. "What did you guys do today?"

"When we finished the duck pens, we..." Sam's gaze slid to Margo and back. "Got to clean a chicken coop." He grunted. "Loads of fun."

"I bet."

The foster boys' eyebrows twitched, but like Sam, their weary gazes remained impassive. Her heart went out to them. So young, so tired.

"I snuck a look at the horse pasture," Sam murmured. "This place has some nice-looking horseflesh."

His use of horse lingo made Kasenia smile. On the way home from their first riding lesson, he'd said he liked horses, a lot, and wanted to have his own horse someday. Once they escaped Shadow Ranch, she'd find a way to make it happen for him.

She turned to the boys. "What are you studying in school?" They didn't speak much English, but they seemed to understand the language.

Margo slapped the table. "Summertime is for work, not school."

"What about play?" Kasenia asked.

Margo's glare said it all. "Here at Shadow Ranch, our work *is* our play. We're privileged to serve Spirit Father with our labor. It gives us joy, right, boys?"

Two boys mumbled something. The others nodded.

Eyes flashing, she raised her voice. "I said, 'Right, boys?'"

Cesar bobbed his head, "Es verdad." The others echoed him.

"Sam." Margo's eyes narrowed. "Do you agree?"

"I, I don't know the Spirit Father thing."

"You'd better learn and learn fast." She stabbed a piece of roast. "First lesson, he's not a thing." She sawed into the meat so hard Kasenia feared she'd slice through the paper plate and disposable tablecloth into the table.

Eyes lowered, Sam pushed a carrot slice around his plate.

Palms on the table edge, Kasenia peered at Margo. "Are you threatening my brother?"

Margo jutted her chin. "Are you questioning my authority?"

"I asked if you're threatening my brother."

Sam shrunk into his chair, as if to avoid being hit by their volley.

"My conversations with Sam do not concern you."

"Oh, yes, they do. I'm his legal guardian."

"When you married into this family..." Margo narrowed her eyes. "Brewster and Lorraine became Sam's guardians, like they're guardians for these foster boys." She spoke slowly, as if to a child. "I serve as the proxy when the family leaders aren't available."

"I did not marry into Lorraine and Brewster's family, and neither did you." Kasenia pounded the table with her finger. "Their *supposed* guardianship of Sam is a farce that wouldn't hold up ten seconds in court. My guess is the situation is similar for these other wonderful young men."

Margo jumped up, yelling, "Lorraine, I need to speak with you. Now." All eyes were on her as she hurried to Lorraine's table.

Kasenia sighed. She'd blown it again.

Sam nudged her with his knee and lowered his fist between their chairs, his way, she knew, to remind her of the strength and solidarity they shared.

Sensing the boys' stares, Kasenia turned with a shrug. "I'll hear about that comment." She lifted her palms. "But what I said was true."

"Es verdad, true?" Cesar asked.

She nodded. "Yes."

The boys looked at each other, eyes wide.

Moments later, Margo plopped into her chair, her mouth twisted in a smirk. "Eat, people, eat. We don't waste food at Shadow Ranch."

How anyone could eat in the nasty woman's presence, Kasenia didn't know. She'd lost her appetite, yet tomorrow would be as demanding as today. She had to maintain her stamina. Now that she knew the drill, she'd pay better attention to the customers and be ready when an escape opening presented itself.

She took a bite of roast, barely tasting it. She hadn't seen Tomás today, but maybe he'd wake her tonight with something more than, "Es importante, la paciencia." Whether she ever saw him again or not, she was even more determined to extricate the boys from Brewster's clutches—and Margo's.

After dinner, Lorraine told Kasenia to go to the craft room to help Brittany organize the products for Sunday's sale. "You don't have a skill to contribute, so you'll help load sale items."

Kasenia thought of everything she'd learned from her grandmothers. Babushka Irina had taught her to quilt, crochet and garden. Grandma Clara had taught her to cross-stitch, arrange flowers and bake lemon meringue pies. She also knew how to can vegetables and make borscht, sauerkraut and applesauce.

But the less Lorraine knew about her, the better. In fact, if Brewster's women considered her a simpleton, despite her degree, all the better. She'd remain *under the radar*, as Grandpa Gordon would say, watching and waiting for a chance to return to the real world. If Tomás didn't have answers tonight, she'd be on the lookout tomorrow.

Women, girls and boys were already busy in a craft room that smelled of fabric and leather. Some manned the cutting tables, sewing machines and ironing boards. Others threaded beads and stones onto thin wires, stamped designs on leather or punched holes and hand-stitched leather pieces together. Sewing machines whirred, steam irons hissed, and scissors snipped, punctuated by the strike of mallets against the metal punches.

But no one spoke, unless to ask for a tool or supplies. The kids, some as young as four or five, yawned from time to time and rubbed their eyes.

Background music would be nice. Kasenia suppressed a smirk. *But only if Spirit Father approved, of course.* On second thought, music might put the tired children to sleep, which would disrupt the all-important workflow and likely result in punishment.

After she and Brittany finished loading the carts—and Brittany handed her a dress from the costume closet, Kasenia returned to the camper. Once again, someone had switched off the AC. Too tired to waste energy on anger, she opened the front curtain, trusting the sunrise to wake her, and reached to restart the AC.

Seeing movement, she screamed and jumped back. A scorpion, its long, segmented tail curled over its brown body, clung to the paneling just above the switch. Kasenia groaned and opened the closet to pull out her hiking boots and the broom. Her grandpa sometimes had scorpions in the garage but never in the house. Encountering one in her sleeping space was disgusting, though she shouldn't be surprised to find one in the desert, its natural habitat.

She checked the boots. Finding no scorpions inside, she smacked the intruder with a boot, smashing it against the wall. The scorpion fell to the floor but immediately scuttled toward the open doorway, reminding Kasenia that scorpions were notoriously hard to kill. She exchanged the boot for the broom, opened the screen door and swept the unwanted arachnid onto the metal steps. Before it could get far, she stepped out of her sandals and into the boots then stomped the scorpion until it no longer moved.

Satisfied it was dead, she swept it off the landing, searched the entire trailer for its relatives, and finally fell into bed fully dressed. She'd shower and change in the morning. And try to learn what Sam wanted to tell her.

Please, God, if you can hear me, help Sam and the boys to sleep soundly tonight. They need it, and so do I.

⟨⟨⟩ ··◆··⟨⟨⟩

A loud noise awakened her. Kasenia opened her eyes. Yard light through the front window outlined a hulking form. She sat up. "Who, wha—?"

The trailer lurched and swayed, and then Brewster was at the bed. She knew it by his cologne and his clothes' sickening dry-cleaner scent.

Grabbing her shoulders, he pulled her to her feet and shook her. "You ungrateful whore."

The camper rocked and groaned on its axle.

He threw her against the wall. "Thankless traitor."

"I don't under—"

"I gave you my name and a beautiful home with a beautiful family, showered you with gifts, treated you at the best restaurants, yet you turned on me." He slugged her in the stomach, knocking the wind out of her.

She doubled over.

He shoved her to the floor and kicked her until darkness overtook her vision. Eyes closed, she curled into herself and prayed he'd stop before he killed her. Sam needed her.

"Nothing escapes my notice, *darling*."

His hateful tone hurt her more than his kicks.

"You should know that by now." He crouched beside her. "Your selfish behavior and your critical attitude have earned you disciplinary action."

He grabbed her by the hair and yanked her head back, bending so close she could feel his sour breath. "Look at me."

She did not want to see his face, but maybe it would make him stop. Kasenia forced her eyes open.

"Until you prove your allegiance to me and to Spirit Father, to my entire family, I cannot allow you to be near Sam, who is now in my custody." His empty black eyes glinted in the yard light coming through the window. "I cannot allow you to taint his stubborn spirit with your lack of appreciation and respect for me, the patriarch of this family and your guarantee of heaven."

"Please..." she whispered.

Brewster's loud maniacal laugh knifed through Kasenia's chest. She began to shake.

He dropped her head, jumped to his feet and marched to the door, jarring the floor. Again silhouetted by the yard light, he flexed his biceps and stretched his back. "You stink, Kasenia. Clean up before the customers come tomorrow, or your stench will drive them away."

Head nearly touching the ceiling, he ran his fingers through his hair and straightened his clothes. "Now, I'm ready for Chloe. She's anxious for me to give the family another child."

He opened the door and left but stuck his head in again. "If you had exhibited loyalty rather than disloyalty, you could have been the one to have me tonight."

Kasenia retched, sending her battered ribs into painful spasms. The man got off on violence. That's how he controlled the Shadow Ranch women and children. "Dear God," she whispered, "please don't let him harm Sam."

11

— • —

K ASENIA DIDN'T KNOW HOW long she lay sobbing in her vomit, but when she heard voices and flashes of light flickered through the window, she knew she had to move. Or suffer the consequence. What that would be, she didn't know, but she didn't have the wherewithal to endure another round with Brewster.

With effort, she maneuvered to her hands and knees and crawled to the camper's front end. Pushing upright, she balanced a knee on the padded seat and reached to close the curtains. The pain was so intense, she cried out and had to sit for a minute to renew what little strength she had.

Finally, she shuffled into the bathroom, but the cold shower did nothing to relieve her pain. In fact, she hurt worse. She rinsed her hair, turned off the water and stepped out. The sight of her red swollen flesh reflected in the wavery full-length mirror on the outside of the bathroom door sickened her. The bruising would be extensive.

But like Rachel promised, he hadn't touched her face.

You bastard. She squinted at the mirror, seeing Brewster's visage, not her own. *I may stink on the outside, but you reek through and through, from your black heart to your twisted brain.*

With effort, Kasenia pulled on the cotton print dress that covered her from her neck to her wrists and ankles. She was grateful it would hide the welts, yet she hated herself for not having the courage to display her injuries for the customers to see and report. Deep down, Brewster's beating humiliated her.

More than that, she was ashamed of herself. Ashamed she'd allowed his cruelty, ashamed she hadn't fought back. She didn't want Sam or the other boys to know she'd succumbed to his abuse, even if he'd caught her unaware.

His suggestion she *could have had him* sent painful chills through her body. She'd sworn to never let him touch her again, but her refusal would only make him angry, and he'd do whatever he wanted to her. Maybe she should start the birth control pills again. Last thing she wanted was his baby. Better yet, she'd slip away today, contact authorities, and make sure he was locked up where he couldn't hurt or impregnate anyone for a long, long time.

She used the damp towel to wipe the puke from the floor then rolled it tight. Holding it away from her body, she slowly sidestepped down the camper stairs vaguely lit by the porch light. A rooster crowed twice.

The sight of yard light reflecting off Brewster's Corvette drew an involuntary groan from somewhere deep inside her aching ribs. He was still here, the man she never wanted to see again.

A cloudless sunrise had barely silvered the eastern mountaintops, but residents were already pushing cartloads of products and produce over the packed dirt and through the front gate. Kasenia ignored them, hoping she wouldn't be drafted to help, and walked around the lodge to the back porch. Clinging to the handrail, she pulled herself up one step at a time.

She stopped first at the laundry room, but it was locked. Checking both ways, she dropped the towel in front of the door and made a mental note to grab a clean towel later. Then she shuffled to the bathroom to wash her hands, and from there, hobbled into the big room where she'd first met Brewster's fake family.

Margo, Sam and their seven dormmates were busy prepping the breakfast serving table. Fighting through a fog of pain, Kasenia forced a smile. "Good morning."

Margo ignored her, but the boys said, "Buenos días."

Kasenia gathered an armful of paper tablecloth packets and made her way to the empty dining room. She appreciated the boys leaving table duty for her. The more distance between her and Margo, the better.

Sam came alongside her, whispering, "You okay, Sis?"

"I'm sore, that's all. Busy day yesterday."

"Right." He nodded. "And more of the same today."

"What were you going to tell—?"

"Separate, you two, and get to work."

Margo stood in the doorway, shaking her finger at them. "Serve Spirit Father, not your evil desires."

Sam took three tablecloths from her stack, murmured, "Love ya," and walked to the other side of the room.

Kasenia smiled. Her brother didn't tell her he loved her often, but when he did, it made her day. His words reminded her to not give up hope. She would do whatever it took to free him from their desert prison.

Breakfast plate in hand, she was pulling out a chair to sit with the boys, dreading the actual act of sitting, when Margo held up a hand. "Stop right there."

Kasenia raised her eyebrows. *Now what?*

"Brewster doesn't want your rebellious spirit to taint these vulnerable children. You belong over there, at Wanda's table."

Kasenia eyed her for a moment and then turned away. No sense making a scene. She wasn't up to it this morning.

Sam pushed back his chair and stood.

"Samuel," Margo barked. "In your chair."

"My name isn't Samuel."

"It is now. Resume your seat."

Sam searched Kasenia's face. "What should—?"

"Stay here." She smiled. "I'll be close."

The other boys watched with furrowed brows and rounded eyes.

The separations they'd endured as foster children must have been terribly painful. She winked. "See you guys later."

Turning, she surveyed the dining room. This was a sale day, yet everyone was in place, not running in and out, like yesterday. Hands in their laps, they seemed to be waiting for something. For her to sit?

Like the other women, Wanda sat at the head of her table. The only empty chair was one beside her. Kasenia set her plate down and eased into the hard seat one muscle at a time. Wanda's arrogant smirk spoke volumes. No sympathy from this crowd.

Hearing a rustling sound, Kasenia looked around. The other women's postures straightened and their faces tightened as they gazed toward the head table. Kasenia twisted in time to see Brewster seat Chloe. Both sported Cheshire cat grins, as if they had a wonderful secret. He kissed her, long and hard, aimed a thumbs-up at the onlookers and sat. Without comment, he popped the top of the soda can beside his plate.

Kasenia turned away, trying to forget how his kisses stirred her emotions, and caught glimpses of other women's reactions. Disgust, anger and jealousy flitted across their faces. Lorraine appeared resigned—and sad. Paradise had sprouted more than a few thorns.

Most of the children, including Sam, were looking down. What were they thinking? What were they learning from the pervert?

"The E.D. must have taken a break," Wanda muttered. "Chloe'll be crowing, for sure."

Oh... Kasenia scanned the room again. Of course, Brewster's E.D. issues would be common knowledge among these women. Along with the hand tremors, erectile dysfunction had several possible causes. Sugar, diet sodas, high-fat foods and alcohol. Pornography was also a suspected trigger.

He'd tried to hide his porn habit from her. However, she'd seen enough to know he was a regular online viewer. When she told him it made her feel like she wasn't attractive to him, he'd scoffed. *Don't be silly. This is art. Bodies are beautiful. Besides, it makes me a better lover.*

"Prayer time." Brewster rose, hands in the air, and everyone jumped to their feet, chairs scraping the floor. Supporting herself with the chairback and the table, Kasenia slowly pushed upright.

"Move it, Kasenia." Brewster's harsh words were followed by an impatient growl.

She clamped her jaw, aware all eyes were focused on her.

Brewster rushed them through the Spirit Father prayer then told them to sit, though he remained standing, his face long and serious. "I am severely disappointed In every one of you. Our income from yesterday's sale barely reached twenty-thousand dollars."

You greedy jerk... Kasenia pressed her lips together. *You pocketed twenty-thousand dollars from our labor, yet you have the nerve to complain.*

He sipped from the Diet Dr. Pepper can and licked his lips. "Today, I expect you to take in twenty-five thousand dollars. Anything less, and I will not be pleased."

"But how?" Chloe asked, apparently emboldened by their amorous night. "We worked hard yesterday."

"By working harder, that's how." He glared down at her. "Use your brain, woman, if you have one."

Chloe dropped her gaze. "S, s...sorry.' Her lips quivered.

Someone snickered.

Kasenia checked the other women, not surprised to see contempt rather than sympathy on their jealous faces.

"I'm leaving soon." Brewster adjusted his lavender tie. "Lorraine will report sales numbers to me tonight. If you achieve the goal, I'll return the popcorn popper I took from the kitchen after last weekend's dismal sales. And..." He lifted both hands in emphasis. "Bring in twenty-five thousand dollars, I'll return the popcorn popper *plus* buy ice cream bars for everyone."

Extending his arms, he added, "Kids, what do you think of that? Do you want Daddy to bring you ice cream? I'm that kinda guy, you know." Kasenia wondered if the others saw the tremor in his fingers.

The younger children hopped in circles, waving their arms and shouting, "Ice cream, ice cream." The older ones clapped, but by their demeanors, Kasenia got the impression they didn't have much hope of making the goal or receiving a reward.

"What if the ice cream melts?" a little girl asked.

"Have no fear, Penelope, sweetheart. My friend Izzy the Ice Cream Man told me he'd be happy to drive his truck all the way from Tucson to help us celebrate. He *loves* little children."

Something about the way he said *loves* turned Kasenia's stomach. What kind of deal did Brewster swing with the man?

❦ ❦ ❦

After breakfast, Lorraine directed Kasenia to restock supplies as needed, like she'd done yesterday. She was relieved to know she'd be outside the fence again, yet she longed to sleep away the pain. Somehow, she had to ignore the throbbing ache, keep moving, and watch for an escape from Shadow Ranch hell.

Clutching the handrail, she was slowly descending the veranda, when Sam came up beside her. "What's wrong, Sis? I can tell you're not okay. Did Brew—?"

She nudged him. "Shh."

"I hate him." His voice shook with rage.

"Don't waste your thoughts and energy on him. Concentrate on finding a way out."

Twenty minutes later, Kasenia was painfully pushing a loaded wagon steered by pregnant Alana, when Brewster's car passed them and sped out the open gate. Her spirits lifted. No matter how much she hurt or how tired she was, his departure made it possible for her to face the day.

Through the dust churned by the car's tires, she spied Sam walking with three boys toward the highway. He and another young teen had sandwich boards hanging from their shoulders. Sam's advertised discounted quilts, and the second board offered free coffee.

The remaining two youths carried orange flags. They appeared to be dressed in normal clothing. No knickers. She was glad to see they wore hats with brims and carried water bottles.

So that's how they hope to drum up the extra five-thousand dollars. Flag down passersby and pass out free coffee. That method must have worked before. Why else would they have those flags and boards on hand?

Kasenia did a doubletake. *Free coffee?* Brewster's harem didn't drink the "addictive substance," yet they used it to lure shoppers to their roadside market. Margo's "do as the Romans do" comment came to mind. Anything to earn another dime for the master.

The guard named Smith had a swollen cheek and a black eye and moved with care. Brewster must have done a number on him too. When she and Alana drew near, he quickly averted his gaze, not bothering to check for badges. Kasenia almost felt sorry for him, but the guy was still around, which suggested he was either not very bright or Brewster had a reason to keep him.

Alana rolled the cart behind the vegetable stand to the glass-fronted cooler and started loading bottles into it. Kasenia clamped her teeth to keep from groaning every time she bent to lift the heavy bottles.

"Good thing the cows give milk like clockwork," Alana said. "We sold out yesterday."

"Right." Kasenia was aware demand had exceeded the supply. "Does he do this every weekend?"

"Does who do what?" Alana asked.

"Does Brewster always expect more sales the second day?" Once again, she was surrounded by the market's inviting aromas.

"No, not always. Rumor has it he's been listening to get-rich-quick CDs. Maybe that's where the push came from this morning."

"But five thousand more. What if it doesn't happen?"

"He'll holler and kick a chicken or two." Alana shrugged. "And we won't get ice cream." She sighed. "I don't usually care for ice cream, but my tastes change when I'm pregnant." She patted her belly. "I was hoping to make us a banana split."

"That's all he'll do?"

Head down, she etched a circle in the sand with the toe of her sandal. "Unless he's in a really bad mood."

"And then...?"

Alana shook her head. "We need to talk about something else."

"The little ones will be terribly disappointed if they don't get ice cream."

"That's why we'll try our hardest to meet the goal—for our children. Actually, it's why we do most everything we do here—for the children, to bring joy into their lives."

Veronica approached, carrying a cage with a chicken in it. She set it on the ground and stretched her arms. "This cage is heavy."

"Do you sell chickens too?" Kasenia asked.

"Of course not." Veronica bristled. "It's for show, to enhance the farmers' market mystique and sell a few more eggs." She elbowed Alana. "I lucked out. No E.D. last night."

"They were both gloating this morning," Alana grumbled. "Like they'd returned from paradise."

"Then she was spared a temper tantrum," Kasenia said.

Every time Brewster had a failed moment, he blamed her. She was too skinny, she was too fat. She wore too much perfume, she wore the wrong kind. She was focused on her own pleasure, not his. She was thinking about a former boyfriend, not him.

"How do you...?" Veronica's brow furrowed. "Oh, yeah, you've been with him a couple months. Wait till it's been years and you're no longer the cute new toy. And you've run out of tricks to make him tick, if you know what I mean."

"Hush." Alana lifted another milk bottle from the ice chest. "Lorraine's headed this way."

Midday, Kasenia was restocking eggs when she felt a gaze and turned. The tall cowboy with the concho-ringed hat stood at the far end of the long market stall. He offered a quick nod before he took a wrapped pastry from Lorraine. Coffee cup in hand, he sauntered behind the crowd her direction. Shadow Ranch women greeted him, and he replied with a grin. Like yesterday, he sat at a picnic table not far from her.

Kasenia returned to her work, craving his coffee. She'd smelled the wonderful aroma emanating from the big pot at the other end of the market stand all morning. Or maybe she just imagined it. But, oh, how she'd love a cup to boost her flagging energy, even if it'd make her hotter than she already was in the long dress.

She glanced at the man. Two days in a row. Did he live nearby? He seemed to know everyone. Too bad. That meant she couldn't ask him for a ride to freedom. Right now, merely sitting on a soft car seat would feel like floating on a cloud. The two of them shared one more smile before he tossed his cup and napkin in a trash barrel and left.

Finished with her load, she returned to the compound for more honey. Next trip, she'd pick up quilted items and wander over to mingle with customers shopping in the booths. Maybe, just maybe...

Halfway to the craft hut, she met Rachel and Glenise with a cart of potholders and other small fabric creations.

Kasenia sighed. They were one step ahead of her. "Perfect timing, ladies. After you unload your wagon, can one of you help me with honey jars?"

"I'll help." Rachel patted Glenise's back. "This girl can handle the quilted items by herself. Right Glenise?"

"Of course," the girl responded. "It's lightweight stuff."

"Thanks," Kasenia said, "but aren't you needed at the stand, Rachel?"

"Lorraine decided Wanda's oldest daughter should have produce experience." Rachel swiped her long sleeve across her sweaty forehead. "I'm okay with it, really. Never hurts to have a change of pace."

They were almost to the honey hut when a blue pickup truck with a matching topper rolled alongside them. The driver was the man who'd made a point to catch her eye. He tipped his hat and continued toward the horse barn.

12

— · —

"**W**HO IS THAT MAN?" Kasenia turned to Rachel. "Everyone here seems to know him."

"Trent Duran. His place, the Crimson Arches Ranch, is several miles east of here. Takes him almost an hour to make the drive over the washboard roads. But he says it's worth it 'cause his cooking is so awful even his dogs won't eat it." She giggled. "I doubt it's that bad. He buys fresh fruit, vegetables and baked goods from us, most everything but beef, 'cause he raises his own cattle."

"What's a neighbor doing inside the fence?"

"Trent is the Shadow Ranch farrier."

"Farrier?"

"He shoes our horses."

"Oh, now I remember." Kasenia pulled the wagon into the honey hut. "Sam and I learned about farriers when we took riding lessons."

They finished loading the cart, and before they stepped out into the sunshine again, took a minute to stretch their backs and drink from water bottles. "Rachel..." Kasenia aimed her water bottle at her. "You're not like your sister wives."

"How so?"

"You seem content, not angry like they are—and you talk to me as an equal. Most act like I'm poison."

"They'll get over it." She lifted her chin. "Why shouldn't I be content? I'm married to a wonderful man who's given me five beautiful children. They're gifts from him and Spirit Father to help me reach my highest potential in this life, and the next. In fact, without him, I could never attain the afterlife."

"Really? I never heard that before. Is it in the Bible?"

"I'm not sure. Maybe it came from one of the visions Spirit Father gives Brewster."

Kasenia refrained from rolling her eyes. "Isn't it hard to share him?"

"You'll get used to it." Rachel touched Kasenia's arm. "I mean, he's so charming and..." She lowered her voice. "Sexy." She giggled. "He has enough love for all of us. We call it *big love*. One day soon there'll be twelve sister wives. I'm so excited. Spirit Father will be pleased with the dozens of children we'll produce. The bigger our family, the more we can help him rule the universe."

Big love? Dozens of children to help rule the universe? Had they considered the E.D. or sexually transmitted diseases that could seriously affect their plans? Kasenia had so many questions, but she sensed logical responses would not come from any of the women.

She rolled the cart out the door and down the short ramp.

"Because I'm married to Brewster," Rachel said, "I get to live amidst this beauty, and so do you. What's not to love about Shadow Ranch?"

Kasenia eyed the dry flat expanse. Heat waves rippled in the distance. *What's not to love? Let me count the ways...* She rolled the dress's long sleeves up her forearms. "Do you really believe you'll rule the universe?"

"Of course." Rachel's eyes widened. "If Spirit Father says it, we believe it. You'll rule, too, now that you're in our family. In fact, without Brewster's priestly blessing, you'd be doomed to wander the underworld for eternity."

This was getting weirder by the moment. "What if it's all a big lie?"

Like a hawk tracking prey from atop a fencepost, Rachel jerked her head from side to side. "Don't say such things,' she hissed. "Someone might hear. I know you don't understand yet, but you must be careful. Or you know what Brewster will do..."

Kasenia looked away, sorry the conversation had taken a turn. For a few moments, she'd forgotten the pain.

Back at the stand, Kasenia was pleased to see Sam and his companions seated at a picnic table, drinking lemonade and eating cookies. Between the awnings, she could see other Wiley boys had replaced them out at the highway. She wanted to talk with Sam—he still hadn't told her what was on his mind—but they needed a private setting for that.

The boys hadn't been there long when they got up and started to walk away.

She grabbed two water bottles and hurried to Sam as fast as her sore legs allowed. "Leaving already?"

"We're going for seconds." He lagged behind. "You're still walking funny."

"I'm fine." She lowered her voice. "You watching for a way to escape? I am."

He murmured, "Thought I might try to hitchhike, but I can't leave you."

"If you get a chance, do it. You can send the authorities for me."

"I don't know..."

"Whatever it takes, we've got to get out of here."

"I found out what niños de la noche means...it's so sick my ears are wilting."

Kasenia recognized the phrase her babushka used when she heard something rude or obscene.

He swallowed. "Mateo's uncle says—"

"Sam, Kasenia." Lorraine stormed toward them. "You know you're not supposed to be together." She stopped in front of them, fists on her hips. "What were you two talking about?"

Kasenia raised the water bottles. "I brought my brother water. He forgets he needs lots of water in the desert."

"You tend to your work. I'll monitor his hydration."

"By law, I'm his guardian, the person responsible for his wellbeing, not you."

"Man's law doesn't count here." Lorraine's eyes flashed. "We serve a higher law."

A middle-aged couple seated at a nearby table eyed them over their hamburgers, brows furrowed. The man lowered his burger. "Ma'am, did

I hear you right? You think you don't have to obey the law because you live in the middle of this God-forsaken hot-as-hell desert?"

"No." Lorraine swiveled. "You did *not* hear correctly. Mind your own business."

Kasenia stared at her, shocked she was impolite to a customer.

"Let's go." The man elbowed his wife. "This is no place for law-abiding citizens."

Kasenia watched the couple gather their food, wishing she had the courage to beg them to take her and Sam with them. But she feared the innocent pair might end up in the crosshairs of Marlin's rifle.

"Kasenia." Lorraine's icy blue eyes flashed. "Get busy." To Sam, she said, "Obviously, you can't be trusted. I gave you a privileged opportunity to work with Wiley boys, but by your behavior, you belong with the Mexicans. Come with me."

Taking him by the ear, she led him off.

Kasenia started after them. Sam didn't deserve that kind of treatment. He hadn't done anything wrong. And neither had the foster boys.

"He'll be fine." Rachel came up beside her. "Lorraine is trying to prove she's in charge. She gets this way when Brewster ups the pressure."

Kasenia was returning for more vegetables when another vehicle came onto the property, this one a delivery truck with *Rendezvous Office Furniture* painted on the side. The driver pulled in front of Sam's dorm and parked. Margo met him and his passenger, another man, at the door.

Stepping to a bush-shaded corner beside the veranda, Kasenia watched them carry sections of what appeared to be a reception desk into the building. Her heart sunk. So Tomás's story was true. He'd said opening day was Friday, five days away. Sickened, she trudged to the greenhouse, pulling the wagon behind her, and telling God he needed to do something, fast.

On the way to the stand with a wagonful of vegetables, she saw a second vehicle in front of the dorm. This one was an *Arroyo Cash Register*

Sales & Service van. The back doors were open. Several good-sized boxes were stacked inside. *What if...?* She pulled the cart closer.

What if I slip inside and hide behind the—?

"What're you staring at?"

Kasenia turned.

Marlin was striding toward her, hand on his pistol.

She almost laughed out loud. Like he would shoot one of Brewster's women. "I was wondering what those vans are doing here. Do they have permission to be on the property?"

"That's none of your damn business. Stop your loafing and get to work." He spat in the dirt and stomped to the gate.

Kasenia wanted to kick herself. She'd made sneaking into the van twice as difficult. But if she did get inside, they could pick up Sam on the way. Oh, right, Sam was no longer flagging customers at the highway. Where was he, anyway? She stopped, took a breath, and told herself to slow down and wait for another opportunity.

Moving between the women, she refilled the refrigerated bins with chard, green beans, snap peas, onions, broccoli, cauliflower and cabbage. The tomatoes and melons, which were in high demand, were not refrigerated. Her arms ached from lifting the basketball-size melons, and her ribs rebelled. But she had no choice. She had to keep going.

From there, she walked over to the booths to check supplies. They were low on jams and jellies, earrings, creosote sachets, baby clothes and pottery vases. Observing the ever-moving crowd from beneath the quilt awning, Kasenia murmured, "I can't believe it."

Jacintha frowned. "Believe what?"

"I can't believe so many people come to buy stuff out here in the middle of the desert in the middle of the summer." *And that no one sees this abusive polygamous prison for what it is.*

"Thanks to our quilted products," Jacintha said, "we somehow got a reputation for being Amish. That's why we put our hair up and wear cotton dresses. When people see a sign advertising half-price quilts, they think Amish and get excited for a good deal." Like Corrine and Glenise, she had an odd way of speaking.

Jacintha fingered the top quilt on a nearby rack. "Our quilts are just as nice as theirs, of course, maybe better. Daddy has spread our country market fame far and wide. He says we have billboards all along the highway. Did you see any when you drove here?"

"I might have, if I hadn't been asleep." That Brewster had sired such a sweet girl made her want to gag, but Jacintha couldn't help her parentage. Like she'd vowed to help Sam and his dormmates escape, Kasenia silently pledged to somehow free this girl and her siblings from their father's insanity.

On her way to the craft hut, Kasenia met Corrine and Glenise, who were exiting the canning room with a load of jams and jellies. She was about to greet them when she heard a noise and turned. Margo was opening the horse barn's big door. A moment later, Trent Duran drove out, and she closed it.

To Kasenia's surprise, Trent stopped. "Hey, Glenise, hey, Corrine."

They replied in unison. "Hi, Mr. Duran."

Glenise motioned to Kasenia. "This is Kasenia. She's our new..." The girl looked at Kasenia, who said, "Resident. I'm a new resident. Nice to meet you, Mr. Duran."

"Call me Trent, please. Mister is too formal for a desert rat like me." He doffed his hat. "Nice to meet you, Kasenia." To the girls, he said, "Good to see you two. Tell your dad 'hi' for me."

"We will," they chorused.

He put the truck in gear. "See you ladies next week." With a wave, he motored toward the front gate, driving slowly enough she barely smelled the dust his tires stirred.

Kasenia turned to the girls. "I'm surprised you're allowed to speak with strangers."

"He's not a stranger." Corrine shook her head. "He's like family. He and his wife used to come once a month, but after she died a couple years ago, he started coming every weekend. Says that way he doesn't have to go to town. I think he's lonely and wants someone to talk to."

"Too bad his wife died. She couldn't have been very old." Kasenia watched Trent go, sorry he'd lost his wife and sorry he was Brewster's friend. Mostly, she was heartsick she hadn't found a way to hide in the topper. She could have snuck out of his vehicle somewhere along the way. But she wouldn't have food or water or shelter. What if she got dehydrated and had a heat stroke? Or lost her way in the desert? Or encountered wild animals?

She thought of Beth dying with her children. Despite the torrid temperature, Kasenia shivered. Her and Sam's loved ones would never know what happened to them.

"Kasenia..."

She blinked. "What?"

"You're a married woman." Glenise shook a finger at her. "You shouldn't be staring at another man."

"I am *not* a married woman, and I was *not* staring at a man. I was looking at his pickup, wondering what's inside that topper. It's full of stuff."

"Unless you take back your words, I'll have to tell Lorraine you said you're not married."

Kasenia shrugged. "Whatever." Like with the boys, she needed to stand strong before these girls—and trust they'd forget to tattle on her.

"Trent keeps his horseshoeing equipment in there," Corrine said, "including a forge and an anvil, like a blacksmith uses. We learned about blacksmiths in school."

"Let's go, Corrine." Glenise elbowed her half-sister. "They're waiting for this stuff."

Kasenia rounded the big house with a wagonload of soft goods and saw Trent Duran's pickup idling inside the gate. Marlin leaned against the fender, chatting with Trent as if they were old friends. And they probably were, if Trent and his wife had been coming to the weekend markets for years. Too bad. Trent seemed like a decent guy. Marlin straightened and stepped away, and the pickup merged into the crowd of people and vehicles.

Pulling her sunhat low over her eyes, she shifted her gaze to the dormitory in the far corner. The furniture truck was gone, but the cash register van was still there. If she crawled inside—

The door opened, and two men came out. One climbed in the driver's side and the other opened the back doors. He set what could be a tool case inside, closed the doors and got in the passenger side.

Kasenia's heart dropped. What could she do short of run after them? Marlin would never let her leave with them, even if the men were willing to give her a ride.

The moment they pulled away, she spied a box they'd left behind. Dropping the cart handle, she ran toward the van, waving her arms. The vehicle stopped, and the passenger lowered his window. Mariachi music blared from within.

"You left a box." She smiled her sweetest smile.

The driver said, "Probably trash."

"I'll get it for you." Before they could object, she took off. When she lifted the basketball-sized cardboard box, it was so slight, she knew the driver was right.

A mini dust devil spit dirt in her face. Her eyes teared and she coughed, wiping her cheeks. Through the dust and tears, she saw Marlin approach the van. "What's the holdup here?"

She hurried to the vehicle.

"Left something behind," the driver said. "This kind lady volunteered to get it for us. Sorry to litter."

Marlin stared from him to Kasenia. "Give it to him."

The passenger jumped out. "I'll take it."

Kasenia met the man at the rear of the van.

He opened the door and started to take the box. "Thank you—"

Though she felt Marlin's presence behind her, Kasenia held tight.

The man lifted his eyebrows.

She mouthed "help" and released her hold.

Marlin elbowed her. "Get to work."

The man's gaze switched from Kasenia to Marlin, who shoved her away. "She's paid by the hour."

Kasenia stumbled to the wagon.

As the vehicle passed, the men eyed her, their eyebrows tight above their sunglasses. Kasenia smiled and waved, attempting to act natural for Marlin's sake. Who knew what the stone-faced man might report to Brewster?

The rest of the day passed in a blur. By suppertime, every bruise on Kasenia's body burned, and every muscle ached. With a sigh of relief, she sank into her chair at Wanda's table. She didn't care where she sat tonight, as long as she sat and could see Sam, who looked fit but sun-burned.

She was too tired to be hungry. What she really wanted was to bury her head in her arms and sob. Without a moment to connect with even one customer, she hadn't found someone to drive them to safety. The following weekend might provide a new batch of customers, but it would be too late for the boys.

Kasenia awoke the next morning surprised she'd slept through the night. Her injuries hadn't awakened her. And neither had Brewster, thank God. Or Tomás. But maybe he'd tell her today how they would protect the boys.

At breakfast, in a tired voice that matched the dark circles beneath her eyes, Lorraine announced their Sunday earnings. Twenty-five thousand, two-hundred seventy-six dollars and fifty cents. Everyone cheered, and the children screamed, "Ice cream bars, we get ice cream bars."

For the kids' sake, Kasenia hoped Brewster would keep his promise. But would he, like the Egyptian taskmasters in the Bible, demand more every weekend? She knew the story because she'd asked her babushka about a painting on her church's wall.

Amidst fake flower garlands, flickering candles and shrines, a variety of Biblical illustrations lined the nave. This one was of two shirtless brown-skinned men with towel-like cloths around their waists. A man in a weird hat was whipping a man with straw in his arms. Babushka Irina told her the hat guy was an Egyptian taskmaster beating a Hebrew slave. She then explained that Hebrews were God's chosen people.

"Why did the Egyptians beat God's people?" Kasenia had asked.

"Hate, the same reason they killed Jesus." Her babushka pointed to an equally disturbing painting on the opposite wall. A scantily clad man with long ugly thorns around his head was being whipped by a man wearing a silver helmet.

Both pictures repelled yet fascinated her. She tried hard not to look at them during the priest's long homilies, but she couldn't stop. How did a person do something so awful to another person? And how did Brewster beat her without remorse? He was temperamental, she knew, but it was like a rabid beast climbed down his throat and took over his body.

Did everyone have such a horrid creature residing within? Did she? Was it self-control that kept the monster at bay, or something else? All day, she'd fought the urge to rage against Brewster and plot his demise. But like she'd told Sam, she had to focus on finding a way out of the compound, not on revenge.

"Brewster is immensely proud of us," Lorraine was saying. "He's traveling now but will be home in two days. Be prepared for a party."

The children clapped and shouted, "Ice cream party, ice cream party."

"Keep in mind..." Lorraine warned, "we cannot become lazy. We must work hard every day and do our very best to not let Spirit Father down. He's watching our every move and keeping track of our bad deeds as well as our good ones."

Kasenia scratched her nose to cover a yawn. Spirit Father was sounding a lot like Santa Claus. She murmured to the child beside her, "Know who Santa Claus is?"

"Of course," he muttered. "He's an evil fallen angel worshiped by dumb people who waste money on a dumb holiday."

"Hmm." Kasenia pursed her lips. Between her two countries and family travels, she'd heard plenty of Santa Claus legends, but never had anyone suggested he was a fallen angel. Leave it to Brewster to concoct a bizarre theory. Brewster, the man who'd wined and dined her through the Christmas break, who'd treated her to Christmas concerts and a holiday-lights tour. He'd given her gifts, nice gifts—all part of his seduction.

But why did he deny his God-fearing family an opportunity to celebrate Christ's birth and to have a happy, fun time together?

She answered her own question. Because they worshipped Spirit Father, whoever or whatever that was, not the true God and his Son. She didn't know a lot about the Wiley family religion, but she'd figured out that much.

13

— · —

Aſter breakfast, Lorraine assigned Kasenia to assist Margo
with the horses. Horses, she liked. Margo was a different story.

Kasenia followed the grim woman out the door, struggling to match
her stride, which was difficult when she was so sore. This would be
another day to forget at Shadow Ranch, yet one she had to remember.
When she reported the group's polygamy, slave labor and locked compound to the authorities, she would need details.

Ballcap in hand, Margo slowed to walk alongside Kasenia. "I learned
late last night horse buyers are coming this afternoon. Brewster wants
his stock to appear their best, so you and I are going to groom horses
this morning." Swearing under her breath, she kicked a rock. "Doesn't
matter to Lorraine that my children are experienced groomers."

So, I'm not your first choice? Well, you're definitely not mine. Kasenia
gave Margo a side glance. *Children? Here at Shadow Ranch?* Why didn't
she sit with them at meals? She'd had too many run-ins with Margo to
ask the obvious. Instead, she asked, "How many horses does the ranch
have?"

"Twenty-nine, at the moment. Brewster likes to move stock. He hears
of a good deal and sends me a photo. If the horse appears to be in good
shape, he has a vet examine it. If the vet gives the animal a clean bill of
health, we'll buy it, work on any issues, and sell it."

"How long do you keep the horses he buys?" For the first time, she
was having a civil conversation with Margo. She would continue asking
questions as long as the horsewoman answered them.

"I prefer to have them here a month or two to observe their health and behavior, monitor their eating, study their gaits," Margo said. "But that doesn't always happen. We've turned around a purchase and made a profit within a couple weeks. But these new fillies..." Lips pressed tight, she shook her head. "They were delivered two days ago. Not what—"

Pregnant Alana opened the door to the trailer they were passing and sidestepped her bulk down the metal stairs. Without acknowledging them, she waddled toward the lodge.

Kasenia snickered to herself. So much for sisterly love.

Margo tucked her long red hair into the ballcap and pulled a ponytail through the opening at the back. "These buyers are after registered quarter horse fillies—female horses less than four-years old. Ours are three- to four-years old, and most of them are ready to breed. Some are purebreds, so they'll go for a hefty sum. We have seven fillies. The buyers want five. Brewster will no doubt talk them into taking all seven. He usually does."

She stared Kasenia up and down. "He says you have experience with horses. You don't look the type."

"I don't know about type, but Sam and I took riding lessons a couple years ago. We do photoshoots on ranches and pose with horses."

"You can ride." Margo lifted her chin, eyelids low. "But can you groom a horse?"

Kasenia met her gaze. "Before and after each lesson, we wiped our mounts, brushed them and picked their hooves."

"Good. I won't have to train you."

Kasenia tugged a hairband from her pocket, slipped it around her wrist and wove her hair into a long braid. Securing it with the hairband, she marveled at the change in Margo. The woman was almost nice today. Was she setting her up for an attack?

Margo led the way to the horse barn. Like the dairy barn, it was painted green with a white metal roof. She opened the side door and they stepped into the huge dusky building. At this early hour, it was still cool. Stalls lined the wall across from them, and the other two walls supported big sliding barn doors, one at the front of the building and one at the rear.

Light shafts streamed from small openings in the ventilation ridge high above. Dust motes danced in the light. The air held hints of manure, urine and straw, as well as the sweet scent of hay and the musky scent of horse.

A horse whinnied, and another answered. Kasenia smiled, wishing Sam was with her. He'd love being in the barn with the horses. The ambience was so peaceful, like stepping from Shadow Ranch madness into another much more pleasant world.

"Where are Sam and the foster boys?" Kasenia closed the door behind them. "I thought you were in charge of the dorm kids."

"Dung disposal is Wanda's department. Lorraine thinks I should be with the boys twenty-four-seven, but Brewster wants me to care for the horses." She shrugged. "Their problem, not mine. Are you familiar with American quarter horses?"

"I've been on ranches with quarter horses, but that's the limit of my knowledge."

"They're not only loved in America..." Margo walked to the middle of the hardpacked clay floor. "They're the second most popular horse in the world. Arabians are the most popular, but Brewster favors quarter horses because they're easy to sell here in the West. They're intelligent, hardy, trainable, more even-tempered than Arabians and not readily spooked. Plus, they're energetic and adapt quickly to new situations."

Kasenia could tell Margo liked to talk about horses. Not only was she nicer, she seemed happier.

"Ranchers and farmers like them," Margo continued. "Quarter horses have what's called "cow sense." They instinctively know what a cow is going to do, almost before the cow does. They're also good family horses because they're friendly and gentle, curious yet calm. And if they get loose and wander away, they can find their way home, a good trait in a horse."

Kasenia glanced around the barn. It was beautiful, finished inside with light-colored wood, and as nice as any guest-ranch barn where she'd done photoshoots. Only the best for Brewster. "Why are they called quarter horses?"

"Good question." Margo smiled.

Kasenia blinked. She'd never seen the testy woman smile.

"They're called quarter horses because they run a quarter-mile race faster than any other breed, up to fifty-five miles an hour, if you can believe it."

"Hard to imagine." In her head, Kasenia converted the distance into meters. The metric system she'd learned in Russia made more sense to her than America's imperial system. A quarter mile was four hundred and two meters.

"They were bred in Colonial America to race through the main streets of villages. The country roads they had in those days were poorly built, but the main streets were usually straightaways a quarter mile long. The horses had to run fast from the get-go."

"Interesting history."

"I've been studying horses since I learned to read." Margo walked over to the stalls, which were empty, except for two. "First, we'll release these yearlings I brought in last night to worm. Then we'll move the fillies in from the corral. I had the men gather them early this morning."

When Kasenia tried to clip a lead rope to a yearling's halter, it swung its head away.

"Be careful," Margo warned. "After being cooped up overnight, these youngsters will be frisky. We'll give them a little rope to kick up their heels, but not too much. Keep a firm grip on the rope."

Finally, Kasenia was able to snap the carabiner into place, and they led the horses out of the stalls. Sure enough, Margo's horse wanted to run around the barn, and Kasenia's pranced from side to side. When both animals had settled, Margo handed her horse's lead to Kasenia and pushed the barn door open just far enough to walk the yearlings through the opening and into a corral.

The instant they were through, she closed the door. "When we go in and out, we do what we can to retain as much cool air as possible."

Kasenia caught her first glimpse of the vast expanse beyond the compound. A surprising abundance of greenery grew alongside the tall saguaros that distinguished the Sonoran Desert from other deserts. The valley was bordered by mountains on every side, some within four or five miles. She had to admit the desert held a certain allure.

Cattle and horses were scattered over the distant flat stretch, grazing or resting. Several cows and a horse drank from a stock tank beneath a tall windmill. Its blades rotated lazily in the slight breeze.

They walked the anxious horses through the empty corral. Fillies in the next corral nickered and came to the rail. Kasenia smiled, enjoying their bright-eyed curiosity.

Margo opened a gate and led her horse out of the corral. Kasenia followed. Both animals were chomping at the bit and tossing their heads, ready to run.

Another windmill with slowly circling blades sat inside the fence not far from the gate. The pump rod creaked and groaned as it pumped. "Exactly how I feel," Kasenia whispered. All morning, she'd nearly moaned out loud every time she moved.

Lifting her cell phone from her belt, Margo tapped it and a moment later said, "Please come open the back gate. We have two horses to let out to pasture."

Margo said please. Kasenia lifted an eyebrow. *Why the dual personality?*

The horsewoman had barely clipped the phone onto her belt when a man on a loud ATV sped around the outside of the fence. He motored to a metal box on one of the gate posts, leaned over, and punched in a code. The gate clanked loose and rattled open. And there before Kasenia lay freedom.

She had a horse. She had an open gate. She had—

"Some people," Margo murmured, "when they see that gate open, they think they can walk through it, away from the *security* of Shadow Ranch. But it's a mistake, always a mistake. If snakes, scorpions and wild animals don't get them, Brewster will. He's the wildest animal of all."

Kasenia said nothing. What could she say? She appreciated the warning, but she couldn't let fear stop her from ushering Sam to safety. Maybe not now, but soon.

"Jump out of the way when you remove the halter," Margo said. "Or you'll get trampled."

Murmuring, "Easy now, easy now," they unclipped the halters, slid them off and stepped back. Without a moment's hesitation, the yearlings galloped through the gap.

The man tapped in the code again, and the gate rolled shut, connecting with a clang on the tall metal post. The sound jarred Kasenia's psyche like a fire alarm. She clenched her fists. Once more, she was locked inside the Shadow Ranch compound. She forced her fingers open. Broad daylight wasn't a good time to run away in a desert.

"We can move the fillies into the barn now." Margo turned to the other horses. "I added a bit of hay to the stalls to entice them, so they should cooperate."

"None of them have the same coloring." Kasenia rubbed her sweaty hands on her jeans. "But they're all quarter horses, right?"

"We do have quite a mix, don't we?" Margo pointed them out. "Chestnut, black, buckskin, gray, palomino, blue roan and pinto—the one with the large white patches." She lifted more halters from a fence post and led the way into the corral. "The American Quarter Horse Association recognizes seventeen colors, the base colors being either black or red."

"Amazing. They're beautiful."

One by one, they haltered the horses and led them inside. The fillies behaved better than the yearlings, though not without an occasional nip or head toss. Their sleek coats, neck nuzzles and inquisitive natures enthralled Kasenia. What a pleasant change from a weekend of hauling supplies to the market stand.

She ran her fingers through the buckskin's dark silky mane. "You're a sweet baby," she whispered. "You make me feel almost human again."

But only with coaxing and a firm hold on the lead rope did she convince the horse to step into the stall. Kasenia empathized with the reluctant animal. Like her, it was one of Brewster's prisoners. Yes, it was just a horse, but today she sensed an affinity with all caged creatures.

Margo showed her the big wooden box where the grooming equipment was stored. They took out rubber curry combs, brushes and hoof picks and went to work. Kasenia started with the last horse she'd led inside, a beautiful palomino with three white stockings. The repetitive motion of combing with the curry comb and brushing the smooth coat soothed her soul and loosened her sore muscles.

The animal's closed eyes and gentle snuffling suggested it relished the brushing as much as she did. She knew from experience not all horses liked to be groomed. "You are a true beauty." She brushed the filly's chest. "I love the diamond on your forehead and your pretty feet. When I'm done with you—"

"Mornin', ladies."

Kasenia flipped around.

The Crimson Arches guy.

What made him drive to Shadow Ranch on a Monday? Couldn't be pastries. Or maybe it was.

"Heard you have some horses for me to look over."

"Good morning, Trent." Margo met him in the middle of the barn. "Thanks for coming by on such short notice." She led him to the stall where Kasenia was working. "I'd like you to meet Kasenia, our newest resident. Kasenia, this is Trent Duran."

Without mentioning they'd met earlier, he reached over the gate to shake her hand. "Nice to meet you, Kasenia. Welcome to the Sonoran."

"Thank you." His handshake was firm and his warm brown eyes kind though sad.

She searched his face, knowing better than to trust a friend of Brewster's but longing to trust Trent Duran. "Nice to meet you, Trent."

Margo opened the gate to the next stall. "This is the filly I mentioned." She brought the gray horse out and walked it around. "Notice how she walks? I'm thinking something's wrong with a shoe."

Trent squatted on his heels, observing the horse's gait. "I see what you mean. Let's trot her in here on the hardpack and then take her out to the corral. I want to watch her on both surfaces."

Margo mounted the filly bareback and circled the open area several times before exiting the barn. When they returned, she tied the horse outside its stall, close enough Kasenia could watch them while she groomed her horse.

Talking softly to the filly, Trent ran his hand down her right foreleg. She tilted her hoof and he lifted it higher to examine it. "You nailed it,

Margo. This shoe wasn't fitted correctly." He lowered the hoof to the ground, patted the horse and stood. "She needs a new shoe. And as you know, when I reshod one front foot, I prefer to do both to ensure good balance and even wear and tear. Want me to inspect the other fillies before I get my truck?"

"Yes, please do."

Kasenia gave her a side glance. *Please* again? Margo was a different woman in the barn. Was that how the other wives were? Did they become civil in their comfort zones, like Rachel was in the garden?

Working in tandem, Margo and Trent checked each horse, including the one Kasenia finished grooming, and decided the first filly was the only one that needed new shoes. "I'll open both barn doors partway for ventilation," Margo said, "so you can work in here in the shade."

"Thank you." He left the barn to get his pickup, and she opened the big front door wide enough for him to back in then walked across the barn to pull the other door open several feet.

Trent stopped his truck just inside the door, not far from Kasenia, and killed the engine. When he got out, he gave her a thumbs-up. "Nice work. That filly's looking good."

Kasenia grinned. "Thank you." Was it the compliment that warmed her cheeks or the man's friendly smile? Either way, he probably had no idea how much he'd brightened her day. And made her heart do a strange little flutter.

He hung his hat on a post nail. "Better get my forge going. Gotta heat the shoes before I can shape 'em." Stepping to the back of the truck, he lifted the topper window, dropped the tailgate, and swung out a platform that held a small propane tank and a forge shaped like a toaster oven. He turned the tank valve, and with a click of a butane lighter, lit the forge. Then, after sizing a couple horseshoes against the filly's hoof, he used long metal tongs to place one inside the forge.

In the quiet barn, the propane hiss sounded loud. Kasenia could smell the heated air emanating from the forge, but the horses didn't seem to notice. They were apparently accustomed to farrier noises and aromas.

Margo was walking toward them when her phone rang. She answered it with a disinterested, "Yes, what now?" And then, "That woman... I told her—"

Kasenia focused on her work, her ribs aching with the effort, but she heard every word. Was this more sister-wife "love" in action?

Another pause was followed by, "I'll be right there." Margo marched across the barn and out the side door, slamming it behind her.

Now, that's more like the Margo we all know and despise.

Trent set a metal toolbox on the ground. Its upright slots, angled for easy access, held an assortment of tools. He placed a three-legged stand beside the toolbox then lifted a large iron anvil from the truck, seemingly without effort, and placed it on the stand. As he belted a leather apron around his jeans, he walked over to Kasenia.

His eyes were as dark as his hair, which was creased where his hat rested. With or without a hat, he was a good-looking man. For a brief second, Kasenia felt guilty she'd entertained such a thought, but then she remembered she was a single woman, no longer married—*never* married.

He adjusted the apron. "You've had experience with horses. The filly is comfortable with you."

"I'm glad she's relaxed and not fighting me." Kasenia smiled. "I took riding lessons, but other than that, I haven't spent a lot of time around horses." She indicated his leather apron. "That's like the chaps cowboys wear but somehow different."

"It's called a farrier apron or horseshoeing chaps. Protects my legs from hooves and kicks as well as from scraping myself with the hoof rasp or getting burned by a freshly forged horseshoe."

"Ouch. That would be a terrible burn." She stroked her horse's blond mane. "Can I ask you a question?"

"Shoot." He folded his arms and leaned a shoulder against the stall post.

"I've seen horses without shoes," Kasenia said, "while others have them on all four feet. These fillies wear them on the front. Why the differences?"

"Good observation." He nodded his approval. "Could be several reasons, some related to how an animal is used, what terrain it's ridden on, if it has injuries or balance issues. In general, owners shoe the front hooves because sixty to sixty-five percent of the animal's weight is on the front feet and those hooves wear down faster than the back. A horse has better traction when the back legs are unshod. Also, when shod horses get into kicking matches, metal shoes can cause serious damage."

"Oh." Kasenia cringed. "I had no idea."

"The barefoot versus shod debate is ongoing and can get heated, though front-feet only is the most common practice. From my limited experience—" He lifted a hand. "This isn't my regular work. I took up the farrier trade as a side business to help out my neighbors. The nearest fulltime farrier lives sixty-five miles away."

He aimed a thumb at the back door. "I raise cattle east of here at the Crimson Arches Ranch."

She smiled. "I like the name."

"The neighbors suggested my great-grandfather name it Double Arches Ranch because it has two tall arches. But when he saw the way the setting sun turned the red sandstone a deeper red, he chose Crimson Arches. The name was a reminder, he said, of the blood Jesus shed for us on the cross."

"He must have been a deep thinker." Trent's mention of Jesus told Kasenia he probably wasn't a Spirit Father acolyte like Brewster's tribe, but this wasn't a good time to ask about his beliefs. "What's involved with being a farrier?"

The horse she was grooming lifted her head and snorted, like she felt neglected.

Kasenia grinned and brushed her side.

"Knowledge of horse anatomy is important," Trent said. "First thing I do, after getting input from owners, is evaluate a horse's gait, like I did with these fillies. I also check for leg injuries and hoof damage in order to produce a correctly balanced hoof. Oftentimes, I merely trim, clean and shape. Today, I'll do all that plus give her a new pair of steel shoes."

He combed his fingers through his hair. "You asked a question, and I think I rabbit-trailed without answering."

"I sidetracked you." She laughed. "You were talking about the barefoot versus shod debate."

"Oh, right, thanks." He grinned, and once again, Kasenia's heart flipped. Without his hat, Trent appeared younger than she'd first thought. He seemed like an honest, trustworthy kind of guy who would help her and Sam if she told him their plight. On the other hand, he was friends with everyone at Shadow Ranch, including Marlin and Brewster.

"My personal belief," he said, "is horses that jump, race or pull loads, or are ridden on rough or hard terrain should wear shoes on all four feet. But those that are pets and mostly hang around the farm probably don't need shoes."

"Makes sense."

"I'd better go fill my water bucket before I get started." He straightened. "Was nice talking with you, Kasenia. Give me a buzz anytime day or night if you need anything. Neighbors out here watch out for one another." He moved his toolbox, which was on wheels, closer to the horse, grabbed a bucket from his pickup and walked over to a faucet on the other side of the barn.

When he returned, Kasenia motioned with the brush. "You've got more tools than women use for their fingernails." Seeing her own broken, dirty nails and chipped polish, she lowered the brush.

"You sound like my wife." He chuckled. "She offered to loan me her nail file and clippers."

"She was just trying to save you money." Kasenia grinned, glad he could talk about his wife, even though she'd passed away. "What do you do with your tools?"

"First thing I'll do is use the clinch cutter to cut the clinched nail ends from the hoofs and a pull-off tool to remove the shoes. I also have nippers to cut down the hoof walls and tools to clean hooves plus trim and file the frogs. I use other tools to shape the shoes and punch nail holes in them, nail them on and snip and clinch the nails where they poke through the hoof wall."

He turned to the gray filly, scratched her nose, and stepped around to her right side. Talking softly to the horse, he rubbed down her neck and all the way down her foreleg, where he tugged gently on the fetlock. Again, she obediently cocked her hoof. He scooped it into his hand then straddled the leg, securing it between his thighs. Knees bent, torso angled over the hoof, he reached into the toolbox for the clinch cutter.

"It's good to know you look out for your neighbors, Trent." Kasenia glanced from one partly open barn door to the other. She'd take a chance on the man, but she wouldn't be direct. "I might surprise you and call sometime, but I'll need your—"

The side door flew open, and Margo rushed in.

14

---·---

K ASENIA SLIPPED TO THE other side of the horse she was grooming, heart racing. She'd taken too long to muster the nerve to ask for Trent's phone number and missed her chance. Maybe it was for the best. She didn't know the man, and the fact he worked for Brewster was a huge strike against him. Besides, how could she call him without a phone?

Margo talked with Trent for a moment then turned to Kasenia. "I want to show you how to polish hooves. After that, we'll detangle, brush and trim the manes and tails. But we need to hurry." Once she'd shown Kasenia how to clean and polish hooves, the three of them worked without talking, though they murmured reassuring words to the horses.

Hearing a snap and then another and another, Kasenia peered over the stall gate.

Trent was bent above the hoof he'd clamped between his knees, clipping away the edges with the nippers, which to her looked like long rounded pliers. Black and white clippings fell to the clay floor.

"The filly doesn't seem to mind you doing that," she said. "I assume it's not painful for her."

"Right." He ran his fingers around the hoof. "The outer portion of a hoof wall is constructed of specialized hair follicles. Like human hair, fingernails and toenails, it's mostly keratin, always growing but without any nerve endings."

"Wow, I had no idea."

He lowered the hoof and walked over to the forge. Using the tongs, he reached into the fire to turn the horseshoe over. A hot metallic aroma filled the air.

Trent exchanged the nippers for a long file, straddled the hoof again, and began to smooth the edges and scrape across the hoof base in quick even strokes. Hoof shavings drifted to the barn floor.

Kasenia returned to brushing out the filly's long creme-colored tail. Trent's rhythmic rasps provided steady background noise along with the propane's wind-like whoosh and the sound of equines munching hay, along with their nickers and snorts. Like downy feathers, the comforting ambience settled on her troubled soul, soft and soothing.

An unpleasant odor broke the spell. She peeked over the gate to see what Trent was doing. "That's a strange smell."

"Yeah." He chuckled. "Some compare it to rotten eggs. Horse hooves are comprised of connective tissue proteins rich in sulfur. This hoof has a hint of thrush." He showed her. "The white area you see here. It consumes the connective tissue proteins and excretes sulfur compounds as waste, which is what you smell."

He aimed the file at Margo, who was exiting a stall. "You'll need to inform potential buyers about the thrush. Left untreated, it could penetrate deeper into the hoof."

"I agree, but you know Brewster." She shrugged. "He'll wait until he has cash in hand, if then, to tell the new owner."

Trent shook his head and, without comment, pulled a small bottle from an apron pocket.

"Oh, good," Margo said. "You brought Thrush Buster."

He squeezed the purple liquid into the hoof, waited a moment for it to dry, then released the filly's foot. Stepping to the forge, he grasped the glowing red-orange horseshoe with the tongs, set it on the anvil and, with the same tongs, grabbed another horseshoe from the rack in his truck. He quickly shoved it into the forge, picked up a hammer and began to pound the first horseshoe. Sparks flew like a July 4th sparkler.

The sound of steel hammering steel reminded Kasenia of the blacksmith who lived down the road from her babushka. A big man with massive biceps, he made iron fences and railings, fixed tools and farm implements, and shoed the local horses. From sunrise to sunset, the ring of his hammer echoed through the village.

Kasenia wanted to watch Trent shape the horseshoe and nail it to the filly's hoof, yet she had to concentrate on her own work. Using the grooming scissors Margo had handed her—with instructions to trim no more than four inches, she began trimming the horse's tail. One eye on what she was doing and one eye on Trent, she observed his actions as best she could.

As he worked the hot metal, turning it this way and that, the orange color faded. Apparently satisfied with the shape, he fitted the still-warm shoe to the prepared hoof. Smoke billowed, along with a caustic stench that smelled like scorched hair.

Kasenia wrinkled her nose.

Trent pounded the shoe some more.

She peeked over the gate in time to see him lower the shoe into the water bucket. The resulting sizzle was sharp and quick as a snake's hiss.

With the filly's foreleg gripped between his thighs, Trent pulled horseshoe nails from his farrier apron and nailed on the shoe. When he finished, he clipped the nail points that protruded through the hoof and clinched them down. His final step was to file the outer hoof's rough edges, including the nail stubs, before he went to work on the second hoof.

Kasenia was nearly finished grooming her last horse when Trent said, "I'm outa here, ladies." He pushed the cooled forge back inside the topper, loaded his equipment into the truck and pulled off the leather apron. "I might want to get my hands on one of these fillies, Margo." Lifting his hat from the nail, he added, "You've got some beauties here."

"You sure?" she asked. "Brewster Wiley drives a hard bargain."

Trent set the hat on his head. "I don't doubt you for a moment, but I'm tempted to give it a shot anyway."

"I know you'd provide a good home. If you're serious, hang around. Brewster texted a moment ago. He's on the way, and the buyers are right behind him. Should be here in a couple hours."

Kasenia pressed her lips to keep from groaning out loud. Lorraine said Brewster would be gone for two days. Had the opportunity to sell a few horses caused him to change his plans? She sighed and tried to appreciate the fact he'd be busy with the horse sale. She wouldn't have to be anywhere near him.

Using the tailgate as a table, Trent handwrote an invoice and gave it to Margo. She set it on the grooming box then walked toward the rear of the barn.

Trent watched Margo for a moment then unsnapped a shirt pocket and pulled out a business card. Eyebrows raised as if to say, *You asked for my number,* he extended the card.

Kasenia mouthed, *Thank you,* and shoved the card into her back pocket. His guarded actions told her Trent Duran understood the need for caution. But how much did he know about Shadow Ranch's shady secrets?

He winked, shut the tailgate, and climbed into his truck.

Margo closed the barn's back door then hurried to roll the front barn door shut behind the pickup.

Kasenia sighed. Trent had brought peace and maybe even a little joy into her morning, despite the sorrow she sensed in him. Was it because he'd lost his wife? He'd mentioned her but not her death.

Turning again to the filly she'd been grooming, she patted her neck and stepped out of the stall. A horse nickered, and another responded. Kasenia smiled, wishing she could stay in the barn all day, basking in the quiet shuffles and snorts, listening to cows moo in the distance. The animal smells and sounds reminded her of her grandparents' village, where everyone had a horse and a cow, maybe a donkey or sheep, and always, chickens.

Margo picked up the invoice. "We'll leave the fillies in the stalls until it's time to show them." She folded the paper and stuck it in her back pocket. "If we put them in the corral, they'll be sure to roll in the dirt."

Kasenia giggled. "That would be a travesty."

"You'd better believe it." Margo's frown was stern. "Brewster would *not* be pleased."

Brewster. Just the sound of his name made her skin crawl. He governed every breath these women took. "Anything else to do?" Kasenia hated to leave the tranquil barn, but she didn't care to hear Brewster's name mentioned one more time.

"You'll get used to it." Margo's voice was low.

"Used to what?"

"Life here. Being one of the wives. You'll learn to love the desert as well as your sister wives and their children."

Kasenia started to respond but closed her mouth. What could she say? She might befriend a couple of the women, but she'd never accept being a so-called sister wife.

"You have no choice." Margo stepped closer. "Brewster will make your life miserable until you accept his conditions."

"Conditions?"

"Complete obedience to him and cooperation with the sisters. Be assured your every hint of rebellion will be reported to him and subsequently punished, as you've already experienced."

Kasenia looked away.

"Watch your p's and q's and you'll be fine. But one more misstep, and... Well, be warned."

With a sigh, Kasenia turned back. "So, what's a *misstep* around here?"

"Never say anything bad about Brewster."

"But I've heard other—"

"Keep your mouth shut until you've been here long enough to be accepted by everyone, or most everyone. Lorraine will never accept any of us. And why should she? She thought she was Brewster's one true love, and now she's sharing him with eight women, soon to be eleven or more. Some resent her bossiness. But I figure all she's got left is a little power."

"What else is a misstep?"

"Refusing Brewster sex or neglecting to tell him how amazing he is in bed. It's a big deal to him."

Kasenia nodded. Yes, it was a big deal, especially on the nights he couldn't perform, though he refused to believe he might be losing his prowess. Was that why he wanted to add a fifteen-year-old to his harem? Did he think a fresh body would fix his problem? Would he stop with a dozen women? Or keep searching for the perfect turn-on?

"Anything else?" She hated to ask, but she needed to know.

"Be grateful for his gifts and the time he spends with you. Shower him with praise. He thrives on adulation."

Margo was trying to help, but her well-intentioned advice set Kasenia's teeth on edge. *What Brewster really needs is solitary confinement, where he can't harm anyone other than himself.*

"In a nutshell, don't make waves. Cooperate, smile a lot, and settle in."

Kasenia tilted her head. "If you don't mind me asking, why do you stay? You talk like you're not one of the wives, and you seem to have a separate life out here with the horses." *Plus, you're a far nicer person in the barn.*

"You're very observant." Margo raised an eyebrow. "I came to Shadow Ranch through a different door than most."

"You mentioned children."

"Yes." Her features softened.

"Are they here with you?"

Margo sighed. "I owe you an apology."

Kasenia furrowed her brow. "For what?"

"You might not believe it, but I was a decent person before I came to Shadow Ranch." She glanced at her watch. "We have a couple minutes. Let's take a break in my office."

Once inside the sparsely furnished office, Margo closed and locked the door. "Have a seat." She indicated the couch, then sat at the desk.

Though Margo's behavior mystified Kasenia, she did as she was directed, easing her sore body onto a soft well-worn cushion that smelled like a horse had sat on it.

"We can talk in here." Margo lifted a cooler lid, pulled out two bottles of water and handed Kasenia one. "But we need to keep our voices down."

"Thank you." Kasenia opened her bottle, took a long sip and screwed the cap back on.

Margo set her bottle on the desk and pulled out a desk drawer. "You like almonds?"

"I do."

"You won't get lunch today." Margo took a bag from the drawer and walked over to pour a handful of almonds into Kasenia's palm. "These'll help keep you going. Eat as many as you like."

"Thank you."

Margo dropped the bag on the desk and settled into her chair. "My husband, Nate, and I had a beautiful marriage, a beautiful family, and a beautiful horse ranch in western Wyoming. But, like many ranchers, we barely broke even. When Nate died three years ago from a brain aneurism we didn't know he had, I..."

She looked down, blinked a couple times, then swallowed.

"I'm sorry." Kasenia offered a sad smile. "His death must have turned your world upside down."

Margo sighed. "I was left with a broken heart, three grieving kids, two big dogs and forty-five expensive horses. As you probably know, their feed and care add up fast."

"So I've heard."

"I did the only thing I could do, considering the ranch was mortgaged to the hilt. I sold the horses and the ranch."

"And that's how you met Brewster."

"I was lonely and vulnerable, afraid to face the future by myself."

Margo's confession surprised Kasenia. She would never have guessed the brusque woman was afraid of anyone or anything.

"He was a sympathetic listener, kind, helpful." Margo rubbed her neck. "Until he moved us here. Like you, I had no idea what I was getting into. The worst part..."

She stared at her hands. "My children, two boys and a girl, have suffered the consequences of my rash decision. We were a close family, very close, which bothered Brewster. The day the foster boys were delivered, he had me move with them out here to the barn until the dorm renovation was finished. And now, I have to live with the boys there."

"That's terrible, especially after what your family's been through."

"I'm angry day and night. Furious." Margo pounded her thighs. "So mad, I fear I might have a stroke and leave my kids to face Brewster's fury on their own." She rocked back and forth, clutching her ribs. The chair creaked. "I'm angry at him for what he's done to my family, angry at the women who agreed to this ludicrous lifestyle. Mostly, I'm mad at myself for letting him dupe me. My kids are paying the price."

"I feel the same way." Kasenia released a shaky breath. "Look what my gullibility did to Sam."

"But you're young. I was old enough to know better." Margo rubbed her eyes. "It'll get worse. Already, I see Lorraine's attempts to pair my boys, who are sixteen and seventeen, with her daughters. To avoid the inbreeding thing, I'm sure. And I swear Brewster has his eye on my daughter, Marisa, who's fourteen."

Kasenia gasped. "That's despicable."

"Makes me sick to my stomach. As you saw, I can get someone to open the gate anytime I want. But how far could we run before Brewster got wind and came after us?

"Before I came, one of his wives, a woman named Beth, ran away with her children. A couple weeks later, a rancher at the Saturday market was overheard saying he'd come across the strangest thing in an arroyo—a woman's severely bruised dead body along with the corpses of two young children sprawled on top of her."

Kasenia groaned. "I know he has a temper, but—"

"Fighting the system is futile, unless one has a death wish." Her face almost as red as her hair, Margo sucked in an unsteady breath and dropped her head. Finally, she lifted it again. "My anger is like a volcano. It spews all over everyone. Part of it is an act to make people think I'm onboard with the culture here. Part of it, I'm ashamed to admit, has been a release valve for my rage—very unfair to you and the boys." Rubbing her temples, she blew out a raspy sigh. "I'm terribly sorry and will do my best to ease up."

"I'm sorry for the pain and sorrow you've suffered." Kasenia was tempted to suggest Margo and her children flee with her and the boys. But this was too early in their changing relationship to trust her.

"Have you heard about Eva, the other sister wife who died?" Margo asked.

"The nurse who killed herself?"

Margo nodded.

"Rachel mentioned her but didn't offer details."

"I heard from a couple sources that Brewster got a Tucson woman pregnant before he learned she was part Puerto Rican. You've probably noticed we're all light-skinned around here. He didn't want his 'seed' tainted with dark skin, so he insisted Eva abort the pregnant woman's baby. She and the mother-to-be both begged him to let the child live, but he refused. Rumor has it he didn't wait for the woman to recover before he dumped her at the border later that same day."

"How awful, but at least she escaped this place."

"Eva escaped too, by suicide."

"Such a tragic ending." Kasenia shook her head. She could only imagine how distraught Eva must have been to end her life in such a horrible way. Gripping the water bottle with both hands, she moved to the edge of the cushion and leaned closer. "I saw a cash register van at the dorm." Keeping her voice low, she asked, "Do you know Brewster's plans for the place?"

"He hasn't said, but it can't be good." Margo rubbed her forehead. "I fear for the boys. They're sweet kids, your brother included."

"He's planning to pimp them, Margo, to offer their bodies to pedophiles. Very likely, you'll be the person who takes the johns' money."

"Oh, no. I was afraid of that." Margo covered her face with her hands. "What am I to do? If I cooperate, the boys will suffer terribly. If I don't, he'll punish me *and* my children because he knows how much I love them."

"We can't let it happen."

Margo looked up, eyes wide. "But how can we stop it? When Brewster decides to do something, he doesn't let anyone or anything stand in his way." She checked her watch. "Oops, I talked too long." Jumping to her feet, she said, "We'll talk more about the boys' later. Right now, we only have a few minutes to shower and change. Brewster and the buyers will be here soon. Come with me. I'll grab your outfit from my trailer."

Kasenia blinked. "Outfit?"

"Our *dearly beloved* expects us to dress for the occasion."

"What occasion?"

"You and I are showing horses this afternoon."

"Why me? I don't—"

"Never ask why." Margo waggled her finger. "Just do as you're told."

She led Kasenia out the side door and over to a nearby mobile home. "Wait here." A moment later, she returned with a garment bag, a hatbox and boots that smelled new. "Brewster had these delivered. Put them on and hurry over to the barn."

Kasenia reached for the hanger, but Margo held firm. "To be clear..." She spoke just above a whisper. "If you share what I said in the barn, I'll deny it, call you a liar and say you're trying to make me look bad to gain favor with Brewster."

"Never." The last thing Kasenia wanted was *favor with Brewster*.

Margo raised an eyebrow. "Don't forget to wear makeup."

Kasenia hurried toward the barn, fluffing her still-wet hair behind her shoulders and ignoring the scandalized stares of Wileys on their way to lunch. The flashy royal-blue pants and shirt adorned with sequins and flower appliques, so unlike the fringed-leather earth-tone outfits she modeled for guest ranches, was something she'd never purchase for herself. But she wasn't going to trigger jealousy by telling them the outfit came from Brewster.

Everything fit perfectly, from the white hat down to the blue boots. He hadn't forgotten her sizes. Did he remember the other women's sizes too? Maybe that was expected with *big love.* She huffed. *Big ego* was more accurate.

Slipping in the side door, she thought of Trent and wished she could have taken a moment to read his business card before she tucked it beneath her hiking boot insole.

Margo was already in the barn, pacing before the horse stalls, stunning in a purple getup. Intricate gold-and-silver designs adorned the shirt. She wore purple boots, and like Kasenia, a white hat crowned her long red hair.

Kasenia walked over to her. "What's the plan, boss lady?"

Margo's eyes shuttered like a boarded-up house. "My name is Margo."

"Oh..." Kasenia stepped back. She should have known better than to get chummy with the volatile woman.

The sound of a door opening was followed by, "Ah, now that's the look I was hoping to achieve with my two beautiful ladies."

Kasenia pivoted in time to see Brewster exit the corner bathroom and stride toward them. He wore a wide-brimmed straw cowboy hat and a colorful Aztec-patterned shirt tucked into dark Levi's. He was incredibly sexy in western attire.

Disgusted by her reaction, she reminded herself he was an ogre who beat and murdered people. How could she have fallen for him? She'd learned early in the fashion world all that glitters on the outside is not necessarily gold on the inside. But she'd been so dazzled by his charm she'd ignored her misgivings.

"Margo, sweetheart..." Brewster put an arm around Margo's shoulders. "Let's take a look at the fillies. You can fill me in on their finer points."

Kasenia was glad he was businesslike and didn't kiss her or Margo. In fact, he barely acknowledged her presence, which was okay with her.

The pair moved from stall to stall, Margo talking, Brewster making notes on a small pad. They discussed the age and condition of the horses, the price to ask and the lowest offer they'd take. They also decided what order to show the fillies. Brewster would announce and describe each one as it was brought from the barn.

A constant insistent mooing from the pasture seemed to be coming closer. What was going on? Did a cow need to be milked, or had one been injured? Neither Margo nor Brewster seemed concerned, so Kasenia didn't mention it.

Margo's interaction with Brewster fascinated Kasenia. They appeared compatible, like sister and brother, or maybe longtime friends or business partners. Was a business relationship what he expected of her—a modeling agency and little more? She lifted her hat and fluffed her hair. She wasn't going to hang around long enough to find out.

15

B REWSTER LED THE WAY from the barn into the first corral. Kasenia and Margo followed.

"The buyers will be on the other side of the railing. I'll stand inside, over there." He pointed to the rails opposite the barn. "You'll lead the fillies in front of the buyers, toward me, then turn so they can see both sides of each animal."

He studied the women, from their hats to their boots. "I want you two to flirt—smile, wink, wiggle your butts. Be sexy. And don't forget to hand out cold water bottles. You have those ready, Margo?"

"They're on ice in my office."

"Am I hearing you right?" Kasenia furrowed her brow. "You want me to flirt with other men, when I'm supposedly your wife?"

Margo sucked in a breath, and Kasenia knew she'd crossed a line. But her words were out, hanging between the three of them like a storm cloud.

Brewster glared at her. "The object of this exercise, Kasenia *Wiley*, is to sell horses. If a little harmless flirtation gets some dude's engine running, all the better."

Remembering Margo's advice, Kasenia nodded her agreement. "Whatever you say."

"What's wrong with that cow?" Brewster demanded.

The mooing sounds Kasenia had noticed earlier were getting louder. She searched the pasture and saw a cow weaving their direction, shaking its head, obviously unhappy about something.

"My guess is a rattlesnake bit her face," Margo said. "She's coming closer, probably hoping we'll give her some relief."

"We can't have that racket during the sale." Bending, he lifted a pant-leg, reached into his boot and pulled out a handgun. "I'll go put her out of her misery."

"Brewster..." Margo touched his arm. "A dead cow gathering flies in your pasture might give buyers the wrong impression regarding how we care for our animals."

"Whatever." He grunted. "Have a better idea?"

"Get one of your men to move her into the dairy barn and tranquilize her. If she awakens before our visitors leave, he can give her another dose."

"Call right now." He replaced the gun. "We need to shut that cow's mouth."

Margo lifted her phone from her belt and walked toward the dairy barn.

Brewster eyed Kasenia, as if noticing her presence for the first time. "I knew royal blue was right for your coloring. Do you like what I chose for you?"

Breathing his potent aftershave and staring into his hard gray eyes that dared her to defy him, Kasenia heard Margo's words again. *Be grateful for his gifts. Shower him with praise.* She swallowed, hating herself for stroking his insatiable ego. "Thank you for the compliment, Brewster, and thank you for this fun outfit. It's, uh, colorful."

"And a perfect fit, I might add."

"Yes, perfect." She smiled. "From the hat to the boots."

"Of course. I'm that kinda guy."

Oh, for the day she never heard those words again.

The man who'd earlier opened the gate drove up in a pickup. He leaned out the window and punched the keypad buttons. When the gate clinked and began to roll open, he motored away.

"Gotta check for rattlers." Brewster pulled the pistol from his boot. "Don't need any slithering in during the sale and startling the horses." He turned and hurried toward the ever-widening opening.

Kasenia watched with envious eyes, wishing she could slip through the gap. But knowing Brewster, he wouldn't hesitate to use his gun. One of these days, she'd find a way to walk out that gate and never look back.

"Don't think of it as flirting." Margo came alongside her. "Just put on a show. Wave at the buyers, exaggerate your movements, kiss the horse."

"Eww."

"Then hug the horse." Margo blew out a weary breath. "At the end of the day, the only thing that'll matter to Brewster is a sizable profit."

I'd kiss a horse before I'd willingly kiss Brewster again.

Tomás came around the barn on an ATV, slowed to a stop and shut off the engine. Reaching behind his seat, he grabbed a rope. Step by careful step, he approached the mooing cow. When he was within range, he twirled the looped rope above his head and threw it over the cow's head.

"Nice job, cowboy." Margo nodded, obviously pleased. "He got her on the first try."

Kasenia folded her arms. Was Tomás a security guard or a vaquero? Or both? If he was an illegal immigrant, how could he help them without getting deported? He cared for his nephew and seemed to care about Sam and the other boys. Maybe that was all that mattered.

Waiting at the partly open barn door, Kasenia watched Margo sashay with the feisty filly she was leading, exhibiting energy she didn't have a moment ago. Like the other women, she knew how to come alive when her phony husband was watching, no matter how tired she was. Her purple outfit not only highlighted her beautiful hair, it complemented the animal's dark coloring.

"I call this magnificent animal Black Beauty," Brewster declared, "though her registered name is Firecracker out of Prince Horacio." The shiny black with two white socks pranced and put on a nice show for the onlookers. After Brewster finished describing the horse, Margo secured it to a rail and returned to the barn.

Kasenia rubbed her horse's neck. "Your turn to show how pretty you are, little girl." The brassy chestnut filly had inquisitive eyes and bright attentiveness. Her perky auburn mane and tail flashed gold highlights.

The horse dutifully followed her from the barn, head high. Kasenia waved to the handful of men watching from the far side of the corral. They looked like a Wild West travel ad. Cowboy hats on their heads, forearms resting on the top rail, one booted foot propped on the bottom rail. Pickup trucks and horse trailers were lined up behind them, with the chain-link fence and a mountain range as backdrop.

Seeing movement in her peripheral vision, she glanced to the side and caught sight of a lizard scampering along the top rail. Evidently, the filly saw it too, for she snorted and shied, nearly wrenching the lead rope from Kasenia's fingers.

The sudden jerk jabbed pain through Kasenia's already sore body. She winced but quickly plastered a smile on her face. Gripping the rope with both hands, she sidestepped to protect her feet. The horse tossed her head and circled away, but Kasenia held tight, murmuring, "It's okay, it's okay. Just a harmless lizard. It can't hurt you, girl, can't hurt you."

Finally, the filly settled. Kasenia took a breath, adjusted her hat and paraded the horse before the men. Too focused on regaining her composure to sashay, she smiled. "Sorry for the show. A silly little lizard gave us both an adrenaline rush."

"Good job working her through the fright," someone called.

Recognizing Trent's voice, Kasenia grinned and waved.

He gave her a thumbs-up.

The men clapped and cheered. "Way to show her who's boss."

All she'd hoped to do was calm the horse, not dominate it. She reversed the filly to display the horse's other side.

Without commending her actions or even mentioning the event, Brewster finished his litany, describing the horse's pedigree, including her name, Sugar Pop out of King Willie, as well as her history.

⋙ ⋯ ✦ ⋯ ⋘

Later, after the buyers had left with their horses, Margo slammed the cash box closed and stood. "Not bad for a day's work. Brewster should be pleased." She motioned to Kasenia. "Please fold this table and take it inside. I'll carry the chair and the cash box."

Kasenia tilted the table onto its side, then snapped the legs into their stowed position. Relieved the sale was over, she couldn't wait to change into cooler clothing, no matter if her bruises showed or not. Her normal summer attire did not include boots and long pants, let alone a long-sleeved shirt and a hot hat. But then, normal flew out the window the moment Brewster drove her and Sam through the compound gate.

"Here, I'll get that for you."

Kasenia glanced up, eyes wide. Brewster rarely volunteered to help her do anything. Normal had truly flown the coop, as her grandpa would say.

He picked up the table and walked with Margo into the barn. "I'll help you count the money."

Of course. She should have known it was about the money.

"That was a fast, profitable turnaround." He sounded excited. "We'll have to do it again, Margo."

"Brewster, I need time with—"

They entered the barn and Kasenia stepped to the nearby corral. The horse that had been spooked by the lizard was standing with her head over the railing, eyeing a small patch of dry grass that had somehow not been trampled.

"Exciting day for you, little girl." Kasenia ran her fingers through the horse's golden mane. "A good home is in your future. Trent Duran will treat you like a czarina."

The filly flung her head up and down. Her mane flashed fire in the sunshine.

"I'm glad you agree." Kasenia wrapped her arms around the horse's sturdy chestnut neck and laid her head against it, reveling in her solid strength and horsey smell. "I wish I could go with you."

As if the horse understood her anguish, it quieted, allowing Kasenia to linger.

"Nice job, Kasenia."

She looked over the filly's neck.

Trent had pulled his pickup alongside the corral and was getting out. "Thank you."

He shut the door and came to stand beside her. "You handled those horses like a pro."

"My lucky day, I guess. I've done photoshoots with horses but never anything like this." She stroked the filly's forehead. "I was loving on your acquisition. She's the sweetest and prettiest of the horses we showed today."

In contrast to Brewster's overdone aftershave, Trent smelled like warm spices.

"That was my thought." He stepped back to study the horse. "I'm surprised no one outbid me."

"Do you have plans for her?"

"I've started a small herd and am hoping to grow it horse by horse. I'd rather raise my own than..." He jutted his chin toward the barn. "Flip horses like people flip houses." He shoved his hands in his pockets. "Personal preference, that's all."

And maybe because you're not greedy like Brewster.

Tomás walked the suffering, moaning cow out of the dairy barn and over to a water tank. **BWSR** was branded on its side.

"Ah, too bad," Trent said, "another rattlesnake victim."

"How can you tell?" She didn't remember him being nearby when Tomás moved the cow from the pasture into the barn.

"See those rubber tubes hanging from her nose?"

Kasenia adjusted her hat to shade her eyes. "Oh, I see what you mean. Weird."

"The venom swells their nostrils shut. Unlike horses, cattle can breathe through their mouths, so they don't normally suffocate when they get bit on the face. But providing an airway lessens the trauma and makes eating and drinking easier. Some ranchers use PRID ointment to draw out the poison or DMSO for the swelling and antibiotics for potential infection. Rattlesnake fangs can inject bacteria along with the poison."

"Sounds awful."

"It is, but livestock usually survive without long-term side effects."

He stroked the horse's neck. "I hate to leave Sugar Pop..." He grunted. "Worthless name. Dumb as a fur coat in the desert."

Kasenia laughed. "I think it's cute."

"Yeah, well, anyway, I didn't bring a trailer and can't get back here for a couple days."

"Margo will take good care of her."

"I'm sure she will. In the meantime, I'll be thinking of a better name. Got any ideas?"

Kasenia grinned. "Like I said, I think Sugar Pop is cute, but we can do better." She studied the horse for a moment then wrinkled her nose. "You probably won't like what I'm thinking."

"Try me."

"She's curious as well as smart and sweet."

"Right." He scratched the filly's forehead beneath her forelock. "Go on."

The horse lowered her head, as if begging for more, and Trent obliged.

"This is silly," Kasenia said, "but her coloring reminds me of my babushka—that's grandma in Russian."

He glanced from her to the horse. "Did your hair color come from your grandmother?"

"Yes, though mine is darker than hers. My babushka hasn't grayed—she's still a ginger redhead. And she hasn't lost her spunk or her curiosity."

"Ah, my kind of lady. What's her name?"

"Irina."

"Whoa..." He reared his head, startling the horse.

The filly shied away but then returned.

Kasenia scuffed the toe of her boot in the dirt. "Just an idea."

"That's my great-grandmother's name."

"Oh..." She looked up. "Was she Russian too?"

"She immigrated from Spain with my great-grandfather and home-steaded my ranch with him—my family's ranch, that is. My parents moved to town and my sisters don't have the slightest interest in country living. I'm the only Crimson Arches resident these days."

"What a wonderful heritage." Kasenia stroked the horse's cheek. "What do you think, Sugar Pop? You want a new name?"

The horse nickered.

"She agrees." Trent laughed.

"Thinking of her coloring, how about Firestorm Irina or Irina Afire? Or..." She paused. "*Princess* Irina Afire because she's from a royal bloodline."

"Princess Irina Afire... I like it." He raised his palm. "High five. Princess Irina Afire out of King Willie, it is."

Kasenia slapped her palm to his, feeling a tingle down to her toes. "May your Princess Irina be as fun and delightful as my Babushka Irina."

"What're you two doing?" Brewster came up beside Kasenia and put an arm around her waist.

She dropped her hand.

"We're celebrating, dude." Hands on his waist, Trent gave him a hard stare. "I asked Kasenia for a better name for this filly, and she came up with a perfect one, first try."

"So, why's the horse still here?" Brewster squeezed Kasenia's bruised ribs, hard.

She gasped and coughed, worsening the pain. Tears balanced on her eyelids.

Eyebrows tight, Trent studied her for a moment before focusing on Brewster. "Like I told you, I..." Anger flickered in his dark eyes. "I drove over this morning to shoe horses, not haul one home. I'll get the filly later in the week."

"You do that."

Margo, who'd followed Brewster from the barn, said, "I'll have the registration paperwork ready for you. You'll need it to submit a name change request to the American Quarter Horse Association."

"Thank you." Trent strode to his pickup, fists clenched, shoulders taut.

The moment Trent drove out of the compound, Brewster shoved Kasenia against a post. "You *ever* touch another man, I'll do more than crack a couple ribs."

She grasped a rail for support. First, he told her to flirt with the buyers, then he threatened her because she touched one.

Gripping her chin, Brewster jerked her head upward until they were eye to eye. "Because..." he growled, "I'm that kinda guy."

⊰⊱ ·•✦•· ⊰⊱

Later that night, Monday night, Kasenia sat on the edge of the camper bed, debating. Should she change her clothes—a painful, slow process—or wait, fully dressed, for Tomás to throw rocks at the window? She hoped she'd hear him over the AC's rumble.

She also hoped Brewster wouldn't come after her again. If he hit or kicked her one more time, she might lose the will to live and beg him to kill her. Shaking her head, she pushed the thought aside, for Sam's sake.

They hadn't had to work after dinner, a definite *plus* after a long day. However, sitting on a wood floor when she ached all over, watching Brewster pontificate on the TV screen above the piano was an exhausting *minus*. His "Papa's Place" check-ins from a hotel room or the front seat of his Corvette were supposed to be live interactions with his family when he was out of town. From what she'd observed, the conversations were one-sided.

Her body craved sleep, but if tonight was the night to escape, Kasenia didn't want to miss it. Worst-case scenario, she'd help the boys leave and sneak away later, maybe on a horse. Trent Duran said his Crimson Arches Ranch was east of Shadow Ranch. When the opportunity came, she'd ride east as fast as the horse could gallop.

Kicking off her shoes, she pulled her feet up and leaned back against the wall. Trent seemed like a nice guy, and her heart lurched every time she saw him. Yet, she refused to let her hormones lead her into trouble again. Her recklessness regarding Brewster had gotten her and Sam into this nightmare.

Knees bent, she laid her head on her folded arms, smelling her dusty clothes. Why hadn't she listened to Grandpa Gordon, who'd mistrusted Brewster from the beginning? And to her mother, who'd said, "This relationship is happening awfully fast, sweetie."

She'd never really loved Brewster. Just thought she did. Now, she could see her feelings for what they were, infatuation.

From the honeymoon on—earlier, if she was honest with herself—he'd been evasive, yet so smooth, so charming. Once he'd bagged her, like a hunter who downed a deer just to hang a trophy on the wall, he'd become a different person. Or, apparently, his real self.

And then there was her stupid arrogant belief she was a better guardian than either of her parents. Thanks to her, Sam had been kidnapped and imprisoned. Could they ever forgive her? Could *he* ever forgive her? Would their loved ones ever learn what had happened to the two of them?

Worse than their disappearance was the horrid fact her brother could be forced to service pedophiles. Kasenia rubbed her temples. Brewster was evil personified. How had she been so easily duped by him? When people did dumb stuff, her grandpa would say they lacked horse sense. Evidently, she was no different.

She pushed to her feet to pace the narrow corridor between the bed and the shower. Five steps. Pivot. Five steps. Pivot. Five steps... Finally, she fell to her knees beside the bed, something she hadn't done since she was a little girl at her babushka's house. *God of the universe,* she prayed, head on her arms, *or wherever you are, please give me courage and strength—and show me how I can save my brother and the other boys from a terrible future. Amen.*

She and Sergei were in Babushka Irina's garden, picking green beans with her and laughing at the barn cats chasing butterflies between the plants. Kasenia didn't know why, but she sensed she was happier than she'd been in a long time. She dropped a handful of beans in the basket. Her babushka would boil the beans then fry them with eggs for lunch, one of her favorite—

A loud clatter splintered her dream.

Instantly awake, Kasenia was on her feet and out the door faster than she'd moved since Brewster beat her. Sidestepping down the stairs, she slowed and tiptoed toward the camper's rear bumper. If it was Marlin, she didn't want to look anxious, just curious.

She felt exposed in the porchlight. But she had a legitimate reason to be out—a frightening noise. Her pounding heart was proof.

When she reached the trailer bumper, she stopped to let her eyes adjust.

"Señorita, es Tomás."

Kasenia whispered, "Buenas noches, Tomás," and stepped into the trailer's shadow. "You have news?"

Though she could barely distinguish his silhouette from the horse behind him, he was standing at the fence, fingers wrapped through the links. "Sí," he murmured. "Los chicos lo saben."

"Chicos means boys, right?"

"Sí. Boys, they...comprenden."

"Oh, they comprehend, understand? They know about the men coming?"

"Sí." His hat bobbed up and down. "Vamos a escapar pronto."

Soon. They would escape soon, thank God. "Tonight?"

He shook his head. "No es posible."

"Tomorrow night?"

He shrugged. "Sólo Dios sabe."

She groaned. "Only God knows."

"Sí." He turned, settled his foot in a stirrup, swung his leg over and straddled the horse. "Rezar a Dios, Señorita Kasenia."

"Yes." She nodded. "I will pray."

16

— • —

WORKING ALONGSIDE SAM AND his dormmates at breakfast calmed Kasenia's spirit. She couldn't have a conversation with any of the boys. But seeing them healthy and whole was a relief and renewed her determination to snatch them from Brewster's greedy fists.

Sam elbowed her as he passed. "Mornin', Sis."

"Mornin', Bro."

That was the extent of their conversation, but it was enough to give her the courage to face another day inside the Shadow Ranch confines.

Assigned to work in the laundry room with Chloe and two teenage girls, Kasenia followed them to the other end of the lodge. The big room was hot and smelled like detergent and dirty socks. Sorry she'd dressed in jeans and a t-shirt, not shorts and a tank top like the girls, Kasenia rolled her shirt sleeves higher but immediately lowered them. The bruises had taken on an ugly yellow-green hue.

The laundry room reminded her of the Usva dry goods store that sold everything from razors to curtains. Here, racks and shelves had signs indicating what clothing items were for what size person, whether boys, girls or women. Large canvas bins marked "dirty" lined one wall, the clothing shelves another, and commercial-sized washing machines and dryers the other. Clothing racks and folding tables occupied the center.

The work was mindless, but that was okay with Kasenia. She and the girls filled and emptied washers and dryers and folded and hung clothing without speaking, which allowed her to think about escape options. The entire time, Chloe sat at the desk near the door, doodling.

At lunchtime, Kasenia returned to the camper to wash her hands and have a moment of privacy. After handling dirty laundry, she felt filthy. From there, she crossed to the big house but stopped when she saw the silver Corvette parked in front. Not Brewster again. Wasn't he here yesterday? And didn't he preach at them last night on the TV screen?

She had to muster every ounce of fortitude in her being to keep walking. Whether she wanted to or not, she had to look the truth in the eyes. Brewster was one big bundle of lies. And that was the truth.

Nearing the house, she spotted him on the veranda outside the front door. Dressed in Levi's and a plaid western shirt with a turquoise bolo tie, he welcomed each person like they were guests. Whether women or boys or girls, he shook their hands and kissed their cheeks, murmuring in their ears and bringing smiles to their faces.

Kasenia didn't know what to think. Was this a kinder, gentler side? Or was he faking it? If so, why? One thing she knew, his presence instilled a quiet tension in his family. Another Russian saying came to mind. *Without a cat, mice feel free.* Shadow Ranch mice were never truly free of the tomcat, but they acted freer when he was absent.

A surprising fast-food aroma wafted through the doorway. Was this another attempt to please Brewster? Despite his gourmet tastes, he loved hamburgers and fries with fry sauce.

She joined the line, dreading the moment she reached Brewster. But when she did, he wrapped an arm around her shoulders. "Dear, dear, Kasenia. How I've missed you in Tucson."

She stared into his gray unreadable eyes, eyes that didn't match his soft voice or sweet words. Had he already forgotten the beating? Or how he'd duped her and Chloe?

He kissed her cheek and shook her hand. "Go have a seat, my love."

My love? She shuffled behind Chloe and her children to the food line. Tapping Chloe on the shoulder, she whispered, "Does Brewster do this often?"

"No." Chloe shook her blond curls. "Something's up."

◆》◆·◆·◆·◆◆

Brewster ended the communal prayer with a final "so be it" and told them to sit, though he remained standing. Today, Rachel and her children shared the head table with him, all with Diet Dr. Pepper cans before their plates.

"I have an important revelation from Spirit Father for you," Brewster declared.

Something about his ear-to-ear grin made Kasenia's stomach lurch.

"This is wonderful news, for all of us. You'll no doubt remember Spirit Father instructed us to have a family like our Old Testament forefather, Jacob, and establish *twelve* tribes." He held out his hands. "His goal, my goal, *our* goal is twelve sister wives. Then we will be complete, one big happy family."

Babushka Irina's priest had once talked about Jacob during one of his homilies. The Jewish patriarch had twelve sons, but they were from two wives and two slaves, not twelve wives. Kasenia scanned the room. By the resigned expressions on the women's faces and the way they picked at their French fries, they'd heard all this before.

He sipped from his Diet Dr. Pepper, licked his lips and set the can down. "I informed you a couple days ago the Tucson neighbor girl is destined to be my number ten wife. She's a darling. We recently had quite a lively conversation."

Your neighbor? Does that mean you're still living in my grandfather's house? If only she could call Grandpa Gordon and beg him to warn Denika's parents. For the first time, the thought that Brewster might harm her grandfather entered her mind. If they got into an argument, he might beat him the way he beat her.

"What I haven't yet mentioned..." Brewster adjusted his bolo tie. "Are Spirit Father's other intended additions to our growing family. For several months, I thought Julie, the unmarried business department admin, was to be my next bride. I even went as far as to take her to dinner not long ago."

Julie? She was a sweet lady who always greeted Kasenia when they crossed paths at the university. Sometimes, they stopped to talk. *You took Julie to dinner while you were married to me? Or supposedly married to me...*

"But then," he continued, "I noticed she had photographs of two adorable young ladies on her desk. Julie said they were her twelve-year-old twins, identical twins at that." He rubbed his hands together. "There you go, folks, numbers eleven and twelve, and we'll be complete. As soon as I bring Denika to Shadow Ranch, I'll start courting the twins. They're a bit young, but they'll fit into our family like two peas in a pod."

Are you out of your mind? You have daughters that age.

Silence greeted his announcement.

He jutted his chin. "Where's the enthusiasm, the praise to Spirit Father?"

"Brewster." Lorraine jumped up. "That can't be right. Our Guiding Principles command men not to marry sisters."

Others in the room nodded, but no one spoke in support.

"You are so right, my love." Brewster took another drink of soda, ran his tongue over his lips and wiped his mouth with his shirtsleeve. "I questioned Spirit Father's wisdom in this and was told in a beautiful follow-up revelation—oh, how I wish I could describe the rainbow colors, the ever-weaving textures, the delicious aromas—so heavenly." He sighed dramatically. "Spirit Father patiently explained to me identical twins are not sisters because they come from the same egg and are basically the same person."

"I see." Lorraine sat, eyes flashing, jaw clamped.

She may see... Kasenia studied the woman. *But she doesn't like what she sees.*

"I'll continue the quest," Brewster said, "in case I heard wrong regarding twins—or that a dozen wives is Spirit Father's *final* plan for our family."

On the other side of the room, Sam was intent on Brewster, taking in every word. Did he believe the lies? How did the mothers in the room feel when Brewster spewed his craziness at their children? Surely, they could see he made up the stories to give credence to his lust.

"What do you think, family? Is this monumental news or what?" He waved his arms. "We'll soon be a dozen, maybe even a baker's dozen, if

Spirit Father so leads." His eyes glittered. "And babies, more and more babies."

Lorraine stood again. "Where are we going to put all these people?"

"Oh, sweetheart..." He chuckled. "You should know by now we'll cross that bridge when we get to it."

Kasenia felt sorry for Lorraine and her sister wives. As Russians would say, a hedgehog could see how Brewster manipulated his clan. His empty soul would never be filled and his craving for more and more fresh flesh and younger and younger children would never be satisfied. She ran her hand over her eyes, sickened by the thought.

He had to be stopped. But how? He looked the model citizen, always smiling, always charming, always dressed to the hilt. Always hobnobbing with powerful people.

Every time her dedushka mentioned the glib-talking Moscow officials he dealt with while mayor of Usva, he'd say, "The devil lives in still waters." On the surface, Brewster was an influential professor, but beneath his polished exterior, he was a monster. She had a feeling she didn't know the half of what he'd done to make these people so subservient.

After lunch, the younger children gathered around Brewster for a story. Seeing him with two children on his lap and more at his knees was more than she could bear. How could he be so loving to his kids when he planned to pimp Sam and the Hispanic children? She shivered and strode out of the building into the afternoon heat.

Sam and the foster boys were ahead of her. This afternoon, they were assigned to clean the pigpen. Funny how their work always involved manure. Brewster's kids never shoveled the stuff.

Kasenia stopped by the camper to grab her sunhat—and to make sure the AC was on before she headed for the garden. Again, it was off. Who did that, anyway? Not only was the act malicious, it was an invasion of privacy.

When she exited the trailer, two young girls came running to her. "Our daddy wants to talk to you. He's on the veranda."

She thanked the girls and set the hat inside the camper. What now? Couldn't be good. Her stomach roiled.

She found him seated on a bench with two toddlers on his lap, a boy and a girl.

He hugged them both. "Time for you to go, my sweeties. I must speak with this lady."

"Who's she?" The boy pointed at Kasenia.

"She's your mom's newest sister."

"Oh," the girl said. "Mommy have sisters."

"Yes, she does, and she's gonna have more." Brewster kissed each towhead on the cheek and set them down. "I'll walk you to the door, then you can run to your mamas."

Stooping low, he took their hands, led them to the door and opened it for them. "In you go. I'll see you later." For a long moment, he gazed inside the house, and then he turned to Kasenia, motioning to the bench. "Have a seat."

She sat at the far end. "Such sweet, adorable little ones you have, Brewster." As much as she hated the man, she couldn't deny he had beautiful children.

"I'm a proud papa, proud of every one of them." He settled on the bench and slid close. "I have something to show you."

"Have you talked with Grandpa Gordon?" Kasenia breathed through her mouth. Brewster's aftershave seemed stronger than ever. Or maybe it was because the smell now repelled rather than attracted her. "He's probably worried."

Brewster rested his arm on the back of the bench. "I saw him for a few minutes yesterday. When he questioned your whereabouts, I told him, 'Last I heard, you and Sam were planning to fly to Russia to surprise your babushka.' He said he didn't know anything about that. I told him you'd been discussing the trip for a while. He should pay better attention. Your babushka was anxious to plan the wedding and you thought it would be easier in person than long distance. School's out, so this seemed like a good time. I promised to let him know if I heard anything."

With a sneer, he added, "Gordon isn't the least bit concerned about you and Sam. He's too busy tinkering with the rust heap that litters the garage and listening to redneck music on his ancient cassette deck. Face it, Kasenia, he doesn't give two hoots about you—or Sam. He and his golf buddies are lazing around the living room, drinking beer and watching golf reruns."

Kasenia didn't respond, didn't want to admit Brewster was probably right. Her parents would call Grandpa Gordon after they'd tried her cell phone several times. But their calls were random, and she didn't talk often with Babushka Irina.

Mostly, she wrote her Russian grandmother letters because after a few minutes on the phone, she'd say, "This is your kopek, dear, and kopeks add up fast. I'd better go. Long distance across the ocean is too expensive for a college student. Write me a letter. I read them to my friends and your Uncle Sergei. They enjoy them as much as I do."

"Your phone disappeared with your purse," Brewster was saying, "and the other items you left in the car. If your parents bother to call my phone, I'll be shocked they haven't heard from you. We'll call the cops then, when no one knows what happened to you, including little ole me."

Kasenia searched his gray eyes for the love he'd showered on his toddlers. His gaze was hard and empty of any emotion, except perhaps arrogance. Had he never loved her?

Something struck her in that moment, beside the fact he was trying hard to destroy her hope. He had perfectly straight, perfectly white teeth, unlike most of the Shadow Ranch residents. Some of the older children and a couple of the women had gaps where teeth should be. Was that due to Brewster's abuse? Or did they handle dental problems by pulling the teeth? Very likely Brewster didn't want his so-called family to use dentists because they'd have to leave the compound—and dentists kept records. Thirty or forty people with the same address, same last name and similar features would likely trigger an inquiry.

Brewster took her hand. "Change of subject."

And change of tone.

Every cell in her body screamed for her to run from him and his unspoken threat. Yet, she had nowhere to hide. Kasenia planted her feet and fought the urge to rip her hand from his.

"What do you think of Shadow Ranch so far?"

She took his steely grip as a signal to choose her words carefully. Smiling, she waved her free hand to indicate the flowers and bushes that lined the flagstone walkway and the big cottonwoods that shaded the well-kept lawn. "You've made the desert bloom, Brewster. Quite an accomplishment, I'd say."

She almost said *bloom in this harsh environment* but decided that would be a poor word choice. "It's so well designed—pink oleander bushes alongside rose bougainvillea, purple Russian sage, lavender, pink and magenta butterfly bushes, and my favorite multi-colored lantana. Absolutely beautiful. I love it."

Brewster tweaked an eyebrow.

Oops. Maybe she'd gone a bit far.

"I have to agree." He relaxed his grip. "I singlehandedly created a paradise from this dry unforgiving desert."

You call this a paradise?

A faraway look came into his eyes. "It's taken a lot of backbreaking toil and hardship."

Toil and hardship for your women and children, not you. She hated to think what Lorraine had endured over the years since he brought her out here far from civilization.

He lifted her chin with his thumb, pressing hard. "What about you, Kasenia? Are you willing to do your part to support my growing family?"

You mean your growing enterprise?

She ignored the pain. "I've groomed your horses, weeded your gardens..." Talking was difficult with her chin shoved upward. "I've bottled yogurt, washed laundry, delivered goods to the weekend market, set up breakfast every morning. I work hard all day, every day."

For a long moment, he studied her, his hooded gaze so like a lizard's. "But is your heart in it? Do you do it for me, Kasenia? For our family?" He pinched her chin.

She recoiled, but he held tight.

"I thought you and I had a family." Kasenia wanted to swallow but couldn't. "You, me, Sam and Grandpa Gordon."

Brewster snorted and released his grip. "That old man was never in *my* family."

"You admit our marriage was a sham."

"I didn't say that." He glowered at her. "My marriage to you is as sacred and binding as my other marriages."

"That's not saying much."

He shoved her off the end of the bench and towered over her. "The Wiley family is *your family*. Not Old Man Clarke. Not your mommy and daddy, not your Russian granny. They're out of your life. Forever." He spit on her. "I, Brewster Wiley, am your husband. Shadow Ranch is your home."

Kasenia pushed upright and stood before him, willing her shoulders to relax, her fingers to hang loose, and her face to remain impassive. Despite the drool sliding down her cheek. Despite the pain. He'd hurt her, again, but she refused to cower before him.

"You're about to learn an important lesson in respect for sacred institutions." He squinted. "One you failed to learn in either Russian or American schools—*or* from your irresponsible parents. That's why I don't care to ever meet them or your precious babushka."

Kasenia narrowed her eyes. Where were his insults leading?

Brewster unsnapped his shirt pocket, reached inside, and pulled out a folded tissue. Opening it, he said, "Recognize these?" The edges of the paper fluttered, as if in a breeze, reminding her of his ever-present tremor.

She glanced at the dirt-encrusted jewelry on the plain white tissue, and her heart plummeted. She should have buried the necklace and rings rather than throw them at the fence. Wordless, she met his gaze.

His eyes hardened to flint ready to spark. "You discarded the symbols of my love and my eternal union with you. You disrespected me." He snarled. "I should dismember you and throw your stinking traitorous parts to the coyotes." He spat at her again, hitting her other cheek.

Resisting the urge to swipe his saliva from her face, Kasenia whispered, "I'm sorry, Brewster. I didn't mean—"

He grabbed her shoulder and shook her. "You Russian commie slut." His sour Dr. Pepper breath turned her stomach.

Her head hit the log wall, jarring her brain. She blinked, fighting to focus. "Stop, please stop. I, I couldn't help myself."

"What do you mean you couldn't help yourself?" He shoved her against the wall.

"You remember, Brewster, don't you?" she pleaded. "Remember how distraught I was the night you left me here? I thought it was all over between us, that you were lost to me. We'd never be together again." She held out her palms. "But now..."

His eyes narrowed. "Don't try to con me."

"It's why I threw the necklace, a necklace I dearly loved—you know how much I loved it—and my beautiful wedding rings. You were my world—and you were gone, forever. It felt like divorce or death to me. I was so upset. Yet..." She gave him a tremulous smile through tears. "Here you are, just like before. I am so sorry I hurt you."

Her words were partially true. She'd had that same abandoned feeling every time her parents left her behind. Kasenia stopped before she overplayed her fake regret. "Can you forgive me?"

He handed her the rings. "Put them on."

17

—·—

"**P**LEASE," KASENIA WHISPERED, "WOULD you...like before?"
She held out the rings.

At first, she feared he'd refuse. But then, he took the rings from her, rubbed them on his jeans, and slid them one at a time onto her finger. Still holding her hand in his quivering hand, he murmured, "Promise me you'll never remove these again." His probing gaze never left hers.

"I promise."

He polished the necklace with the tissue and handed the tissue to her. "Wipe your face and turn around."

Without speaking, she obeyed, like a horse accepting a bridle.

Before he clasped the necklace, he pulled it tight on her throat, cutting off her airway. "This necklace must *never* be removed by anyone but me. That includes you. Understand?"

She nodded.

"Say it."

A garbled "understand" was all she could manage.

He released the chain from her throat and clasped it behind her neck.

Kasenia sucked in a breath and closed her eyes. *Forgive me, Father, for I have sinned.* She'd heard that prayer in her babushka's church. *I have lied, over and over. For Sam, for the boys. For them I have to say the words Brewster wants to hear.* She made the sign of the cross over her heart.

Brewster spun her around. "What did you just do?"

"I, I was confirming my promise to you and to God."

His iron gaze softened, and he held her by her arms. "You have much to learn regarding my family's beliefs, my love. Spirit Father finds the sign of the cross repugnant."

"He does?"

"Of course. It's a foul, bitter taste in his mouth. A terrible memory of how his son died. He wants it erased from the history books, but that takes time."

"I had no idea."

"That's why Spirit Father gave me new scriptures for our family. Churches get it wrong. His son's death is to be pitied and reviled, not worshiped or revered. In obedience, I've deleted every reference to the son from our doctrine and covenants. The document isn't quite finished but will be ready for you to proofread soon."

"I see." Kasenia swallowed a disparaging retort. Of course, he hadn't finished it, like he hadn't finished his other writing projects. But that was good. The fewer of his warped ideas to infiltrate the world, the better.

"Lorraine assigns you to a variety of duties because you need to learn the ropes here before you take up your proofing duties again. And before we launch the Shadow Ranch modeling agency. You must be available to serve the family as needed. You won't be modeling or proofreading every day."

Modeling. She'd forgotten he stole her dream. An on-site job elsewhere with Sam might be their ticket out of Shadow Ranch.

His cell phone buzzed. He released her, lifted the phone from his belt and listened a moment. "Let him through."

The compound's front gate clanked.

Kasenia turned to see who was coming. Visitors were few and far between at Shadow Ranch, except during the weekend markets.

"Off with you." Brewster swatted her rear. "Time to get busy, Kasenia Wiley. This is a ranch. Everyone works here."

Everyone but you.

As she descended the veranda steps, a black Cadillac Escalade came through the gate, crunched over the gravel, and stopped in front of the railing. A broad-chested, big-bellied man wearing aviator sunglasses rose from the car like a bear exiting its den. His white snap-front western shirt was open far enough to reveal gray chest hair and a gold chain around his wide neck.

He plopped a tall black Stetson on his bald head and closed the door. "Howdy, folks."

Brewster moved to the porch railing. "Sheriff Guy Childers. What brings you to Shadow Ranch?"

Lowering his sunglasses, the man peered between the cottonwood branches and let out a low whistle. "This a new one, Wiley? Nice work."

Kasenia gave him a disgusted glance and started around the veranda, but then she slowed her steps. Brewster called the man *sheriff*. He could arrest Brewster and open the gate for her and Sam and the boys, except...he acted like he was Brewster's friend.

"Eyes off my woman, Childers." Brewster folded his arms. "How can I help you?"

"Thought I'd check on my investment, see how the renovation is going. Me and our investors can't wait for the grand opening."

Kasenia stopped. *Renovation, investors... Grand opening?* A man whose job was to uphold the law was funding Brewster's brothel. Bile rose in her throat.

"Go on." Brewster waved Kasenia away. "We're done here."

She stumbled ahead, but behind her, she could hear him take the stairs down to the flagstone path and tell Childers, "We're on schedule for the Friday opening. Video cameras will be installed Thursday. I hear the residual income is outstanding."

"Brilliant move, Wiley."

Video cameras? Kasenia stifled a groan. *Residual income...*

"If everything falls into place, I may be able to offer the investors a sneak preview Thursday evening."

"Whoa, doggie. I'm for that."

"Come on over. I'll show you how it's coming together."

At the veranda corner, Kasenia knelt behind a bush and pretended to retie her shoelace, all the while trying not to lose her lunch. Peeking between porch spindles, she saw Brewster lead Childers toward the boys' dormitory, which was all she needed to see. Could anyone be more wicked than those two men? She jumped to her feet, scanning the compound.

Where was Tomás? She had to talk with him. Maybe he'd trim trees while she worked in the garden, and she could tell him what she'd just witnessed. She started for the garden and was passing the big house when she remembered she was supposed to work in the laundry room.

Kasenia groaned. With the railing for support, she slowly climbed the stairs to the back porch. As tired as she was, she would watch all night for Tomás. They needed to talk, needed to act before the boys were forever traumatized, maybe even killed. She'd read the articles her mother wrote about prostituted children around the world and the terrible things done to them in the name of "pleasure."

Walking the hallway toward the laundry room, she rubbed her throat where the chain had notched her skin. She had to stop thinking the worst. Dwelling on the what-ifs was not helpful.

Early that morning, she'd read Psalm 34 in the travel Bible. It said God's ears are attentive to his people's prayers but against those who do evil. She didn't know if she was one of God's people or if he heard her prayers. However, she did know Brewster's plan was evil, and that meant the God who created the stars was against him *and* the sheriff. If he could make and hold the heavens in place, he could thwart their vile plans.

Kasenia opened the laundry room door and stepped inside. The temperature was almost as hot as outside.

Chloe lifted her gaze from a sketch she was drawing of a desert cardinal. "Bout time you showed your sorry face."

"Brewster wanted to talk to me." She would have complimented Chloe's artwork if the woman hadn't been so nasty.

"I heard." She made a show of scrutinizing Kasenia's neck. "Guess he taught you who runs the show around here." She called to the two girls transferring laundry from the dryers into wire-basket carts. "Can you believe she threw your father's symbols of his undying love in the dirt? Like the Good Book says, she tossed her pearls before swine."

What does that mean?

Eyes wide, the girls covered their open mouths in what Kasenia perceived as mock horror.

Chloe caressed her own *B+C* pendant. "Not for one moment have I *ever* considered removing this everlasting treasure. I will wear it to my grave and beyond."

You want to wear that noose for eternity?

Raising her wedding rings to her lips, Chloe kissed them. "My most cherished possessions."

Kasenia folded her arms. "Want me to do the same thing as this morning?" She couldn't stomach any more adoration of a man who was planning to pimp children and who'd just shoved her off a bench, spit on her, choked her and threatened to dismember her.

"Go sort the clothes the girls are pulling from the dryers. They can move laundry from the washers to the dryers."

Kasenia walked to a folding table piled high with warm clean-smelling clothing and lifted a purple blouse similar to one she'd been given by a designer friend. But this one was wrinkled and seemed to have shrunk. She checked the label.

Same label. It had to be her silk blouse, which was supposed to be handwashed in cold water. The sight of its deformed condition made her heartsick, but it was only a blouse. She had more important concerns, far more important concerns.

By the time she'd sorted, hung and folded everything, she'd found several of Sam's shirts and jeans that could have been his, three of her blouses, two dresses, underwear and a pair of pants. Some items had been given to her by Brewster, who said he liked to shop for her. Had he really been shopping for his other women? Did he tell them the clothing was new?

Clothes had disappeared before, but this was ridiculous. He must have emptied their dressers and closets right after he dumped her and Sam in the compound. Surely, when the police investigated, they'd notice the lack of clothing in the bedrooms.

She bit her lip. Brewster was slick. Slimy slick. He probably already had an answer prepared for the detectives.

Holding a shrunken beige camisole that had cost seventy-five dollars and been well worth the price, she momentarily mourned the loss.

Already, the lace was torn. She sighed. Her favorite item of clothing wouldn't survive many more washings.

"Quit fondling the underwear," Chloe called from her perch at the desk.

The teen girls working at the opposite end of the folding table giggled.

Kasenia threw the camisole into the girls' size-twelve slot, smiled and blew the teenagers kisses.

Their shocked expressions made her smile even more. She hung three t-shirts in the boys' section then strode to the door. "I'll be in the restroom."

Chloe frowned. "You didn't ask—"

Kasenia walked out, not about to ask permission to tend to bodily needs.

The three-stall bathroom was empty. Rushing to the farthest stall, the one by the window, she locked the door and raised the window casement. If she saw Tomás, she'd slip from the building to talk with him. To anyone who tried to stop her, she'd say she wasn't feeling well and needed fresh air.

From her limited perspective, she couldn't see Tomás, but she did see Sam and the foster boys. They were hauling rocks and gravel to the back of the dormitory, hard work in the overwhelming heat. Though they wore hats, she worried they might get heatstroke.

Hearing giggles, she twisted her head. Beneath the tree branches overhanging the fence, several blond kids with plastic jugs were throwing water at one another. So unfair. While they played in the shade, soaking each other with cool water, Sam and the others were shoveling dirt, hauling rocks, rubbing their backs, wiping their brows. Slave labor.

The bathroom door creaked open. Kasenia flushed the toilet, quietly lowered the window, and exited the stall.

One of the girls from the laundry was standing by the bathroom door, a suspicious scowl on her face. "Chloe is wondering what's taking you so long."

Kasenia smiled. "I'm wondering why she would have you ask me such a personal question."

The girl opened her mouth and then shut it.

Kasenia walked to the first sink, washed and dried her hands. "I'll walk back with you, unless you're staying."

The girl hurried into a stall. "Tell Chloe I'll be there in a minute."

After supper, the residents once again gathered in the living area to watch "Papa's Place." She didn't like seeing Brewster bigger than life on the large screen, but she was glad he'd left the compound. His empty eyes barely veiled the malevolence that saturated his soul. Did the others see it? She glanced at Lorraine, who sat beside her, her features limp and resigned. Whatever bond she and Brewster had when they were young was long gone. Kasenia felt sorry for the exhausted woman, for every woman and child trapped in his tortuous web.

When she escaped and reported Brewster to authorities, the gates would open. His women would be free to regain their lives and introduce their children to reality. But would they? Where would they go? She and Sam had a home in Tucson, but these women had been forced to sever connections with their families and friends. Maybe social services would help them get on their feet.

"I liked what I saw today," Brewster was saying. "Clean, well-kept property will ensure the buyers coming tomorrow can be confident our stock has had good care. Best of all, they'll be willing to pay a premium price."

More buyers? Did they want horses or cattle? And would she and Margo be expected to put on another show?

"First thing tomorrow," he continued, "the stalls and corrals must be thoroughly cleansed and the horses groomed. My women, my children and my animals must appear their best." He chuckled. "Even the pigs...and the foster boys."

Kasenia frowned. Did he really say what she thought he said?

Snickers popcorned about the room, telling her she'd heard correctly.

She clamped her jaw. Any shred of love she'd ever had for the nasty man evaporated like raindrops on a Tucson sidewalk. No doubt he felt the same disdain for Sam who had light skin and hair but wasn't one of his precious offspring.

Scanning the crowd, she wondered how those snickering children would act when their father was imprisoned, and they discovered he wasn't really married to their mother. And that they were illegitimate. Lorraine's children were likely legit, but not the others. What a mental, emotional mess they'd be when the truth surfaced. Would they seek counseling or be so brainwashed they couldn't comprehend their need for therapy?

"See you bright and early tomorrow." Brewster blew kisses at the screen. "May Spirit Father meet you in your dreams and fill your sleep with my face and my love for each of you."

Kasenia crossed her eyes. That would give her nightmares, for sure. Sam caught her eye and curled his lip. She grinned. He hadn't fallen under the Brewster Anton Wiley spell after all.

On the way out, Mateo bumped her elbow. *"Mi tío,"* he whispered, *"esta noche."*

"What?"

But he was gone.

Sam breezed by, murmuring, "Dark clothes, hide your hair."

And he, too, continued on, jogging with the boys toward the dorm. *Esta noche.* Tonight. *Really?*

Though her heartrate accelerated, she slowed her steps. *"Dark clothes,"* Sam had said. *"Cover your hair."*

Her jeans and hiking boots were dark, but both her sunhat and cowboy hat were light-colored. She pictured her t-shirts hanging in the camper closet. They were either white or pastel. Her sweatshirt was light blue.

But she'd seen several dark sweat jackets in the laundry room, unused during a Sonoran summer. She walked around the lodge to the back. A hoodie, as Sam called the jackets, would cover her arms *and* her hair. It might be hot, but it would make her less visible at night.

Kasenia slowly climbed the stairs to the door, walked the hall to the laundry room, and discovered it was locked again. Why? People needed to deposit dirty clothes and pick out clean items.

Hearing footsteps, she turned. "Oh, hi, Chloe."

Chloe, who had two young children with her, gave Kasenia a half curious, half-irritated look. "What're you doing here?"

"I need underwear and shirts, but the door's locked."

"Is it your time to select clothing?"

"I didn't know I had a specific time to do that."

Chloe pivoted to a chart posted on the opposite wall, a chart Kasenia hadn't noticed. She studied it for a moment then said, "Guess I haven't added your name. Lucky for you, I came to pick up pajamas for my kids. I'll let you in this once, but *only* this once. Get it?"

"I get it." Kasenia bit back further response. This was laundry they were discussing, not government secrets.

Chloe narrowed her eyes. "Are you the one who left the nasty towel by the door?"

Kasenia responded with a confused look. "Nasty towel?"

"Never mind." Chloe used the key dangling from the lanyard around her neck to unlock the door. She switched on the lights and stepped inside.

Kasenia and the kids followed her.

"Here are your pjs, kiddos, in my bag." Chloe stretched the wide strap over her head and onto her shoulder then took her children's hands. "Grab what you need, Kasenia, and turn the doorknob button to lock it before you leave. I've got to get these two and their siblings ready for bed."

"Thanks. I'll lock the door, although I don't understand why it's locked when everyone needs to deposit laundry and get clean clothes. This compound is supposedly a safe place."

"Beats me." Chloe shrugged. "I learned long ago not to ask why." She leaned close. "Thing is, Lorraine wants first pick. Have you noticed how she wears the best that Brewster brings us?"

Kasenia shook her head. She'd only noticed her own clothing on certain women.

"She's the queen bee, and she finds her ways to stay on her throne." Chloe bent to talk to her children. "Let's hurry and get your jammies on so you can have a night-night story."

The children, who'd been quiet, came alive. "Story, we want story."

Kasenia watched them go. Chloe was a nicer person with her kids in tow. She closed the door and snatched bras and panties from their respective slots in case she ran into Chloe again. From the teen boys' rack, she selected two dark t-shirts and an oversized hooded black sweat jacket.

Draping a towel and a washcloth over the entire selection, she twisted the lock before she switched off the lights, shut the door and headed for the back entry. But before she could exit the building, Veronica walked in. She eyed the towel like it might grow legs and attack her. "You the one who left a filthy towel in the hallway?"

Kasenia responded with the same confused look she'd used moments earlier. "Filthy towel?"

Veronica rolled her eyes. "What are you doing in here this time of night?"

What does it look like I'm doing? "I needed fresh clothing and clean linens."

"You have assigned days and times to access the laundry room."

"Chloe let me in. She hasn't added my name to the schedule yet. I appreciated her kindness."

"Chloe? Kind?" Veronica snorted. "That'll be the day the Sonoran melts into a rainforest. Get to your trailer."

18

— · —

K ASENIA DROPPED THE UNDERWEAR in a kitchen drawer then traded the t-shirt she wore for a black one. She hung the jacket on the hook by the door, stuffed socks into her hiking boots, after checking for scorpions, and set them on the floor below the jacket. Not knowing what else to do to prepare for their escape, she paced the camper floor, from the bench seat to the bed and back. The trailer floor creaked and groaned.

Finally, she gingerly knelt beside the bed and folded her hands on the mattress. The AC's steady throb vibrated her knees and worked upward through her torso. Her quavering words melded with the rumble.

Dear God...This may be the stupidest thing I've ever done. Yet, I can't ignore a chance to help Sam escape Shadow Ranch. We might be captured. We might be beaten within an inch of our lives. We might be killed.

My Bible says you're against evil, and Babushka Irina says you're more powerful than the most evil person or force on earth. You're our only hope. Please help us all. Amen.

Getting up, she turned off the AC, opened the curtains, windows and door and locked the screen door. She needed to hear Tomás, but she didn't need any surprise visitors.

Clouds and a rare cooling breeze had moved in that afternoon. The air coming through the windows smelled of dust, but it had lost some of the day's heat.

Seated on the edge of the hard bed with yard light for illumination, she loosened her hair from the braid and brushed it out. She had a feeling this could be her last chance for a while to wash her hair.

Mi tío...esta noche rang in her brain. *My uncle, tonight.* She couldn't think of any other way to translate Mateo's words.

Her long hair crackled with electricity. The desert, she'd discovered, was even drier than Tucson. Her hair had become so flyaway, she had to keep it in a ponytail or a braid. She dropped the brush on the bed and washed her hair in the tiny kitchen sink then rebraided it. Last thing she needed was out-of-control hair when they broke out of the compound.

Lifting the hoodie from the hook, she tried it on for size. Her reflection in the mirror was dim, but she could see enough to know the jacket covered her hands to her knuckles and her hair was hidden by the hood. It also covered most of her face. Perfect. She ran the zipper up and down, grateful it worked. She hadn't thought to check it earlier.

Now, all she could do was wait.

Kasenia sat on the bed and leaned against the wall. She was so tired she might not awaken if Tomás threw rocks at the trailer. Maybe she should spend the night on the rear bumper like she did before. But cool air was wafting through the trailer and the bed was so, so inviting.

Still dressed, she stretched across the thin mattress. Every muscle in her body ached, including her eyelids. She'd relax for just a few minutes.

A high-pitched scream jolted Kasenia upright. Eyes wide, heart pounding, she searched the trailer's dark interior. Where did that come from? Was Brewster hurting someone?

Clutching her collarbone, she held her breath.

The scream came again from behind the trailer. It ended in a yelp followed by three more yelps.

"A coyote," Kasenia breathed. "Just a coyote."

She leaned against the wall, hoping the animal would leave and let her return to sleep. "Oh, no." She straightened. What if Tomás had thrown rocks, but that hadn't awakened her, so he howled like a coyote to get her attention?

Sleep-haze fogged her brain as she stumbled from the trailer, squinting in the porchlight. She felt her way along the camper's side, came to the back corner and stopped to let her eyes adjust.

A horse snorted.

Tomás, thank God.

She took another step.

"Evenin', *Missus Wiley*." The gravelly voice came from the other side of the fence. "Like my coyote imitation?"

Marlin.

"My way to initiate the new brides." He snickered. "Welcome to Shadow Ranch."

She flipped around, stomped up the metal stairs and into the trailer, slamming both doors behind her.

He laughed out loud. "Sweet dreams, *Missus Wiley*."

Swallowing a nasty retort, she closed the curtains and locked the door. What a jerk. She fell onto the hard bed. If only he'd been Tomás. She rolled to her side. Mateo had said, *Mi tío...esta noche.* Surely, he meant tonight. But if Marlin was on the prowl...

This time, loud pounding awakened her. Kasenia bolted upright. Brewster?

"Sis, wake up." Sam's whisper came from the window near her head. "Hurry and dress. Margo's out at the barn, but she could show up any minute."

She slid the curtain back. "Thanks, Sam. I'll be right there." What happened to Tomás? Had she slept through his signal? But Sam was still here, and he was hurrying her to the dining room. He and the other boys hadn't left the compound.

She pulled the black shirt over her head, changed to another t-shirt, then splashed water on her face, swished toothpaste around her mouth and rinsed. Wiping her lips, she moved the boots to the bottom of the closet and dropped the sweat jacket on top. Intruders might become suspicious if they saw a jacket and boots by the door. With a quick scan to make sure she'd left no other telltale items out, she stepped from the trailer into a rose-streaked dawn. The morning air was dusty, yet fresh, and tinged with creosote.

"You're the best." She squeezed his arm. "I overslept."

"If it wasn't for Margo," he grumbled, "I'd sleep for a month." He started for the big house.

"Wait." Kasenia grabbed his elbow. "We never get to talk. About last night…" She glanced around. "I thought the uncle—"

"Shh." He frowned. "We'd better go help the guys."

"I saw you and the boys hauling rocks, while Brewster's kids had a water fight. So unfair." Illuminated by the porchlight, he was more tanned than she'd ever seen and his arms and shoulders more buff.

"They make us work harder 'cause we're not Brewster's kids." He grunted. "I tell the guys we're lucky. I'd rather do slave labor than be stuck with him for a dad the rest of my life." He clenched his fists. "Some of his kids are just as mean as he is. They call us nasty names."

"I hope you consider the source."

"They tell the guys from Mexico their dark skin is a mark of the devil. That's why nobody wants them and why Brewster's kids avoid them. They say Mom and Dad don't want me. It's why I lived with you and Grandpa before Brewster dumped us here." He paused. "I sorta believe them. I mean—"

"Sam, that's not true." She turned to look him in the eyes as best she could in the dim light. "They were so excited when you were born, so excited I was jealous and felt left out. I loved holding you and giving you your bottle, but I did naughty things to get their attention. Right now, they're engrossed in their careers. Did you know their goal is to retire by the time they're fifty?"

"Hadn't heard that."

"Last time I talked with Mom about the wedding we were supposed to have in Russia, she told me she couldn't wait to hug us. She hoped we'd have lots of family time before we returned to Arizona."

He kicked a rock and it hit the fence, clanging like a dull bell.

"I'm not making this up, Sam." She leaned closer. "Mom said she and Dad miss us, a lot. We've been separated far too long."

"They fly around the world. Could have flown here for a weekend now and then."

"I know, I know." She sighed. "We expected the Russian wedding would be in late spring and we'd be together at Babushka Irina's house. Then it was early summer, then late summer, then... Well, you know how it went. I should have suspected something when Brewster delayed it the first time."

He snorted. "Good thing the *real wedding*..." He made air quotes. "Never happened."

They crossed the yard and climbed the veranda stairs together. Risky behavior, Kasenia knew, but it was worth the gamble to spend a couple minutes with her brother. She could smell toast before they opened the screen and stepped inside. Sam's dormmates were hard at work, prepping for breakfast. They nodded but said nothing.

"It's our lucky morning," Sam muttered. "She's not here yet. I'll get the salt and pepper shakers." He strode toward the walk-in pantry just off the kitchen.

Kasenia grabbed paper tablecloths and hurried as best she could into the dining room. The boys liked her to arrange the tablecloths because they had trouble centering them. She was straightening chairs when Mateo came in with more table coverings. She gave him a questioning glance.

"You want?" he asked, holding out the packets.

She took them and he leaned close. "Mi tío lo siente. He, uh, him say sorry. Vaca enferma. He help Wanda y Margo."

Kasenia frowned. "Vaca?" She would take one word at a time.

"Sí, vaca." He looked behind him then emitted a low guttural sound.

"What...?" She gave him an apologetic shrug. "Sorry, I don't understand."

He made the sound again, and again.

"Oh, you mean 'cow'?"

"Sí." His face lit. "Enferma." He stuck out his tongue and made a gagging motion.

"A cow," she whispered, "a cow is sick?"

"Si, mi tío—"

"Almost time." Margo barged into the room. "Everything ready for breakfast?"

"Just about," Kasenia said.

"Two minutes."

She thanked Mateo. Tomás didn't need to report his actions to her. But knowing why he didn't come last night renewed her faith in him, what little she had. Trusting anyone at Shadow Ranch was risky. Unfolding a tablecloth, she asked, "Want to help me spread this?"

He moved to the other end of the table.

An early ray of sunlight through the window grid spilled a cross-shaped shadow over the wood floor.

"Señorita, mire la cruz," Mateo murmured. "La cruz de Cristo."

Kasenia smiled. "The cross of Christ." She wasn't sure why, but the familiar symbol from her babushka's church settled peace on her soul. She smoothed the tablecloth, covered the remaining tables with Mateo's assistance, and returned to where people were already queued at the serving table, chatting quietly among themselves.

Though most ignored her, Rachel offered a cheery, "Good morning."

Kasenia returned her greeting and picked up a paper plate, painfully aware standing in line to eat with Brewster's women and children felt almost normal. Beyond the big window, the chain-link fence loomed above the trailers, the razor wire catching the early morning light. *Never, never, never,* she reminded herself. *Never forget who you are or where you are.*

Like the others, she and Sergei were trapped inside a compound patrolled by heartless security guards. This was *not* a normal way to live. This was a prison. Polygamy was unlawful in Russia *and* in Arizona. And so was jailing innocent women and children.

Surprised she was assigned to work in the bakery rather than the horse barn to prepare for the sale, Kasenia caught up with Margo on their way out of the lodge. "Do you need help grooming the horses?"

"The potential buyers cancelled." Margo, who was dressed in shorts and a t-shirt, threaded her hair through the back of her ball cap and pulled the bill low over her eyes. "Good thing. Running around in that hot getup yesterday afternoon was more than enough horseshow for me."

"I agree." Kasenia stopped at the bakery door. "Have a good afternoon."

Margo nodded and kept walking.

Despite the woman's mercurial temperament, Kasenia was disappointed she wouldn't be spending the afternoon in the peaceful barn. But maybe the bakery would be interesting and make the day go fast. Tonight had to be the night. This was Wednesday, and the "sneak preview" was a day away. *Please I...*

Alana met her at the door. "What do you know about baking?"

"I've done it." Kasenia glanced around the spotless room that smelled of yeast, flour and sugar.

"What kind of answer is that?"

"The truth." If Alana didn't have the courtesy to greet her, she could be curt too.

"Have you made bread?"

"Yes."

"What else?" Hands on her bulging belly, Alana huffed like Kasenia was an irritating child.

"Cookies, muffins, scones..."

"Pies?"

"Yes."

"Good." Alana pointed to a pan of dough balls at the end of the wide butcher block counter. "You'll roll out pie crusts from those dough balls."

Kasenia walked to the sink to wash her hands. *She could have told me to roll the dough and skipped the interrogation.* Oh, well. One more day, one more crazy woman, one more chore.

The exact size for the pie shells had been drawn onto the wooden counter. And Alana had an exact method for pressing dough to an exact thickness and shape. Kasenia redid the first shell four times before Alana was satisfied.

By lunchtime, her shoulders and arms were sore, and she was tired of standing. But then, she hurt everywhere, thanks to Brewster's beating and the Shadow Ranch culture of work till you drop. Sitting to eat felt good.

After lunch, Lorraine gave assignments to everyone else first. Then she asked Kasenia if she'd ever operated a sewing machine.

"Yes."

"More than once?"

"Yes."

"Can you sew a straight line?"

Kasenia didn't bother to answer.

"Well..." Lorraine sniffed. "Brewster insists you be exposed to every facet of our family business, so we'll take a chance on your sewing skills."

Kasenia folded her arms.

"Brittany will appraise your skills—or lack thereof—and report her findings to me."

"I'm sure she will." Without waiting for Lorraine's reaction, Kasenia left the building. For once, no one else was around. Taking the veranda stairs to the ground, she heard a high-pitched call and saw a bald eagle circling above the ranch.

Soaring through the cloudless blue sky, it dipped and swooped as if it was enjoying the sensation of free flight. Most likely, it was hunting, but seeing the majestic bird, an American symbol of freedom, filled her with hope. Was God giving her a sign she would soon fly free too? She watched the bird sail higher and higher until it disappeared from sight.

When she reached the craft room, several boys and girls were already assembling jewelry and leather items, painting tree ornaments or ironing quilt sections. Brittany led Kasenia to a sewing machine, the only one of six not in use. Small fabric squares were stacked beside it. "Sew this piece to this," Brittany said, "and then that one to the next one. Quarter-inch seams. Understand?"

Kasenia quickly calculated. One-fourth inch was around six-and-a-half millimeters. "Yes."

"When you have ten sections of twenty, press the seams, then sew the sections together. Does that make sense?"

"Yes." She'd helped her babushka assemble many a quilt for village newlyweds and newborns. They'd used a treadle sewing machine until the village got electricity.

Stitching quilt pieces together was a welcome change from rolling dough under Alana's watchful eye. Sewing machines whirred, steam irons hissed, rubber mallets pounded holes into leather, and beads and metal clinked. The smell of steamed cotton blended with that of leather and paint.

Kasenia's mind wandered as she worked. She hadn't had a chance to talk with Sam since earlier that morning, but she'd seen him and the other boys at lunch. They appeared tired. The kids around her worked hard and rarely spoke, but they labored in air-conditioned comfort protected from the sun's harsh rays. The dorm boys' treatment wasn't fair, but soon, life at Shadow Ranch would be a bad memory for them. She had to keep believing Tomás would rescue them—or devise her own plan.

What if she befriended one of the men who knew the code? For sure, that would be playing with fire. If Brewster found out, he'd beat her worse than before, or kill her, like he killed Beth. Her heartbeat raced and so did her sewing machine. She eased the pressure on the foot pedal. Once again, she had to rein in her imagination before panic overtook reason.

Following supper, dining room cleanup and more sewing in the craft room, Kasenia joined the "family" in the big room for Brewster's latest Papa's Place episode. "I didn't forget my promise," he declared from the front seat of his Corvette. "Izzy the Ice Cream Man and I are bringing you ice cream bars and Diet Dr. Pepper tomorrow night. I'm that kinda dad."

His audience cheered.

A broad smile on his tanned face, he waited until they calmed. "He'll play music from his truck, and we'll have a dance. You know how I love to dance."

For a moment, Kasenia was transported back in time to the romantic honeymoon she'd shared with Brewster and the magical night they danced beneath sparkling chandeliers. She closed her eyes, burying the memory before humiliation, loss and rage overwhelmed her. She'd grieve later. This was neither the time nor the place.

The younger children giggled and waved their hands. The older ones clapped and tried not to appear overly excited. Sam and the Hispanic boys showed no emotion.

Brewster admonished the listeners to speed up production for the weekend sales, then blew kisses and hugged himself, which Kasenia thought appropriate. The children, and some of the wives, hugged themselves and blew kisses in return. "Bye bye, Daddy." "Bye, sweetheart." "See you tomorrow."

Exhausted by the time she reached her trailer, Kasenia changed to a dark t-shirt and plopped onto the bench by the door. What did she need to do to prepare for tonight? Sleep was tempting, but she didn't dare.

She rehung the sweat jacket on the hook by the door and set the sock-stuffed boots on the floor beneath it. *Will it be tonight, God?* Heart pounding, she rummaged through her satchel until she felt the travel Bible the bookstore clerk had given her. The jacket's pockets were large enough to hold it. Maybe it would somehow protect her and her companions.

She fell to her knees, elbows on the bench. "God, we're running out of time," she whispered. "Brewster's perverts will be here soon. I know you know, but—"

Sh-wee, sh-wee, sh-wee. A shrill whistling birdcall resounded nearby, the chirp much like that of a desert cardinal. She hadn't heard one at the ranch, and she'd never heard one sing this late at night.

The call came again, more urgent than before. *Sh-wee, sh-wee, sh-wee!*

And she knew.

Yanking the socks from her boots, she slid them on and shoved her feet into the boots, tying them tight before she lifted the jacket off the hook. She slipped her arms into the sleeves and the hood over her head, and with trembling fingers somehow managed to connect the zipper halves and zip it to the top.

She opened the door partway to check for observers. An insistent *sh-wee, sh-wee, sh-wee* rang out from behind the camper.

I'm coming, Tomás, I'm coming.

19

— · —

S TEPPING FROM THE CAMPER, Kasenia carefully closed both doors behind her, took the stairs to the packed dirt and tiptoed to the corner, her porchlight shadow preceding her. She'd considered turning the light off but decided the wrong person might question why. She reached the bumper and hesitated.

"Señorita," came the words, barely a whisper in the wind. "You fly like un pájaro al molino, bird to windwheel...agua tanque. Follow fence. Stay down, en las sombras, shadows."

With a click of his tongue, he leaned into the saddle and the horse hurried ahead, not trotting, but walking faster than before, the pair mere phantoms in the hazy moonlight.

Kasenia pulled the hood over her forehead and crouched behind the camper. She wasn't sure exactly what Tomás had said, and she didn't have time to work through a translation. But she understood *windwheel* to be windmill and *agua tanque* to be water tank. She would follow the fence that direction, and she would stay down.

Were the boys doing the same thing? Would she meet them at the windmill? *God, help us all.* She leaped from the camper's yard-light shadow into that of the neighboring trailer.

Hunched beneath the window, she waited and listened. Hearing no sound except the horse's steady movement through the brush ahead, she scooted far enough to peer around the trailer. Nothing stirred.

She scurried behind the next mobile home and checked every direction, fearing a guard or vaquero might step from a doublewide for a smoke and see her furtive movements.

A baby's cry came through the air-conditioning unit, calmed by a mother's muted voice. Kasenia couldn't tell who the voice belonged to, but it didn't matter. She was leaving the harem, and soon they could do the same.

Trailer by trailer by trailer, she skirted the compound then darted from behind the last mobile home to the horse barn, moving as fast as she dared. Breathless, she pressed against the barn wall. An owl hooted in the distance. Another answered from farther away.

She stifled a dusty sneeze.

Step by step, sliding noiselessly along the wall, she grew closer to her destination. It was only the beginning of their journey to safety. But it was a beginning. All she could do was follow Tomás's instructions to meet at the windmill and hope for the best.

Angry shouts shattered the silent night.

Kasenia gasped and froze.

Her already elevated heartrate spiked, pounding her ears. She dropped to a crouch, willing her dark form to meld with the barn wall.

Peppered with profanity, the shouts continued but didn't come closer. After a long, tortured moment, she located the source. The angry exchange came from the doublewides. Had a poker game gotten out of hand? She released the breath she'd been holding. Disturbing as the argument was in the still night, it meant the guards weren't chasing after her.

At the corner, Kasenia knelt to find her bearings. The moon hovered above the mountains to the southeast, slightly wider than last night's sliver. Though it didn't offer much light to guide them, it might make them more visible. Not good.

The big lights mounted near the peaks of the barn roofs were both turned off, which was good, because three corrals stood between her and the windmill across from the dairy barn. She would stay low and work her way around each corral.

Out in the pasture, a horse whinnied. Nearby, something rustled in the underbrush. Stirred by a breeze, the revolving windmill blades reflected glints of yard light. Below the blades, the pump powered by their rotation cranked a steady beat, metal grating and clanking against metal.

Stooped down, she hugged the rails and felt her way toward the windmill.

Checking every direction.

Listening.

Hardly daring to breathe.

The cardinal call came again, this time from near the windmill. *Sh-wee, sh-wee, sh-wee!* Urging her to *hurry, hurry, hurry.*

Kasenia reached the last corral, the one outside the dairy barn. The manure smell was stronger here and the pump's rhythmic clang sounded loud in the quiet night. Creak, groan, bang, pause. Creak, groan, bang, pause.

Something flew past her head. A bat? She shuddered.

Gazing up the windmill's legs, she had to wonder what Tomás's plan was. The pump tower was tall, nine to twelve meters in height, with a platform just below the blades. Did he expect them to climb up to the platform and jump over the razor wire to the ground on the far side? Surely not. Maybe he had a rope.

Sh-wee, sh-wee, sh-wee!

Right. She needed to move. Now.

Kasenia checked her surroundings then scuttled to the tower, swung one leg then the other over a crossbar and crouched beside the noisy pump centered beneath the pump rod. The smell of rusted metal and earthy hay filled her senses.

"Over here, Sis." Sam's whisper came in the pump's pause.

Kasenia squinted, seeing only hay bales she didn't remember being there earlier.

"Through the bales."

Now she could see a narrow gap between two stacks five or six bales high. She clambered over a second crossbar and slipped through the opening.

Bent forms hunkered by the fence. She drew close. "How do—?"

The fence opened and someone was pulling her through. "Stay down." Sam's voice.

She squatted.

"Hold still." He touched her face.

"What—?"

"Close your mouth."

He patted something on her cheek that felt like moisturizing cream, but she had a feeling it wasn't because it smelled like burnt rubber. Only the whites of his eyes showed. He whispered, "Used axle grease to hide our gringo faces."

Oh... She hated to think what it would do to her skin. And Sam's. But a bad complexion was a small price to pay for freedom.

Others knelt nearby, but no one spoke. As far as she could tell, they were wearing hoodies. The darkhaired boys might not need to cover their heads, but she was glad they took that extra precaution. Behind them, a horse grazed, its shape vaguely visible in the muted moonlight.

One horse for ten people? She counted again in her head. Tomás, seven foster boys, Sam, and herself. That made ten.

Hearing quiet clinks, Kasenia shifted her gaze. Someone was doing something to the fence. Wiring it back together?

Moments later, Tomás hovered near her shoulder. "Go now."

Sam dabbed her chin, sealed the plastic bag he'd been holding, and handed it to Tomás, who murmured, "Walk low. No talk."

He spoke to the others, his soft Spanish barely louder than a sigh, then stepped to the horse and hung his hat on the saddlehorn. Leading the horse, he started across the pasture.

Stooped like aging monks, the boys followed single file behind him. Kasenia took up the rear after Sam. Bent down, she turned again and again to check the compound. So far, no sirens, no flashing lights, no Marlin charging at them on a horse or in a pickup.

Thank goodness she'd worn her hiking boots. She hoped Sam was wearing his. So many kinds of cacti grew in the desert, they were sure to step on one. The sound of their footsteps crunching through dry vegetation seemed extra loud. But maybe from afar, listeners would assume the animals were searching for taller grass, or whatever livestock did at night.

Though barely visible, the tall wind turbines stood like silent sentinels on the cliff above the compound. Their long white blades rotated slowly, reflecting hints of moonlight. Darkness hid the stubby satellite dish and the cell tower frame, yet the blinking red light on top was bright in the night.

Wild melodic yip-howls erupted from up on the ridge. A shiver ran down Kasenia's spine. *Coyotes.* Some people called them "song dogs." As romanticized as the name was, the animals were too close for comfort. Coyotes supposedly avoided horses and humans. But was that always the case?

The closer they got to the pasture pump, the louder its clank sounded. Ahead of her, one of the boys tripped and let out a cry. Everyone halted.

Tomás whispered, "Down."

As if one organism, the group crouched, and he walked the horse back to the boy. After a brief, quiet Spanish conversation, Tomás turned toward the windmill again.

They stopped at the watering tank beneath the tall wooden structure. A horse nickered, and she caught sight of more horses bunched around the windmill legs. Tomás untied one and handed the reins to Ulises. He did the same with the other horses, motioning to Sam, Cesar and Kasenia to take the reins.

Without speaking, he returned to his horse and indicated Kasenia and the boys should follow him single file. Those without horses to lead were to trail directly behind him.

The farther they walked from the ranch, the better Kasenia felt, though she knew at any moment their absence could be discovered and... She swallowed and tried not to think about what might happen.

The next time they stopped, Tomás assigned two riders to each horse. He asked Sam, "Ride no saddle?"

Sam shrugged. "I can try."

"Hold el pelo. Jorge hold you."

"El pelo?" Sam asked.

Cesar whispered, "It mean hair."

"Oh, the mane, right."

"We go fast," Tomás added, "No demasiado rápido."

"Not too fast," Cesar translated.

Tomás helped Sam mount the horse and then boosted Jorge behind him. "Hold to Sam."

Next, he had Kasenia place her left foot in his clasped hands and swing her right leg over the horse. She grabbed the mane and adjusted her seating, muffling a sneeze in her elbow. The horse smelled like it had been rolling in the dirt.

Tomás lifted Benicio and settled him behind her. "Hold la señorita."

Benicio put his hands on her waist, barely touching. Kasenia knew hanging onto her was awkward for the young boy, but she had a feeling his grip would tighten later.

Tomás paired Raúl with Ulises, Ismael with Cesar, and had his nephew, Mateo, ride with him. He took the lead and Kasenia brought up the rear, moving away from the ranch at a quiet walk. Every few minutes, she twisted to observe the Shadow Ranch headquarters but saw no sign of life. Around them, the desert was alive with cricket chirps, coyote yips, owl hoots, and rustles and crackles in the bushes. Once, she thought she heard a growl but wasn't sure. Something flew over them, and she was fairly certain a rabbit hopped past.

The horses ahead broke into a trot.

Kasenia nudged her mount with her knees, and it took off. Pressing her thighs against the horse's sides, she gripped the mane. Benicio hugged her bruised ribs so hard she could barely breathe, but he was out of sync with her and with the horse.

"Benicio," she whispered over her shoulder, "hold with your knees, legs around el caballo. *Before we bounce off into the cactus.* "Move with el caballo. Me entiendes?"

"Sí."

He relaxed his arms and tightened his legs, and together they matched the horse's rhythm.

Flying through the night, she longed to push her hood back and feel the wind in her hair. But she couldn't take that chance, not yet. A wispy cloud floated overhead, blurring the moon's vague light and obscuring their departure. She hoped Tomás and the horses could see better than she could.

And that he knew where he was going.

She couldn't see Sam, didn't know Tomás, had no idea where he was taking them, no idea what would happen to her and her brother and the foster boys. She and Sam had a home to return to, if they could find their way there. But the boys didn't.

What if Brewster and his men caught up with them? She was still bruised and hurting from the beating. And he'd threatened her with worse. She hated to think what he'd do to the boys, besides offering their bodies to pedophiles, like ancient worshippers who sacrificed children to idols.

As if he felt her tension, Benicio spoke softly through her hood. "Señorita, Jesús, he make libres."

Libres? Kasenia mouthed the word. It sounded similar to "liberated." She turned her head. "Sí, Benicio. Hay-sus made us free." She had to leave her fears with Jesus. If he could free them from Shadow Ranch, he could get them home.

The air cooled and she felt a breeze on her cheeks. Along with the dust the horses stirred, the gentle wind carried a fresh sweet smell she couldn't identify. Was it a harbinger of better things to come?

Her horse snorted and flung its head then sidestepped as if something had crossed its path. She and Benicio held tight, and when she urged the horse ahead, it responded.

She wasn't sure how much time had passed when their mounts slowed to a walk. And then they were beside a barbed-wire fence and Tomás was dismounting. He tied his horse to a post and helped the boys and Kasenia slide off their mounts.

Cesar stretched the bottom two fence wires apart and signaled for them to crawl through.

Kasenia scooted between the wires, and from the other side, watched wide-eyed as the horses wandered away. Now, she and the boys were on foot on a dirt road that very likely led straight to Shadow Ranch. Brewster's men could easily catch them. They had vehicles.

Sam, whose face she could barely see, came up beside her. "Sis," he murmured, his white teeth accented by his darkened features, "We're free."

"Yes, we are." She didn't dare share her concerns with him or the boys and ruin their joy.

The moment Tomás was through the fence, he muttered, "Vamos," and charged across the road and up a treed incline. She and the boys followed, weaving between the sparse trees, staying close enough to see the person ahead in the dim light.

Kasenia was about to beg for a few minutes rest, when Tomás stopped in front of a framed black opening that appeared to be an abandoned mine entrance. They gathered round, resting their hands on their thighs and inhaling the pine-scented breeze.

"Señorita y amigos, por favor esperen, you wait," Tomás whispered. "I come pronto." He pulled a knife from a belt sheath and cut a branch off a scrub oak bush. Swishing it on the ground, he began retracing their route.

Kasenia sat on a rock.

"What's he doing?" Sam asked, his voice low.

"Make zapato, shoe mark go away," Cesar whispered.

"Wiping out our shoeprints," Sam said. "That's smart."

Kasenia agreed, though she didn't like being left alone. She could see the ranch lights from where she sat. Marlin and gang were too close for comfort. The boys' jittery glances every direction told her they were nervous too. Maybe they should formulate a backup plan in case Tomás didn't return. She was about to motion Sam over to discuss their options, when Tomás appeared from a different direction than he'd taken down the slope. She shook her head. The man was a mountain goat.

Hardly taking a breath, Tomás pointed at the mine opening and muttered something in Spanish.

Cesar translated, "This place they try find us."

Kasenia frowned. *So why...?*

"We go different into mine."

Oh...

"If hear noise," Cesar continued, "maybe guards, maybe El Jefe."

"El Jefe?" Kasenia asked. "Who's that."

"Hah-gwahr. Gato grande, big cat. Es jaguar en Inglés. It mean *The Boss.*"

"Cool," Sam murmured. "I didn't know jaguars lived in Arizona."

"Come from Mexico," Cesar explained. "El Jefe here long time."

"And we're going inside?" Kasenia blurted.

"Señorita, no…" Tomás shushed her. "No worry."

"We're making more tracks," Sam said. "Will the Shadow Ranch guys notice?"

"Los hombres no son buenos…no good trackers. Pero…" He shrugged then handed the branch to Sam. "We go, tu barres, you sweep. I show you."

Sam looked at the branch, looked at Tomás. "Okay."

Tomás pointed into the valley. "Gracias a Dios, guards no wake."

"Thanks to God," Cesar said.

Everyone seemed to breathe a little easier.

"Will they wonder where you are, Tomás?" Kasenia asked.

"Hombres, they beben, they drink cerveza, jugar al póquer, fumar peyote. Sleep long."

"The men, they drink beer," Cesar said, "gamble, smoke peyote."

"I see." But when Margo went to wake the boys to prep the tables for breakfast and found them missing, Shadow Ranch would erupt. No matter how hungover the guards were, they'd be galvanized into action.

Tomás demonstrated to Sam the best way to erase their tracks yet not leave suspicious streaks and then motioned the group forward.

They walked single file past an old ore cart on a short section of tracks and onto a trail. Winding between trees and rocks, again keeping each other in sight, they climbed ever higher. Other than their quiet footsteps and heavy breathing, the only sounds were occasional twig snaps and stumbles accompanied by grunts. And the rustle of Sam's tree branch as he brushed away their shoeprints.

Tomás stopped at a tall boulder stack near the top of the mountain. The trees had thinned, and the moon was no longer obscured by clouds. He motioned for them to wait and scrambled up the rocks.

Thankful for a moment to catch her breath, Kasenia unzipped the jacket partway. The air was cooler at this elevation, but she couldn't drop the hood or remove the jacket. Not yet. Minutes ticked by. She tried not to think the worst, like she'd done earlier.

A shadowy figure materialized in the gloom.

Kasenia jumped and knocked against Sam, who murmured, "It's Tomás."

"We go." Tomás nudged Sam and made the brushing motion again.

They circled the boulders until he stopped beside a blackened tree trunk with a handful of bare branches and a huge nest at the top. Tomás scrambled onto a big boulder and slipped between two more. Mateo followed, then Jorge, and then the others. Kasenia wanted to go last, but Sam waved her ahead. "Gotta sweep."

Kasenia hated to lose sight of her brother in the dark dangerous night, but she had to keep up. Once again grateful for her hiking boots, she clambered over the boulder and squeezed through the narrow opening. Ahead of her, one of the boys skirted a tree that had sprouted between rocks.

Sam scrambled behind her.

Hurrying ahead, she felt her way over boulders large and small, stumbling, slipping, bumping her elbows and knees, glad she wore a sweatshirt and jeans. On her feet, then on her knees, she scraped her hands on rough metallic-smelling stones that still held a hint of the day's heat and wormed through a narrow channel sideways, breathing hard. Only the stars glimmering beyond the passageway's exit kept her from panic.

Escaping the corridor's confinement, Kasenia stepped into a circle of truck-size boulders and nearly stumbled over the boys crouched around Tomás. She could barely see him, but he was tugging at something below a narrow rock overhang. Kasenia quieted her huffs and sat by the boys, catching whiffs of rock, dirt, pine—and sweaty bodies. Sam joined them, still panting.

An inch at a time, Tomás slid a short stubby log from beneath the overhang. A tiny glint of moonlight reflected off the silent two-way radio attached to his belt.

The towering boulders made her feel safe and hidden, yet any sound she and the others made could be heard in the quiet night. Tomás was wise to keep noise at a minimum.

An owl hooted in the distance, and a bat fluttered over their heads.

Kasenia's insides jumped. But those were good sounds, normal sounds on a mountain. Surely, they'd cover whatever Tomás was doing.

He sat back. "Es suficiente." He took a small flashlight from his belt and shined it under the overhang, revealing a narrow gap. "We go."

20

—·—

K ASENIA STARED AT TOMÁS. The hole didn't appear big enough for a child, let alone chunky Jorge.

Just as quickly as he switched the light on, Tomás turned it off.

"Señorita," he murmured, "you primero, luego los chicos."

Cesar touched her arm. "You first, then boys."

"Go, Sis," Sam said. "I'll be right behind you."

"But..."

"Ladies first."

Had they switched roles? She'd always watched over him. Was he watching over her now?

"Sí, ahora," Tomás whispered, his voice urgent.

"That means *now*." Sam nudged her.

Kasenia scooted closer.

"I show." Tomás gave her the flashlight and squatted. In one swift motion, he went from all fours onto his stomach. Feet first, he slid into the cavity and disappeared. A rattle of pebbles accompanied a soft thump.

"Señorita," came his soft call, "la luz, por favor."

Balanced on her knees, Kasenia lowered the flashlight into the black void. She couldn't see Tomás, but she felt him take the flashlight and heard him whisper, "Gracias. Venga, come."

Before she could change her mind, she swung around, flattened on her stomach, and pushed backward, letting her feet drop into nothingness. Without warning, Tomás grabbed her legs and pulled her in and down.

Kasenia gasped then landed on solid ground. She crouched and looked around, seeing nothing. "La luz," Tomás whispered, and light blazed in the narrow, rugged chamber where he stood at full height. Kasenia straightened.

"Lo siento, sorry, señorita." He handed her the flashlight, aimed downward, and urged the boys to join them.

Kasenia stepped away, but not too far into the mountain's pitch-black bowels, and drew a shaky breath. How in the world did Tomás find this place?

Mateo came next. Tomás helped him get his footing. One by one, the other boys joined them, Sam at the tail end, branch in hand.

Tomás grasped a metal handhold affixed to the wall and maneuvered upward, using a second handhold and toeholds in the craggy wall. He grabbed a stubby branch on the log he'd pushed aside and slowly pulled it over the opening, plugging the hole and hiding them from Brewster's men.

Kasenia hoped that was the case, that Marlin and gang didn't know about the hideout. And no bobcats, mountain lions or jaguars could move the log and follow them in.

She offered Tomás the flashlight.

"Un momento, por favor." He stepped to a pile of branches by the wall and grabbed what looked like a giant black cotton swab. Pulling a lighter from his pocket, he lit the thick end, and it became a smoky torch. "Gato grande, no like."

Even with her limited Spanish, Kasenia knew *gato grande* meant *big cat*. So, big cats *were* a concern. Lucky for her and the boys, Tomás had obviously been here before. She had to believe he knew what to expect and how to handle whatever came their way. She had no other choice.

Pocketing the lighter and the flashlight, he led them along the pebble-strewn, downward-sloping shaft. She assumed the rear position behind Sam. The oily smoke made her cough, but she muffled it in her elbow.

She was about to shove back her hood to enjoy the corridor's cool air when she saw Sam hunch. If his head nearly touched the ceiling, hers would also. The hood would protect her from spiders and other creepy-crawly things. She tried not to think what those might be.

Their footsteps and muted coughs echoed. Or maybe the sounds came from behind. Kasenia pivoted for a glimpse of who or what might be trailing them but saw an inky void and quickly swung around, careful not to bump her head or slide on the rubble.

She should have been relieved the entrance hole was blocked. But with a little effort, the log could be shoved aside by man or beast. Staring ahead, she should have been glad for torchlight and a place to hide from Marlin and his men. But the black tunnel seemed to close in on her. Dread constricted her chest.

Only once had she ventured into a cave, and that was when she was a little girl. She hadn't like the experience, at all. She'd been with her parents in some tropical country. Everything was bright green outside the cave but black as midnight inside, except where the guide's light shone. To her, the dank, dark, muddy chamber felt like being locked in a stuffy closet, but far worse.

Before the cave incident, she hadn't cried much, according to her parents. But that day, she'd screamed until her father apologized to their guide and rushed her out. Now that she thought about it, the moldy smell might have been what set her off. It made her head pound and her chest hurt. Every breath was painful.

Beneath the smoke cloud, this tunnel smelled earthy, maybe musty. But not moldy. She fought her mushrooming panic. It was far better than being trapped at Shadow Ranch the rest of her life, watching Sam and the foster boys being used and abused day after day, night after night. Never having a chance at real life.

For them, she had to take herself into her hands, as her babushka used to tell her, and not panic. Seeing the boys' hazy forms ahead calmed her heart and slowed her breathing. *Thank you, God in heaven,* she prayed, hoping he could hear her inside the mountain. *You answered my prayers for these boys.*

Tomás stopped at a juncture of three tunnels. Here, the ceiling was higher, and she and Sam were able to stand upright.

"Ah," Sam whispered. "Feels good."

For a brief moment, all was quiet, except for a melodic trickle of water somewhere nearby.

Something skittered past. Kasenia gulped a shriek, only because it might have echoed through the mine and out onto the hillside. The creature was a rat. Just a rat. A small one by the sound of it...maybe.

Tomás gave the torch to Mateo and handed the flashlight to Jorge, directing him to focus the beam on a small protrusion in the tunnel wall. He jiggled the chunk loose then reached inside the hole. With a murmured, "Alabar a Dios," he held a big cast-iron skeleton key to the light.

The Hispanic boys echoed, "Alabar a Dios," and Sam translated for Kasenia. "They're saying, 'Praise God.'"

"Yes," she whispered, "praise God." She didn't know what door the rusty key would open, but Tomás appeared pleased.

He replaced the rock and retrieved the flashlight and torch.

Narrow, rusted, ore-car tracks ran through the left and right tunnels. Tomás led them into the middle tunnel and resumed the hasty pace. Here, the trackless floor had plenty of gravel-size rubble to trip through, but it was flat, not inclined like before, and they could stand at full height.

Ten, maybe fifteen minutes later, they arrived at a timeworn wooden door with tarnished hinges and a rounded top cut to fit the curved ceiling. Rough lumber framed the door, securing the space between it and the irregular walls. Coarse cement filled the gaps.

This time, Ulises took the torch, his orange-streaked hair catching the light, and Raúl focused the flashlight on the vintage lock.

Kasenia held her breath. She had a feeling the others did the same.

Tomás twisted the key. In the underground silence, the loud click resounded like a hammer blow. Wood rasped against wood when he pulled the heavy door open. He reclaimed the flashlight and motioned. "Entrar."

Releasing the breath, Kasenia followed Ulises, who led the way with the torch, and the other boys into the mystery chamber.

Tomás closed the door. "Señorita..." He held out the flashlight. "Por favor." The torch provided some light, but Ulises had walked to the other side of the cavern.

Kasenia steadied the beam on the lock. "I'm surprised the hinges didn't squeak. Does someone oil them?"

"Sí." He locked the door then lifted a long metal bar attached to one side of the doorframe and dropped it onto a metal catch on the other side. Kasenia had a feeling only dynamite could break through the barrier. She pushed her hood back, glorying in the freedom and cool air.

Tomás slipped the key onto a nail in the doorframe and hung his hat over it. Taking the torch from Ulises, he rolled it up and down the rock wall until the flame was extinguished and then laid it on the cavern floor. Motioning for Kasenia to follow with the flashlight, he stepped to an antique lantern hanging from a hook in the wall, pushed a lever to raise the glass and pulled the lighter from his pocket. After the flame caught, he adjusted the wick and lowered the glass then did the same thing with a lantern several feet away.

Kasenia recognized the oily kerosene smell. Her babushka used kerosene lanterns during power failures, a regular occurrence throughout severe Russian winters. The flickering lamplight reminded her of snuggling with her babushka beside the fireplace on cold snowy nights.

He led her between bunkbeds and behind a curtain to a narrow chamber, where he lit a third lantern.

A breeze fluttered the flame and ruffled Kasenia's hair. She raised her hand. Feeling a draft on her fingers, she asked, "Tomás, where does the wind come from?"

He took the flashlight from her and shined it at a two-foot-wide hole above them. "El viento, wind." Then he aimed the beam toward the end of the short corridor, illuminating a wooden seat. "El baño."

"A toilet. That's amazing. Where does, you know, everything go?" She gave him a side glance. What an embarrassing question to ask a man she barely knew.

He grabbed a stone from the rubble that had been swept to the edges of the shaft, walked to the wooden lid and lifted it. "Escucha, listen."

She moved closer, getting a not-so-pleasant whiff of the latrine contents.

Stone in hand, he held it over the hole, nodded to her and released it.

Unlike the outhouse her Russian grandparents used before indoor plumbing, the plop was delayed and sounded hollow. Some ingenious person had devised the perfect combination of toilet and ventilation from the mountain's natural features, either when the mine was in use or in more recent years.

"Amazing, Tomás. Someone thought of everything."

"Es verdad, truth." He closed the lid and extinguished the flashlight. They stepped from behind the curtain, which hung from a wire several inches above her head, into the main portion of the cave. The cavern wasn't huge, yet it held eight bunkbeds with thin vinyl-covered mattresses. Torch smoke hovered along the ceiling, tainting the air.

More torches were stacked beside the door, along with thin branches, rags and a large can of torch oil. A metal trunk and a cooler sat beneath the side-by-side lanterns. Several feet from them, a rivulet of water trickled down the craggy wall, disappearing into a thin gap between the wall and the floor.

Sam walked over to Kasenia, his auburn hair haloed by lamplight, his face dark. He snorted. "You sure look funny with that grease on your face, Sis."

"I was thinking the same thing about you." She laughed. "How long do we leave this stuff on?"

He shrugged. "Don't know."

"Agua?" Tomás asked.

"Sí, sí." The boys gathered around him.

He opened the trunk and took out a V-shaped metal piece and a dipper, both stainless steel by the looks of them. Pressing the V into the channel, he funneled water into the dipper and handed it to the first boy, speaking softly. "No toques tu boca."

Cesar motioned to Sam and Kasenia then tapped his lips. "No touch mouth."

Sharing the dipper wasn't Kasenia's idea of healthy living, but she was incredibly thirsty, and she had no idea when they'd have access to water again.

"Tomás," Sam asked, "do you know what kind of mine this is?"

Tomás handed the dipper to another boy. "Plata."

"What's plata?"

"Plata es..."

"Es silver," Cesar said.

"Cool, I always wanted to see inside a silver or gold mine." Sam surveyed the room. "I like it down here. Maybe I'll be a miner someday."

Kasenia grinned. "I'm sure there's a song about a guitar-playing silver miner."

And then it was Sam's turn to drink. He took one sip and said, "Sis, it tastes just like Babushka's well water."

"How is that possible?" They both liked the water at her house better than any other water they'd ever tasted.

He handed her the dipper, and she had to agree. Was it the minerals in the rock? Did the Ural Mountains have the same minerals as the Arizona mountains? She swiped at the water on her chin. Surely not.

Tomás was the last to quench his thirst. The more Kasenia was around the man, the more she saw how selfless he was. And the more she trusted him. "What is this place, Tomás? I have a feeling this isn't how the miners left it."

He smiled. "Es por coyotes y inmigrantes después de cruzar la frontera. Dormir. Beber. Comer."

"For coyotes and immigrants come across border," Cesar interpreted. "Sleep, drink, eat."

"Oh." Kasenia saw the cave in a new light. "Explains the beds." Having spent half her life in Arizona, she knew they weren't referring to the animal but to someone who smuggled immigrants from Mexico into the United States. Like many people, they pronounced coyote *ky-oh-tey*, though her grandfather, an Arizona native, said *ky-yote*.

Was Tomás a coyote?

After he'd drunk several dippers of water, he said, "Ismael, ven a la luz, voy a curar tu mano."

"He wants Ismael to come to the light," Sam whispered. "Something about his hand."

Ismael walked over and held out his hand.

Despite the poor lighting, Kasenia could see cactus spines protruding from the back of the boy's hand. No wonder he'd cried out in the pasture, yet he hadn't complained since.

Tomás produced pliers from a back pocket and set to work, carefully removing the long spines one by one and placing them on the trunk lid.

Ismael clamped his jaw and twisted his thick eyebrows, but no sound escaped his lips.

When Tomás finished, he had the boy drop the spines down the commode hole. Then he lifted a flat plastic bottle from the trunk.

Kasenia elbowed Sam. "What's that?"

"Beats me."

Squeezing the bottle, Tomás covered the back of the boy's hand with a thick white substance. "Seque y luego tire para quitar pequeños pedazos de púas."

"Es what you call glue." Cesar chuckled. "Tomás say dry and pull. Remove más cactus pieces, small pieces."

"Good idea." Sam gave him a thumbs-up. "I'm going to remember that trick."

Ismael fanned his hand in the air, and Kasenia could smell the glue.

"I go now." Tomás returned the glue to the trunk. "Put radio y saddle en el establo...barn. Make fence better."

Kasenia stared at Tomás. "You're leaving us?"

"I come pronto." He lifted the heavy iron bar to its original position.

"Tío..." Mateo tugged his sleeve. "Margo, she say, 'Take...'" He turned to Sam. "What she say?"

"Take me with you."

His comment triggered a rapid-fire conversation between the Spanish-speakers, a conversation Kasenia couldn't follow except for occasional mention of Margo. She nudged Sam. "Sounds like they're arguing. Do you know what they're talking about?"

He shrugged. "They talk too fast, but I'm pretty sure it's about whether to help Margo or not."

"How did you guys get away from her?"

"We made a plan." Sam's eyes danced, reflecting lamplight. "First, I cut my pillowcase into long strips with Jorge's knife."

"Jorge has a knife?" Kasenia was shocked he'd been allowed to have a weapon at Shadow Ranch.

"He keeps it in his boot. No one knew he had it, except us boys. We all hid in Mateo's room, then he pretend-cried really loud. And just like we knew she would, Margo threw open the door, mad as a wet cat, and screamed for him to shut up."

Kasenia rolled her eyes. "I can only imagine."

"Cesar tripped her, and the moment she landed on the floor, we jumped on her. While the others held her down, I gagged her and tied her hands to one bed leg and her ankles to another, just like we planned." Sam snorted. "That bully's not going anywhere."

"Brilliant." Kasenia was proud of the boys' ingenuity. Together, they'd come up with a simple but effective escape strategy. "When did she say, 'Take me with you'?"

"Right before I gagged her. We ignored her."

"Good for you. She's trouble." Margo had two sides. Kasenia had seen more of the nasty than the nice.

The others quieted, and Tomás said, "I get Señora Margo ahora, now, antes de Señor Brewster...he hurt her, bad."

He wasn't exaggerating. Kasenia knew full well Brewster would beat Margo within an inch of her life, maybe even take her life, for letting eight moneymakers go free. Still, Margo was Margo. "Tomás, she treats these boys like trash. How can you bring her here to hurt them more? Or trust she wasn't tricking them when she said take me with you?"

"She tell me she want be free but afraid Señor Wiley. Now she ready. I bring her."

"Please, I don't trust her—"

He shook his head. "I bring Margo. She okay señora."

Understanding dawned. Tomás had known Margo longer than she had and had a formed a different opinion of the woman than she had. Plus, he'd obviously made up his mind. "She has children," Kasenia said, "two boys and a girl. I can't imagine she'd leave without them."

"I call policía." He lifted his hat off the nail. "They take away."

"That might be too late. If Brewster can't punish her, he'll punish her children."

"I'll help." Sam raised his hand. "They're my friends."

21

"**W**HAT?" KASENIA EYED HER brother. "Margo's children are your friends?"

"Casey, Ross and Marisa are outsiders like we are. I snuck into their trailer once to play a game on the Xbox Brewster stole from me. He gave it to one of his kids who didn't know what to do with it." Sam jutted his chin. "*Told you* he stole my stuff. Casey traded ice cream for it."

To Tomás, he said, "They hate Shadow Ranch and can't wait to leave."

"How you help?" Tomás asked.

"I'll take Jorge's knife, cut Margo loose and show her the way out. Then I'll go talk to her kids. They know me, and I speak good English. They might not understand you, Tomás."

"It has to be two or three in the morning," Kasenia whispered. "People get up early at the ranch. It's dangerous for you to return there."

"Tomás left his horse tied to the fence. We'll ride it and fly like the wind. Right, Tomás?"

"Sí." Tomás was already at the door, key in hand. "Fly rápido como el viento."

Jorge handed Sam his knife. "Fly con Dios."

"No, Sam. Nyet." Kasenia shook her head. "You can't—"

Sam hugged her. "I'll be right back, Sis. Don't worry." He pulled his hood over his red hair. With his blackened face, only his eyes showed.

"I should go with you."

"No, señorita. No go." Tomás unlocked the door and handed her the key. "You aquí con los chicos. I bring Sam to you." Speaking Spanish, he pointed to the cooler, telling Mateo something she couldn't understand.

After he instructed her to lock and bar the door, he grabbed a torch from the floor and lit it.

Kasenia watched the two disappear, leaving only smoke and darkness behind. Their running footsteps echoed through the tunnel before she closed and locked the door. With Jorge's help, she lowered the bar then hung the key on the nail.

Pacing the gloomy chamber, she chided herself for allowing Sam to leave. *It's late. The guards will catch him. And then Brewster will...* She hated to think what he'd do to her brother. Kasenia reached for the key. She should run after Sam, stop him from this insanity. Grandpa Gordon would say Margo made her bed—with Brewster. She could lie in it.

"Señorita Kasenia."

She turned.

Mateo smiled and raised the cooler lid. "You hungry?"

"I have to go after Sam."

He frowned. "Está oscuro, sí?"

"Dark," Cesar said. "Muy dark."

"I'll take a torch."

"Know where they go?"

She leaned against the door, arms folded, head bowed. The boys were right. If she didn't get lost in the mine, she could easily lose her way on the mountain. Besides, by now, Sam and Tomás were too far ahead to catch.

When she raised her head, the boys were watching her, their eyes wary and worried. How many times had they been left behind? She straightened. Tomás would watch over Sam. She would stay with the boys.

"Barra energética, señorita?" Mateo held up a small object. "You like energy bar?" He offered her a sweet, dimpled smile.

"Yes, please." She walked over to him.

"Papel, paper go here." He lifted a plastic grocery sack from the cooler. "Nosotros no queremos ratónes, mouse...chew."

"Thank you." Kasenia quickly scanned the floor. "We certainly don't want to attract vermin." She removed the wrapper, shoved it into the sack and sat on a bottom bunk to eat the bar. Despite the thin mattress, she was happy to sit again.

The boys each took two and three bars.

Kasenia smiled. *Growing boys. Always hungry.* Not until she bit into the chocolate-coated bar did she realize how famished she was. Sam and Tomás had to be equally hungry, but they hadn't taken water or food with them, which wasn't smart. On top of that, they were risking their freedom, maybe their lives for Margo—of all people. What if she screamed for the guards?

Jumping up, Kasenia began to pace the room again, from the bunks to the door and back. Why didn't she go with Sam and Tomás? She could have gathered horses and held them for Margo's family. She could have—

"Señorita?"

Kasenia swiveled. The boys had knelt beside two lower bunks, hands folded on the mattresses. In the faint flickering light, they looked like a painting, so peaceful and trusting.

Cesar beckoned to her. "We pray a Dios, to God in heaven...truth God, not Señor Brewster Spirit Father. You want?"

Yes, she wanted. She wanted to pray to the real God, to do something other than fight her imagination for hours on end. Kneeling beside Ismael on the hard cave floor, she rested her elbows on the bed, folded her hands and lowered her head.

"Señor Dios, Jesús, Espíritu Santo, te amomos. You we love," Cesar began. "You eres bueno, good. Be good Tomás and Sam, por favor. Gracias."

Amidst quiet flowing words, few of which she understood, peace filled the room, calming her spirit and softening her tight, weary shoulders. "Thank you," she whispered, "thank you." Sam was in God's hands. The Creator of the stars could take better care of her brother than she could. Even while endangering his life to rescue Margo and her kids. Kasenia didn't know how long they knelt on the hard rock floor, but her knees were stiff and cold when she got to her feet.

Mateo walked over to a lantern. "Tío Tomás, he say, 'drink, eat, pray, sleep.'" He lowered the flame until it was barely a flutter and did the same with the other lantern in the main chamber.

Mateo took thin wool blankets from the trunk and handed each person one. Kasenia knew she couldn't sleep until Sam returned, but resting while she waited was better than pacing the floor. The boys, who looked as exhausted as she felt—one of them had snored through the prayers—chose their beds, and she fell onto a bottom bunk.

Sam could sleep on the upper bunk when he returned...*if* he returned. She stopped her mind before it stampeded down that path, trusting God had heard their prayers from deep inside a boulder-topped mountain.

Lying on her side, she shifted to find a more comfortable position for her bruised ribs and examined the shadowy room. Who created this stopover for people seeking a better life in America? And how did they keep it clean? Who stocked the cooler with energy bars? How did Tomás know about it? Were he and Mateo illegal refugees?

Truth was, she and Sam were no different. They, too, were foreigners searching for a better life, a *much* better life than Shadow Ranch offered.

She'd barely stretched out when she heard a noise, like sniffing, that seemed to come from the door. She lifted her head. Had she imagined it? Mice didn't breathe loudly, not the ones at her babushka's house, anyway. When the boys didn't stir, she lay back on the mattress.

Then she heard what sounded like scratching. She was sure of it. "Anyone hear that?"

"Sí," came a soft response, and then another.

A low guttural growl vibrated through the door, followed by a louder noise, like something clawing the door.

A shiver ran down her spine.

Someone whispered, "El Jefe..."

The jaguar. Kasenia's heart leaped to her throat. They were trapped. No way could they defend themselves against a jaguar.

"Por favor, Jesús, ayúdanos."

"Help us, Jesús."

"Dios, El Jefe go."

"Dios envíe God jaguar lejos."

"God, send jaguar away." Cesar's voice shook. "Por favor, Jesús..."

The animal sniffed again then was quiet.

Several moments passed before Cesar said, "El Jefe no come. Big door, shut hard. Jesús make jaguar go."

Kasenia blew out a long breath, willing her heart to settle. Yes, they were safe from El Jefe, for now. But what about Sam and Tomás when they returned through the tunnels? Was the torch protection enough?

Once again, she slammed the lid on her fears and prayed for the brave pair. God in heaven had brought them this far. He would continue to protect them all.

⇒⇒ ·◆· ◄◄

The birdcall out her Tucson window was familiar. And then she recognized it, a desert cardinal. The red-chested blue-gray birds with their tall mohawks and short stubby beaks never failed to amuse her.

The call came again. Sh-wee, sh-wee, sh-wee.

Someone whispered, "Tomás."

Kasenia sat up, hitting her head on the top bunk. And reality returned. *Sh-wee, sh-wee, sh-wee.*

Ulises sprang from his bed and hurried to the door.

She jumped to her feet. "It might not be him."

"Es Tomás." Ulises lifted the heavy bar and reached for the key.

"Before you open the door, ask who it is."

"Es Tomás." He stuck the key in the lock.

"Please, Ulises, I beg you. Ask first." The birdcall could be a signal all the coyotes used. One of them might want the cave for his group and shove her and the boys out into the dark tunnels. Or worse.

"Sí, señorita." Through the keyhole, he asked, "¿Quién eres?"

She grabbed a torch from the stack, grasping it with both hands, ready to defend them.

"Es Tomás," came the soft familiar response.

Ulises unlocked the door and Kasenia dropped the torch. Thank God it wasn't El Jefe or a band of immigrants—or Brewster's men. But was Sam with him?

Multiple forms entered the room, blocking the light and bringing an assortment of smells—perfume, horse, sweat and smoke.

Were these people illegal immigrants? Faint lamplight haloed long red hair. Margo? Had Sam and Tomás really brought her and her kids into the mine?

"Sam...?" She'd barely breathed his name when he was at her side, a smoky torch in his hand.

"Sis, I came back, like I said I would."

"Thank God. I was so worried." She hugged him until he pulled away.

"Hey..." His voice was hoarse. "Don't get emotional on me."

"I want to hear all about it." She swiped at her tears. "What happened to your eye?"

"Later." Sam pushed his hood back. "I'd better douse this before people start coughing." Like Tomás had done, he rolled the torch on the rock wall until the flame was extinguished.

Tomás closed and locked the door then lowered the bar. "We hablar, talk." He slid the key onto the nail and hung his hat over it. "First, drink, eat."

Eyes wide, the newcomers surveyed the cave.

Tempted to ignore them, Kasenia swallowed her resentment and extended her hands, palms up. "Welcome to our humble abode." This was a night of new beginnings, for all of them. Against her wishes, Margo and her family had joined them. With any luck, they wouldn't be together for long. But whatever the case, she'd make the best of it.

"Oh..." Margo peered at her. "Is that you, Kasenia?"

"Yes, it's me under all this grease." She touched her cheek and then wiped her finger on her jeans.

"We didn't have time to grease their faces," Sam said. "Had to take a chance they wouldn't be seen."

"Thank you for welcoming us." Margo smiled. "Helps to make this a bit more real. I'm having a hard time believing we actually escaped Shadow Ranch."

The other boys climbed from their bunks, rubbing their eyes and running their fingers through their hair. Ulises joined them. In the dim light, Kasenia couldn't see their expressions, but the fact they huddled together on the opposite side of the room said a lot.

"Oh..." Margo gasped. "I didn't see you boys at first, but I should have expected you'd be here. I'm...well, how wonderful for you, all of you."

Tomás raised the flames on both lanterns, brightening the dark cave. Raúl walked over to a cooler. He lifted the lid and pulled out the dipper. "Agua, Señora Margo?"

"Thank you, Raúl." She sounded surprised. "That's very kind of you." She glanced from him to the other boys. "First, I must apologize. I've been horribly unkind to you boys and to Sam and Kasenia. For a long time, I blamed Brewster and the Shadow Ranch environment for my behavior. But while I lay on the floor—"

"We sorry," Cesar interrupted. "We not want hurt you."

"No, no." She shook her head. "I'm the one who needs to apologize. Lying on that hard floor, contemplating my life and what a witch I'd become, my anger drained out of me. I realized I'd had a choice. I could have done my best, despite the dire circumstances, to help you all adjust to the ranch. Instead, I made it an even worse hell for you. For that, I'm deeply sorry."

She looked down and then up again, her cheeks wet with tears. "I don't expect you to forgive me now, but I hope someday you can."

"Oh, Mom..." The girl next to her put her arm around her mother.

"Jesús, he say we forgive," Cesar said, "like he forgive us." He turned to the other boys. "Sí?"

Their faces solemn, they nodded. "Sí." "Es verdad."

Again, Raúl offered Margo the dipper.

"I'd love a drink, Raúl, but my children can go first."

The girl drank greedily and handed the dipper to her brother who appeared a couple years older than she was. He drank and handed it to the oldest boy who insisted Margo drink first. After they'd had their fill, Jorge gave them energy bars.

Then Sam drank from the dipper and handed it to Tomás.

Kasenia was proud of her brother for letting others drink first, but when the lamp shone on his face, she frowned. His eyelid was swollen and red. She hadn't imagined it.

Jorge gave Sam two energy bars and offered Tomás two.

Tomás pocketed them then drank three dippers of water, returned the funnel and dipper to the cooler, and faced the group. "We must speak."

Something about his serious tone made Kasenia stand taller.

"Señorita Kasenia y Señora Margo, tienes familia aquí, here, help you?"

"Yes," Kasenia said, "our grandfather lives in Tucson."

"Bueno." Tomás eyed Margo.

"No one nearby." She covered a yawn with the back of her hand. "Most of our relatives are in Florida."

"We can't go to Tucson," Sam blurted. "Grandpa's house is the first place Brewster will look. He has a key."

Kasenia sighed. "Sam's right."

"Inglés..." Tomás motioned to Cesar. "Por favor."

Cesar moved to stand by Tomás, who spoke in rapid Spanish.

"Wife, sister—la madre de Mateo." Cesar nodded at Mateo. "And children, they drive van carro...take us, go Mexico."

Kasenia smiled, happy to hear Tomás had a wife and children waiting for him. He'd sacrificed a lot to save his nephew—and the rest of the group. What a happy reunion he and Mateo would have with their family.

Margo glanced at her daughter and the two tall boys who stood on her other side. Kasenia assumed they were her sons. She could see their furrowed brows in the lamplight.

"We can't go to Mexico," Margo said. "Brewster took our passports."

"Ours are in Tucson," Sam said. "Right, Sis?"

"Last I knew." Kasenia pressed her lips together. Their passports were in the safe deposit box with the Russian coins and family wills. But Brewster knew where she kept the key and had likely emptied the box by now. Why did she give him access to everything in her life, including her heart?

Because he asked, she reminded herself. *That's why.* And like a fool, she'd trusted him.

Balanced on his heels, Tomás folded his arms and stared at the floor.

Everyone was quiet. How he planned to sneak fourteen people out of a mine shaft this close to Shadow Ranch and lead them to safety was a mystery to Kasenia. Every single mercenary and vaquero had to be scouring the countryside by now.

He lifted his head. "I call," and started for the door.

Kasenia whispered, "Be careful."

"Tío." Mateo stopped him. "El Jefe, él rayó la puerta."

Sí." Cesar pointed at the door. "El Jefe scratch door."

Tomás grabbed one of the rag-topped sticks in the corner and lit it from a lantern. When the flame was steady, he murmured, "Lock," and strode out the door, followed by an oil-tinged smoke trail.

Two boys hurried to do as he instructed.

One of Margo's boys asked, "What is El Jefe?"

Mateo's eyes grew big, and he spread his hands wide. "El Jefe grande gato...big cat, jaguar."

Marisa sucked in a breath. "A jaguar?"

"Sí...pero no like fire."

"Thank you, Mateo." Margo sounded relieved. "I'm glad to know that."

Kasenia grinned. Margo's new deference to the foster boys warmed her heart. She walked over to her. "You know all of us, Margo, but I haven't met your children." She'd seen them at the ranch, but not with their mother.

"I'll be happy to introduce my sweet threesome. Thanks to Sam and Tomás, we're together again. I'd almost given up hope." Blinking back tears, she put her arm around her daughter. "This is Marisa. She's fourteen."

Kasenia reached out her hand. "Hi, Marisa."

"Hi." Marisa squeezed Kasenia's hand. "I'm sorry Brewster tricked you and Mom into marrying him. It's been awful, for both of you."

"Thank you. The good news is we're not *legally* married to him."

"Really good news." Margo wrapped her other arm around the boy beside her. "This is Casey. He'll be sixteen in a couple weeks, and we'll be free to celebrate his birthday."

"Wonderful, Casey." Kasenia shook his hand. "It'll be the best celebration ever. My grandpa would call it a *happening* worthy of fireworks, wild music and crazy dancing."

"My kinda party." He gave her a thumbs-up.

She motioned to the others. "Hey, everybody, let's sing an early *Happy Birthday* to Casey and a late *Happy Birthday* to Jorge, in whatever language you prefer. But remember, we can't be loud."

They gathered around the two boys. Kasenia and Sam sang in hushed Russian, the Mexicans in Spanish, and Margo's family in English. *Happy birthday to you, happy...* Hands in their pockets, Casey and Jorge glanced at the singers and at each other, embarrassed half-smiles on their faces.

By the time the song ended, everyone was laughing. Kasenia relished their joy. For a brief moment, they'd forgotten the Shadow Ranch terror and enjoyed a normal human experience again.

Margo took Jorge's hand. "I apologize for being so mean about your birthday. I knew if we started singing, Lorraine would call Brewster and we'd never hear the end of it. But I should have been nicer. Please forgive me."

"Es okay." Jorge's gaze was soft. "Te perdono."

"He forgive you," Mateo said.

"Thank you." She hugged Jorge and turned to her children. "I can't believe we're a family again, a dream come true. I'm so sorry my stupidity got you trapped at Shadow Ranch." Her voice broke. "Every time the others treated you like trash, my heart shattered." She sniffed and swiped at her tears.

"It's over, Mom." The older boy put his arm around her shoulders. "I should have told you I suspected Brewster might be mentally unstable before you married him."

"Might be?" Casey snorted. "That's an understatement. Wiley's a certified nutcase."

"Yeah..." The older boy shrugged. "But he can put on a good act, appear as normal as the next guy."

"We love you, Mom, and you love us." Marisa held out her arms. "It's the only thing that matters. Group hug?"

The four of them embraced, heads together, until Casey stepped away. "This place got a bathroom?"

"Yeah." Sam pointed. "Behind that curtain."

Casey left, and his brother held out his hand. "I'm Ross."

"Nice to meet you, Ross." Kasenia shook his hand. "Sorry I got us singing the birthday song and overlooked you."

"No problem." He grinned. "This is the best day of my life. I'm out of Brewster's cage."

"I know the feeling." She raised her arms. "I'd like to stand on top of this mountain and shout, 'I'm free,' and hear it echo, *'I'm free, I'm free, I'm free.'*"

"Don't know about you, Kasenia..." Margo unzipped her jacket and tapped her *B+M* necklace. "As long as I'm wearing this and these worthless wedding rings, I won't feel free. I thought of tossing them in the pasture, but yours were found after you threw them away, so I didn't dare leave any clues on our escape route. Do you plan to keep yours?"

"No way. Nyet."

Sam shook his head. "So weird how Brewster put his initials on everything."

"And on everybody." Margo sighed. "The women, anyway."

Casey came around the curtain. "That's the coolest toilet ever."

Ignoring his brother, Ross asked, "What're you talking about, Mom?"

She removed her hoodie and slipped her t-shirt neck off her shoulder, revealing a black **BWSR** tattoo as high and wide as the one on Rachel's shoulder.

"Oh, Mom..." Marisa burst into tears.

"Why did you let him do that to you?" Casey asked.

"I begged him not to, but he got that look in his eyes..." She glanced at Kasenia. "You probably know what I mean when I say coyote's eyeball."

"Right." Just the memory of Brewster's veiled threat made Kasenia flinch.

Turning again to her children, Margo said, "He named each of you and listed the terrible things he'd do to you if I didn't cooperate." She shuddered.

"You did it for us." Ross's expression was a mix of horror and gratitude.

"Yes, but I plan to have it removed once we're settled."

Casey, who was already taller than his mother, enfolded her in his arms. "Thank you, Mom." Ross and Marisa joined them for a second group embrace.

Sam and Mateo turned away, apparently embarrassed by the emotional display. The other boys lowered their eyes, shifted from foot to foot and rubbed the toes of their tennis shoes against the rock floor.

Kasenia swiped at a tear. If only the foster boys could be reunited with their families too. But their birth homes must not be good. Could she become their foster parent? She served as Sam's surrogate mom. Why not add six more boys to the household? They were great kids who had become like brothers to Sam. She could tell they'd grown close in the few days they were together.

Margo kissed her children's cheeks, wiped her eyes, and then smiled at Kasenia. "Sorry. I think we were discussing what to do with our jewelry."

22

"COME WITH ME. I have an idea." Kasenia led Margo to the curtain and held it for her.

Margo murmured, "Cozy," and stepped into the lamp-lit tunnel.

Kasenia showed her the opening above their heads. "It's a fresh-air source. Don't know where it leads. We'll need to keep our voices down." She lifted the lantern from the hook, walked to the wooden lid and opened it. Holding the light over the latrine, she said, "Here's the deepest, darkest, stinkiest hole you'll ever encounter."

One hand on the rock wall, Margo eyed the hole. "Can't see the bottom, but I can sure smell it." She wrinkled her nose and straightened. "Are you thinking we should drop our jewelry in there?"

"Why not?" Kasenia grinned.

"It would be symbolic." Margo lifted her auburn eyebrows. "A way to show what we think of the snake and the vile things he's done to us."

"Even if he somehow discovered this cave, he'd never look down there. Our rings and necklaces will be buried forever in the *bowels* of the earth." Kasenia snickered. "An intentional play on words. And if some future archaeologist happens to discover them, they'll be totally mystified as to how such similar pieces of jewelry ended up in the privy."

"Let's do it." Margo's eyes sparkled in the lamplight. "Want to go first?"

"You can. I'll hold the light."

Margo unfastened her *B+M* necklace and dangled it over the opening. "Here goes." She released the chain. It disappeared in the darkness, landing with a barely discernible splash.

Kasenia whispered, "Love that sound."

"Music to my ears. Now, for the best part." Margo slipped the rings from her left hand and threw them at an angle into the hole. The rings pinged from side to side until the final plop.

"I'm free." Margo lifted her head and waved her hands in the air. "Even with the tattoo, I'm a free woman."

"Yes, you are." Kasenia gave her the lantern and unclasped the chain on her own neck. Brewster had warned her not to remove the necklace. But he no longer controlled her life.

Like Margo, she let the necklace swing for a moment. The *B+K* heart glittered in the lamplight. She opened her fingers, and her once-loved necklace hit bottom with a satisfying splat.

"Ah..." Staring at the dark hole, she rubbed her throat—still sore from Brewster's stranglehold with the necklace—and inhaled the toilet's putrid odor. Unpleasant as it was, she wanted every sensation, good and bad, imprinted on her memory as a reminder to never again allow a man to own her. "Feels so good, Margo, as if my soul was just unshackled."

"I agree." She grinned. "Thanks for suggesting this. It's like we escaped Shadow Ranch a second time. Or maybe we escaped Shadow Ranch's *shadow*."

Kasenia removed her wedding rings and held them to the light. "Here in America, they say diamonds are forever. In Russia, we say, *diamond cut diamond*, which means *you have met your match*."

She raised the rings high. "Brewster Anton Wiley, you have met your match in Kasenia Anya Clarke and..." She glanced at Margo. "What's your full name?"

"Margo Suzette Barton."

"Brewster Anton Wiley," she said as loudly as she dared, "you have met your match in Margo Suzette Barton and Kasenia Anya Clarke."

Margo pumped her fist in the air. "Yes..."

With all her strength, Kasenia slammed the rings into the craggy cavity. They plinked from one side to the other before hitting bottom with a wet slap. She held out her bare left hand and Margo did the same.

"It's over." Margo's voice shook, and her hand trembled. She lowered it to her side.

"Yes, it's over." Kasenia dropped her hand. "You and I just turned the pages of our lives to a new chapter."

"Beauty from ashes." Margo hung the lantern on the hook. "This ceremony has helped me so much, like chains were removed and my heart has begun to shed callouses. I've been a witch, but that's not the real me." Tears glistened in her eyes.

Kasenia wrapped her arms around the remorseful woman. Her own few days inside the Shadow Ranch fence had been harrowing, but Margo had suffered so much more. Forced separation from her children and worrying about their safety as well as their future well-being must have been hell, not to mention dealing with Brewster and his wives. She'd built a barrier around her heart to protect it. Kasenia knew she would have done the same.

"Thanks." Margo straightened and wiped her cheeks. "I needed that."

"Me, too." Kasenia dabbed her eyes. Hearing a commotion in the main chamber, she pushed aside the curtain. "What's happening?"

The boys had gathered around the door again. Marisa, who stood nearby, said, "Tomás is here."

"Good." Margo joined her daughter. "Maybe he figured out how to keep us homeless people off the streets *and* off Brewster's radar." She dried her eyes with her jacket sleeve.

Kasenia grabbed a torch, just in case Tomás wasn't the person at the door. Had the boys checked first?

Ulises, his scraggly chin hairs highlighted by lamplight, pulled the door open, and Tomás stepped inside. After instructing the boys to lock and bar the door, he doused his torch, but not before its pungent smoke infiltrated the chamber. "Sit, por favor. We speak more."

Kasenia coughed and laid her torch on the floor. This was it, the next phase of their journey to freedom.

Cesar moved to stand beside Tomás.

"Primero..." Tomás said, and continued in Spanish.

"First," Cesar translated, "he say gracias you wait. He talk wife. She y su hermana, sister, no take los niños...make más espacio, more room, en el auto van."

Kasenia chewed her lip. Tomás wife must be as kind and caring as he was to leave their children behind to make room in the vehicle. But could it hold *everyone*?

"Tomás walk Mateo, Señora Margo y familia en montañas...uh...mountains," Cesar said. "Go to van. Drive speedy Florida."

"That's really kind of you," Margo said, "but—"

"Tomás give you phone, call familia. They come to van."

"I can arrange that." Margo nodded. "My cousin and her husband will be happy to help us resettle. But what about these boys and Kasenia?"

Tomás spoke at length, pointing at the door.

"We go," Cesar said, "a Crimson Rancho Arcos. Señor Duran bueno good man. He help."

Kasenia nodded. "Okay, but how do we get there?"

"Go mountains, hide árboles...trees. See arches."

"Brewster's men will find us."

"Go por la noche."

"These boys are in the foster program." Kasenia addressed Tomás. "Under Arizona state jurisdiction. I can't legally take them anywhere. I'm Sam's guardian, but not theirs. Plus, I'm from Russia. Authorities might think—"

"No..." Tomás frowned. "No chicos foster."

"What?" She stared at him and then the boys. "You're not—"

Margo completed her thought. "Foster children?"

"No, nunca, never." Cesar exclaimed. "Nuestras familias viven en Phoenix."

"Dude..." Sam gave them a thumbs-up. "But how did you get here?"

"Los hombres malos, bad men," Cesar said. "We go in van to montañas, what you call retreat. Pastor Eduardo, he drive, stop for luces, lights de emergencia. Put down window and bad man, he—"

Cesar slugged the air with his fist. "Hit Pastor Eduardo en la cara..." He knuckled his own cheek. "Push him out van, get in. Bad man come other side with gun, put en la cabeza, head of Raúl. Tell us no yell, no get out or..."

Everyone glanced at Raúl, who shrugged without comment.

"Bad men drive us Shadow Ranch," Cesar concluded. "Brewster pay mucho dinero."

"That's terrible." Kasenia's heart hurt for the boys. They'd been kidnapped and purchased like slaves to do slave labor. "I'm so sorry. Your parents must be worried sick."

The boys nodded, their faces sad, except for Mateo, who wrapped his arms around Tomás's waist and smiled up at his uncle. "Nuestra familia vive en Bisbee."

"Sí. Our family live in Bisbee." Tomás laid his hand on the boy's shoulder. "Somos inmigrantes legales."

"You're legal immigrants?" Sam asked.

Tomás nodded.

Cesar indicated the other boys. "Nuestras familias también son inmigrantes legales...also legal immigrants."

"How wonderful your families are nearby." Kasenia smiled.

"Mateo, how did you get to Shadow Ranch?" Sam asked. "And you, Tomás. I don't understand."

"I throw basketball by house por la noche," Mateo said. "Bad man put hand on mouth, take me to car." He mimed being dragged away with a hand over his mouth.

"I ask people," Tomás said. "They say talk coyotes. Coyotes say look Shadow Ranch. Es un mal rancho, bad ranch. I talk Marlin. Tell him I know animales, I know guardia de seguridad, security."

"Wow, Tomás," Kasenia said. "That's amazing. Thank you for rescuing all of us, not just Mateo."

The others nodded and murmured their gratitude.

Tomás dipped his head. "De nada."

"You're going to lead us through the mountains, Tomás," Margo said. "But are you saying Kasenia and the boys will be on their own, without a guide?"

"Dos arcos, they see," Tomás said. "Not far."

"It's dangerous." Margo folded her arms.

"Sí. También es drive to Florida."

"Does Trent Duran know we're coming?" Kasenia asked.

"No sabe." Tomás shook his head.

"How do you know he won't drive us right back to Shadow Ranch?"

He tapped his chest. "En mi espíritu, lo sé."

"What?" She squinted at him.

"His spirit," Cesar said. "En his spirit, he know."

Kasenia scrunched her eyebrows. "What do you know, Tomás?"

"Sé que Brewster y Marlin son hombres malos, bad men. Trent es un buen hombre, good man. Mi espíritu..." He searched for a word. "Conoce su espíritu."

"Tomás say," Cesar interjected, "his spirit know Trent spirit."

"We hermanos cristianos," Tomás added.

"Christian brothers?" Kasenia asked.

"Sí." Tomás smiled. "I ask Trent Duran, 'You love Jesús?' He say, 'Yes.'"

"He could have said that to please you. It doesn't mean—"

Tomás lifted a palm. "Trent Duran es un buen hombre. You must trust."

"Okay, Tomás. Because I trust you, I will trust Trent Duran." She had trusted Tomás to lead them out of Shadow Ranch. She had to accept his assessment of the Crimson Arches rancher. Trent seemed like a nice guy when they talked in the barn and after the horse sale. A really nice guy. But she'd once thought Brewster was a nice guy, too.

Kasenia knelt, one knee on the floor, untied her boot, took it off and lifted the insole. Despite the hiking and climbing they'd done, Trent's business card was still legible. When she straightened, everyone was staring at her like she'd lost her mind. She held up the card. "I have his phone number. We can call him."

Tomás shook his head. "No." And rattled off a string of Spanish words.

"Not yet." Cesar said. "Maybe Trent with Brewster or Brewster see phone."

"Unlikely."

"No more discuss." Tomás mumbled something to Cesar, walked over to a bottom bunk and dropped onto it.

"Poor guy," Margo whispered. "He's exhausted."

Kasenia replaced the card, slid her foot into the boot and bent to tie it. She needed to trust Tomás's judgment, not argue with him. In her spirit, she knew he was a trustworthy man.

Cesar cleared his throat. "Tomás say we sleep now. Is day soon. No go out. They see us. We rest. Go en noche." He lifted the cooler lid. "Eat, drink, pray a Dios, sleep."

The boys gathered round the cooler, anxious for more energy bars. Kasenia sat on the bottom bunk. Sam joined her, already chewing. She could smell the chocolate.

"I'm glad we have water," he said. "These things make me thirsty."

She glanced about the cave. "We should look for something to carry water in when we leave here."

"Maybe we'll follow a creek."

"Nice idea, but this is the Sonoran Desert, in the summertime. Remember?"

Ulises, who was lowering the lantern flames, whispered, "Dios nos dará agua."

Mateo translated. "He say God give us water."

Kasenia smiled. If only she had the boys' faith. An oft-quoted Russian proverb came to mind. *Hold your children with your heart but teach them with your hands.* These sweet boys had been taught well by moms and dads who held them in their hearts and longed to hold them in their arms again. She couldn't wait to return them to their parents.

"Phew." Sam blew out a breath. "All of a sudden, I'm done for." He stuffed the wrappers in the trash bag then climbed to the top bunk.

"About your eye..." Kasenia stood to talk with him. "What happened? And how did you and Tomás get everyone out without being caught?"

Sam lay on his side, cheek against the vinyl mattress cover but quickly lifted his head. "Yuck, the grease is rubbing off."

"Hang on." She hurried over to the torch supplies, grabbed two unused rags and handed him one. "We can clean our faces with these." The rags would remove most of the axle grease, but she had a feeling her complexion would never be the same.

When they finished wiping their faces and the mattress cover, she folded the cloths and returned them to the pile. The extra grease would help a torch or two burn brighter. Back at the bunk, she started to ask her brother about his second escape from Shadow Ranch, but he was already asleep.

Kasenia covered Sam with her blanket, patted his shoulder and sat on the bottom bunk. His story could wait. Right now, she was content to listen to the sleepers' steady inhalations. They were safe and sound, every one of them. *Thank you, God in heaven.*

Two bunks away, Margo got up and walked over to the cooler. She lifted out the funnel and dipper, drank from the trickling stream and then sat beside Kasenia. "I can't sleep," she whispered. "Too much excitement, I guess. How about you?"

"I slept earlier. Right now, I'm appreciating this peaceful moment, something foreign to Shadow Ranch, as you well know."

Eyes soft in the flickering glow, Margo murmured, "It's an impossible dream come true. I'd kiss Tomás's feet, if he'd let me."

"What about the other women?" Kasenia asked. "Behind their fake smiles and Brewster worship, do they long to escape to the real world too?"

"You gotta wonder." Margo shook her head. "But don't forget, they're depending on him to get them to heaven."

"That's like depending on the devil, which makes no sense."

"Does anything at Shadow Ranch make sense?"

For a long time, neither woman spoke. Kasenia broke the silence. "Do you have any idea how Brewster became so evil?"

Margo flipped her long red hair behind her shoulders. "Just a guess based on the night he visited me in Wyoming and got drunk on our neighbor's chokecherry wine." She chuckled. "Stout stuff, but delicious."

"I've seen him drink but never saw him intoxicated."

"For whatever reason, maybe because he was far from Shadow Ranch, he rambled on and on, describing his childhood. Apparently, his grandmother was forced to raise him after his parents dumped him at her house and then disappeared. A bitter woman who barely had enough welfare income to feed and clothe herself, she resented having to care for him and made it clear with abuse and neglect."

"How old was he?"

"Nine or ten."

"That would be rough." Kasenia rested her hands on her knees. "It doesn't excuse his actions, but I have an idea how he felt. Our parents abandoned us to our grandparents' care. However, they didn't disappear from our lives, and they made sure our needs were met." Funny Brewster never mentioned their similar backgrounds.

Sam stirred above them.

Margo waited until his breathing leveled out before she resumed her story. "He ran away so many times and stole so much food and clothing, a judge finally put him in a home for wayward boys. Brewster said he hated the discipline and being forced to study and do chores, although later, he was grateful because it prepared him for the military. He stayed at the home because the sheets were clean and the food was good—and they didn't serve pickled beets. His grandmother grew and pickled her own beets, which they ate every night. Sometimes, that's *all* they ate."

"Ah, that explains why he hates borscht."

"After several months, they sent him home to his grandmother, who was not at all happy to see him. The feeling was mutual. He went straight to his room but didn't unpack his suitcase. Instead, he sat on the edge of his bed until dark then took off the moment he heard her first snore. This time, he made sure he wasn't found and didn't *surface*, as he said, until he joined the military."

"Interesting."

"Along the way, he vowed to never again eat out of garbage cans, wear secondhand clothing or let a woman tell him what to do. He alone would be the master of his fate, and he would surround himself with people who loved and obeyed him."

"Oh..." Kasenia nodded and then nodded again. That little bit of information explained so much. Yet, Brewster had a choice. He could have searched for opportunities to help neglected children like himself, to give rather than take. Instead, he chose to fill his empty soul by using people, including children, to satisfy his bottomless lust for money, power and sex.

"I know, I know..." Margo breathed. "I should have considered his confession a red flag, but I felt sorry for the unloved, unwanted little boy, and thought he was exaggerating the obedience part. Now, I don't feel anything but abhorrence for the monster."

"Do you know how he and Lorraine met?"

"I've heard her say they met in college. While he was working on his doctorate, they bought the ranch with money she inherited from her parents after they died in a car crash."

How like Brewster to use Lorraine's money for his benefit.

"You've probably heard him say he built Shadow Ranch from nothing."

Kasenia nodded. "He's quite proud of the ranch."

"It's a flat-out lie. The lodge and barns were already there when they bought the ranch, plus some of the outbuildings. The lodge had a restaurant in it and suites for overnight guests. That's why it has a commercial kitchen. Lorraine planted the garden, trees and grass, bought some animals and started making products to sell in a little gas station up the road. I guess it began with prickly pear jelly when Brewster said, 'This is so good, we ought to sell it.'"

"She probably had a handful of kids to care for by then."

"Right."

"What I don't understand..." Kasenia yawned. "Last year was Brewster's first year teaching at UA but not his first professorship. He also taught in Montana and Utah. If they were living out here, how did he—"

"He commuted. Only came home once a month or so."

"Poor Lorraine, stuck in the middle of the desert with just her kids for company."

"It was in Montana he discovered the Spirit Children and their weird beliefs, including Spirit Father worship. In fact, that's where he picked up Wanda."

"For some reason, I thought she came from a brothel. Maybe it was his *pretty woman* comment."

"Rumor has it the locals called their commune a brothel." Margo yawned and rubbed her eyes. "Now that I've unloaded on you, I'm starting to feel sleepy."

"Did you ever dream of what you'd do if you escaped?"

"All the time. That's what kept me sane, imagining the riding school I hope to start, deciding what I'd offer and how much I'd charge. I even designed a sales brochure in my head."

"You're so good with horses. Your school will be popular."

"What about you? Do you have plans?"

"I had ideas for a couple businesses," Kasenia said, "before…well, before Brewster. He claimed one idea for himself, opening a modeling agency. I doubt it'll come to fruition without Sam and me, but he might try to pull it off anyway. Right now, my sole goal in life is to reunite these boys with their parents."

"I've had equine-assisted therapy training and would love to offer it to help them overcome the trauma they experienced at Shadow Ranch." Margo blew out a long sigh. "Trauma that includes my terrible mistreatment. Can't believe what a nasty bully I've been. I doubt I'll ever be able to forgive myself for the heartache I caused those boys as well as my own children."

"Like your children, the boys seem to have forgiven you. And God will forgive you, if you ask. I read that in here." Kasenia pulled her travel Bible from her pocket. "Just this morning. Or was it yesterday morning?" She pushed loose hair away from her eyes. "I've lost track of time."

Opening the little Bible, she squinted to read the small print in the muted light. When she found Psalm 86:5, she read it to Margo. "For You, Lord, are kind and ready to forgive, rich in faithful love to all who call on You." She looked up. "I'm not a Bible scholar, but according to this, all you have to do is ask because he's kind and loving and ready to forgive."

"Hmm, I'll have to think about that." Margo stood and stretched. "Thank you, Kasenia. You're a great encourager."

"I'm talking to myself, too." She shrugged. "I feel terribly guilty for getting my brother into this mess. But this seems to suggest I should accept God's forgiveness and Sam's, if he chooses to forgive me, which I think he will. He's always been quick to forgive."

"I will be forever grateful." Margo turned to go. "Goodnight."

"Have a good nap." Kasenia got a blanket from the trunk and stretched across the bunk. She pictured her Russian grandfather with his long white beard, his glasses perched on the end of his nose. After village meetings, Dedushka Abram would wander the house half the night. When Babushka Irina asked in the morning why he was so blurry-eyed, his response was always the same. *The more you know, the less you sleep.*

Margo had given her plenty to think about. Kasenia understood her pain and anger and had readily forgiven her for how she treated the boys. But she couldn't bring herself to feel sorry for Brewster or to forgive him for what he'd done to her and Sam and so many others. Surely, God didn't expect that of her. After all, he was against evil people.

Sam stirred when she rolled to her side on the crinkly vinyl, but he soon quieted, and she drew the blanket over her shoulder. Snores and snuffles drifted about the room. She was glad everyone was sleeping soundly. But she was wide awake and might not be able to sleep, though she needed to rest before their trek to Crimson Arches Ranch—and Trent Duran. Could he help them? Would he?

His ranch was too close to Shadow Ranch for comfort. And his connection to Brewster and the Shadow Ranch women too strong. Yet, she and the boys had nowhere else to go.

23

— · —

A WAKENED BY AN UNFAMILIAR sound, Kasenia opened her eyes. Across the cave, Tomás was funneling water from the wall into the dipper. Was it time to leave, or was he getting a drink? Their windowless sanctuary offered no clue as to whether the sun or the moon was shining.

Tomás drank from the dipper, laid it and the funnel on the cooler, and then bent over a bottom bunk. "Cesar, despierta."

Cesar groaned and pushed upright. Seated on the edge of his bunk, he rubbed his eyes.

"Tell them, por favor," Tomás said, "es hora de irnos."

"No hay problema, Señor Tomás." Cesar stood and slowly faced the bunks. "Amigas y amigos..." He yawned. "You wake. Is time we go."

Kasenia watched dim forms stretch and shift, accompanied by grunts and moans and crackling vinyl. Above her, Sergei muttered, "Already? I just fell asleep."

Marisa climbed down from a top bunk. "Are we leaving for Florida now?"

"Soon." Tomás raised the wick on a lantern, his features animated by the flickering flame before he sidestepped to the second lamp to brighten its light as well. "Muy pronto."

Kasenia threw off the blanket and swung her feet to the cave floor. This was it, their final moments hidden from Brewster's fury. She felt cocooned and safe here, yet they couldn't remain buried inside the mountain forever. Before the two groups parted ways, before they ventured out into treacherous territory again, she had questions for Tomás. Lots of questions.

She stood, undid her braid, and was about to ask her first question while she rebraided her smoke-laden hair, when Tomás launched into a rapid-fire Spanish conversation with Cesar.

"Sí." Cesar nodded and then nodded again. "Sí, señor."

By now, everyone was sitting on their beds or standing beside the bunks, their hair spiked, their clothes rumpled, and their focus on Tomás. Nervous shuffles, sniffs and throat-clearing replaced the cavern's quiet calm.

"This is it," Sam whispered, eyes bright above smudged cheeks.

Kasenia ran her forefinger across her jaw then checked it. Greasy black residue smeared the tip. Soap and water and Grandma Clara's favorite skin toner, witch hazel, would be needed to completely cleanse the grease from their faces.

Who was she kidding? She wiped her finger on her jeans. They'd be lucky to find drinkable water on their trek through the mountains, let alone soap and witch hazel.

"Es de noche," Tomás said. "We go ahora, now. Después de ir al baño, bathroom, drink agua, eat food y speak adiós, goodbye." He pointed at the door. No speak en el túnel."

"Do we need more axle grease?" Sam asked. "To hide our gringo faces?"

"Sí." Tomás pulled the baggie from a pocket and gave it to Sam, who swiped a black blob with his finger and handed the bag to Kasenia.

She groaned. "I can't believe I'm doing this again." After scooping a fingerful of the greasy stuff that still smelled like burnt rubber, she dangled the baggie before Marisa. "Your turn."

Marisa wrinkled her nose. "Do I have to?"

"Yes." Margo's voice was firm. "We must do as Tomás instructs."

Tomás spoke to Cesar, who said to the others, "No take comida...food. Fall on trail or animals, they..." He put his nose in the air and breathed in and out.

"Sniff?" Kasenia asked, dabbing the grease about her face.

"Sí, they sniff, smell. Not good."

"Señorita Kasenia..." Tomás focused on her. "Baja por el sendero de la montaña hasta el carro minero y gira hacia el este, a la derecha."

"I'm sorry..." Kasenia held out her palms. "I don't understand.'"

"Go down mountain to mine cart," Cesar explained. "Go east, right."

"Lo intiendes?" Tomás asked.

"Yes, sí, I understand." Kasenia hoped she sounded more certain than she felt. "The boys and I will take the trail down to the mine cart and then go east, or right, and follow that trail."

"Bueno." Tomás nodded and murmured in Spanish to Cesar, who turned to Kasenia. "Be very careful at cart. Es dangerous place."

"Thank you for the warning."

Those who didn't line up for the bathroom reached into the cooler for energy bars and ate quietly while they waited to drink from the dipper. Everyone seemed lost in their own thoughts.

When the Hispanic boys and the gringos with their blackened faces reassembled, Tomás picked up a torch but didn't light it. "Es hora de decir adiós."

"We say goodbye now," Cesar said.

For a moment, no one moved, then Margo hugged Cesar. "Thank you for translating for us and for being such a wonderful young man. I will never forget you."

Murmuring something in her ear, he returned the hug and Margo moved to the next "foster" boy.

Sam exchanged awkward hugs with Margo's boys. "Wish we could have spent more time together. Maybe someday."

"Yeah," Casey said. "Next time, I'll beat you at that Xbox game."

Marisa hugged Sam. "I'll watch for you on social media." Beneath her brother's grease smears, Kasenia thought she detected a blush.

She shook Ross and Casey's hands. "I wish you a wonderful new life in Florida. Take good care of your mom."

"We will." Ross dipped his head, his expression somber.

Though she didn't know Marisa, Kasenia embraced the girl then stepped back. "I will tell you what I'm trying to tell myself. Please don't assume all men are like Brewster. Instead, remember the good guys you met here—Tomás and Mateo and the boys from Phoenix—and Sam."

"Okay."

"My brother may be ornery..." Kasenia winked. "But he's a gem. And so are your brothers, but you already knew that. And your dad. From talking with your mom, I'm convinced he was a wonderful man."

"So true." Margo put her arm around Marisa. "He was a kind, loving husband and father."

Marisa smiled at her mother.

"In Russia," Kasenia continued, "they say mistrust is an axe in the tree of love. Don't let one rotten apple spoil the whole bushel."

"She's right," Sam interjected. "Our Dedushka Abram always told us we should judge men by their hearts, not their clothes."

"All good advice." Margo nodded her approval. "Brewster is a good example of a wolf in sheep's clothing."

Marisa's brow furrowed as if she couldn't absorb one more idiom.

Kasenia laughed.

"I couldn't resist." Margo chuckled and turned to Sam. "Thank you for saving us from the nasty wolf—after I'd been nasty to you. You didn't have to do that."

He shrugged. "When I found out you wanted to get away, I couldn't leave you there, knowing what Brewster would do to you and..." He glanced at her kids.

Margo gave him a quick embrace. "Sam, you deserve nothing but the best in life." Turning to Kasenia, she grasped her hand. "We may not be sister wives, but we're sisters in trauma. I hope we find each other again someday."

"I'd like that." Kasenia hugged Margo, inhaling her hair's citrus scent. "Thank you for gifting me with a peaceful morning with the horses in the quiet barn. You can't imagine how much it calmed my tortured soul."

Tomás cleared his throat, and the women separated. He opened the trunk lid, pulled out a handful of flat rectangular items and handed one to every other person. "Put...pocket. Share con tu amigo."

"What is it?" Sam asked.

"Manta de supervivencia."

"I don't—"

"Blanket to survive," Cesar explained.

"Oh, a survival blanket." Sam examined the one in his hand. "Cool camo colors."

"Leave pocket," Tomás insisted. "No play. Solo emergencia. Entiende?"

"Yes." Sam shoved the folded Mylar packet into his back pocket. "I understand. Only emergencies."

Kasenia and the others who'd been given packets followed his example. When they quieted, Tomás focused on each person one at a time. "No speak en el túnel." He paused. "Lo intiendes?"

With one whispered, solemn voice, the Hispanic boys responded, "Sí, Señor Tomás."

"I understand, but I need to know..." Kasenia stepped closer to their leader. "How far do the boys and I walk on the trail?"

"Look dos arcos."

"That's all? Just look for the arches?"

"Sí."

"We'll need water."

"Dios proveerá."

Kasenia turned to Cesar who chuckled and winked. "God will provide."

"Whatever you say." She addressed Tomás again. "You and God got us this far. I can't begin to thank you enough for endangering yourself for our freedom. You are a truly wonderful human being."

He pointed at the cave's dark ceiling. "Toda la gloria a Dios."

"May I hug you?"

He blinked, as if startled by her change of subject and then hesitantly opened his arms.

"I will never forget you." She hugged him and he returned the embrace. Kasenia stepped back. "Please tell your wife and children *muchas gracias* for sharing their wonderful husband and father with us, even when you could have been killed." To the others, she said, "Right?"

Whispered "sí" and "yes" and somber nods followed. Ross added, "My family and I are also grateful to Sam for helping us escape. Took a lot of courage."

Sam shrugged. "I'm just glad we didn't run into Marlin."

Her brother's happy grin made Kasenia smile. To think she tried to keep him from going back to Shadow Ranch with Tomás.

She squeezed Mateo's shoulder. "Adiós, Mateo. Come see us in Tucson when you return from Florida. And bring your uncle with you."

He grinned. "Sí, señorita."

Tomás walked behind the curtain. The light shining above it dimmed and then died. Back in the big room, he lowered a lantern wick until the fire sputtered out.

Darkness enfolded them like a blanket, wrapping around the cavern's final flickering flame.

Tomás pushed the lever to raise the second lantern's globe and spoke to Mateo in Spanish.

The boy grabbed a torch, lit it from the flame and held it high. Tomás turned down the wick, waited for the fire to dissolve into a spark and lowered the glass. He glanced at the dark smoke crawling across the ceiling. "We pray. Mateo, rezas en Inglés, por favor."

Mateo stared up at his uncle. "Yo?"

"Sí."

Mateo gave the torch to Benicio beside him, closed his eyes and pursed his lips as if thinking before he lifted his hands.

From behind the group, Kasenia took in the surreal snapshot, reveling in the craggy, smoky, otherworldly cavern—the stuff of adventure films. But this scene was peopled with real individuals, precious brave friends stepping into uncertain futures.

This moment, she sensed, would frame the rest of her life, constantly reminding her how priceless freedom is—and how easily it can be stolen. And how family and friends were the most precious treasures of all.

"Padre, Hijo y Espiritu Santo," Mateo prayed, "Father, Son and Holy Spirit. We love you y nos amas, you love us. Danos alas, give wings, por favor. We fly far away. No Brewster, no Marlin, no El Jefe see. Gracias, amén."

Tomás's murmured, "Gracias, amén" was echoed around the cavern.

He reached for the key, which was none too soon because the smoke had begun to burn Kasenia's eyes. And the boys were muffling sneezes and coughs in their elbows.

Once more, Tomás said, "No speak in el túnel."

Mateo whispered, "No cough."

Murmurs of "Vaya con Dios" followed but quickly hushed when Tomás stuck the key in the lock. The metallic click chimed in the silent chamber.

Sam whispered, "The sound of freedom," and pumped a thumb in the air.

Kasenia pursed her lips. *Maybe...*

Raúl raised the bar and slowly opened the door, wood rasping against wood.

Tomás had Mateo take the torch from Benicio, thrust it into the black tunnel and wave it. Kasenia assumed the purpose was to discourage the jaguar from coming close. She would have thought El Jefe was a myth if she hadn't heard the big cat growl and scratch the door. That was one animal she didn't want to meet in the dark—or the light.

They filed from their safe haven into the murky tunnel illuminated only by torchlight. Tomás quietly shut and locked the door, switched his flashlight on, gave it to Sam, and moved toward the head of the line. Kasenia and Sam remained at the rear, like before.

Stirred by a twinge of nostalgia, Kasenia ran her fingers over the old door just to remember its rough texture smoothed by time. Though anxious to move on, she was reluctant to leave the peace and safety the cavern had provided. Her fingers caught on a ragged ridge. She nudged Sam and motioned for him to shine the light at the door.

Like someone had scored the wood with knives, four parallel grooves ran from near the top of the door downward.

Wide-eyed, they stared at each other. Sam mouthed *El Jefe* but turned away when Jorge grabbed his sleeve.

Kasenia swung around. Illumined by smoky torchlight, Tomás waved the group forward and took off. Fourteen people treading gravel sounded as loud as the rocks that pummeled the camper roof, but it couldn't be helped. Ore dust stirred by their feet mingled with the smoke and made breathing hard. Certain it clung to her clothes and greasy face like a dirty mist, she fought the urge to brush it off. The darker her skin and clothing, the better.

Tomás stopped at the juncture where the three tunnels met and motioned for Sam to aim the flashlight beam at the wall. Moments later, he found the loose stone and wiggled it outward. Like their footsteps, rock grating against rock sounded loud in Kasenia's ears. She glanced about, fearing some person or animal would hear the noise and come running.

Tomás replaced the key in its hiding place and inch by grating inch pushed the rock into place.

They'd just started to move again when one of the boys tripped and fell and let out a loud cry. The others gathered round.

Kasenia stepped closer. *Benicio.*

Tomás whispered, "La luz."

Sam focused the flashlight on the boy's knee. Already, blood pulsed through a split in his pant leg. Whatever he'd fallen on had cut through his jeans and into his flesh.

Marisa gasped and covered her mouth.

Kasenia pressed her fingers against her lips. How was he going to make it out of the mine and through the mountains on a knee gushing blood?

In the stillness, a faint but familiar male voice called, "I know you're hiding in here, people. I hear you. Face it. Your ridiculous little escapade is over."

24

—·—

K ASENIA FROZE, EYES WIDE. A jaguar's growl couldn't have terrified her more.

"You're getting hungry, aren't you? And thirsty. *Real thirsty.*" Oily
and smooth, Marlin's words oozed through the mine's myriad tunnels,
distant yet sinister. "Come out, people. I'll give you water—*all* you can
drink—and ice cream. Cold, creamy, sweet, strawberry ice cream. You
like ice cream. I know you do."

Tomás murmured, "He no find," and pulled a red bandana from his
back pocket.

The onlookers eyed each other as if they wanted to believe Tomás but
weren't sure they should. A smoke cloud hovered above their heads.

After creasing the bandana on the diagonal, creating a triangle, Tomás
folded the middle point to the crease to make a long rectangle with
pointed ends. He folded it lengthwise one more time then had the boy
pull up his pant leg.

"Tomás," Margo whispered, "use this." She slipped a tissue packet
from her pocket and extracted the tissues. "Cover the wound with these
and put the plastic over them, then the bandana."

Tomás laid the soft tissues on the wound, placed the plastic cover
on top and wrapped the bandana twice around the boy's skinny knee,
securing the ends with a double knot. He patted Benicio's shoulder. "Es
okay?"

Benicio nodded and wiped tears from his cheeks.

Slowly and carefully, Tomás slid the boy's pant leg over his bandaged
knee.

"Come on, quit dragging your feet. Get your sorry asses to the mine entrance." No longer cajoling, Marlin's faraway call was demanding. Kasenia thought she also detected weariness as well as uneasiness.

Tomás grunted. "Estúpido."

He and Margo helped the boy to his feet.

Kasenia felt a sneeze coming and pinched her nose. She could not, would not endanger her friends.

"If we have to come in after you..." Marlin's words were menacing and low. "You-will-be-sorry. Brewster will beat you to a bloody pulp."

Someone moaned. Apparently, they'd also experienced Brewster's brutality. She knew Marlin was bullying them, yet her insides quaked. She could only imagine how angry Brewster was right now.

"No listen." Tomás insisted. "Marlin not find." He raised a palm in the hazy torchlight. "Jesús cierra los ojos del estúpido Marlin." Though his words were soft, they were firm. "Cierra su gran boca, haz que se moje los pantalones. Amén."

Cesar whispered a quick translation. "Jesús close stupid Marlin eyes, close big mouth and... Pants wet?" He peered at Tomás, eyebrows raised.

"Es un cobarde."

"Marlin is coward," Cesar said.

Kasenia glanced at Sam who shrugged as if to say, *Who knew?* Maybe cowardice explained the hesitation in Marlin's voice, but if he feared Brewster's fists like she did, he'd go to any length to capture them. For the moment, at least, he had quieted. Maybe God had shut his mouth, like Tomás prayed.

Tomás took the torch. "Jorge y Ulises, ayuden a Benicio a caminar."

In response, Jorge and Ulises, both big boys, took Benicio's arms and stumbled after their leader.

Kasenia was glad to be moving, not just to distance themselves from Marlin but to escape the haze amassing around them. Her eyes burned, and she wasn't the only one who struggled to contain coughs and sneezes.

Tiptoeing through the gravel, barely breathing, Kasenia checked behind every few seconds but saw nothing in the blackness. The crunch of twenty-eight feet on the rubble was incredibly loud in the tunnel. Marlin probably heard their every step. For sure, the jaguar did.

Sam turned on the flashlight and flipped around. But he quickly switched it off and pivoted forward again.

Startled by his behavior, Kasenia glanced back, heart racing.

Everyone hurried. No one spoke. With his friends' help, Benicio managed to keep pace. After what felt like an endless climb up the slanted shaft with torch smoke burning their eyes and noses, they finally reached the exit.

Tomás raised his finger to his lips and pointed from person to person. Each one nodded their understanding. He motioned to Sam to focus the flashlight downward, then he extinguished the torch flame in a blackened sand pile. Climbing to the opening, he slowly pushed away the log that covered the hole they'd slid through hours earlier.

Kasenia swallowed, staring down the dark shaft then up at Tomás's back, what little she could see of it. She knew why he didn't rush their exit, but still, she wished he'd hurry. This was just the beginning of a different kind of terror.

Finally, he crawled up and out the hole. For a brief moment, Kasenia heard him fumbling for a foothold. And then he was gone. The group's uneasy breathing and rustlings were loud in the stillness he left behind. Fresh air wafted from above, stirring the smoke.

The dark rock wall absorbed the flashlight's beam rather than reflected it. She could see vague outlines of the others in the murky gloom and feel their nervous tension. Oh, how she longed to say one more goodbye, to thank them for their bravery and wish them safe travels and lives filled with joyous freedom.

She thought she heard a noise far down the shaft and twisted her head to hear better. Marlin? El Jefe? A mouse? Mice and big cats were quiet. That left Marlin...

Tomás slid feet-first through the hole and landed before them, a short tree branch in his hand. He pivoted to face them. "No hay ningún hombres en las rocas. Solo Marlin's truck camino muy abajo."

"No men on rocks," Mateo translated. "Only Marlin truck on road far down."

"But..." Margo's voice was hushed. "Other men could have come with him in his truck."

"Sí." Tomás nodded. "No vi más hombres, pero, no sé."

"No see more men," Mateo murmured. "But don't know."

Tomás took the flashlight from Sam and gestured for him to retrieve the branch he'd left earlier. He gave Mateo the second branch.

"We go ahora, now." Tomás aimed the light on the wall below the exit. "Esperar, wait en las rocas."

Marisa climbed out first, then Benicio—with help—then the rest of the boys and Margo.

Before exiting the shaft, Kasenia hugged Tomás one more time and whispered, "Gracias." He reeked of sweat and horse, yet he was the sweetest-smelling, kindliest man she'd ever met. She was a stranger to him. He had no reason to risk his life for her. The scripture inscribed below the ornate cross at the front of her babushka's church flashed through her memory.

Greater love has no one than this, than to lay down one's life for his friends.

For the first time since her early questions about the cross with a man nailed to it, she was beginning to understand the meaning. Tomás was that kind of friend.

He murmured, "Vaya con Dios," and with the flashlight, highlighted the iron handholds protruding from the shaft wall.

With the two handholds and the natural footholds, she quickly ascended the short, jagged wall and wormed through the narrow opening. Sam helped her out into a pine-scented night. Seated beside him, she captured another mental snapshot, this one of their faint moon shadows flung across the flat stone.

Inhaling the fresh air, Kasenia rested her hands behind her on the warm rock and stretched out her legs. Between two big boulders, she could see the moon hung low in the eastern sky. The night was young, yet the moon sliver offered more illumination than the night they'd come. Was that just last night?

The added light would make their journey easier but also make them more visible. Moving together down the mountain, they'd be easy to spot. What if Marlin's men—? Her jacket dropped from her shoulders, and a gentle breeze caressed her bare arms, reminding her she had no control over the elements or her future. She couldn't dwell on what-ifs.

Tomás exited the hole and carefully pushed the log into place beneath the overhang.

Kasenia pulled the hood over her hair, zipped the jacket and stood.

Signaling for Mateo and Sam to brush the surface around the hidden passageway, Tomás disappeared between boulders. Sam motioned Kasenia ahead so he and Mateo could sweep away all hints of their momentary presence.

She was surprised to discover descending the boulders was as difficult, maybe more so than climbing them. The sound of fourteen people scrambling, slipping, scraping rough surfaces with their shoes, and dislodging pebbles that bounced down the boulders exploded in her ears.

But Tomás had said Marlin's men were *not* monitoring the mountain's crest, which made sense if they believed the fugitives were inside the silver mine. That could change at any moment, she knew, but she had to trust Tomás—and God.

Kasenia stopped. *Benicio. Where is he?* The descent had to be especially difficult for the injured boy. Slipping through a narrow gap between two tall boulders, she found the others clustered on a huge rock not far below them.

Sam crouched beside her. "What are they doing?"

"I don't know."

Together, they crab-crawled closer.

Jorge and Ulises slowly rose with Benicio cradled between them. Then Tomás stood, pivoted, and grasped the boy's feet, placing one on each side of his ribs. Bent low, he carefully steered the human stretcher through the mountain's stony crown to ground level and set Benicio on his feet.

Kasenia smiled. *Teamwork.* Tomás always knew what to do. But he wouldn't be with them for long. How could she deliver the boys to Crimson Arches?

They didn't have food, didn't have water, didn't have explicit directions to Trent Duran's ranch. If they happened to find it, they didn't know if he would help them. She wasn't a hiker, didn't know the mountains, didn't have medical supplies *or* medical training.

Releasing a long breath, she remembered her childhood hesitation to try the rope swing that hung above the Usva River and her dedushka's encouraging words. *Fortune favors the bold.* She had gathered her courage, swung out over the river and let go. The plunge into the cool water was exhilarating on a hot summer day. This plunge into the unknown was far more terrifying, but she would gather her courage and do her best for the boys.

Sliding off the final boulder, she joined the others. This was it, the moment they parted ways. The moment she shouldered the responsibility of leading seven boys through Brewster Wiley's hornet nest to safety.

Using hand signals in the pale moonlight, Tomás indicated his Florida-bound group should wait while he led Kasenia and boys to the trail they'd hiked earlier.

Deeper into the trees the dark figures slipped ahead of Kasenia, moments later arriving at the barely visible path. Tomás pointed heavenward and disappeared around the rock outcropping. Kasenia watched him go, saddened she might never see her kindhearted rescuer again. She mouthed, *Vaya con Dios,* took a breath and turned to the boys.

This time, Cesar and Raúl took Benicio's arms. Sam stayed at the rear, pine branch in hand. Kasenia moved to the front. The only sound other than their barely discernible footsteps was the quiet swishing of Sam's branch. They crept through the woods like soldiers on a mission.

They *were* on a mission, a mission to escape Shadow Ranch hell.

Halfway down the mountain, she spotted the antique ore cart that marked the intersection of trails. She motioned for the boys to stay behind, ducked low and hurried to the cart. Peeking over the top, she could see the dark hole that was the mine's entrance.

Marlin was still inside the mine, she assumed, and other Shadow Ranch mercenaries likely patrolled the hillside. Tomás had warned her to be extra cautious at the juncture.

Crouched behind the cart, she held her breath and listened. But all she heard was her pulse pummeling her eardrums. Nothing more. She looked around. The boys had melted into the trees. She couldn't hear them, couldn't see them. They were good boys, smart boys.

She waited, ears tuned to catch the sound of voices, horse noises, the crunch of footsteps, even that of vehicles on the road below. Again, nothing, except the skitter of something small in the underbrush.

Anxious to be far, far away from the mine and Shadow Ranch by sunrise, Kasenia rose and was about to motion the boys forward, when a roar erupted from the mine entrance followed by the most terror-filled scream she'd ever heard.

El Jefe! Kasenia gasped and dropped to her knees behind the cart. She should rush the boys to safety, but where could they go? How could they outrun a jaguar?

Guttural screams echoed in the mine, growing louder and louder. A light appeared near the opening, flashing up, down and across the tunnel walls. Scrabbling sounds, as if someone was fighting for footing on a rock strewn floor, intermixed the screams. And then a man's figure burst from the opening, headlamp askew, arms flailing like a windmill on a blustery night.

Shrieking, "El Jefe, El Jefe," he slip-slided down the scree that over-spread the hillside below the mine and sprawled face-first in the dirt, less than ten feet from the cart.

Kasenia cringed. *Marlin*. She sank onto her heels, peeking over the rim. She could smell his sweat—and his fear.

Marlin lurched to his hands and knees, breathing hard. With a frantic glance at the mine entrance, he sprang to his feet and charged down the hill, his cry now a rasping sob. But he didn't get far before he stumbled again, rolled, and smacked into a tree trunk so hard Kasenia felt the jolt beneath her feet. Like a bass note on a pipe organ, a loud groan huffed from his lungs as he crumpled in a heap.

Clutching the cart's rusted rim, she stared from the inert man's indistinct form to the mine entrance now vaguely illuminated by his catawampus headlamp. Would El Jefe come after him? She might not like Marlin, but she didn't want to watch the jaguar devour him.

The big man wasn't moving, so maybe he was no longer a threat. But El Jefe was a different story. The grande gato had chased the man out of the mine. It might smell her and the boys—had probably already smelled them—and come after them too. They should leave, now.

One hand on the cart, she was about to return to the trail, when a throaty snarl stopped her. Kasenia gaped at the mine entrance, chills shooting down her spine.

The jaguar, its golden eyes reflecting the headlamp's dim light, stood at the opening, rumbling its displeasure. For a long moment, it posed statue-like in the beam, as if contemplating its next move. And then—majestically, deliberately—El Jefe lifted his head, opened his jaws and bared his long yellow teeth.

The deafening growl the big cat emitted reverberated through Kasenia's core and across the mountainside. Her breath seized. Her skin crawled. The hair on her arms rose. The very air quivered, along with the leaves and every other creature within hearing distance—she was sure of it.

The huge animal released another heart-stopping roar, turned its sinewy spotted body and with unhurried disinterest disappeared in the dark tunnel, the fuzzy black tip of its long tail her last view of El Jefe.

Gripping the cart, she clutched her chest and sucked in air, her gaze locked on the mine entrance. Her heart pounded so hard she feared it might burst. Was it safe to leave now? El Jefe seemed to be warning Marlin to stay away or maybe he was letting the world know the mine belonged to him. Could be the big cat wasn't interested in her or the boys.

Marlin's headlight beam wavered and stopped. He moaned. "El Jefe..."

Something or someone nudged her shoulder and she jerked, nearly crying out.

"Sis," Sam whispered in her ear. "Marlin's coming to. We'd better—"

"Right, let's go." She waved her arm, signaling to the others to join them, and stumbled to the trail.

From both sides of the path, the boys' dark forms materialized, silent as specters.

"Smith," came a harsh hiss, "you there?"

Kasenia gasped. Someone was coming down the path they'd hiked moments earlier.

The boys scattered like dandelion tufts in the wind, and just as quiet. She slipped behind a tree.

"Yeah," came a wavering, crackly voice. "Somethin' big 'n' ugly's out here."

"Shh..." The first man sounded closer now. "Keep it down. Run-aways'll hear you."

A male figure came in view.

Kasenia shrunk into the shadows, but not before she recognized him as one of the Shadow Ranch guards. He stopped by the ore cart, holding a two-way radio near his mouth.

"It's El Jefe," he breathed. "I warned Marlin about him. But he never—"

"Who's heavy?" Smith wheezed.

"El. Heh. Fee. He's the big-gest, bad-dest..." He dragged out the words. "*Jag-u-ar* this side of the Mexican border."

"Jaguar?" Smith coughed. "You're pullin' my chain, man."

"Wish I was, 'cause I don't wanna run into him."

"Me, neither." The radio sputtered. "Where are you?" Smith sounded winded, as if he was on the move.

"By the ore cart, where the paths meet."

"I'm comin' down."

Inch by inch, Kasenia maneuvered to the far side of the tree trunk, hugging it with her shoulder blades and wishing she'd picked a bigger tree. She listened for noises on the hillside or footsteps on the path, willing El Jefe to return and scare off the two guards—and any others searching for them. If more Shadow Ranch men were around, they were quiet—not using the radio or reacting to the jaguar's spine-chilling roars like Smith and his buddy.

She'd heard Brewster hired mercenaries to be his guards. Most of them were probably more discreet than these two, but they were all likely to be merciless. In fact, she wouldn't be surprised if Brewster was prowling the mountain in camo right now, night-vision glasses on his nose and a weapon in each hand.

As silly as the mental picture was, she shivered.

Marlin moaned, and the guard spun around, gun raised. "What the—?"

At the sound of heavy footfall, Kasenia turned her head.

A dark form came running on the path she and the boys had been about to follow.

The person slid to a stop by the ore cart, breathing hard.

Kasenia gripped the tree bark behind her.

"Quiet, Smith." The first guard lifted a palm. "I heard something."

Smith pivoted, pistol ready, and scanned the area from side to side.

Fearing he might see the whites of her eyes, Kasenia squinted.

He twisted her direction, and she aborted the breath she'd started to take.

He stepped closer, so close she could smell his sweat-tainted aftershave.

Muscles tensed, she prepared to run.

"Uhh..." Marlin moaned. "Idiots..."

Smith wheeled, gun ready. "Who's there?"

"Help...me, you idiots." Marlin's gravelly order ground into another groan.

"I know that voice," the other guard murmured. "It's Marlin."

"What if the jaguar is close or..." Smith sucked in a breath. "What if it's, you know...chewin' on him?"

"Only one way to find out." The man switched on a flashlight and danced the beam across the open terrain beneath the mine entrance. "There he is," he muttered. "At least I think it's him." Louder, he called, "That you, Marlin?"

"Uhh..." Marlin's moan faded, and the men hurried to his side.

25

S TEP BY STEP, KASENIA edged from the trees onto the path. She and the boys had to leave *now*, before the guards radioed for help.

Sam was at her side in an instant. The others fell in behind her, and he moved to the rear, branch in hand. But only after Kasenia counted seven boys did they creep away from the mine, slinking from tree to tree.

When she felt they'd put enough distance between them and Brewster's men, they walked the trail, maneuvering its twists and turns as fast as Benicio could manage with help. Out of breath, Kasenia stopped at an outcropping and pushed back her hood. The boys followed her lead.

Cupping her ears, she mouthed, *Listen.* At first, she heard their labored breathing, but then night sounds reached her. A car way out on the highway—she could see its lights—coyote calls, cricket chirps, poorwill whistles, and the buzz of nighthawks diving for insects.

No feet tramping after them, no deep-throated jaguar snarls.

Something big swooped overhead, wind whooshing through its wings. A great horned owl, perhaps? The flat expanse below was dark, yet the star-studded sky sparkled with brilliant clarity. A breeze ruffled her hair, cooling her sweaty scalp, but it didn't alleviate her growing thirst. The boys had to be as thirsty as she was.

She crooked her finger for them to come close. "Everyone okay?"

They nodded.

"How's your knee, Benicio?"

"Es okay." He shrugged. "Mis amigos me ayudan."

"We help him," Cesar said.

"Please sit down, so I can look at it." Benicio complied, and she knelt before him to peer through the split in his pant leg. A strong metallic aroma assaulted her senses. Despite the dim lighting, she could see blood had darkened the bandana, but it hadn't dripped down his leg. Considering his injury and all the hiking they'd done, that was good.

"Hey..." Sam leaned into the circle. "Wasn't El Jefe awesome?"

"Sí." "Sí." The boys came alive, all talking at once, hands waving. Kasenia grinned at their sweaty wide-eyed exuberance.

Benicio clutched his chest. "Big noise make..." He thumped his chest.

"Made your heart pound?" Sam asked.

"Sí. El gato grande tiene un gruñido grande."

"You said it..." Sam said. "That big cat has a big growl."

"Really big." Kasenia shivered. "We'll talk more later. You boys ready to go?"

"¿A dónde vamos?" Ulises asked.

"He's asking where we're going," Sam said.

"Crimson Arches Ranch, like Tomás told us." Kasenia stood and helped Benicio to his feet. "We probably won't see the arches tonight, but we should be able to see them tomorrow."

"Then...?" Cesar asked. His voice trailed off.

"Then..." She smiled. "Señor Trent Duran will help us return to our homes, you boys to Phoenix and Sam and me to Tucson. That's our hope, anyway."

"Señorita Kasenia, we no hope." Cesar held up a finger. "We pray."

"Whatever you say."

"Pray now, you like?"

"You pray. I'll watch for trouble."

"Tener los ojos abiertos...eyes open. Dios, he hear." He circled his finger in the air, and the boys faced outward. Kasenia and Sam followed suit.

Cesar, who was next to Kasenia, was the first to pray. Palms lifted to the glittering heavens, he whispered, "Padre, Hijo y Espiritu Santo—Father, Son and Holy Spirit. Nosotros te amamos y tú nos amas, we love you and you love us. Gracias por ayudarnos a dejar Rancho Sombra."

"Thank you for helping us leave Shadow Ranch," Sam translated.

"Yes," Kasenia murmured. "Thank you." *Please, God, may it be a forever goodbye. Don't let them catch us or Tomás's group.*

"Por favor, help Benicio leg," Cesar entreated. "All well, no hurt."

Kasenia smiled. How thoughtful of him to think of his friend.

"Por favor, fix Marlin," Cesar continued.

What? Kasenia frowned.

"Make him okay, e ir lejos del rancho, go away from ranch. Make him good guy, no más hombre malo, no more bad man."

Head back, she stared at the stars. *Maybe God could make Marlin a good guy, but it wouldn't be easy. And why would he bother? Cesar was young and blinded by his faith. Marlin was evil to the core. Changing him would take a miracle on par with raising someone from the dead.*

The other boys asked God for safe travels, for water, for food. To protect them from Brewster and El Jefe. And for all of them to go home to their madres y padres.

Sam squeezed Kasenia's hand.

She whispered, "I know." The boys' hunger for home and family made her miss her parents more than ever. Where were Mom and Dad now? Did they know she and Sam were missing? What was Grandpa Gordon thinking? Had he figured out they didn't fly to Russia? He wouldn't telephone Babushka Irina because he didn't understand her limited, accented English. But surely, he'd talk with their parents.

From where she and the boys stood, the murky moonlight on the treeless path ahead revealed a stone-littered stretch. Then the trail rose, skirted the mountain and disappeared from sight. She and the boys shouldn't linger on the outcropping. They needed to slip into the shadows again and find a place to rest. They were tired, hungry and, mostly, thirsty.

"En el fuerte nombre de Jesús." Raúl paused before concluding his prayer. "Amén."

"Strong name of Jesus," Cesar translated. "Amén."

Kasenia opened her mouth to tell the boys they would stop after they traversed the curve ahead, when Sam began to pray, something she'd never heard him do. Well, except when they prayed in unison with their babushka's Russian congregation and repeated memorized prayers before they ate with her.

"Dear God," he breathed, "make Brewster's eyes blind to keep him from seeing us, and make Trent Duran understand the truth. Brewster is his friend, but he will lie to him." He hesitated, as if not sure how to continue. "Thank you. Amen."

Kasenia glanced at her brother. She hadn't thought of Brewster's influence over Trent.

"We go now, Señorita Kasenia?" Cesar asked.

She directed their attention to the trail descending below them. "Can you walk a little farther, guys?"

Their response was a soft unison, "Sí."

"Benicio..." She raised her hood and tucked her braid inside. "Will your knee be okay?"

"Sí, señorita."

"Let me know if gets to be too much."

He nodded.

"We help." Again, his friends spoke in unison.

"You boys..." Kasenia grinned. "Are the best of the best."

"We help Sam." Cesar acted out sweeping the trail.

"Thank you."

They'd traversed the rocky valley, rounded the bend and entered a dense copse of trees, when Sam hissed, "Sis, someone's coming."

Without stopping or asking questions, the boys slipped from the path into the thicket. Kasenia did the same then pulled her hood over her forehead and peeked around a tree trunk. What had Sam heard?

"...wouldn't have come this far," a male voice was saying, his words accompanied by a scuff of feet.

Lights flashed over the trail and the tree trunks. Though they were some distance away, their words were distinct.

"They've had at least twenty-four hours," responded a second man. "Could a gone clear to Mexico by now."

"Hoofin' it through the mountains?"

"Someone might a been waiting out on the highway to pick 'em up."

"Nobody has a clue, which explains why Wiley is sittin' in his Vette, cruising the blacktop, and we're killin' our feet walkin' around a stinkin' mountain in the middle of the night."

Barely breathing, Kasenia leaned into the tree. She and the boys should climb higher to escape the flashlight beams. But the sound of eight people scaling an incline covered with dry detritus would draw attention in the silent night.

Arms plastered against her sides, hands covered by her dark sleeves, she drew inward, making herself as one with the tree as possible, and hoped the boys did the same. One twitch or cry or visible tennis shoe, and they'd breathe their last breath of freedom. Without a doubt the men had guns and wouldn't hesitate to shoot. She didn't want any of the boys to die, but for herself, death might be better than facing Brewster's manic wrath.

"I need a smoke," one of the men said.

The footsteps stopped.

"I need a drink. Should a stuck a flask in my hip pocket. Didn't know we were—"

A deep rumble sounded nearby.

"What...what was that?"

"Thunder?"

"Sky's clear."

Kasenia furrowed her brow. What was going on?

A silent form emerged from the brush and stopped on the path, tail twitching, spots visible in the pale light.

Oh, no... She stifled a gasp. El Jefe had followed them.

One of the men stuttered, "Wh–what the—?"

The jaguar's snarl jolted her from head to toe, electrifying every cell in her body.

With screeches rivaling the big cat's growl, the men spun and charged back the way they'd come.

El Jefe let loose another hair-raising threat and bounded after them.

Grasping the rough tree trunk behind her for support, Kasenia balanced on shaking knees. Her heart thrummed her ribs, and her breath came in jagged gulps. The jaguar no longer sounded warnings, yet the men's diminishing screams pierced the night air for a long, long time. Birds flapped in the treetops and called out warnings. Wildlife skittered through the underbrush. Deer crashed past.

When all was quiet again, she abandoned the security of her tree, and one foot at a time, worked her way onto the path, softly calling, "Everyone okay?"

Almost as noiseless as the big cat, the boys materialized in the shadows from both sides of the trail. Kasenia counted their hooded heads but came up with six, not seven. She counted again. "Who's missing?"

They looked at each other.

"Estoy aquí..." Benicio stumbled onto the path.

Sam and Ulises ran to grab his arms.

"Beni." She knelt before him. "Can I call you Beni?'

"Sí, señorita..." He fell trembling into her arms. "Estoy muy asustado."

"Benicio," Ccsar whispered, "es muy scared, afraid."

"Me, too, Beni." She rubbed the boy's back. "Me, too. That was El Jefe's loudest growl ever. My bones are still shaking."

The boys drew near, falling on their knees. "Gran boom." "Como el trueno, like thunder."

"But wasn't it cool?" Sam pounded his thighs. "El Jefe blew those guys' minds. Never heard grown men scream like little girls before."

He laughed, and then the others started laughing, as loudly as they dared. Even Benicio.

"Un momento, por favor." Kasenia smiled, proud of her Spanish sentence. Turning him to the meager light, she studied his injured knee through the slit in his pantleg. Blood now trickled from the makeshift bandage down the boy's skinny shin. Though she could smell the blood, it held no unpleasant aroma that might indicate infection. Even so, he needed medical attention. The only way they could get help for him was to continue their trek to Trent Duran's ranch.

"Señorita Kasenia, what you think?" Cesar's brow was knit with concern beneath his thick shock of dark hair.

"I think Benicio is a very brave young man who needs a doctor. I know you boys are tired and his knee will bleed more, but we must keep moving. That's the only solution I see." She stood and the boys followed suit.

"What if El Jefe comes after us again?" Sam asked.

"No–no–no–no–no." Cesar tick-tocked his finger in Sam's face. "El Jefe want Brewster hombres, no nosotros." He indicated the group. "Not you, not me."

"You don't know that. When he's done with them, he might come for us."

Cesar shook his head. "El Jefe es like... How you say, ahn-hel?"

"Angel?" Sam offered.

"El Jefe help like un ángel para Dios."

"Are you saying God up in heaven is making a wildcat down on earth do whatever he wants?" Sam asked. "Like a guardian angel?"

"Like en la Biblia." Cesar grinned. "Daniel y leones, lions. Un ángel shut las bocas, mouths."

Sam didn't look convinced.

"I know." Kasenia shook her head. "Seems crazy. Yet, El Jefe has distracted five men from capturing us, if you include Marlin and the two by the mine cart. Hard to believe it all happened by chance."

Kasenia had no idea how far or how long they walked beneath the stars, up and down inclines, over rocks and roots, between trees, over and under fallen logs. No one spoke, no one complained, though they were thirsty, so thirsty. She and the boys took turns brushing away their trail and holding Benicio's arms. She told him he was strong and courageous. She also told him they could stop anytime.

"No, señorita," he'd say. "Estoy bien."

But he was pale, and she sensed he was weakening.

They reached a short bridge and she stumbled across it, not catching the significance until someone hissed, "S-s-señorita, agua."

Water? She stopped. How had she missed water?

Peering over the bridge railing, she realized the trickle was so small, it made little noise. The boys were already climbing into the creek bed, giggling with excitement. She giggled right along with them, giddy to finally be able to satiate her mounting thirst.

They followed the stream to its source, a spring less than thirty feet up the hill from the bridge. It bubbled like a miniature geyser from the mountainside, forming a small pool at its base. The fountain only reached seven or eight inches at its peak, yet it glinted with moonlight, and it was water, fresh, life-giving water.

"Gracias a Dios." Ismael raised his hands heavenward. "Dios escuchó nuestra oración y nos dio agua."

"What did you say?" Kasenia asked.

"Ismael thank God he hear prayer, give water," Cesar translated.

"He did." She smiled. "Yes, he did."

The boys invited Kasenia to drink first.

"Oh, no, I can't do that. The youngest can have the first drink."

"Go ahead," Sam nudged her arm. "Ladies first, remember?"

"Thank you." Kasenia smiled at the boys. "You are so good to me." She removed her hoodie, hung it on a branch and knelt by the spring. Water seeped into her jeans, but she didn't mind. The cool liquid felt wonderful.

Quickly, so she didn't keep the boys from assuaging their thirst for long, she splashed the cold water on her neck and arms, gasping with shock and pleasure. Tempted to wash her grease-smeared face, she resisted, reminding herself she'd have access to soap and water soon. And then she drank...and drank again. She wanted more, but she'd have time later, after the boys had their fill.

Sam and Ismael helped Benicio arrange his limbs in a position that allowed him to drink but protected his knee. One after the other, the boys gulped the refreshing gift, God's answer to their prayers. Kasenia smiled. Just like in the cavern and outside the shaft, she had another hazy snapshot to add to her mental photo album.

Downstream from the mini fountain, Benicio washed blood streaks from his shin. He told Kasenia the wound had stopped bleeding. For a moment, she considered removing the bandana, but she didn't know what she'd do with the blood-soaked tissues beneath it. They couldn't leave the wad behind. If they buried it under a rock, some animal might dig it up and it could somehow lead Brewster to them.

In addition, Benicio's wound would be open. If he fell in the dirt, it could be injured worse or horribly infected. She decided to leave the bandana in place—Tomás had done a good job securing it—and trust they'd get medical care soon.

She drank once more from the fountain, and so did each boy before they took off again, refreshed and energized for the first time in hours. But it wasn't long before their energy flagged. When Benicio's limp became more pronounced, she knew they had to stop.

The sky had just begun to lighten when they reached an outcropping that overlooked the desert, what little they could see of it. The boys disappeared in the trees to relieve themselves, but Kasenia remained on the path, staring into the heavens. "What next?" she wondered out loud. They were more vulnerable, more easily seen now. Even if they spied the arches, they couldn't walk up to Trent Duran's door in broad daylight.

"Señorita..." Raúl climbed up the hill to join her on the path. "You see." He waved his hand over a massive stone that stretched out before them like a huge a pancake and motioned for her to follow him down the direction he'd come. When he showed her how the flat rock "roofed" a boulder shelf below, Kasenia decided it was a good place to rest until sunrise. They would search for the crimson arches then. She hoped they hadn't passed the formations in the dark. Backtracking toward Shadow Ranch would not be wise.

The gap beneath the overhang provided enough headspace for everyone to sit upright against a rock wall, including Kasenia and Sam. They could give their weary bodies a break yet be hidden from the path. Hard as the stony seat was, Kasenia marveled at how good it felt to sit.

Mountain air sifted through their hideout, cool though not unbearably cold. Grateful her oversized jacket was thick and warm and provided a bit of padding, Kasenia closed her tired dry eyes. She'd rest them until the sunshine was bright enough to search for the arches. The birds would awaken them.

The next thing she knew, however, Sam was shaking her shoulder. "Sis, wake up."

"What?" She jolted upright, knocking the back of her head on the hard stone. Her heartrate zipped into high gear. "What's wrong?"

"Listen."

26

—·—

A<small>T FIRST, K</small>ASENIA HEARD nothing. And then it was as if dozens of tiny feet tiptoed around their hideout.

"Hear that?" Sam whispered.

She nodded.

Outlined by the early morning light, a doglike form trotted past on the rocks below, trailed by another and another. Coyotes! Kasenia stifled a gasp. A whole pack of them. *What do they want with us?* She'd been told coyotes rarely attacked humans. Had she and the boys intruded on their hunting ground?

She glanced at the boys who were all asleep. Should she wake them and have them yell and throw rocks at the coyotes? No, not a good plan. Sound carried on the desert *and* in the mountains. If any of Brewster's men were nearby, they'd be after her and the boys in an eyeblink.

El Jefe, where are you when we need you?

The coyotes circled the ledge, padding below, above and around it, stopping often to stare their direction. Whiffs of urine assaulted her senses interspersed with a wilder, ranker, rotten-meat stench. She'd heard coyotes liked to roll in carcasses. Whatever the source, the smell was revolting.

What were the animals thinking? Were they merely curious or were they deciding when and how to attack? Did they smell the humans' sweaty unwashed bodies? Or the bloody pad on Benicio's knee? She should have buried it back by the spring. What if the coyotes—

Kasenia opened her clenched fists, took a breath, and stopped her downward-spiraling thoughts. She had to plan, not panic. "Sam," she whispered in his ear, "we're trapped. What should we do?"

He leaned close. "We were taught in the outdoor class I took to yell and clap and throw things, to make ourselves look big. But we can't be loud or..."

"Right." The sun's rim was poking above the mountains on the eastern edge of the desert. She wanted to get far away from the coyotes. But she didn't know if Benicio could run or if the coyotes would follow them.

"One thing for sure," Sam said, "we shouldn't run. They'll chase us."

"Oh, too bad..." That answered that question.

Kasenia closed her eyes. *You helped us do the impossible, God—escape Shadow Ranch. And you've helped us all along the way. If you could make a jaguar scare off Brewster's men, you can help us intimidate these—*

A strange sound, like a sudden wind, interrupted her prayer. Kasenia opened her eyes in time to see the sun-tinged silhouette of a huge bird rush at a coyote, wings wide and talons spread. It knocked the yipping animal down then soared upward, fur tufts, dust and loose feathers roiling in its wake. Diving at another coyote, the bird drove it to the ground. One yelp, and the animal slunk into the underbrush, tail between its legs.

With wingtips and white crown glowing in the sun's early rays, the eagle rose again, gained elevation, and plunged at a third coyote, bowling it over. The coyote flipped to its feet, snapping and snarling, yet it cowered before its attacker.

The eagle flapped up, up, up—all the way to the top of a lofty pine tree—and settled on a bare branch. Eyeing the coyotes with fierce golden eyes accentuated by a hooked yellow beak, the winged predator screeched three loud, strident calls. Then it repeated the shrieks, as if giving the four-footed predators a piece of its mind from its all-seeing perch.

Bristling but beaten, the coyotes snarled, whined and bared their teeth at the eagle as they slunk into the woods, scraggly tails tucked between their legs. Kasenia counted seven of them.

"Wow..." Sam murmured.

Kasenia released the breath trapped in her throat and sucked in the dusty wild-animal smells. Silencing a cough with her sleeve, she glanced at the boys. Wide-eyed awake, they gestured and murmured among themselves.

Sam laughed. "God did it again, didn't he?"

Kasenia grinned. She hadn't even finished praying.

With one last chattering call that sounded a bit like a chuckle, the eagle spread its huge wings and flew away—magnificent, mysterious, fearsome and free.

The boys scrambled to the platform's edge to watch the eagle's soaring flight. As the majestic bird faded beyond their vision, Sam's whispered, "Awesome," was followed by murmurs of agreement and Cesar's, "Praise to Dios."

"Yes, praise to Dios." Kasenia smiled at Cesar. "He's taking good care of us."

Birds twittered in the treetops, apparently convinced their world was safe again.

"Señorita Kasenia..." Raúl directed her attention to the flat valley. "You see? Mira los dos arcos."

"You found the arches?" Shading her eyes against the sun cresting the craggy mountain peaks, she strained to see what he saw. "Oh, there they are." Situated at a juncture of dirt roads, the formations were bigger than she'd expected. "Good job spotting them, Raúl."

"This was the perfect place to stop." Sam grinned.

Sunshine backlit the arches, leaving the frontside dark. They towered above a Spanish-style home and outbuildings visible where the sun's rays penetrated between sandstone shadows.

"Trent Duran told me the western setting sun gives them a rosy tinge," Kasenia said. "That's why his great-grandfather named it Crimson Arches Ranch. He also wanted it to be a reminder of Christ's blood on the cross." Not everybody would understand his thinking, but these boys would.

"Ah, sí." Ismael pointed upward. The other boys did the same.

The ranch wasn't far—as the crow flies—one of her grandfather's favorite phrases. Thinking of Grandpa Gordon pained her heart, but she pushed aside her anguish. If all went well, she'd see him soon—and hug him like she'd never hugged him before.

"Boys," she whispered, "how about a bathroom break?"

Amid their nods and murmurs, she said, "Jorge and Sam, please check to make sure we're alone."

The two boys crawled off the ledge in opposite directions. Several minutes later, they returned, signaling the coast was clear. The group climbed from their hiding place then separated to ensure privacy on both sides of the trail. One by one, they reassembled on the flat outcropping.

Basking in the early morning sunshine, Kasenia stretched her back. "We're almost there, guys." She inhaled the fresh mountain air. "We can see our destination. We can do this."

Eyes bright with hope, the "foster" boys mimed excited cheers and fist pumps. Kasenia grinned. She couldn't wait to watch them reunite with their parents.

"Shh," Sam hissed. "Everybody quiet."

Kasenia whipped around.

One hand cupped behind his ear and the other pointing the direction they'd come, he said, "Is that what I think it is?"

And then she heard it, a distant pulsing thrum.

"Es un helicóptero," Cesar breathed, his eyes wide.

They couldn't see it, but the chopper sounded as if it was headed their way.

Visions of her helicopter wedding and Brewster's enthusiasm for the *birds*, as he called them, flashed through Kasenia's mind. It would be just like him to use one to hunt them down. Greed plus fury bolstered by unlimited funds would fuel his determination to find them, no matter the cost.

"Quick." She pulled her hood up. "Into the trees." Whether or not it was Brewster, they needed to hide. The evil sheriff or a hired crew might be searching for them.

"Sis..." Sam yanked the emergency blanket from his pocket. "We can disappear under camo cover."

"No time."

"Right." He shoved the packet back into the pocket and grabbed Jorge. "Cut two branches and help me wipe out our prints."

All too soon, the thwop-thwop of blades could be heard, growing louder each second. Kasenia waited in the trees with the others until Sam and Jorge caught up.

"Just in time," Sam sucked in a breath. "I bet they're gonna land right where we were standing."

She studied the wide, flat ledge. Sam was right. It was a perfect place to land a helicopter, but that put her and the boys in immediate danger. She scanned their surroundings. Another boulder stack, this one as high as a two-story house, jutted through the trees. "Can you two carry Beni to those rocks?"

Sam and Jorge dropped the branches and clasped arms to form a chair for Benicio. He clutched their shoulders and they staggered ahead.

Signaling the others to follow, Kasenia took off. They scurried through the trees, reaching the massive stones moments before the helicopter approached the flat outcropping. The engine's roar shattered the quiet morning and sent birds fleeing its alien presence. Trees and bushes bent with the blades' downwash.

The wild wind pummeled the fugitives with forest detritus. Fearing they'd be impaled by pine needles, Kasenia had the boys maneuver farther around the big rocks and crouch behind them. She touched her face, which itched more than usual. It was crusty where dirt and debris had stuck to the grease. She longed to scratch her cheek, but as awful as it felt, the grime would help her blend into their environment.

One hand on the boulder for balance, she peered between the branches of a bush growing alongside the boulder.

Behind her, Sam murmured, "I'm looking over your shoulder."

Almost as soon as the chopper settled onto the granite shelf, a male voice shouted through the rotor noise, "Head out opposite directions."

Brewster.

A voice she never wanted to hear again. He must have rented the helicopter and hired a pilot. He'd once told her he wanted to take flight lessons, but as far as she knew, that hadn't happened. Otherwise, he'd be flying back and forth from Tucson, not driving.

Kasenia sniffed the air. An oily kerosene aroma, like in the mine, had infiltrated the woods.

"Jet fuel," Sam whispered.

Kasenia glanced at him. How did her brother know the helicopter ran on jet fuel?

"The deserters don't have supplies," Brewster called. "They'll come begging, so be ready to grab 'em and herd 'em to the ranch, where they belong. You're packin' the zip ties, right?"

"Yes, sir," another man yelled.

She could see the pilot but not Brewster or the other man.

"If they take off, you know what to do—last resort. Just remember, they're mine and I need 'em at the ranch, ASAP." He paused. "Meet back here. I'll tell you when. Radios on twenty-four-seven. I'll be monitoring the infrared. Be ready to head where I direct."

Infrared? Kasenia and Sam locked gazes, eyes wide.

"Infrared," Cesar whispered. "What is?"

"Bad news," Sam whispered. "Thermal imaging. A camera that can see our body heat."

Cesar frowned. "No es good."

"You're tellin' me, dude." Sam shook his head. "But it can't see inside hard stuff like houses and cars—or Mylar, like what our survival blankets are made from."

Turning to the other boys, Cesar spoke in soft Spanish.

"We'll find the defectors," Brewster called. "No way fourteen people can hide in these mountains for long without being spotted."

"Wanna bet?" Sam muttered.

The helicopter's whine changed pitch.

"Sis," Sam hissed, "it's about to take off."

"Move." She motioned for the boys to shift around the boulder stack. "We have to keep the rocks between us and the helicopter, so Brewster's camera can't see us." If he spied even one of their thermal images, he'd have his men charging at them in an instant. The question was, could they move fast enough on the rugged mountainside to avoid the camera's scrutiny?

"Señorita..." Ismael pointed to a gap in the rocks. "Go en las rocas."

"Good, go." The hooded youth ducked into the cleft, followed by the others. Sliding on pine needles, Kasenia squeezed after them, Sam at her heels. The boys crowded farther in, breathing hard. Did the crevice have room for everyone?

By the time the chopper left the ledge, they'd jammed into the hollow, out of camera view. At least she hoped so. Finally, the helicopter was off the mountain and flying away. The air stilled, as if waiting for the birds to return. A kaleidoscope of odors drifted through their cramped hideout. Bad breath, sweat, Benicio's blood, and the sweet earthy scents of their surroundings.

One of the boys started to speak, but Kasenia shushed him. "Listen."

Pulse by pulse, the engine and rotor sounds diminished until a nearby conversation filtered through the trees. The men—sounded like two of them, probably Brewster's mercenaries—were still nearby.

"Just like Wiley to leave us out here all day, maybe the whole night, with one expired MRE for food and a single canteen of water," one man grumbled. "While he loafs in an air-conditioned copter."

"He talks big, but he couldn't make it up here on the mountain." The second man's voice was deep, with a southern drawl. "He's used to sittin' on his ass, ridin' around in that Vette of his, not doin' any real work."

"Bet he don't find nothin' but a coyote or bobcat with that fancy camera on his helmet," the first man said. "Anyone smart enough to break out of the compound—still can't figure how they did it—is long gone. Probably hitched a ride to Mexico by now."

"Bet my bottom dollar Tomás helped hisself to some tourist's van," the other man said. "Friendly enough dude but *way* too quiet. Kept to hisself, never would drink or play poker with us, no matter how many times we asked. Should a known he was up ta somethin'."

"Yeah, but..." Man number one snorted. "Why take two broads plus their brats and all those Hispanic kids with him?"

"Maybe he's makin' his own harem, like Wiley."

"Don't seem the type."

For a long moment, they were quiet. Then the first man asked, "You ever off a woman or a kid?"

After a pause, the second man, the one with the southern accent, offered a monotone response. "We leveled entire villages in Nam. Hated every moment, 'specially the screamin'. To this day, I have flashbacks and dreams where I hear 'em all over agin. And agin and agin. Don't mind takin' down an enemy soldier, but innocent women and children? Not my game."

Above them, a hawk's harsh cry was answered by another.

"Wiley don't consider those women and children innocent. He calls them defectors, traitors, apostates."

Kasenia sighed. She hated to think what other words he might have used.

"Truth be told," the first man continued, "I don't care what he calls them, I'm not going to send a woman or a kid to an early grave, a grave I'd have to dig myself."

"He'll have your hide if you let jus' one of 'em get away alive."

"I'm thinking it's about time I found a new employer."

"You keep on thinkin' that, Duvall. You go AWOL while Wiley's mad as a cornered rattler, he'll send me after you in a heartbeat." His tone dropped a notch, and his words were slow and even. "I *always* get my man."

For a long moment, Duvall didn't respond. When he spoke again, his voice had changed pitch. "Thought you didn't like the screaming."

"You wouldn't scream 'cause you wouldn't see me comin'."

Kasenia grimaced. These guys were as nasty as Brewster.

"I'm shaking in my boots." Duvall sounded half convinced. "We better get moving. Got a lot of territory to cover. Wiley'll be crisscrossing these mountains all day long, antsy as a caged wolf. With that thermal-heat lens, he can see us as clear as he can see a coyote or El Jefe."

"Wish I could a watched El Jefe tear into Marlin. Sure bunged him up bad."

"Couldn't a happened to a more deserving dude."

"No shit. I'm outa here."

"Watch out for rattlers."

Except for the sound of feet pounding the trail, quiet descended on the clearing.

Kasenia blew a long breath through pursed lips though she remained motionless. Not until the men's running footsteps receded and the birds began to sing again did she allow the boys to worm out of their hiding place.

They glanced warily about as if expecting the mercenaries to come hurtling through the trees, guns ready. After the stress the youths had experienced, no food, little water and just a couple hours of sleep, they were exhausted, hungry and thirsty. Benicio seemed especially ragged, and his limp was worse than ever.

Beckoning the boys close, she murmured, "Let's see how far we can get before the helicopter returns—or those two guys." She knelt before Benicio and took his hands. "You going to be okay, Beni?"

His only response was a weary nod.

"This is hard for everyone, but especially difficult for you." She squeezed his hands. "I appreciate your determination. We'll help you as much as we can. The sooner we get down this mountain, the sooner we can find someone to tend to your knee."

Standing, she added, "Wish I could fix you guys a big breakfast, along with all the orange juice you can drink. That'll come later, once we conquer this hill. Everyone ready to go?"

"What do we do if the chopper comes back?" Sam asked.

"Good question." She sighed. "I have no idea."

"We pray, ask Dios," Cesar suggested. "He show us."

The boy's faith amazed Kasenia. And God seemed to hear and answer his prayers. "Great idea, Cesar. Would you do that for us before we go? Ismael can be our lookout."

Ismael climbed onto a boulder, checking every direction.

Cesar held out his arms. The group joined hands and bowed their heads.

"Padre nuestro que estás en los cielos ...Our Father in heaven," Cesar began, "you help mucho. El Jefe make Marlin afraid." His voice grew louder. "Coyótes leave, hombres not see. Muchas gracias."

Kasenia was about to quiet him when he lowered his volume. "Por favor, help Benicio go down montaña. Ayuda a todos, help everyone go down. Nosotros te queremos mucho, we love you very much. Amén."

"Thank you, Cesar. What a wonderful way to start the morning." She held up a hand. "Before we go, let's get our survival blankets ready, just in case."

Cesar, Ulises and Sam slipped the packets from their pockets. Kasenia did the same. Together, they examined them, front and back. The contents had been folded and inserted into zip-top bags. "Open the top," Kasenia said, "so we can pull the blankets out fast, if needed."

She elbowed her brother. "What were you saying about Mylar?"

"These are made from Mylar sheets. They'll reflect our heat signatures back to us, which might get hot, but it'll keep Brewster's camera from seeing our thermal images."

"I'm so glad you know outdoor stuff."

"And I'm glad you paid for the class, after I begged and begged to go."

Kasenia laughed. "You and I are about the same height. Want to take a turn at being Benicio's armchair?"

Sam grinned, his teeth white in his blackened, debris-plastered face. "Did you forget I'm taller?"

"You won't ever let me forget, will you? By the way, your eye is more colorful this morning than last night. Kind of a yellow-green." He still hadn't told her how he got the black eye.

"Good. Then I won't need the camo blanket 'cause I have a camo face."

"But you want to use it, I know you do."

They grasped forearms and bent down so Benicio could back into their human chair. His arms tight around their necks, they took off. Lurching downhill sideways around trees and over rocks and fallen branches was not a walk in the park, as her Grandpa Gordon would say. At this rate, they wouldn't reach the bottom until nightfall.

We're in no hurry, Kasenia reminded herself. They had all day to make their way down the mountain.

Ulises and Cesar went before them, holding branches aside and guiding them on the best path for their awkward descent. The boys who followed were silent, other than their huffs and puffs and the noises their shoes made as they trudged through dry leaves, needles and pinecones.

Kasenia wasn't sure how long or how far they'd carried Benicio when her back began to throb and she could no longer feel her hands. Finally, she said, "Sorry, guys, I have to stop." Though Benicio was the smallest of the boys, she needed a break.

She and Sam lowered him to the ground then shook out their hands. "My arms are tingling," Sam said. "Must have lost circulation."

"Mine, too." Kasenia rubbed her arms.

"Lo siento mucho." Benicio hung his head.

"Don't be sorry, dude." Sam elbowed the boy. "Not your fault your knee got cut." Kasenia wrapped an arm around Benicio's shoulders. "You'd do the same for us, Beni. I just need to rest for a moment, and then we'll start again."

Sam walked to a big tree with red-brown bark that looked like thousands of overlapping puzzle pieces. He scratched at the bark then sniffed it. "Yep, smells like butterscotch."

"Butterscotch?" Kasenia raised an eyebrow.

"I learned about these trees in the class. Arizona mountains have lots of them. They're called ponderosa pines. Take a whiff."

She leaned close. "You're right, it's a sweet aroma. But to me, it's more like vanilla than butterscotch."

"That's how it was in the class. Everybody smelled something different. Some said butterscotch or vanilla. Others said cinnamon or coconut."

Benicio scratched at the tree. "Galletas."

"What's that?" Sam asked.

"Cookies." Cesar stuck his nose on the tree. "Sí, es cookies."

The other boys crowded around, excited for a new experience.

"Shh, we must remain quiet." Kasenia hoped the food reminder wouldn't make the boys' stomachs growl any more than they already did. Hands on her waist, she stared up through the tall ponderosa's thick branches, admiring the long green needles and pinecone clusters. She and the boys might lack food and water, yet they had shade and a relatively cool morning, considering they were in the desert.

"S-s-señorita..." Ulises tugged her sleeve. "Helicóptero, it come."

27

"**B**oys." Kasenia motioned to the group gathered around the tree. "Ulises hears a helicopter."

Mouths agape, they gawked up at the tree branches.

"Sis," Sam hissed, "time for survival blankets."

"Right." She slipped hers from her pocket.

"Come on, guys." He waved his packet. "Let's see how fast we can disappear. Brewster's camera can't see us or our heat signatures under these things."

Those with the emergency blankets pulled them out and started to unfurl them.

"Put the plastic bags in your pockets." Kasenia shoved hers into a back pocket. "We can't leave any evidence behind."

"Be careful," Sam added. "They have a shiny side."

"No es good." Cesar frowned. "Brewster see."

"Sit in pairs." Kasenia held up two fingers. "Two beneath a blanket, camo side up. Near a tree trunk. The branches will provide some protection. Every inch of your body should be covered by the blanket. Benicio, sit with me."

A thwap-thwap of chopper blades rumbled in the distance.

The boys separated into three groups of two and unfolded the Mylar sheets, shiny sides down. Benicio helped Kasenia open theirs and then sat on the ground, his injured leg extended. She tucked the blanket around him and instructed the other boys to sit back-to-back, knees at their chests.

"Drape the blankets over your heads, anchor them beneath your feet and backsides and pull your arms in. I'll check to see if you're covered, so be quick." Thank God they all understood English.

The boys did as she instructed, drawing the blanket edges under their shoes.

The helicopter's rhythmic beat grew louder.

Kasenia rushed from one camouflaged mound to the other. "Keep your hoods on, fold your arms and lower your heads to your knees." She wasn't sure why she said that, but it seemed the best way for them to hold still.

"Good thinking, Sis," came Sam's muffled comment. "Our faces against the Mylar sheet could reveal an outline."

Once more, she checked the blankets. They needed to be far enough under the boys' shoes and buttocks to withstand the rotor wind that was growing stronger by the second. If just a corner got loose, and the sheet blew—

"Sis," Sam urged, "hurry, hide."

Treetops swayed. Debris swirled.

Squinting into the gale, she crawled under the camo sheet with Benicio, bent her knees and secured the blanket around them. How long would Brewster linger over the trees? Just knowing he looked down on them like some sort of god made her stomach lurch. He was the devil incarnate, not a god.

Please, God in heaven, don't let him see us. They were so, so close to Trent Duran's ranch.

The helicopter hovered above them for what seemed like forever, and then, from the sound of it, continued up the mountainside. Kasenia didn't move for fear it would circle around. And sure enough, it did, weaving back and forth above the treetops.

Something charged through the brush not far away. A deer? A bear? One of Brewster's men?

She sucked in a choked breath, arms tight around her shins, head on her knees. The air inside their tent was suffocating. If only she could remove her jacket, but she didn't dare move. What did Brewster see that brought him back? Did his camera spot movement? Were his guards storming down the hill after them, guns and zip ties ready?

The Mylar quivered with the rotors' pulsing throb—or maybe it was her trembling body. An untethered sensation overtook her, rattling her psyche as if she, along with the entire forest, would splinter into a million pieces. She drew tenuous, gasping gulps of the muggy air. *I can't take any more, God. Make him go, make him—*

Benicio patted her arm. "Es okay, señorita."

"Oh, Beni, I..." She'd forgotten he was there. She needed to be strong, for him, for the others.

The helicopter lifted and took off. Kasenia waited until the rotors' whop-whop and then the engine's rumble faded before she shoved away the sheet, threw back her hood and drew a deep breath.

Benicio grinned. "Jesús make okay."

Hardly able to croak out the words, she called, "Come out, guys."

"About time." Sam flipped the blanket aside. "I was getting so hot I was afraid the infrared would pick up my heat signature through the blanket."

When they'd gathered in a circle on the ground, crumpled camo blankets in their arms, Cesar excitedly announced, "I pray Brewster go far, bother no more."

"I do same." Jorge's wide grin dimpled his chubby cheeks.

Ismael lifted his dark eyebrows. "I pray he no see Tomás y Mateo y Margo familia."

"God got an earful from us," Kasenia said. "I was praying, too. But I didn't think of Tomás and Mateo and Margo's family. Thank you for remembering them, Ismael."

"Do you know him?" Cesar asked.

"Who?"

"Dios, God."

Kasenia rubbed neck. "Do I know God?" What a strange question and what an odd time to ask.

"Sí." He waited for her reply, hands clasped.

"He answered our prayers." She lifted her eyebrows. "But it doesn't mean we can know him or be friends with him, like you and I are friends." She wasn't sure what Cesar wanted from her, but she knew he expected honesty. "I mean, he's somewhere up there, or out there. And we're down here."

"La Biblia, the Bible, it tell how we know him."

"Really? In those words?"

Cesar nodded, eyes bright with certainty.

"Where does it say that?" She pulled the tiny travel Bible from her jacket pocket.

"I not sure. Maybe los salmos."

"The psalms?"

"Sí. It say, 'Quedaos tranquilos, y sabed que soy Dios. Stay still and know I Dios...God.' Jesús, he say, 'You know me, you know mi Padre, my Father. I am way to Father.' Jesús is way to heaven, not Señor Brewster. Jesús die for you, save you from pecados, sins...bad things you do. If you say sorry for pecados, he make heart clean and take you heaven—because he love you, not because you Señor Brewster wife."

"Thank you, Cesar." Kasenia smiled. "And thank God I was *never* Brewster's real wife. Let's talk more about Jesús and God later, okay? Right now, we need to get off this mountain."

Ismael pointed at her Bible. "Mira tu Biblia," and Cesar said, "He want see Bible."

Kasenia gave it to him, and the two boys turned pages until Ismael announced, "Aquí está mi nombre."

Finger on a page near the front of the Bible, he showed her the name *Ishmael*.

"I remember you telling us you have a Bible name, Ismael. Very cool. I'd like to read Ishmael's story with you after we get to Señor Duran's house. Would you like that?"

Ismael grinned and nodded.

She stood, brushing debris from her jeans. "We'd better move on."

"Señorita, por favor, please." Cesar took the Bible and leafed through it. "Aquí," he said, "here it say children of light." He showed her the verse. "We no niños de la noche. We children of light. See?" He gave her the Bible.

Kasenia read the verse aloud. "You are all children of the light and children of the day. We do not belong to the night or to the darkness." She gave him a thumbs-up. "It's true. You boys belong to the day, not the night."

"Jesús make chicos del día, boys of the light," Cesar said, "when save from pecados, sins."

"Chicos del día. I like it, Cesar." She pocketed the Bible, helped Benicio to his feet and handed him one end of the survival blanket. "Let's see if we can fold these things to their original size. Remember to keep the shiny sides toward the ground."

They wrestled with the blankets, folding and refolding until they could cram them into the plastic packets. None of them could zip the closures shut, but the sheets were now small enough to fit into their pockets, which was what mattered.

"I'm so proud of you boys." Kasenia raised her hood over her braided hair. "Good job making yourselves invisible just now. I'm still trembling inside, but you were all calm and brave."

Ismael and Raúl volunteered to be Benicio's "chair" for the next leg of their slow descent. When they tired, Cesar and Ulises took over, followed by Sam and Jorge. Kasenia did her best to eliminate their tracks.

By now, the trees were thinning and the temperature had risen. The boys' body odor intensified. Kasenia knew she didn't smell any better. A wild animal could smell them a mile away, which would be good if their rank aroma repelled the animals. But if a wolf or coyote were hungry...

They were approaching a clearing when Cesar, who was in the lead, held up his hand, waited for the others to stop, and pointed. "Una cabána." His whisper seemed to echo in the quiet woods.

Kasenia peered through the trees at a log cabin nestled in an aspen grove. No one had lived in the house for a long time. The windows were broken, the roof had caved in on one end, and tangled brush choked the perimeter. The weatherworn outhouse behind the cabin leaned precariously to one side. She hated to think what residents now occupied the structures.

"Brewster come, nosotros hide en la cabána," Cesar said.

"Good thinking." Sam high-fived Cesar. "His fancy camera can't see us in there, unless the roof has a big hole."

"Sam, Cesar..." Kasenia indicated the clearing beside the cabin. "That open space has enough room for a helicopter to set down. If Brewster happens to land there, where's the first place he'll look?"

"Oh, right." Sam frowned. "It'd be the cabin."

Cesar furrowed his brow. "No es good."

"It may be a place to spend the night," Kasenia said, "if we're unable to get off the mountain for some reason." She hoped that wouldn't happen. The boys were hot and exhausted and had gone too long without food or water.

"Señorita," Raúl exclaimed. "Dos arcos."

Below the meadow, the reddish-brown formations rose from the desert floor like giant picture frames.

"Oh, wow, Raúl." She grinned. "The crimson arches. We're really close."

"Yes." Sam punched his fist into the air. "Almost there."

The others cheered softly.

"Esta noche, Señor Duran..." Ismael mimed knocking. "Esta noche, nosotros knock your door."

Ulises tugged her sleeve, like he'd done earlier. "Señorita, agua."

"Water?" Kasenia turned to where he pointed. Sunlight sparkled off a small stream that meandered from the forest into the meadow.

The boys looked from her to the water and back again, eyes shining like the rippling creek.

"Yes, go." She smiled. "But stay in the trees and keep your voices down."

They ran through the woods, noiseless as squirrels hopping from branch to branch, except for Benicio and Cesar, who grasped one of Benicio's arms. Kasenia took the other. Their pace was slow, but soon they could hear a waterfall. Moments later, they were drinking cool clear water as it splashed off a ledge not much higher than her head.

Along with the boys, she whispered, "Gracias a Dios, gracias a Dios." God had met their needs again. Maybe they *would* make it to the Crimson Arches Ranch tonight and sleep in safety.

The stream pooled below the waterfall. The boys removed their shoes and jackets and sat in the water then dunked their heads and came up gasping and giggling.

"Get in, Sis." Sam waved her over. "You won't believe how good this feels."

"I will. But first, I'm going to take off Beni's bandana."

After she removed the bloody wrapping, Benicio grinned. "I like." A moment later, he was in the water with the others.

Kasenia was glad for him but wondered if she'd made the right decision. What kind of germs were invading his open wound? She moved farther downstream to bury the tissue under a rock and scrub as much blood as she could from the red bandana. *Germs or no germs, the poor kid feels better.* She squeezed the water from the cloth and hung it on a branch.

Back at the waterfall, where the boys were happily soaking in the cool water, she said, "I'll keep watch first." She pointed a forefinger at her brother. "Try not to get water on your face."

"I want to scrape the grease off, but I haven't touched it."

"I know the feeling."

She hung her jacket on a branch and rotated a slow circle, peering through the trees and brush, grateful the boys had an opportunity to relax and refresh. Yet, knowing Brewster hunted them like animals never left her mind.

The evergreens on the lower slope weren't as thick or majestic as the ponderosas. Disappearing beneath their slender branches would be difficult, with or without camo blankets. And she saw no rocky ledges or caves to hide in. The water was a possibility but not a good one. *What can we do, where can we go?* Kasenia rubbed her temples. It was too much to think about. Surely, Brewster would abandon the hunt at dusk, and they'd be able to leave the mountain.

She stopped, sensing someone or something watching her. Her pulse pounded her ears, dulling the creek sounds and the boys' soft laughter. She scanned the nearby foliage, thought she saw movement, and scanned again. This time, she made out a deer's dark curious eyes barely visible between branches. The moment she made eye contact, it burst from the bushes.

Kasenia drew a startled breath and watched the doe bound up the hill as nimble and graceful on land as the eagle was in the air. She blew out the breath. Thank God it wasn't one of Brewster's men. Pulse still in high gear, she resumed her revolving search for intruders. Once again, the cabin came into view.

Who built it and why? Had it been it a getaway or a miner or rancher's home? Why had it fallen into disrepair? From this angle, she could see a mound of dirt not far from the outhouse. Was it a root cellar like her babushka had behind her house? Of course, they couldn't hide in there, but...

She hurried to the boys. "I'm so sorry to interrupt your fun, guys, but I think I figured out how to make a shelter to hide in if Brewster comes this way again."

"We could submerge in the water," Sam said, "where thermal imaging can't pick up our heat."

"I thought of that, but this stream is too shallow. The helicopter's downwash would likely blow water off our bodies and expose us."

"Or it'd hover so long we'd run out of breath and have to surface." Sam pursed his lips. "We could make straws from reeds, so we could breathe."

"Let's try my shelter idea first. If that fails, we'll figure out how to be safe in the water." She paused, hating to pull the boys from a rare peaceful moment. Yet, they couldn't waste any more time. "Use your jackets to dry your feet, then put your socks and shoes on. You can hang your jackets on a tree branch near the shelter we're going to build by tearing apart the outhouse and the cellar door. Just remember to watch out for spiders and scorpions."

A couple hard shoves by the three biggest boys and the outhouse fell over, folding in on itself. Then they tackled the cellar door. But when Cesar pulled the door up, the other boys yelped and jumped back, whispering, "Lo ves, lo ves?" "You see it?"

Kasenia tiptoed to the edge of the cavity, fearing she'd be greeted by a horde of scorpions or a big ugly snake. Instead, a Gila monster hissed up at them, it's long orange-and-black-striped body glistening in the sunshine. A gray forked tongue flicked from its wide-open jaws.

"Can we keep it for a pet, Sis?" Sam crouched at the edge, ogling the creature. "We'll be home soon."

"Are you kidding?" Kasenia stared at him. "It's a reptile."

"It has cool stripes."

"No want," Jorge warned. "Monstruo de Gila es venenoso."

"Venomous?" She quirked an eyebrow at Sam. "Not my idea of a pet."

The Gila monster waddled behind a rubbish pile.

"We'd better leave it alone." Kasenia clapped her hands. "Let's get busy, guys."

Their thirst quenched and their bodies cooled, the boys set to work. "This feels good," Sam said, grabbing one end of the cellar door. "A lot better than run-hide-run-hide." Jorge took the middle and Cesar the opposite end. With one loud, united grunt, the boys wrenched the door from its hinges.

The weathered lumber that formed the cellar door and the outhouse walls separated without much effort. The holes left behind were dank and dark but not as smelly as she'd expected. Though she couldn't do anything about the trampled grass, Kasenia insisted the boys carry the lumber rather than drag the boards and create paths that might be seen from the air.

The next challenge was to find two trees with branches close enough together, low enough and strong enough to support the salvaged boards in a roof-like fashion. The longer they searched, the more discouraged she became. Potential tree pairs either didn't have low branches or the branches weren't strong enough to hold the heavy boards.

Finally, she called the boys together. "This isn't working. Anyone have a better idea for a quick and easy shelter?"

Ismael touched his fingers together, looked at Cesar and said, "Tienda."

"Sí, tienda. Bueno." Cesar turned to Kasenia. "Ismael say tent."

"Okay..." She tried to visualize what he was picturing. "But how?"

Ismael walked the area, examining fallen branches, and finally chose one that was eight or nine feet long and five or six inches in diameter.

Balancing the branch on his shoulder, he returned to two trees they'd considered earlier. With Cesar's help, he settled the branch into the crotches formed where live branches connected to the tree trunks.

"Good thinking, dude." Sam gave Ismael a high-five. "That's what we need, a ridge pole."

Ismael had the others grab boards and lean them against the ridge pole, forming a wooden tent just big enough to hold the group.

"Perfect," Kasenia exclaimed. Not only would it protect them from the infrared camera, they could sleep in it, if they had to.

Jorge suggested they cover the boards with emergency blankets to hide cracks that might reveal their body heat. They tugged the Mylar sheets from the packets and laid two across the tented boards, silver side down, securing them at the base with rocks. The other two were hung over the open ends.

"Nice work, guys." Kasenia gave them a thumbs up. "Put your jackets in the tent and pick up the extra boards. We'll crisscross them on top the holes and cover them with branches, so they aren't obvious from the air. Remember, carry, don't drag the boards."

When they'd camouflaged the holes and Sam and Raúl had brushed their prints as best they could, Kasenia said, "All we can do now is wait for dark. You guys worked really hard. Want another dunk in the creek?"

The sweaty boys grinned as if she'd offered them tickets to a pro ball game and hurried to the water, everyone but Sam, who walked with Kasenia. "I'll stand watch this time."

"Thanks." She gave him a side hug. "I'm so glad we're in this together." She hesitated. "I mean, it's my fault—"

"Stop it, Sis." He scowled at her. "I'd rather be here with you than wondering where you disappeared to. Besides, other than Brewster and his creepy family and those mercenary dudes, it's been a..." He lifted his chin. "Gra-a-and adventure."

"Grand adventure? I don't think so."

"Go dunk your head, but..." He shook his finger at her. "Don't you dare wash that gunk off your face before I can wash mine."

Kasenia sat on the bank to remove her shoes and socks, inhaling the creek's intoxicating mix of wet earth, vegetation and fresh mountain water. Almost as soon as she stepped into the pool, she lost her balance on the slick rocks and fell in with a splash.

Sam laughed. "Sis, it's too shallow for diving."

The boys giggled then put their hands over their mouths.

"No problemo." Kasenia grinned. "I'm okay." Until they could laugh freely again, she appreciated how hard they tried to rein in their normal boyish responses to life's joys and disappointments. She rested her head against the big rock behind her. The water filtered through her t-shirt and jeans and felt incredibly good.

Sam straightened his shoulders. "Better go report for duty."

Cesar's brow furrowed beneath his thick dark hair. "Who you report to?"

Sam winked. "Dios." He climbed on a boulder, saluted the sky, and did a three-sixty of their surroundings.

Kasenia smiled. Her little brother wasn't joking.

28

— • —

T HE SUN WAS LOW in the west when Kasenia coaxed her charges
out of the water. "We need to be dry before nightfall and ready to
climb down to the road and run to the ranch." *Or ready to spend another
cool night on the mountain.* She didn't mention the possibility.

She wiped her feet and donned her socks and shoes, all the while
considering their situation. Here she was, hanging out in the wilderness
with adolescent boys. The sun was setting behind the mountains. Under
normal circumstances, this would be the time to build a campfire and
enjoy the American ritual of roasting hot dogs and marshmallows.

They'd sing silly songs and tell scary stories. While they told their tales,
she'd boil some rice, add dried fruit and nuts plus a little honey and make
Russian rice pudding for the boys to enjoy with their hot chocolate.

Kasenia shook herself from her dream world. Instead of telling frightening tales, they were living a horror story, one more terrifying, more
treacherous than anything she could concoct. Their destination was
nearby, yet real and imminent danger threatened, whether wild animals
or Brewster and his henchmen, the vilest predators of all.

They were standing by the burbling creek in the waning light, letting
the warm sweet-smelling breeze dry their clothes, when Cesar hissed,
"Escuchar...listen. Something, it come."

Kasenia looked to where he pointed but didn't see anything. She'd
heard the occasional whine of a vehicle driving on the road at the mountain's base. But this engine growl was different and growing louder. A
thumping crescendo of rotors quickly followed, as if the helicopter had
come around the mountain.

Her heart leaped. "Boys, run for the tent as fast as you can."

Jorge headed into the meadow.

"Jorge…" She waved him back. "Through the trees." He might make it across the open stretch with time to spare, but they couldn't take the chance.

Kasenia tore after her charges, ignoring the branches that whipped her face and scratched her arms. Sam followed behind her, doing his best to cover their tracks. Breathless, they ducked into their makeshift tent moments before the helicopter flew past.

Huddled with the boys on the forest floor, she caught her breath, inhaling the earthy smells tinged with a lingering outhouse tang. She peered between a plank and the camo blanket that hung over the end, relieved the chopper didn't hover above them.

But then it circled back.

Someone said, "Uh-oh."

"Boys…" She could barely see their hooded forms in the dark enclosure. "If that thing lands, be prepared to disappear in the woods. You're good at that. It's getting darker by the moment, which is to our advantage. Be as quiet as you can but climb as far away from Brewster as you can. Understand?"

"Sí, señorita."

"We pray," Cesar said.

"Okay." Kasenia slipped on her jacket and pulled the hood over her head. She was hot from running and their shelter was plenty warm, but she had to hide her hair.

"God in heaven," he prayed, "you see todos, all. Brewster es el diablo, devil. No let see. Amén."

Murmured améns were muffled by the helicopter's thrum.

To Kasenia's dismay, the chopper slowed. She looked out in time to see it settle in the meadow. Its brilliant searchlight bleached the hillside white, capturing the frenetic flutter of tree leaves and detritus stirred by the rotors. The stream slithered through the pale landscape like a silver serpent, as if racing to escape Brewster's scrutiny.

From her limited vantage point, she saw only one fatigue-clad man exit the copter. It had to be Brewster. Her stomach knotted. She didn't want the monster anywhere near the boys, yet the fewer the men hunting them, the greater the possibility they wouldn't be discovered.

"I'm going to the cabin," Brewster shouted. He had what looked like a weapon in one hand and a flashlight in the other. "Something's not right. Not sure what but stay alert."

The pilot yelled, "I'll be there as soon as I shut this thing down."

Kasenia began unlacing her hiking boot. If Brewster captured her and somehow found Trent's card, he'd think the worst. Both she and Trent would suffer horrific consequences.

Their shelter was some distance from the cabin, yet the men's voices carried across the meadow. She could hear their shouts and see Brewster's flashlight beam dart over the cabin walls. Above it, the sky had darkened, and several stars had appeared. Kasenia turned to the boys. "Get ready to run like deer up the hill."

The boys responded with grunts and stomach growls.

She slipped her boot off, lifted the insole and retrieved Trent's card then peered through the gap again.

Brewster was inside the cabin. Light flashed through the cracks and the windows. Within moments, he'd come around behind it, see the fresh tree branches piled over the holes and know something was amiss.

Kasenia shifted, ready to send the boys up the mountain, when she heard the pilot call, "Hey, Wiley, over here."

Heart in her throat, she stared at the now-silent helicopter. Its blades spun slowly, as if propelled by a breeze. A man stood in the searchlight beam, staring at something on a branch.

Kasenia squinted. Had one of the boys left a sock behind?

Brewster charged out of the cabin and across the meadow faster than she'd ever seen him move. He lifted the object off the branch. "Huh, a bandana."

Benicio's bandana... Kasenia sucked in a breath. *I can't believe I forgot it.*

He held it to the light. "Some hiker must have left it." He threw the bandana on the ground. "Wouldn't be any of the renegades. I don't allow bandanas at Shadow Ranch. The symbols have meanings to attract the devil."

She raised her eyebrows. That was a new one. But she was happy he believed his own absurdity. She pulled on her boot and retied it.

"It's getting late." Brewster glanced at his watch. "Time to pick up my men."

The pilot climbed into the chopper, and the rotors began to whir.

"*Good,*" she whispered, "*fly away now.*"

Brewster approached the helicopter then paused and yelled, "I didn't finish checking the cabin. Toss my helmet down. I'll need the infrared camera."

Kasenia's heart sank. She slid Trent's card under a rock just outside the makeshift tent, wishing she'd memorized his phone number, and turned to the boys. "We have to go. The chopper noise will cover us for a bit, but please be careful. Beni, where are you?"

"Aquí."

"Oh, right behind me." She touched his arm. "I'm so sorry about the bandana. You'll have to keep moving the best you can until Trent Duran can help you."

"I be okay."

"Señorita," Cesar murmured, "where we go? Señor Brewster see us go Crimson Arcos."

"As high as you can climb. If he starts up the mountain then hide in the rocks and bushes, behind trees. You boys like to pray. Don't stop. God got you this far, he'll get you home to your families."

"But—"

She pushed aside the camo sheet just far enough to see. Brewster was striding across the meadow, swinging his light back and forth. Any moment now, he'd see the holes they'd covered and put two and two together. He might be delusional, but he was no dummy.

"Go now." She motioned to the boys. "Vaya con Dios, my friends."

They returned her farewell and one by one slipped out the other end of the shelter.

Tears sprang to her eyes. *Dear God, please lead your children home.*

She was the last to exit the shelter. Everyone but Sam had disappeared. "Go, Sam." She handed him her survival blanket, one more item Brewster didn't need to find in her possession. "Don't wait for me."

"Sis, we're in this together."

His hood had slipped down. She pulled it around his face, though he was no longer her *little* brother. But, oh, how she loved him. "I have to distract Brewster, Sam. And you have to get the Phoenix boys to Crimson Arches. You can call Grandpa from there."

He clutched her shoulders. "Brewster will lock you in his compound again, beat you like before."

"I won't be there long. You'll tell the authorities the truth about Shadow Ranch, and they'll make Brewster open the gates."

"What if—?"

"Go. Before it's too late." She hugged him. "I love you."

"Love you, too, Sis." He gave her an extra squeeze. "See you soon." Already a master at stealth, he slipped from tree to tree until he was out of sight.

Staying inside the tree line, Kasenia hurried toward the helicopter with no idea how to capture Brewster's attention or what she'd tell him to throw him off the boys' trail. Should she say she tried to catch up with Tomás and the boys but got lost? Or that she'd gone with Tomás at first then changed her mind because she missed Brewster?

She ducked under a low branch. Just the thought of seeing him again twisted her insides. How could she say she missed him without spewing what little food remained in her stomach?

She was almost to the creek when she tripped and sprawled headfirst, scraping her hands and hitting her head on something hard. For a long moment, she lay face down in the dirt, unable to breathe or think.

Somewhere in the dark recesses of her mind she knew she had something important to do, something urgent. She turned over and gulped the mountain air, one breath after another.

The helicopter's pulsing thump brought everything back. She had to get to the chopper, fast. To save the boys.

Now, she knew what to do.

Kasenia pushed to her hands and knees. Startled by the pain, she groaned but rose to her feet, teetering on the edge of consciousness. She blinked to clear the cobwebs in her brain, shoved her hood away and sucked in another breath.

Before she lost her nerve, she undid her braid, ran her fingers through her hair and stumbled down the hill into the searchlight's blazing beam. The helicopter's engine and rotor noise resounded in the clearing like a dozen choppers.

She narrowed her eyes against the bright light and the debris stirred by the blades' frenetic rotation. Her long auburn hair whipped about her head, sticking to her face and coloring her view of the black-and-white night. Her temple throbbed and a headache mushroomed behind her eyes.

"Wiley, over here," the pilot shouted. "You gotta see this!"

Startled by the amplified voice, Kasenia lurched backward and crashed into a bush.

Brewster tore across the meadow, his gun aimed at Kasenia like she was his enemy or his prey—or both.

She'd barely regained her footing when he slid to a stop in front of her. The camera mounted on his helmet made him look like a giant bug. Kasenia gawked at him, smelling his sweat, sensing his paranoia. This was the man who told her he loved her, yet he'd deceived, imprisoned, and beat her, belittled her family—and threatened to kill her brother. Now, she was his target.

He dropped the flashlight and ripped off the helmet. "Kasenia?"

She angled her head like she didn't understand him.

The engine died, and the rotors slowed.

"Where have you been? You're filthy. What happened to your face?" Brewster stepped closer. "Where are the others?"

"Others?" Feigning confusion, she touched her temple and flinched. It was swollen and tender. She felt something wet and stared at her finger. Blood glistened in the spotlight.

"Kasenia," Brewster barked. "Listen up."

She jerked and slowly focused on him again. Strange. With light hitting him from the side and his eyes squinted with suspicion, he reminded her of the Gila monster.

"Answer me," he demanded. "Did Tomás abduct you for his brothel?"

Kasenia gaped at him. "Brothel?" She could hear the rising rage in his voice, but she didn't care. His anger was his problem, not hers.

He slapped her.

Kasenia's head flipped to the side, and she fought for balance. Okay, so his anger was her problem too. A desire to retaliate rather than run, to shove him to the ground and kick him senseless surprised her. This wasn't the time nor the place, but someday... She touched her cheek, opened her mouth, and stared at him like a confused child who didn't understand why she was being punished.

"Wiley..." the pilot called through the door, "the woman has a head injury. She doesn't understand you. Slappin' her around will make it worse."

Brewster brandished his gun. "She's faking it."

"I'm telling you, Wiley," the pilot insisted, "I've seen head injuries like hers. No way can you bully her to connect the dots. I'll fly her to a hospital. She'll be back to normal in a few days. You can get the info you want out of her then."

Brewster grasped Kasenia's arm and dragged her toward the helicopter.

Gratified to think she'd soon be in a place where she could tell people the truth and get help, Kasenia nearly grinned at the fortuitous change of events. Instead, she whimpered, "No, no..."

He thrust her up and into the helicopter, his rough manner so unlike the care he'd taken when he helped her into a different "bird" the night of their fraudulent wedding. Her head pulsed with the rotors and her vision blurred, but she could see the helicopter had five seats. Brewster shoved her into the back row's middle seat, and before she could decide whether to clasp the seatbelt or pretend she didn't remember how, he forced the shoulder straps around her arms.

"Damn you, woman," he muttered, "this may be a game to you, but you should know by now I always have the last word." Repeating his threat to feed her parts to the coyotes, he buckled the seatbelt and yanked it tight across her hips. Climbing into the front, he told the pilot to head out.

Kasenia focused on the front window, relieved to be away from Brewster's sweaty stench. No matter what he did to her, the boys and Marisa were safe from his perverted plans.

"We're picking up your men on the outcropping, right?" the pilot asked. The engine noise changed, and the blades twirled faster.

"They can wait." Brewster closed the door and fastened his seatbelt. "First, we deal with her." He aimed his chin at Kasenia behind them.

"Bisbee hospital?"

"County jail. I'm going to get my reward money back."

The helicopter lifted off the ground.

"Jail? Reward money?" The pilot stared at Brewster. "You pullin' my leg?"

"She's a wanted woman. I put up ten-thousand dollars for her capture."

The pilot glanced back at Kasenia. "Nah..."

"Along with another white woman and a Mexican man, she's wanted for kidnapping the eleven children we've been searching for."

"But she's injured—"

Brewster's voice took on a hard edge. "My wife's head injury is none of your business. The detention center medic will examine her."

"She's your wife? I didn't know. Seems you'd want—"

"I hired you to fly this bird, not call the shots."

29

THE DEPUTY WHO TOOK Kasenia's picture and fingerprints was a young Hispanic woman of few words. The silver-haired nurse who met them in the intake processing room was also Hispanic, but she was more talkative. "You can call me Nurse Gabby. It's short for Gabriella, but my husband insists I was born with the gift of gab and that's how I got the name."

Any other time and place, Kasenia would have smiled and engaged in conversation with the friendly woman, but Brewster's perverted pal ran this jail. Any sign of mental alertness from her, and the word would get back to Brewster.

The nurse led Kasenia and the deputy into a separate room that smelled like rubbing alcohol. The deputy remained near the closed door, but Gabby had Kasenia sit in a chair. She pulled disposable gloves from a box on a shelf and slipped them on. "Kasenia...that's an unusual name."

Kasenia didn't respond.

The nurse held up a penlight. "I'm going to shine a light in your eyes to check for a concussion." She moved closer, her light aimed at Kasenia's eyes.

Kasenia moaned and jerked away.

"I know it hurts. Bear with me for a moment." Gabby flashed the light in both eyes and switched it off. "Have a headache?"

She nodded. *You just made it worse.*

"Blurry vision?"

"Uh-huh."

"I'll give you something for the headache in a bit." She sat at the desk to type notes into a computer then turned to Kasenia. "What's on your face?"

"Face?" Kasenia touched her cheek then gazed at the grease on her finger, doing her best to appear baffled by it.

"We'll have you wash in a bit." She typed something more into the computer before she swiveled her chair around. "Now comes the part where we ask you to remove your clothing."

What? Kasenia stared at her.

Gabby checked the computer screen. "I understand this is your first incarceration. Our procedures are no doubt new to you, but we are required by law to do body searches."

Kasenia glanced at the deputy, who said, "Please stand."

Slowly, hesitantly, she complied.

"Also required," the nurse added, "is for two officers of the same gender to conduct the search." She eyed Kasenia's hoodie. "Go ahead, take off your jacket, and then everything else."

"But first," the deputy said, "empty your pockets and put the contents in this bag then seal it." She set a clear plastic bag on the chair.

Kasenia had already been patted down and her travel Bible taken from her, but she dutifully pulled pebbles and pine needles from her pockets and dribbled them into the bag. She thought about the mountain and the boys and what they'd endured together. Were they in Trent Duran's care yet?

Both women leaned close to examine the bag's contents. The deputy straightened and stepped back. Gabby smiled. "Appears you were in the hills, Miss Clarke, like your intake paperwork says."

The deputy tossed a large plastic bag onto the chair. "For your clothes. But first, we need to look over your boots."

Kasenia dropped her jacket into the bag then bent to untie her dusty boots, thanking her lucky stars she'd removed Trent's card. For sure, Sheriff Childers and Brewster would hear about it and do their best to ruin his life, if not take it. Slipping the boots off, she handed them to the deputy, who had donned disposable gloves. First thing she did was take out the insoles and look them over. Then she proceeded to inspect the boots inside and out.

"Miss Clarke..." Nurse Gabby dipped her head. "Your clothing, please."

Piece by piece, Kasenia added items to the clothing bag, embarrassed not only by her nudity but by her filth and how she smelled. After three days on the run—or was it four?—she was head-to-toe dirty. But at least she'd been able to sit in the creek and run water through her hair. Was that yesterday or today? She wasn't sure.

Though neither woman touched her, the body search was more extensive than Kasenia expected. She did as she was asked but stared straight ahead throughout the ordeal, shivering beneath the AC vent.

Afterward, Gabby told the deputy, "I would like Miss Clarke to shower before I treat her wounds. Do you think it's possible at this time of night?"

Kasenia lowered her head, embarrassed the nurse had noticed her need for a shower.

"Yes." The deputy checked the clock above the door. "The women should be in their cells. I'll grab clean clothes on the way."

Gabby walked over to a cabinet, pulled out an orange jumpsuit and rubber sandals and gave them to Kasenia. "Put these on for now."

Kasenia slipped on the jumpsuit, grateful to be clothed again, and stepped into the sandals then took the towel Gabby offered.

The deputy opened the door, motioned for Kasenia to exit the room, and led her through a long hallway to an empty restroom with metal mirrors hanging above a row of sinks. The toilets were separated by half walls, and the showers had shoulder-high partitions and open fronts. Despite the lack of privacy, the brief shower felt so good Kasenia almost forgot the humiliation—almost.

The deputy handed her clean clothes. Kasenia didn't care that the t-shirt and pants were orange and stamped with the detention center's name, or that the underwear and slip-on orange sneakers were too big. To wear clean clothing again was a pleasure she wouldn't soon forget. On top of that, her hair was squeaky clean and smelled like coconut.

From there, they returned to Nurse Gabby's office, so she could medicate Kasenia's headache, scrapes and bumps before the deputy took her to an interrogation room. There, a man and a woman grilled her regarding the whereabouts of the other thirteen people who disappeared from Shadow Ranch.

Again and again, the detectives, a man and a woman, asked, "Where are the others?"

Each time, Kasenia squinted and repeated, "Others?" The truth was, she didn't know their where they were, but she hoped they were all safely hidden from Brewster's men and his infrared camera. At one point, too tired and in too much pain to think straight, she almost blurted what little she knew. She had to bite her lip to keep the words from escaping.

Finally, she was led to a jail cell.

"You're in luck," the deputy said. "Single occupancy tonight, but don't expect it to last."

Barely hearing the cell door clank shut behind her, Kasenia kicked off the sneakers and fell onto the bed. She pulled the solitary blanket over her head to block the bright light outside the cell, trusting the aspirin Nurse Gabby gave her would soon dull the pain behind her eyes.

She'd scrubbed hard to remove the grease on her face, leaving it raw enough Gabby applied medicated lotion that still stung. Along with her headache and worrying about the boys, Kasenia was certain she wouldn't be able to sleep. But to lie on a mattress, even a thin one, was a pleasure as gratifying as the shower and clean clothing.

A loud buzzer and an echoing clang awakened her. Kasenia eyed the pale-green cinderblock before her, unable to comprehend what she was seeing until someone walking past whispered, "Breakfast in fifteen minutes, girl. Better get up or you'll miss it."

Kasenia pushed to a sitting position on the edge of the bottom bunk and rubbed her eyes. The headache was gone, but her brain felt murky. She ran her fingers through her tangled hair. Seeing the cell door open, she got to her feet and followed a group of women across a commons area.

Most inmates were subdued. Only a couple Chatty Cathy types appeared happy to be awake. She wasn't exactly happy, but she was glad to be alive and far from Shadow Ranch. She would continue her concussion charade at breakfast and communicate as little as possible. No need to explain how she landed in the detention center. The story was too crazy. Plus, the lecherous sheriff was Brewster's brothel partner, which meant she couldn't trust anyone in the department.

A middle-aged woman came up beside her. "Oh, dear, what happened to your face? Your boyfriend pound on you?"

Kasenia looked down. *Something like that.*

"You don't have to tell me," the woman said. "But if you're in pain, you can ask the day nurse for aspirin."

Kasenia nodded.

The line moved quickly, and soon she was seated at the end of a cafeteria table, eating scrambled eggs, bacon and toast. The ladies at her table, each one dressed in orange, glanced her way, but no one spoke to her. They didn't talk much among themselves, either. Deputies guarded both entrances to the dining hall.

She had just downed her orange juice when another deputy walked into the room. After conferring with one of the guards, he walked to her table and stopped beside her. "Kasenia Clarke?"

Eyes squinted against the fluorescent lights' glare, she looked up at him.

"Is that you?" He asked.

Kasenia blinked. "Uh-huh."

"You have an arraignment hearing with Judge Landrith in fifteen minutes. I will escort you there."

"Hearing?" She tilted her head. What was this about? She didn't have an attorney.

As if reading her mind, he said, "If you don't have an attorney, the court will provide one."

"Attorney?"

"Same as a lawyer, to represent you before the judge. Get your tray and let's go."

"Officer," someone said, "a deputy told me she's from another country, Europe, I think. She doesn't understand."

The deputy lifted an eyebrow.

Another woman said, "Cool, but what's she doing in the middle of the desert?"

Kasenia stood and picked up her tray. What *was* she doing in the middle of the desert, when she could be safe and sound in Usva with her babushka, far from Brewster and his manipulative ways? Of course, if he wanted to harm her badly enough, distance wouldn't stop him.

She followed the officer to the counter where the trays were deposited. She was here to protect her brother and the other boys from Brewster. That's why she was in the detention center. If protecting them meant jail time, so be it.

But when she stood before the balding judge who informed her kidnapping children was a serious crime with severe consequences, Kasenia had second thoughts.

"Do you understand, Miss Clarke?" Judge Landrith asked. "You could receive a sentence of twenty years or more for each of the eleven missing children?"

She gaped at him. That was almost three lifetimes behind bars for a crime she didn't commit. She'd die in prison.

Like the eagle in the tree staring down at the coyotes, the judge peered at her over his wide polished bench, a question in his eyes.

She nodded.

The court-appointed attorney standing beside her, a clean-shaven young man with slicked-back brown hair and an Irish Spring aura, whispered, "Say, 'Yes, Your Honor.'"

Kasenia repeated, "Yes, Your Honor."

"How do you wish to plead, Miss Clarke?" Judge Landrith asked. "Not guilty, guilty, or no contest?"

She touched the attorney's sleeve. "Plead?" What was she supposed to say? She wasn't guilty, but until she knew the boys were safe, she had to play Brewster's game. Or did she? Should she say *no contest*?

The lawyer, who looked barely old enough to be out of high school, gave her a gentle smile. "Miss Clarke, I advise you to plead not guilty."

"But..." How could she explain her predicament without endangering the boys—and Tomás and his charges?

"Trust me." He held her gaze. "It's the wise place to start. I can explain more later."

"Okay…" He was young and likely inexperienced, but he was her only advocate. She had to rely on his judgment and advice.

The attorney addressed the judge. "Your Honor, my client wishes to plead not guilty."

Kasenia's headache had returned and was pounding her temples. She longed for her bunk, but the judge was announcing a cash bond of one hundred thousand dollars. "Do you understand, Miss Clarke?" He paused. "You will be detained in our facility until your trial unless you provide the court with a cash bond of one hundred thousand dollars?"

"Yes, Your Honor." The only person she knew with that kind of money was Brewster, thanks to his Shadow Ranch slaves. He'd sneer at the idea of paying to release her from the jail he'd delivered her to. For that, she was grateful. She'd rather be trapped behind bars than behind the compound's razor-topped fence.

Barely able to see through the blinding pain, Kasenia lay with her back to the cell door. Maybe sleep would cure the headache and help her forget her awful predicament. She didn't know why she was so drowsy, but she was glad for a way to escape her current reality.

When she awakened for lunch, she was surprised to see the cell door still open. The headache had lessened in intensity, and she could see better, so she left the bunk to join the others in the cafeteria. Earlier, the dining room had smelled like bacon. Now it was chicken, which explained the chicken salad sandwiches on the trays between potato chip packages and watermelon slices.

Again, she kept to herself while eating. On the way back to her cell, three women in the common's area invited her to join their card game. Kasenia touched the bump on her forehead. "Thank you for the invitation, but I have a headache and need to lie down." And that was the truth.

Not only did she have a lingering headache, she craved sleep. Kasenia crossed the big room to her cell on the far side. Had Shadow Ranch duties exhausted her? Or was it the escape through the mountains?

Thinking of the escape reminded her of Tomás and Margo. Had they met up with his wife and sister yet? Were they on their way to Florida? Had Sam and the others snuck across the open desert to the Crimson Arches Ranch. If so, did Trent Duran agree to help them? Or were they still wandering half-starved through the mountains?

On top of her concern for them, she had her own quandary to consider—she could spend the rest of her life in prison. She needed a safe place to tell the truth regarding Brewster, Shadow Ranch, and the boys. But that place wasn't a jail run by Sheriff Childers and his underlings.

Lying on her side, she faced the green cinderblock. The Phoenix boys' prayers and their sweet, unflagging faith had sustained her in the mountains. Maybe it was time to establish her own faith. But how? Cesar had said, "Stay still and know God." A person couldn't be more "still" than in jail.

Quieting her mind, she heard her babushka's congregation recite the Lord's prayer in Russian. Their rich accents resonated in the small sanctuary and blended like a beautiful symphony. "Our Father who art in heaven, hallowed be thy name. ...Lead us not into temptation but deliver us from evil. For thine is the kingdom, the power, and the glory, forever and ever. Amen."

The memory faded. "Our Father," Kasenia whispered to the wall. "*My Father in heaven, I need you to deliver me—to deliver us—from evil. I can't help Sam or the other boys, I can't help Tomás and Margo. I can't help myself. I'm invisible to everyone I love, lost to my family. Brewster has the upper hand. But you're the one who made the universe.*"

She thought of the night sky and the millions of stars that populated it. Though light years apart, they wove a beautiful twinkling tapestry. "If you can keep stars from colliding and the solar system in place, you can put people exactly where you want them, including me. You did so many amazing things to help us escape Shadow Ranch. Thank you. Like Cesar said, I want you in my life, forever. I want Jesus to save me from my sins, my pecados.

The inscription in her babushka's church came to her again. *Greater love has no one than this, than to lay down one's life for his friends.* My Bible says you are loving—and you are. You gave your life for me to save me from my sins. You're also kind and ready to forgive. Please forgive me for ignoring the warnings about marrying Brewster, for endangering Sam, and for all the other bad things I've done."

Drowsiness about to overtake her, she finished her prayer. "Thank you for loving me, for being with me in this jail cell. I love you back."

⟨⟩⟩··✦·✦·⟨⟨⟩

Hearing someone call, "Inmate Clarke, Inmate Clarke," Kasenia opened her eyes and turned her head.

A female deputy stood at the door. "Couple detectives are waiting to speak with you."

Kasenia groaned. Maintaining her head-injury charade was difficult with the detectives. They seemed determined to trick her into telling them how and why she left Shadow Ranch and where to find the other escapees.

Flipping the blanket off her orange-clad body, she stood and pushed her hair from her eyes. "I'm thirsty." Maybe water would wash the sleep-fog from her brain and help her dodge the detective's verbal traps.

"You can get a drink on the way." The guard led her to a water fountain near the restrooms and then through a double set of barred steel gates. From there, they walked a long hall to the same sterile-smelling interrogation room, where the same serious-faced uniformed officers stood to greet her with the same fake smiles.

"Good afternoon, Miss Clarke." The woman waved her into the room. "I hope you're feeling better today." She resumed her seat at a small table.

Kasenia glanced from her to the man, who nodded and indicated a chair on the other side of the table. "Have a seat." Like last night, he sat to the side—to study her body language, she assumed. The female detective would focus on her eyes.

She took her seat, and the questions began, the same ones they'd asked earlier. "How long did you live at Shadow Ranch?" The woman leaned her forearms on the table.

Kasenia furrowed her brow. "Shadow Ranch?"

"Yes, you lived there, with your brother."

"Brother... I have a brother?"

"Do you know what a brother is?" the man asked.

"Yes." She lifted her chin. "It's a...um...a person."

"Right. When did you take your brother and the other children from Shadow Ranch?"

"Other children? I have children?"

"Yes...no." He shook his head, eyebrows tight. "Not *your* children."

"You took children that don't belong to you," the woman said.

"Where?" Kasenia asked.

"Where did you take them?"

"Uh-huh."

"That's what *you* need to tell *us*." Hands clasped on the table, she steepled her forefingers. "Try to remember. Where are the children?"

Kasenia rested her hands on her thighs, palms up. What could she say to end the inquisition? The detectives were frustrated, though they tried hard to hide it. Surely, they'd realize soon she couldn't provide the answers they wanted. *Help me, Jesus.*

Head down, her gaze on her hands, she began to sing "Jesus Loves the Little Children" in Russian. Her Babushka Irina had taught it to her when she was very young. She'd never sung it in English, but the second time through, Kasenia translated as she sang. "Jesus loves the little children, all the children of the world. Red and yellow, black and—"

"That'll do, Miss Clarke."

She blinked and looked up, startled from her translation and memories of singing with her babushka before she fell asleep at night.

The woman eyed the man. "We need to get a doctor to do an evaluation before we try again. This isn't getting us anywhere."

"Yeah." The man grunted. "Like talking to a wall."

Exhausted by the interrogation, Kasenia slept through dinner but awakened in time for a shower before breakfast. Her brain felt less scrambled than the day before, yet she interacted as little as possible with the other inmates. If she let down her guard, she could endanger her brother plus twelve special friends attempting to escape Brewster's clutches.

Rested, fed and energized, she stopped by the jail library after break-fast. She was too awake to sleep and had to have something to do that didn't involve talking with anyone. The room was small but boasted shelves of books on every wall. One entire wall, she discovered, held row upon row of romance novels.

Kasenia grimaced. The last thing she wanted to read was a romance novel. Maybe she'd try a biography.

She was about to ask the librarian, an older woman in civilian clothing, where the biography section was, when the deputy who'd walked her to the hearing came into the room with a plastic grocery bag. "Miss Clarke?"

Kasenia nodded. *What now?* Did she have to go to the court again?

"You're being bonded out."

"Bonded out...?"

"Yep, right now." He motioned for her to follow him. "Means some-one paid your bond and you're free to go. He brought you clothes. You can change in the restroom. I'll wait down the hall. Don't dawdle."

Who in the world...?

Inside the empty bathroom with its ever-present urine-soap aro-ma, Kasenia examined the bag's contents. A short-sleeved white jacket, a sleeveless emerald-green blouse, navy slacks, a bra and panties that matched it plus leather sandals.

Her heart sunk. Brewster.

He was the one person who knew the right sizes and best colors for her. The clothing was nice but not new. He must have raided the laundry room at the ranch. Of course, he'd bring her clean clothes. He wouldn't want her to dirty his precious Corvette.

In fact... She stopped. These were *her* clothes. Including the under-wear. She'd worn the bra and panties when she modeled for a lingerie catalog. She recognized the lace, handmade in Portugal. How had the laundry girls managed to not ruin the lace? And how did Brewster man-age to pick out her own items from the Shadow Ranch selection? Was it intentional or accidental?

Sliding her feet from the orange sneakers, Kasenia pulled off her socks and released a shaky breath. Would she ever escape his talons? He must have decided she was a liability in the detention center, that if she ever recovered her wits, she'd rat on him—exactly what she planned to do, first chance she got.

But now, he'd have her under his thumb again. He'd punish her for running away and do whatever it took to force her to tell him where to find the others. Her only hope was Sam and the boys. If...*when* they made it to the Crimson Arches Ranch, Trent Duran would help them inform the proper authorities about Shadow Ranch.

Then Brewster would be the one behind bars, not her. *Please,* she whispered, *make it so.*

30

K ASENIA LEANED HER HEAD against the wall. Who was she kidding? Even if Brewster was charged with the crimes he'd committed, justice would likely be slow in coming. He could maim or kill her by then. Was it possible to refuse to leave the jail?

The bathroom door opened.

She lifted her head.

An orange-clad woman walked in. "Your last name Clarke?"

"Yes."

"Officer down the hall said to tell you to get a move on."

"Okay, thanks."

Kasenia removed the detention center clothing, tossed it into the grocery sack and dressed quickly. Standing before one of the metal mirrors, she did her best to make her messy copper-colored hair presentable and hurried from the restroom. Brewster liked her hair to be perfect. She hated herself for trying to please him, but it was one way to assuage his fury.

The officer reached for the bag. "I'll take that." Once again, she was escorted through the barred doors.

Kasenia's emotions careened from gut-deep dread to overwhelming rage to an urge to collapse on the floor in hopeless tears. This was a detention center run by a sheriff's office charged with protecting the county's citizens. It should be a safe place, an institution where she could expect help. Instead, those who were supposed to protect her were sending her back into the lion's lair.

And they knew it. She narrowed her eyes. If no one else, the sheriff knew.

She wanted to believe she would do anything for Sam and the boys. But returning to Shadow Ranch and Brewster's control was a worse nightmare than the threat of spending the rest of her life in prison. She took a deep breath, squared her shoulders, and determined to not give in to the tears hovering behind her eyelids. Brewster wanted everyone to cower before him, yet he despised them when they did.

They approached the reception desk where the morning light coming through the glass doors was so bright, she couldn't make out individuals. She squinted, fearing the moment she looked into Brewster's stony gray eyes. But she had to do it, had to maintain her dignity, no matter his response.

Lifting her chin, she claimed a Russian proverb as her weapon. *Make a friend of the wolf—but keep your axe ready.*

"Senya Girl?"

She stopped. No one called her that but...

A man was walking through the sunlight, loose white hairs haloing his head.

"Grandpa?" Could it be? "Grandpa Gordon?"

He held out his arms and she fell into them. "Oh, Grandpa, it's you." Her resolve to contain her tears shattered and she wept against his shoulder, soaking his vest, smelling his special blend of old dusty car grease and coffee with lots of cream and sugar.

Hugging her like he'd never let her go, he murmured, "Senya, my sweet Senya Girl. I'm tickled beyond words to see you. Seems like you've been gone for months."

Finally, when she could speak, she stepped away, swiping at her eyes. "I'm sorry, Grandpa, for—"

"Nothin' to be sorry about. This is the best day of my life. I can't begin to tell you how bloomin' thrilled I am to take you home." He wrapped an arm around her shoulders. "Let's get you out of this place and do some sightseeing along the way. I haven't been to Bisbee in a coon's age, but if I remember right, the best Mexican restaurant this side of the border sits smack dab in the middle of downtown."

Climbing into her grandpa's dented faded-red pickup revived childhood memories for Kasenia. She could hear him asking, "Wanna go for a spin, Senya Girl?"

She'd grin. "I do, Grandpa. I do, I do." Then she'd grab the rag doll she'd named Tasha after one of her Russian friends and they'd hop in his truck—this same truck that smelled of oil and rust—and take off. The desert would fly past her window like a movie scene. Oldies would sputter from the ancient radio and the engine's rumble would vibrate the bench seat beneath her.

The downside was the truck's au naturel AC. The hot wind buffeting her face and snarling her hair wasn't fun. Today would be hot, but so far, the morning wasn't bad, and she didn't care if her hair tangled beyond repair. Her grandpa had rescued her from jail *and* from Brewster's clutches.

She opened the bag her jailers gave her and sorted through her dusty belongings until she found what she was looking for—the little black Bible. They hadn't forgotten to return it. Forever, it would be a symbol of how God helped her and the boys escape Shadow Ranch.

Cell phone to his ear, Gordon leaned through the driver's side window. "Hang on while I listen to this message."

Kasenia rested her head on the back window. When did the outings with her grandfather stop? Probably when she decided she was too grownup to hang out with him. From now on, once a week, she'd ask him to take her for a spin. No more living in the same house, going their separate ways day after day.

The minute Gordon got in the truck, she asked, "Grandpa, how did you know where to find me? I thought I'd never see you again."

"You made the news, Senya Girl."

"I did?"

"Yeah, two redheaded women and a Hispanic man supposedly kidnapped a bunch of kids from a ranch down by the border. No names were mentioned, but something about the descriptions got me wonderin'. The two women, one tall and slender, and one of the kids, a teenage boy, were all redheads. "And then, just before Sam called—"

"You talked to Sam?"

"Sure did. I was never so happy to hear—"

"Oh, Grandpa..." Kasenia burst into tears. "He made it. Thank God, he made it. I've been so worried. What about the other boys?"

"They're all in good hands, Senya Girl." He reached over to squeeze her hand. "With a guy named Trent Duran."

"They got down the mountain to his ranch." Her heart danced. "I'm so happy for them and so relieved." She released a long sigh.

"You know Duran?"

"Trent's a nice guy. He's a rancher and the farrier who shoes Brewster's horses, the only person we could trust."

"This very moment, he's driving those boys to Bisbee to meet their parents. Reason why we're headed that direction. To pick up your brother who, by the way, filled me in on what you two have been through since you disappeared. Somethin' about escaping from a ranch Brewster owns. Apparently, he was up to no good, which doesn't surprise me."

"I can't wait to see Sam again." She wiped tears from her face. "You were saying you heard about me on the news, but you didn't know it was me."

"Right. Not until a news bulletin the next morning said a Kasenia Anya Clarke had been captured and was being held on bond in the Santa Cruz County Detention Center. That's when I started making phone calls. When Sam called, the puzzle pieces started coming together."

"Thank you, Grandpa." She laid her hand on his arm. "If you hadn't rescued me, I could have spent the rest of my life behind bars. Actually..." She sobered. "A judge told me it's a strong possibility."

"Somethin' tells me after the boys are reunited with their families, the judge'll be singing a different tune."

"I hope so."

Once they were on the highway, Gordon accelerated, and the desert air churned through the truck's open windows.

Kasenia corralled her swirling locks with one hand and opened the metal glovebox with the other. "You still have rubber bands in here, Grandpa?"

"Sure thing. In the Copenhagen tin over to the right."

"Thanks." Holding the canister between her knees, she shook a rubber band loose from the stuffed contents and returned the container to the glovebox. As she'd done in recent days, she braided her hair into a single braid and secured it with the rubber band. "Do Mom and Dad know about us?"

"Your parents know you went missing. They ask every day, sometimes every hour, for updates."

Kasenia sighed. "I feel terrible we gave everyone such a scare." But she had to admit, her parents' concern felt good. They really did love and miss her and Sam. "Thank you for bringing me clean clothes. Where did you find them?"

He lifted an eyebrow. "In your room."

"Really?"

"Where else?"

"I ask because Brewster took a lot of my clothing to the ranch, without my permission. I didn't realize he left some behind."

"He probably snuck a few at a time, like he stole my tools one by one, the crook."

"Sam and I tried to figure out why our things went missing. But I didn't want to believe Brewster was a thief. Now I know he's much worse than just a thief."

"Like I said..." Gordon grunted. "I'm not surprised to learn he's a devil in disguise, but whatever he did to you and Sam was a tough way to learn a guy's real character." He aimed a thumb behind them. "The message I was listening to back there was from Duran. Didn't want to take the call while I was inside. Had enough trouble with those deputy dudes."

He snorted then continued. "Duran left early this morning to take the boys to meet their families in Bisbee, haulin' 'em in his horse trailer. Guess he wants to keep 'em under the radar. A couple kids started up-chuckin', so he had to pull off the highway onto a sideroad. They'd eaten a big breakfast and the trailer was rock 'n' rollin'.

"Duran said he's drivin' slower now. The boys are anxious to see their parents, and the parents are anxious to see their kids, but if he keeps stopping for them to toss their cookies, it'll take even longer. On the bright side, we might be able to catch up with them and watch the big reunion."

"I'd love to be there." Kasenia clapped her hands. "It's going to be great." She cocked her head. "I take it you know Brewster tricked me and Sam and kidnapped the boys."

"Don't know details. Sam didn't talk long, and he talked so fast I missed half of what he said. Mighty good to hear his voice, I tell you."

Kasenia considered telling her grandfather the brothel story, but that was a conversation for another time. Right now, she wanted to focus on the good happening to her and the boys. "Trent was smart to transport the boys in a horse trailer. Lots of people are looking for them, including local authorities, people who intend to harm them, not help them."

"Huh." He frowned. "You can fill me in later, but right now, I'd like to know how your face got bunged up and how you and Sam disappeared almost before my eyes. One day you were there, and the next, you weren't."

"About my face..." Kasenia touched her cheek. "Let's see. Axle grease—"

"Axle grease?"

"Yes, *used* axle grease, and a run through a forest with branches slapping my face. Oh, and then there was the faceplant."

He cocked his chin. "Faceplant?"

"Yes, but it turned out to be a good thing. Gave me a reason to pretend I had amnesia in jail."

"Amnesia?"

She laughed. "Long story. About our disappearance..." Kasenia shook her head, remembering the shock and the horror. "Brewster told us we were going to his country place for the weekend. And then he locked us in his compound."

Gordon swore then quickly apologized. "Sorry, but I never did like the arrogant prick. He was too slick, which told me he had to be hiding something."

"He's more than slick. He's the most horrid, evil man I've ever met. I should have listened to you."

"You were too head-over-heels in love—or maybe professor awe—to hear anything I had to say."

"I'm over it now, whatever it was, believe me."

"You gonna divorce the guy?"

"Don't need to."

"What does that mean?" He gave her a side glance. "He's doin' the divorcing?"

They passed between tall cliffs, the temporary shade a relief in the warming pickup.

"We were never really married."

"But the Vegas wedding... I thought—"

"I need to have that annulled or whatever the legal term is 'cause of his other so-called wives."

"*Wives?* You mean..." Gordon gaped at her, blinking hard. "He's a... Wiley's a polygamist?"

"With me, his harem totaled nine. His goal is a dozen."

"Oh, my stars and garters..."

Kasenia laughed. "That's a new one, Grandpa."

"I like it. Better 'n' hollerin' a string of curse words that'd blister your ears."

"Thanks for sparing me." She giggled.

For a moment, they rode in silence, then Kasenia said, "You mentioned trouble at the detention center. What was that about?" Before he could answer, she gasped, hand over her mouth. "I just remembered you had to pay a lot of money for my release. How? I mean, I didn't think you had that much—" She stopped. "Sorry, it's not my business. I'm surprised, that's all, and grateful."

"Let's just say golfing with a banker has its advantages." He smirked. "I gave Franklin a promissory note with my house as collateral, and he gave me the hundred thousand. Said he knew I'd repay the loan ASAP and wouldn't charge me interest."

Gordon chuckled. "I caught the sheriff's office off-guard by showing up with a cashier's check for the full amount. They acted real funny and called the sheriff over. He looked at me then grabbed his phone from his pocket."

"I met him once." Kasenia grimaced. "He's a slimy lowlife, to use one of your words."

"No kiddin'." Gordon huffed. "I heard him say 'Wiley,' and that perked my ears."

"Uh-oh."

"I pulled *my* phone from *my* pocket." Gordon tapped his pocket. "It has the number for a guy named Joe Watts on speed dial. Joe was one of my golf buddies until he moved to Phoenix to be deputy director for Arizona's Department of Corrections. Earlier, on the way from Tucson, I called Joe and informed him of everything Duran told me about Wiley and the sheriff. He spewed a few choice words and said to keep his personal number handy. If the sheriff gave me any guff, he wanted to know.

"Right then..." Gordon scratched his white mustache. "Right there in the middle of the reception area, I raised my phone and yelled loud enough for everyone to hear. 'My name is Gordon Clarke. I've got the Arizona Department of Corrections deputy director, Joseph Watts, on speed dial.'

"The sheriff whipped around, eyes big as saucers." Gordon grinned. "Highlight of my day, well, except for seein' you walk in. I waved the phone for effect and kept on hollerin'.

"'Deputy Director Watts said to give him a call.' I turned a full circle, eyeing every person I could see. "If you have any confusion about releasin' my granddaughter *immediately*, thanks to my payment of the full bond, he wants to hear from you. Anyone here need to speak with Deputy Director Watts? He's ready and willing to answer your questions. Tell him Gordon Clarke sent you.'

"I would have called him *my buddy, Joe Watts*," Gordon confided, leaning Kasenia's way. "But I wanted to sound professional and not mess things up for you."

"Thank you, Grandpa." Kasenia grinned. She imagined her pistol-toting, mustached grandfather shouting and brandishing the phone, eyes flashing and long white braid whipping from shoulder to shoulder across his leather vest. "I wish I could have seen the sheriff's face." She giggled. "What happened next?"

"I was politely informed you'd be out within a half hour. And you were."

Kasenia laughed. "No wonder the deputy insisted I hurry. If I'd known you were the one waiting, I would have rushed out, but I thought Brewster had come for me. You can't imagine how happy I was to see you."

"Ditto."

The two-lane highway ran between mountain ranges with a fair amount of desert separating them. Much like when she was a child, mesquite and palo verde trees flew past her grandfather's window, backdropping his sun-burnished profile. This was the man she believed didn't care, the man who put himself and his house on the line to rescue her from jail. Her eyes filled with tears.

"Here, take my phone." Gordon handed it to her. "I forgot to tell Duran we're on the way. He's on speed dial. See that little circle with TD in the center? Give him a call for me. He has a two-way system going with the boys in the trailer. He can tell Sam you're out of jail."

Kasenia swiped at her tears and touched the "Trent Duran" icon, surprised by the wave of shyness washing over her. She wasn't usually bashful. Maybe it was because she didn't know what to say to a man she barely knew but who made her heart flip somersaults.

Trent answered immediately. "Hey, Gordon. How'd it go?"

"Hi, Trent." Her words came out more subdued than she expected. "This is Kasenia Clarke. My grandpa asked me to tell you we're on the way."

"Kasenia..." She could hear his smile, and that made her smile. "You just shot my day over the top, lady." He chuckled. "I was praying hard they'd release you, despite Wiley, and despite Sheriff Childers."

"Thank you for praying. Grandpa had to go to bat for me. He'll tell you the story later. Right now, would you please let Sam know I was released?"

"Happy to. Say, do you know what mile marker you're at?"

She turned to her grandfather, who liked to count mile markers when he traveled. "What was the last mile marker, Grandpa?"

He told her and she relayed the information to Trent.

"Great. At the rate I'm going, you'll catch up with us before we reach Bisbee. Blue Dodge pickup, white two-horse trailer. I'll give your brother a buzz right now."

"Thank you. I'm sure we'll talk again soon."

"Can't wait." His baritone voice softened. "Good to hear from you, Kasenia. Bye for now."

Still smiling, she handed the phone to her grandfather. "He's going to tell Sam."

Gordon winked. "Trent's an okay guy, huh?"

"Yes." Kasenia blushed. "He's a very nice man, and I appreciate what he's doing for the boys."

"Amen to that." He pounded the steering wheel. "I promise you, Senya Girl, when this is over, we're gonna set the neighborhood ablaze with lights, music and dancing. I'll invite the neighbors, so they can't complain."

For a while, they drove in silence. Kasenia had questions for her grandpa, and she was sure he had questions for her. But the warm air made her sleepy. It was so nice to lean back on the leather seat, close her eyes and relax. For the first time in a long time, she didn't have to worry about anybody or anything. The boys were in good hands, thank God, on their way to be reunited with their families.

The tires' hum and the tunes wheezing from the radio had nearly lulled her to sleep when the pickup swerved.

She opened her eyes.

"Sorry to wake you." Gordon aimed a thumb behind them. "Almost clipped a fox that ran across the road."

"I'd rather talk to you than sleep. I'm so happy to be with you again." She peered through the front window. "Is that a horse trailer ahead of us?"

"Yeah, and a deputy behind us."

Kasenia twisted to look.

"Been following us since we left the detention center. Rides my tail, slows down, then speeds up to ride my tail again. Not sure what the dude thinks he's doing."

"But why?"

"Your guess is as good as mine. Could be he's harassing me for the sheriff or tracking you for Brewster. Or maybe he figures you'll lead him to the missing boys."

"Oh." She sat back. "That's exactly what we're doing."

"You watch. He'll flip around when we reach the county line. Won't be long now. That's why Duran asked the kids' parents to meet them in Bisbee. It's in a different county. He also requested the parents not notify the media until their boys are safely in their arms."

"Good thinking. I'm glad he's taking such good care of Sam and the others."

As they drew closer to the trailer, she pictured the boys inside. Brave Benicio with his crooked teeth and cute dimples. Raúl, whose pencil mustache and scraggly chin hairs made him appear older than his thirteen years. Cesar, prayer leader and translator, his thick dark hair combed to the side. Scrappy, stoical, yet spiritually attuned Ismael. Stocky, curly haired, always ready to help Jorge. Ulises with his wavy orange-streaked hair and thoughtful ways. And dear, dear Sam. Every one of them had to be incredibly anxious to see their loved ones.

Gordon squeezed her hand again. "Thank you for leading the boys through all manner of harrowing escapades, including a run-in with the infamous El Jefe. To hear Sam tell it, you had quite the adventures."

Kasenia smiled. If nothing else, she'd given Sam memories for a lifetime, memories she'd prefer to forget, at least for now.

Like her grandfather predicted, they soon passed a sign that read "Entering Cochise County," and below it, "Leaving Santa Cruz County." Behind them, the deputy slowed, swung a squealing U-turn, and headed the way he'd come.

"Thank God he's gone." Kasenia turned to face the front. "The tattletale won't be reporting our actions to the sheriff anymore."

The Arizona highway stretched long and straight before them, devoid of vehicles other than theirs and Trent's truck and trailer hauling his precious cargo.

"Guess you could call me a tattletale, too," Gordon said. "I snitched on Brewster a couple days ago."

31

— · —

"You did?" Kasenia tilted her chin. "I assumed he moved to the condo as soon as he dumped us at the ranch."

"Right." Gordon nodded. "Had some lame excuse, like it was too painful to be in the house where you once lived. I could tell he was lying through his teeth, but the cops bought it, hook, line and sinker." The warm wind whipped loose white hairs about his face.

"Anyway, the other day, I was coming around the side of the garage, where I can *finally* park my truck again, headed for the mailbox. And there he was, big and bad as life, parked in my driveway like he owned it."

Kasenia frowned. "Was he waiting to talk with you?"

"You'd think, but he was leaning out the window, talking to the kid next door, the girl with the funny-colored hair."

"Denika?"

"That's the one. From what I heard, he was trying to convince her of somethin'. I said, 'Wiley, what're *you* doin' here?' He took one glance at me and backed out of the driveway without looking. Woulda hit a truck comin' down the street, if the guy hadn't honked.

"Well, I thought that was mighty strange. He wasn't his usual wily self. I asked Denika what they were talking about. 'Oh,' she said, 'he just wanted me to go for a ride with him, but I told him I'd have to ask my parents first. He didn't understand why and kept pushing me to get in his car. That made me feel funny.' Then she kinda ducked her head and said she was glad I came when I did.

"I told her she did the right thing and to go in her house next time he comes around and lock the door, call the cops if he knocks. And then I went inside and called her dad at his job. He was, of course, incensed but grateful I happened along when I did. For good measure, I phoned the police to report suspicious behavior in my neighborhood. You know, Neighborhood Watch and all that."

"Good for you, Grandpa. I happen to know Brewster intended to make Denika his tenth—she finger quoted—'wife.' You saved her from being kidnapped, raped and forced into a harem as well as lifelong slavery for the lucrative business he runs from the Shadow Ranch compound."

Gordon lurched her direction, almost driving off the road. "What?" He maneuvered into the lane again. "Is that what he did to you and Sam?"

"Sam wasn't raped. but it was about to happen."

"*About* to happen?" Gordon's eyes flashed. "How did you know it was coming?"

"Brewster and Sheriff Childers, along with other degenerate investors just finished building a boy brothel near the entrance to the compound. They were about to open for business and planned to use Sam and the six boys you'll meet today plus another boy who should also be reunited with his family soon."

"That..." Gordon gripped the steering wheel like he might wrench it off. "That..." He growled. "Is beyond my comprehension. Wiley and his sicko pals ought to be strung up or at the very least put behind bars the rest of their lives."

"The boys are going to make it happen." Kasenia pointed at the sign they were passing. "We're almost there. Only ten more miles. And then we'll look the truth in the eyes."

"Speaking of the devil..."

"Huh?" Kasenia stared at her grandfather whose gaze was glued to his rearview mirror and then twisted to peer out the back window. A car was coming on them fast, flashing silver in the sunshine.

"Oh, no," she whispered.

"Oh, yes... This could get interesting."

The car drew close enough she could see the top was down. Brewster was wearing the aviator sunglasses he'd ordered direct from Italy. His camo muscle shirt emphasized his toned shoulders and arms. Tanned and well-oiled, they glistened like boulders on a wet beach.

Kasenia faced the front window again. His physique that had once attracted her now repelled her because she'd met the *real* Brewster Anton Wiley. She thought she'd escaped his hold. But here he was again. Was that a holster strap across his chest? Probably. He never went anywhere without a gun.

And why was he chasing them? Did he think he could convince her to return to Shadow Ranch? Or that he could get answers the detectives failed to pry out of her?

Gordon unsnapped his gun holster. "If the dude tries anything funny..."

"Please be careful." Kasenia didn't know whether to tighten her seatbelt to prepare for a rough ride or get ready to bail if bullets started flying. "We should tell Trent."

"Right." He handed her his phone and sped up to follow close behind the horse trailer. "Probably a dumb idea," he said, "but I like to think this'll help stop Wiley from getting to the kids."

Possibly... Kasenia held the phone to her ear. *But if Trent's truck stops fast...*

Trent answered on the first ring. "Hey."

"Hey..." Kasenia smiled. Trent Duran was a wonderful distraction from Brewster and his latest evil plot, whatever it was. She tapped the speaker icon. "Brewster is behind us, Trent. Came speeding out of nowhere."

"Thanks. I wondered why Gordon started tailgating."

"I'm gonna do whatever it takes," Gordon shouted, "to keep the pervert away from them boys."

"Appreciate it," Trent responded. "The meeting place is a gravel parking area this side of the Mule Pass Tunnel, a couple miles before Bisbee proper. It's not big. Basically a wide spot in the road. We'll be there soon, and it'll be Wiley against a dozen angry parents plus the three of us—and my deputy buddy, Carlos. I imagine a few of his pals from the department will tag along."

Gordon took his hand off his gun long to enough to flash a thumbs-up. "Great news, Duran. Gonna to be a rendezvous to remember."

"Grandpa..." Kasenia furrowed her brow. "You sound like Sam. This might be an adventure to you, but we're playing with fire. Brewster is evil to the core. He'll do anything to get the boys."

"You're right." Trent's voice changed from lighthearted to serious. "Rumor has it he's not above murder. I've seen him almost yank a kid's arm off and then slap him so hard he flew across the yard."

Kasenia groaned then checked the window again. Brewster's car was inches from the pickup's bumper. "Now Brewster is tailgating us, Trent."

The words were barely out of her mouth when the Corvette zipped into the oncoming lane and just as quickly fell back behind the pickup.

"Good thing he saw the semi coming over the hill," Gordon muttered. "Or he'd a sent us all to an early grave."

"Watch out, Trent," Kasenia warned. "He's driving crazy."

"I'm keeping an eye on the mirror and praying the kids don't get hurt."

"Me, too."

The semi loaded with new cars flew past, buffeting the horse trailer and then her grandpa's pickup.

Nearly clipping the rear of the car hauler, Brewster zagged from behind the pickup to drive alongside. He shook his fist at Gordon. "You asshole, you stole my wife." He glanced ahead. "Stop now and I won't hurt you." Leering up at them, he added, "Because I'm that kinda guy."

Kasenia rolled her eyes and aimed the phone so Trent could catch the insane conversation. The noise of three engines, trailer and pickup rattles, and wind blowing through the windows would make hearing difficult for Trent, but he might catch some of the conversation.

"What kind of fool do you take me for, Wiley?" Gordon sneered. "Why don't you do the world a favor and drive that tin can of yours to the nearest jail and turn yourself in?"

"Shut up." Brewster screeched, his face as red as the Vette's interior. He checked the road ahead, reached under his arm and pulled out a gun. "Stop immediately, old man, or I'll help you stop. It won't be pretty."

Gordon hit the brake and slowed. "Don't want the kids to get in the line of fire."

Kasenia gripped the seat edge with one hand and the hot window ledge with the other.

Instead of dropping back with the pickup, Brewster pulled even with Trent's truck and waved the gun at him. Kasenia could hear some of what he said through the phone. "Duran, what're you...followed...those two?"

She leaned to see around the horse trailer.

"Those two?" Trent repeated. "I'm the only one in this truck."

"Don't waste my time...idiot." Brewster aimed the gun at Trent. "I asked you... Answer me."

He's out of control. Kasenia cringed. *Please, God, don't let him hurt Trent or the boys.*

"Hey, man, you're driving on the wrong side of the road." Trent said. "Better put that gun down and pull ahead so you don't get hit."

"Don't tell me how to drive..." For a moment, Kasenia heard nothing but engines and wind. Then Brewster swore. "What's in the trailer, Duran?"

"It's a horse trailer, dude."

"I know what..." Brewster slowed and drove alongside the trailer, yelling, "Pull over...see inside."

"Oh, no," Kasenia whispered. Surely the boys could hear him. If they realized it was Brewster, they were probably terrified—and praying.

The infuriated man aimed the gun at the trailer. "Do it, Duran, or I'll drill holes..."

Kasenia gasped.

"That does it." Gordon yanked his handgun from the holster.

Before Kasenia could question his actions, he aimed the pistol, pulled the trigger, and slowed the truck, seemingly all at the same time. A loud bang erupted, and Brewster's car fishtailed, missing the horse trailer by inches.

Gordon slowed the pickup to a crawl, trailing the Corvette but avoiding its unpredictable path.

The sportscar careened from lane to lane across the highway, the burst tire flapping noisily against the asphalt. With a grating squeal of brakes, the Vette lurched off the road, slammed into a rocky ridge on the left and shuddered to a stop amidst a roiling dirt cloud. Brewster flipped forward into the deployed airbag and then bounced back against the headrest.

"Idiot," Gordon muttered. "Shouldn't have hit the brakes."

He checked the rearview mirror and the road ahead. Then, gun ready, he pulled alongside the crumpled sportscar with its shredded tire and deflated airbag that hung from the steering wheel like an empty grocery sack. The car's engine ticked and whooshed—and then silenced.

But Brewster remained upright. With a trembling hand, he reached to adjust his crooked sunglasses now smashed against his face.

Kasenia breathed a little easier. He must have dropped his gun.

The glasses had cut into his nose and face. Blood trickled down his cheeks. More blood oozed from his nostrils. Dust peppered his greased arms.

"He seems okay," Kasenia murmured. Hearing an odd noise, she looked up in time to see a basketball-size rock tumble off the cliff and onto the Corvette's hood, landing with a resounding crunch.

Brewster swore and Kasenia jumped, but Gordon chuckled. "Well, I'll be a horned toad. Couldn't ask for a better finale."

"What did you say?" Trent asked, still on the phone. He had slowed and was parking his truck and trailer on the shoulder.

"Brewster's fine," Kasenia responded. "Not so much his car. How are the boys?"

"I'm about to check. What happened?"

"Grandpa shot the back tire."

"Nice work." Trent hopped from his truck, hurried to the horse trailer and jumped onto the wheel well. "Sorry about my wild driving, boys. You okay in there?" He pocketed the phone and peered through the narrow opening.

"Boys?" Brewster ripped the sunglasses from his bloody face and squinted through the spiderwebbed windshield. "Did I hear *boys*?"

Gordon hit the gas, swerving his pickup over to the trailer. Kasenia dropped the phone on the seat, placed her clothing bag on the window ledge's hot metal for protection, and leaned out the window. "Everyone all right?"

"Hey, Sis," Sam called. "Glad they let you out of the slammer."

"Oh, Sam..." Her eyes filled with tears.

"Hola," the other boys called. "Hola, Señorita Kasenia."

She swallowed. "Hola, mis amigos."

"What's happening out there?" Sam asked. "I thought I heard Brewster's voice."

"You did," she said. "He was driving crazy, chasing us, and crashed into a cliff. Hurt his car more than it hurt him."

"Gotta go," Gordon whispered. "Wiley's climbing out of his car."

"I'm so happy to hear your voices," Kasenia said. "Your parents are waiting, so we're going to hurry to the meeting place. We're almost there."

The boys cheered and Sam shouted, "See you, Sis."

She called to Trent then pointed behind them at Brewster.

Trent caught her hint, hopped off the wheel well and jumped in his truck. He pulled onto the road and took off. Gordon followed close behind.

The last Kasenia saw of Brewster, he was standing in the middle of the highway, shaking both fists at them.

Eyeing his rearview mirror, Gordon laughed out loud. "Now, there's a sight for sore eyes, one I won't soon forget. Brewster Wiley stranded in the desert."

"Try as I might..." Kasenia turned to her grandfather. "I can't feel sorry for him."

"Like I said, he deserves it and worse." He chortled. "I had no intention of hurting him or causing an accident when I shot his tire. I merely wanted to stop him and assumed he could steer through the fishtailing the blowout would cause. Didn't expect him to run into a cliff."

"It was an amazing shot, Grandpa. You hit the tire first try. All those hours at the shooting range must have honed your skills."

"I was a sharpshooter for the military. I go to the range to stay sharp."

"Know what, Grandpa?" She gave him a side glance. "There's a downside to leaving Brewster behind."

"Oh, yeah?" He arched an eyebrow. "I can't imagine what."

"You won't get to watch that *rendezvous to remember* you were hoping for."

"True." He laughed. "But I got something better. I got to see Brewster Wiley stuck high and dry, without wheels, without his fancy duds..." His eyes moistened. "And without you or Sam."

"Aww, Grandpa..."

The trailer blinker flashed, and the truck and trailer slowed.

"Grandpa." Kasenia squealed and grabbed his arm. "This is the place where the boys are reunited with their families. I'm so happy I could cry."

"Don't start bawlin' on me, or I'll be blubberin' too hard to see." He braked to a stop behind the horse trailer.

Kasenia jumped out, ran to the trailer and hopped onto the wheel well. "We're here, guys, we're here. You can stand up now."

"Whoo-hoo!" The boys leaped to their feet, shaking the trailer and yelling, "Nosotros somos libres! We're free, we're free." They were sweaty from the long ride and smelled like they'd been riding in a horse trailer, but they were the most beautiful sight she'd seen since Grandpa Gordon materialized in the jailhouse sunshine.

Their shouts brought people running to the trailer, praising Jesus and calling the boys by name. The boys cried, "Mamá, Papá..." over and over.

Tears coursed down Kasenia's cheeks. She couldn't stop grinning. Somehow, she felt as if she'd spent a lifetime anticipating this incredible moment.

Sam, who was laughing and crying at the same time, grabbed her hand through the opening that was just wide enough for a horse to poke its head through. "Thanks, Sis. You helped save us." Tears trailed over his cheeks that, like hers, had been scrubbed pink. The color around his injured eye had spread and changed to blue-green.

"Who gave you that black eye?"

"Ross." Sam smirked. "After I cut his mom loose from the bed and took her to the windmill, I snuck into their trailer. He was sleeping by the door, guarding it in case Brewster tried to get to his sister. He told me afterward I was lucky he forgot to grab the shovel he'd hidden behind the couch."

Struggling to hear him over the happy din, Kasenia leaned closer.

"He knocked me down and before I could tell him who I was, Casey piled on top of us. Some woman in the next trailer yelled for them to quit wrestling and go to sleep. That's when I whispered who I was. They got up, grabbed Marisa, and we ran to the windmill."

A camera light flashed in Kasenia's face. She didn't care to have her picture taken, but she ignored it. This was the boys' exodus from hell, a long-awaited moment of glorious freedom they'd carry with them their entire lives.

Trent pushed through the crowd that seemed to have tripled in size. "Perdóname, perdóname. Step away, please step away so the boys can come out."

Sheriff's deputies came alongside the trailer to help him clear a space for the ramp. But when Trent lowered it and opened the double doors, pandemonium exploded again. Kasenia released her brother's hand so he could exit the trailer and hug his grandpa. Still grinning, she jumped off the wheel well to join them in a family hug.

"How about us?" a familiar voice questioned. "Don't we get hugs too?"

Kasenia gasped and spun around, screaming, "Mom, Dad!" She fell into their arms. Soon the five of them were happily entangled, laughing and crying at the same time.

"Family pictures," someone shouted. "I'm taking family pictures."

Kasenia and her loved ones pulled apart. She glanced around. People were separating into small clusters, beaming, chatting, arms around each other. Trent was talking with a deputy.

"I'll be right back." She excused herself from her family and hurried over to the two men. "Pardon me for interrupting, but I need to know who's taking the pictures? And why?"

"Ismael's aunt is a professional photographer and journalist," Trent said. "She's been writing articles about the boys' disappearance for the newspaper."

The deputy quickly interjected, "She needs your permission to publish your picture. You can refuse, if that's your preference."

"Kasenia," Trent said. "This is my friend Carlos. He's with the Cochise County Sheriff's Department."

"Carlos..." Trent smiled. "Kasenia is one of three people wrongly accused of kidnapping the boys."

"I see." Carlos held out his hand. "You don't look like a kidnapper."

"Thank you." She shook his hand. "I'm just a little edgy after spending two nights behind bars for a crime I didn't commit. How do I know these pictures won't be used against me? I don't want the authorities to have any reason to put me in jail again."

"You'd have to take that up with your lawyer," the deputy said. "But once this family reunion story gets out, I'll bet my badge the charges will be dropped before you sit down for breakfast tomorrow morning."

Kasenia sighed. "That would be nice."

"Sure thing." He nodded and walked away.

"Thanks for what you did for those boys." Trent aimed his chin at the happy crowd. "They have great respect and admiration for you."

"They're good kids. Thank you for hosting them—and for driving them here."

"Wish I'd been there the night they arrived. I was here in Bisbee, visiting my folks." He chuckled. "The boys had to spend the night in the barn and drink from the pipe that fills the stock tank, but at least they had water. I arrived about ten the next night just as one of Childers's deputies came looking for the runaways, as he called them. Not knowing the boys were in the barn, I made my dogs stay in my truck and followed him inside. Thank God they heard our voices and hid behind haybales. Guess that wasn't the first time the deputies had checked the barn."

He chuckled. "And thank God I picked up some groceries before I drove home. They ate most of that and nearly cleaned out my fridge and pantry. And this morning..." Trent shook his head. "Don't know how many eggs and sausages I fried or how many pancakes I flipped."

"I can only imagine." Kasenia laughed. "How's Benicio's knee?"

"Thanks for reminding me. I need to speak with his folks." Trent surveyed the crowd. "Back in my Army days, I was a medic. I cleaned and stitched his knee, but he should see a doctor who can check my work and prescribe an antibiotic."

Kasenia watched the photographer snap pictures of Ismael and his family. Their huge smiles and the happy chatter around her made her smile—and grab a mental photo for her album. What a happy day this was.

"The boys told me about the mine hideout," Trent said, "and your guardian angel, El Jefe—and Brewster's mercenaries hunting you down. I saw the helicopter flying back and forth along the mountain range and wondered if they were searching for you." He shook his head. "Quite an adventure."

"I'm glad it's over, but I'm curious... Why didn't you take the boys to their parents immediately?"

"First off, the kids needed to eat. Filling their stomachs was crucial. Secondly, they were the focus of a frenzied search. I closed the drapes and fed them by candlelight while my dogs kept watch outside. Then I called Carlos to formulate a game plan—before I let the boys call home."

Movement to the side caught her attention. Jorge was hurrying into the brush, hand over his mouth. "Oh, dear, Jorge..." She stepped toward him.

Trent stopped her. "That boy ate an incredible amount of food at breakfast. He's been upchucking all morning. I doubt he wants your help right now."

"Right." Kasenia averted her gaze. "I forgot I'm off-duty. His parents can watch over him now." She looked into Trent's dark eyes. "I interrupted you. You and Carlos came up with a game plan, right?"

"We decided driving through Santa Cruz County in the middle of the night with a horseless horse trailer might trigger suspicion and that a morning reunion would be better. I gave the boys each ten minutes to talk with their loved ones, then I got on, emphasizing the danger and insisting they tell no one until after the boys were safely in their arms. We couldn't afford any slipups.

"Besides..." He winked. "This way I get to see you again."

Kasenia grinned.

He pointed into the crowd. "There's Benicio and his family. I'd better go talk with them. Glad you're out of Childers's jail." He touched his hat brim. "Nice talking with you, Kasenia. I hope we can talk more later."

She smiled. "I'd like that." She hadn't thought her happy day could get any happier, but it had.

When she returned to her family, Sam was waving his arms and talking a mile a minute, describing their escape from Shadow Ranch detail by detail. Her dad hugged her, his cheek on her head. "Now, I can sleep at night," he murmured, "knowing you two are safe. Though I have to say you both look like you've been through the wringer."

Kasenia leaned into his solid strength. She'd missed his warm hugs.

The moment they separated, her mom wrapped her arm around Kasenia's waist. "We came as soon as we heard you two went missing. I've never been so scared in my life."

"You and me both." Kasenia rested her head against her mother's, savoring her rosewater scent. "I thought I'd never see you or Dad or Grandpa or Babushka Irina again." She straightened. "How's she doing? Does she know about us?"

"We tried to keep the news from her, but she sensed right away something was off-kilter."

"Sorry to put you—"

A gunshot reverberated between the hills, silencing the happy chatter.

32

—·—

K ASENIA SPUN AROUND.
Brewster.

She should have known he'd chase after them.

Brewster stood to the side, one hand over Jorge's mouth and the other holding a gun aimed skyward. Tears trickled down the boy's chubby cheeks and onto his captor's hand.

Kasenia's mother whispered, "Is that Brewster?"

"Yes," Kasenia murmured. "The *real* Brewster Anton Wiley."

Blood striped his face from his eyebrows to his chin and caked the creases around his distended nose and mouth. One eye was swollen shut. Sweat rivulets ran down his dusty oily body. His legs, clad in dark surfer shorts, were spread wide, muscles taut above black combat boots. A holster attached to the left boot held a second handgun.

"Get behind the cars," Deputy Carlos ordered.

Brewster shot another bullet over their heads, its echo almost as loud as the gunshot. "Stay right where you are, people. Kasenia Wiley, get Sam and the Mexican brats and come with me—or I rid the world of this parasite."

A woman cried, "Don't hurt my baby—"

"Shut up!" Brewster waved the gun. "Get over here, Kasenia. Now."

Her mother sucked in a breath. "No, Kasenia. You can't—"

"I have to." She took two steps toward Brewster, fists clenched, eyes narrowed to hide the fury he'd ignited, fury she'd suppressed for way too long.

Behind her, someone came running, breathing hard. "Officer, I gave him a ride here, but I didn't know he was going to—"

Shut your mouth," Brewster roared, "and get outta here."

Retreating footsteps sounded and then a car door slammed. The vehicle churned gravel before speeding away.

With an impatient jerk of the gun, Brewster motioned for Kasenia to join him. "Come on. Where're the boys?"

One step at a time, she moved closer, never dropping her squint from his wild-eyed gaze.

People shifted around her, some inching backward and others positioning themselves to take Brewster down. She sensed more than saw the movement, and so did Brewster, who discharged the gun again. "Back off, people."

Kasenia, now less than ten feet from him, flinched but did not cover her ears.

"Duran, give me the truck keys. Brats, get in the trailer." Brewster waved the gun at it. "You're going with me because you *belong* to me." Giving Jorge a shove, he ordered, "Get inside."

Jorge stumbled away.

"Nooo..." Kasenia dove at Brewster. "You don't own *anyone!*"

She hit headfirst, slamming into his rock-hard abdomen, feeling more than hearing a gun blast vibrate his ribs and resonate into her skull and down her neck. And then they were on the ground, and she was on top of him, pounding his face and chest with all her strength, screaming her pent-up rage.

An animal-like snarl erupted from him. He clawed at her throat, growling, "You'll pay, whore, you'll pay." Seizing her neck with both hands, he squeezed until she saw stars and her vision dimmed.

And then someone was prying his fingers away.

Brewster howled and bucked, knocking her off his torso.

Kasenia rolled to the side, gasping for air, and was about to grab the gun he'd lost when someone kicked it out of reach. A swarm of men fell on Brewster. Even as he fought them, he cursed Kasenia, promising revenge and eternity in hell. Finally, cuffed and relieved of both weapons, he was shoved into Carlos's SUV still spewing obscenities.

Sam shouted, "I hope they make you eat beets in jail!"

Carlos slammed the SUV door shut, muffling Brewster's loud bitter retort then climbed in the vehicle with another deputy and sped away.

Still on the ground, Kasenia watched their departure through a forest of legs. Another snapshot to add to her mental photo album. The final snapshot of Sam's "grand adventure," she hoped.

Breathing hard, Trent separated from the pack and came over to help her to her feet. "Nice work. You took us all by surprise, but that's what was needed."

"Surprised me, too." Kasenia's braid had loosened in the tussle and her hair was falling in her eyes. She pushed the tangles from her face. "He made me so mad, I had to do something."

His eyes wide with concern, he asked, "Your throat okay? That was...brutal."

"I think so." She touched the tender skin where Brewster had choked her with the necklace not that many days ago and then felt her neck. For sure, she'd have bruises, but they'd fade and only be a memory...like Brewster, who was out of her life, forever. "What was that gunshot? Did someone shoot him or did he—"

"His gun discharged when you knocked him over, and then he lost his grip on it."

Jorge came running. "Gracias, Señorita Kasenia." He threw his arms around her waist. "Gracias."

Her brother and the other boys rushed over, followed by their families. Laughing and crying, they hugged Kasenia and Trent and the deputies and each other.

Her dad held her for a long time. "I'm button-busting proud of you, my sweet girl." Her mom whispered in her ear, "You are one amazing woman. The bear dances, but the tamer collects the money."

Kasenia laughed. "You sound like Dedushka Abram."

Her American grandpa yelled above the uproar, "Listen up, people. Party at my Tucson house tomorrow night. Six o'clock. Everyone's invited. See me for an address. We're gonna party 'til the cock crows!"

Arm around her son, Jorge's mother shouted, "I make tortas."

Another woman called, "Haré enchiladas."

Kasenia's mom chimed in. "I'll provide the borscht."

"Borscht..." Jorge's mother repeated, a question in her voice.

Kasenia laughed. "Russian soup made from beets."

One of the men said, "I play música en mi guitarra."

Sam gave him a thumbs-up. "I'll bring mine too. Maybe you can teach me some songs." He rested his arm on his mother's shoulders. "Just so everyone knows, my mom makes really good borscht *and* really good Russian rice pudding."

"Excelente." Jorge's mother nodded. "Es como arroz con leche Mexicano? Delicioso."

"Maybe like Mexican rice pudding," Cesar explained. "Is delicious."

"Come, señoras." She beckoned with both hands. "We think the food."

Trent nudged Kasenia's shoulder. "Apparently, they don't trust your grandfather's cooking."

She laughed. "You coming to the party?"

"If you're going to be there..." He grinned. "Wild horses couldn't keep me away." Laugh lines creased his suntanned temples.

Smiling up into his kind brown eyes, Kasenia captured the moment, collecting one last sweet memory for her photo album.

SHADOW RANCH DISCUSSION QUESTIONS

- Kasenia's fairytale marriage to her dreamy college professor quickly turned sour. What signs that Brewster had a hidden dark side did she miss or ignore? When did your antennae first register alarm regarding his true character? Can you share a time you heeded your own misgivings and were spared pain or a time you wish you had listened?
- What made Kasenia so susceptible to Brewster? How was he able to deceive a brilliant student who had traveled the world? What areas in your life might make you susceptible to manipulation? What can you do to strengthen those areas?
- Reading the Bible gave Kasenia hope, but Brewster used the Bible to gain power. He claimed "Spirit Father" granted him the authority to alter scripture and told him to do things that contradicted the Bible. Have you known anyone who twisted scripture to control others? How can you safeguard yourself against such deception?
- Kasenia's shock at being trapped in the ranch compound turned to dismay when she learned why the other so-called wives were so passive about their prison-like existence. Why were the women unwilling to risk escape? What could rebellion cost them? What had it cost others?
- Many states in the U.S. have polygamous communities. Have you ever known anyone who's lived in one? What was their view of communal life? How was their community similar to or different from Shadow Ranch? Would a less volatile leader make the situation more tenable? Even if a leader was benevolent, would his polygamy be sanctioned by your country's laws or by God?

- After being deceived by Brewster, how was Kasenia able to trust Tomás to lead them to freedom? What characteristics did he have that gave her the confidence to follow him? How were the two men different?
- When Margo joined the group in the cave, she acknowledged her need to ask forgiveness from the kids. Kasenia shared Psalm 86:5 regarding God's rich, freely given forgiveness with Margo, then she pondered whether she should forgive Brewster. Would God ask that of her? Have you ever had to forgive someone you didn't want to forgive? What lessons did you learn from the experience?
- The escapees prayed often and from their hearts as they fled. God orchestrated several interventions during their escape from the cave in response to those prayers. Which event do you think was the most significant? Would you classify them as natural or supernatural? Describe a time God rescued you.
- Kasenia's jail cell became a quiet refuge where she could consider all that God had done and establish her own faith. Following Cesar's advice, she turned her heart over to the God who created the universe. Have you made the same decision? What circumstances led to your declaration of faith?
- Throughout her ordeal, Kasenia was guided and encouraged by her grandparents' faith as well as their proverbs, whether they were English or Russian words of wisdom. Which adage sticks in your memory? How does it encourage you? Whose faith has inspired you? Share some proverbs or scriptures that have gotten you through tough times.

Questions crafted by Pat Watkins

ADDITIONAL READING

- Breaking Free – Rachel Jeffs

- Combating Cult Mind Control – Steven Hassan

- Crazy for God – Christopher Edwards

- Cults Inside Out – Rick Alan Ross

- Escape – Carolyn Jessop

- Escaping Utopia – Janja Lalich & Karla McLaren

- His Favorite Wife – Susan Ray Schmidt

- In My Father's House – Dorothy Allred Solomon

- Take Back Your Life – Janja Lalick & Madeleine Tobias

- The Polygamist's Daughter – Anna LeBaron

- Toxic Faith – Stephen Arterburn & Jack Felton

- Under the Banner of Heaven – Jon Krakauer

- Wife No. 19 – Ann Eliza Young

ACKNOWLEDGMENTS

THANKS TO WONDERFUL, generous, brilliant friends and relatives who gifted me with their time and talents, *Shadow Ranch* arrived at your doorstep or in your eReader in *much better* shape than the original draft. Critique partners Amber Bennett, Laurie Bower, Val Gray, Lisa Hess, Mary McGuire, Michelle Netten and Kathy Schuknecht offered invaluable input all along the journey.

Alissa Ketterling, Jim Ketterling, Shawna Thackrah, Brady Lyles, Steve Lyles and Pat Watkins blessed me with their wisdom regarding certain aspects of the *Shadow Ranch* adventure; plus, they provided excellent corrections and suggestions for the story.

Special thanks goes to Dan Pease, an Idaho farrier, who kindly shared his horseshoeing know-how with me. And to Angela Ericson for expertly checking the Spanish dialogue in the story. Please know that any horseshoeing or Spanish blunders are totally on me. Dan and Angeles did their best to correct my errors; however, I made changes after they reviewed the manuscript that may or may not be accurate. :-)

I also want to thank those of you who encourage me to continue writing and kindly ask when the next book is coming. Some days I have my doubts about this crazy business, but you keep me tapping the keyboard.

ALSO BY THE AUTHOR

FICTION SERIES

Prisoners of Hope Series

- Shattered Dream (Book One)
- Tangled Truth (Book Two)
- Hidden Path (Book Three)

Kate Neilson Series

- Winds of Hope (Prequel)
- Winds of Wyoming (Book One)
- Winds of Freedom (Book Two)
- Winds of Change (Book Three)

Fiction by Rebecca Carey Lyles & Friends

- Passageways: A Short Story Collection

Nonfiction by Becky Lyles & Friends

- It's a God Thing! Inspiring Stories of Life-Changing Friendships
- On a Wing and a Prayer: Stories from Freedom Fellowship

ABOUT THE AUTHOR

REBECCA CAREY LYLES grew up in Wyoming, the setting for her award-winning *Kate Neilson Novels*. She and her husband, Steve, live in Idaho, which borders Wyoming as well as Montana, where her second series, *Prisoners of Hope,* is set. Together, they host a podcast called *Let Me Tell You a Story* (beckylyles.com/podcast). In addition to writing fiction and nonfiction, she serves as an editor and a mentor for aspiring authors. *Shadow Ranch* is the first novel in the *Children of the Light Series.*

- Email: beckylyles@beckylyles.com
- Facebook author page: Rebecca Carey Lyles
- Website: http://beckylyles.com
- Twitter: @beckylyles
- Instagram: rebecca.lyles1

AFTERWORD

I HOPE YOU ENJOYED SHADOW RANCH and will consider leaving a review or rating wherever you share your book thoughts. If you'd like to learn about future releases, I invite you to go to my website – beckylyles.com – to register for my rare-and-random newsletter. You'll receive a free eStory as my thank-you. http://beckylyles.com/newsletter---freebies.html

Turn the page for a preview of *Shattered Dream,* the first novel in the *Prisoners of Hope Series.* Information about *Shattered Dream (*and my other books) is available on my website – beckylyles.com (in case you missed it the first time!). You can find the book online wherever eBooks and print books are sold as well as order it from your local bookstore.

My prayer is that *Shadow Ranch* not only provided you with a refreshing break from the challenges of everyday life, but that it encouraged you to trust Jesus to save you, care for you and direct your life. I also pray the story enhanced your understanding and empathy for those trapped by manipulative individuals and groups.

SHATTERED DREAM

PRISONERS OF HOPE SERIES BOOK ONE

EIGHT ORANGE-CLAD WOMEN—nine, including myself—are waiting to use one of two phones. I'm the last inmate in the slow-moving line. Like the others, I've been standing on the linoleum-covered cement floor for almost an hour.

I shift my weight to the other foot. My feet ache. My back spasms. The jail-issue boots don't help. I'd love to sit, but the only chairs in the room are the stools attached to the phone kiosks. We're not allowed to plop on the floor.

The women grumble and gossip or fidget with their hair and stare at the wall. Two of them argue in hushed tones about who got there first. We're all anxious to connect with the outside world. And we're all frustrated with the newcomer who's exceeded the ten-minute call limit by two minutes and shows no sign of hanging up.

The inmate ahead of me, a gaunt gray-haired woman, turns. Her dull eyes, pinpointed by tangled wrinkles, are unreadable. Contempt curls her creased lips. She aims a thumb at the newcomer, and through broken yellowed teeth, rasps, "She'll learn."

Her smoker's breath assaults my sinuses. We've just come from the yard, where twice a day she chain-smokes and I walk the track. Stifling a cough, I glance at the guard standing inside the doorway, but he doesn't care how long we talk or what we say. He's only there to keep the peace.

The residents of Gallatin County Detention Center are the ones who enforce a ten-minute maximum and "discourage" those who monopolize the phones from repeating the infraction. They'll deliver a crystal-clear message to the new woman tonight, a message she'll remember for a long time. If nothing else, she'll learn not all rules are written.

For the umpteenth time, I check the big black-rimmed clock that hangs above the phones. An hour and five minutes of afternoon phone time left. The new girl has now talked thirteen minutes. Snuggled into the booth, the phone pressed against her cheek, she's probably whispering sweet nothings to her boyfriend.

The other caller, a big muscular woman who works out every day in the weight room, sits ramrod straight on the stool. Elbow out, she grips the phone like a weapon and nods her head in short bursts, as if answering questions. She's either taking care of business or speaking with a lawyer. I'd bet my last chocolate bar her call will be short.

The small room is warm, as always. I close my eyes and fan my face with my hand. But at the sound of footsteps behind me, I pivot, having learned long ago to watch my back. Several clones of myself—women wearing orange t-shirts tucked into elastic-waist pants of the same lovely hue—drift into the room on their sturdy brown boots. My cellmate, Serena, is one of them.

She lifts her chin in greeting and resumes talking to Nelda, her latest best friend. I don't care who Serena has for friends. However, she and Nelda are both heroin addicts who talk nonstop about how much they itch for another fix, an obsession that's not aiding their recovery.

One inmate has a bounce to her step. She stops two feet from me, grinning like I'm *her* latest best friend.

I backstep to regain my personal space.

"Hi, my name is Roxie," she says. "I'm from right here in good ol' Bozeman, Montana." She giggles like she told a joke. "Born and raised here."

I give her the onceover. *Must be new. She's entirely too happy.* Newbie inmates either keep to themselves, cry all the time, or try too hard to fit in.

Roxie, whom I immediately dub Rookie Roxie, is perky and cute, despite the sores on her face and the shadows beneath her red eyes. She doesn't look old enough to be incarcerated with adults. But then, I've seen plenty of eighteen- and nineteen-year-olds in the women's facility.

At twenty-eight, I'm not that much older, yet some days I feel I belong in the nursing home with my grandma. Alcohol can do that to a person.

Roxie extends her hand, expecting a handshake, I assume.

I ignore it. Touching is against the rules at GCDC.

"I'm new here," she says.

Yep, and still high or in shock from your arrest. I catch a whiff of stale perfume, another clue she recently came from the outside.

She grabs the ID card hanging from my neck. "Cassie Anita True. That's a nice name."

Roxie is lucky I'm not the volatile type. Some inmates would knock her hand away, breaking a finger or two in the process. "Remember the rules," I say. "Hands to yourself."

"Sorry." She drops the ID. "I forgot."

"Happens to all of us." I peek at the guard to see if he noticed—he didn't—and tell her, "You can call me Cat."

She glances from my ID to my face. "That's, uh, different."

"My initials."

"Oh." She giggles again. "I get it." Without pause, she adds, "You're so exotic. What's your nationality?"

"You jump in with both feet, don't you?"

She gives me a funny look.

I don't bother to explain. The girl apparently has no filters. "My mother is Jamaican," I tell her, "and my father is French-Canadian." Before she can ask if I grew up in Jamaica, France or Canada, I add, "They live in Oregon."

One of the bickering women shouts the "B" word. I twist in time to see her shove the other woman, who swears and pushes her against the wall. The rest of us step away. Jailhouse squabbles can escalate to the hair-pulling, eye-clawing stage in a nanosecond.

Fists clenched, the enraged duo stand nose to nose, screaming expletives at each other. The room reverberates with their screeches. I cover my ears.

The guard does an about-face, his jaw hard as stone, and strides toward the red-faced pair. I silently plead for him not to kick us all out.

"She started it," yells one of the women, waving her arms.

"No, I didn't," shrieks the other. "She did."

He raises a palm, and they hush, arms stiff, fists tight.

I clasp my hands. The room is so quiet I can hear my heartbeat.

The guard calls in their names and booking numbers on his radio, tells them they can't use the phones for a week, and orders them to return to their cells. Another guard is waiting for them at the door.

I rub my sweaty hands on my pants. Maybe I'll get to talk with my parents after all. This could be my last chance. The line shuffles forward. If the smell that now permeates the room is any clue, I'm not the only one traumatized by the outburst.

The weightlifter slams the phone and stomps away. Another inmate quickly takes her place. We have to act fast. Sometimes people jump ahead and grab a phone the instant it touches the cradle.

The inmate who was monopolizing the telephone stumbles past. Tears drip from her cheeks, forming dark splotches on her orange t-shirt. Along with heartbreak, she's sure to suffer physical consequences for that long call. I'm tempted to pat her shoulder, but I don't.

Now, only three residents stand in front of me.

Behind me, Roxie is chatting with another inmate. I'm glad she found somebody else to talk to. I'm about to leave GCDC, and I don't need anyone bent on self-destruction in my life. Like others I've met in this jail, she's too much like the old me.

To be honest, I can't say the classes and therapy sessions here have transformed me, but they help. I try to believe I'm in transition—eager to move on and anxious to meet the new Cat. Despite my best intentions, however, the "transitioning me" struggles with random alcohol cravings. This is one of those occasions.

I've learned to search for the source of my need, or my *alleged* need, as the jail counselor regularly reminds me. My guess is the current trigger is either boredom or anxiety, probably anxiety. That's partially due to the fight but mostly because I'm excited to tell my parents my good news. For too long, I've been their "bad news" daughter.

I'm now close enough to the phones to catch snatches of one-sided conversations.

"I'm, uh, wondering if I still have my job. I get out on...oh..." The girl's stringy brown hair hides her face.

The other caller tucks a strand of her chin-length blond hair behind her ear. "Mama loves you, darling. I'll be home soon, and we'll bake peanut butter cookies together."

I hate it when people lie to their kids. That woman is not going home. She's going to prison. She told me she's waiting for the judge to decided which one.

The next person punches in a number, waits, and then replaces the handset. Her disappointment is evident in her lowered head and drooping shoulders. I feel her letdown, remembering the times I couldn't talk because no one was home to accept my call. But my empathy is short-lived.

In fact, I'm inwardly cheering. Thanks to her departure, I'm one person closer to calling home. Two people now stand between me and a telephone.

I can't wait to tell Mom and Dad I'm done with denial and ready for rehab. Really ready, this time. I want to put the past behind me, to stop clinging to my addiction like a life raft. For years, I convinced myself alcohol was my salvation, when in truth, it sucked me to the depths and nearly drowned me.

The airless room is suffocating. I gather my hair in a ponytail and fan my neck. Thinking about my dependency makes me think of Eric and where it all started. And thinking about Eric makes me sad. Painfully sad. I drop my hair and step nearer the phones.

For me, *heartache* is not a metaphor. My entire being aches for my deceased husband, but I've gotten to where I no longer cry myself to sleep. Instead, I stuff the hurt and dwell on the magical night we met at the downtown Bozeman coffee shop where I sang and played my guitar on weekends.

Unlike Rookie Roxie, I moved here ten years ago to attend Montana State University on a music scholarship. Music was everything to me, until my sophomore year. That's when a friend introduced me to Eric True. Then my life became music *and* Eric. He was an amazingly talented art major, also a sophomore. I still remember how our artistic souls connected that night, like two ends of a seatbelt clicking firmly into place.

❖❖ ·❖· ❖❖

Thank you for reading! You can find *Shattered Dream,* along with the next books in the *Prisoners of Hope Series* plus other *Rebecca Carey Lyles* novels, wherever books are sold online. You can also find two ministry story collections authored under *Becky Lyles ~ It's a God Thing! Inspiring Stories of Life-Changing Friendships* and *On a Wing and a Prayer: Stories from Freedom Fellowship, a Prison Ministry.*